THE RIVAN
CODEX

DAVID & LEIGH EDDINGS

ThE RIVAN CODEX

ANCIENT TEXTS OF THE BELGARIAD AND THE MALLOREON

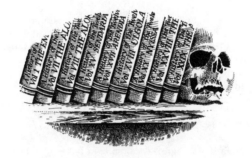

ILLUSTRATED BY
GEOFF TAYLOR

The Ballantine Publishing Group • New York

For Malcolm, Jane, Joy, Geoff, and the rest of the bunch.
It's always a genuine pleasure to work with you.
With all our thanks.

DAVID & LEIGH

A Del Rey® Book
Published by The Ballantine Publishing Group

http://www.randomhouse.com/delrey/

Library of Congress Cataloging-in-Publication Data
Eddings, David.
The Rivan codex: ancient texts of the Belgariad and the Malloreon/David & Leigh
Eddings; illustrated by Geoff Taylor. — 1st American ed.
p.   cm.
ISBN 0-345-42402-6 (alk. paper)
1. Fantastic fiction, American. 2. Fantastic fiction—Authorship.
I. Eddings, Leigh. II. Title.
PS3555.D38R5   1998
813'.54—dc21   98-29234
                                                                                                              CIP

Manufactured in the United States of America

First American Edition: October 1998

10 9 8 7 6 5 4 3 2 1

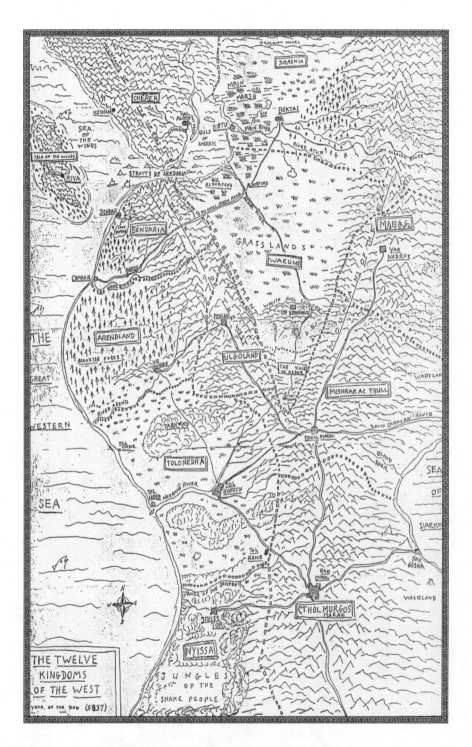

FIRST MAP OF A PLACE THAT NEVER WAS

CONTENTS

PART III: THE BATTLE OF VO MIMBRE

IV: PRELIMINARY STUDIES TO THE MALLOREON

V: THE MALLOREAN GOSPELS

VI: A SUMMARY OF CURRENT EVENTS

INTRODUCTION

My decision to publish this volume was made in part because of a goodly number of flattering letters I've received over the past several years. Some of these letters have come from students at various levels, and to make matters worse, I've also received letters from teachers who inform me that they're actually encouraging this sort of thing. Aren't they aware that they're supposed to wait until I'm safely in the ground before they do this?

The students, naturally, ask questions. The teachers hint around the edges of an invitation to stop by and address the class. I'm very flattered, as I mentioned, but I don't write – or grade – term papers any more, and I don't travel. To put it idiomatically, 'I ain't going no place; I been where I'm going.'

Then there are those other letters, the ones which rather bashfully confide an intention to 'try writing fantasy myself'. I don't worry too much about those correspondents. They'll get over *that* notion rather quickly once they discover what's involved. I'm sure that most of them will eventually decide to take up something simpler – brain surgery or rocket science, perhaps.

I'd more or less decided to just file those letters and keep my mouth shut. A prolonged silence might be the best way to encourage a passing fancy to do just that – pass.

Then I recalled a conversation I had with Lester del Rey on one occasion. When I'd first submitted my proposal for the Belgariad, I'd expected the usual leisurely reaction-time, but Lester responded with what I felt to be unseemly haste. He wanted to see this thing – now, but I wasn't ready to *let* him see it – now. I was in revision of what I thought would be Book I, and since I was still doing honest work in those days, my time was somewhat curtailed. I wanted to keep him interested, however, so I sent him my 'Preliminary Studies' instead – 'So that you'll have the necessary background material.' Lester later told me that while he was reading those studies, he kept telling himself, 'There's no way we can publish this stuff,' but then he admitted, 'but I kept reading.' We were fairly far along in the Belgariad when he made this confession, and he went on to say, 'Maybe when we've got the whole story finished, we might want to think about releasing those studies.'

Eventually, the two ideas clicked together. I had people out there asking questions, and I had the answers readily at hand since nobody in his right mind takes on a multi-book project without some fairly extensive preparation. My Preliminary Studies were right there taking up space, I'd just finished a five-book contract, and I had nothing else currently on the fire. All this thing needed was a brief introduction and some footnotes, and we were off to press. (Just in passing I should advise you that my definition of 'brief' and yours might differ just a bit. It takes me a hundred pages just to clear my throat. Had you noticed that? I thought you might have.)

Please bear in mind the fact that these studies are almost twenty years old, and there are going to be gaps. There are places where some great leaps occurred, frequently flowing out of the point of my pen during that actual writing, and I wasn't keeping a diary to report these bursts of inspired creativity. I'll candidly admit that probably no more than half of these 'strokes of genius' actually worked. Some of them would have been disastrous. Fortunately, my collaborator was there to catch those blunders. Trial and error enters into any form of invention, I suppose. This book may help others to avoid some of the missteps we made along the way, and it may give the student of our genre some insights into the creative process – something on the order of 'connect wire A to wire B. Warning! Do *not* connect wire A to wire C, because that will cause the whole thing to blow up in your face.'

Now that I've explained what I'm up to here, let's get the lecture out of the way. (Did you really think I'd let you get away without one?)

After I graduated from the US Army in 1956, one of my veteran's benefits was the now famous GI Bill. My government had decided to pay me to go to graduate school. I worked for a year to save up enough for some incidentals (food, clothing, and shelter) and then enrolled in the graduate school of the University of Washington in Seattle. (A good day in Seattle is a day when it isn't raining *up*.) My area of concentration was supposed to be modern American fiction (Hemingway, Faulkner, and Steinbeck), but I had those Ph.D exams lurking out in the future, so I knew that I'd better spend some time with Chaucer, Shakespeare, and Milton as well. Once I'd mastered Middle English, I fell in love with Chaucer and somewhat by extension with Sir Thomas Malory.

Since what is called 'Epic Fantasy' in the contemporary world descends in an almost direct line from medieval romance, my studies of Chaucer and Malory gave me a running head start in the field. 'Medieval Romance' had a long and honorable history, stretching from about the eleventh century to the sixteenth, when *Don Quixote* finally put it to sleep. It was a genre that spoke of the dark ages in glowing terms, elevating a number of truly barbaric people to near sainthood. The group that is of most interest to the English-speaking world, of course, is King Arthur and his knights of the Round Table. There may or may not have been a real King Arthur, but that's beside the point. We should never permit historical reality to get in the way of a good story, should we?

Since the issue's come up, though, let's take a look at someone who was historically verifiable and who had a great deal of impact on the fledgling genre in its earliest of days. The lady in question was the infamous Eleanor of Aquitaine.

Eleanor was related to *five* (count 'em) different kings (or pseudo-kings) during the twelfth century. Her father was the Duke of Aquitaine (now known as Gascony) and, since he controlled more land than the King of France, he routinely signed official documents as 'the King of Aquitaine'. In 1137, Louis of France arranged a marriage between his son, Prince Louis and 'princess' Eleanor. Eleanor wasn't a good wife, since she had what's politely known as a 'roving eye'. Evidently, it was more than her eye that roved. Her husband, who soon became Louis VII of France, was a pious man, and his wandering wife not only failed to produce an heir to his throne, but also became notorious as an adulteress. He finally managed to have their marriage annulled in 1152, and two months later Eleanor married Henry Plantagenet, Duke of Normandy, who incidentally also happened to be King Henry II of England. Eleanor, as it turned out, was not barren, and she bore Henry several sons. Aside from that, Henry and Eleanor didn't really get along together, so he took the easy way out and locked her up to keep her out of his hair. After he died, Eleanor stirred up trouble between her sons, Richard the Lionhearted and John the Incompetent, both of whom became kings of England. They *also* locked Mother away to keep her out of mischief.

Thus, Eleanor spent a lot of her time locked up. Embroidery didn't thrill her too much, so she read books. Books were very expensive in the twelfth century because they had to be copied by hand, but Eleanor didn't care. She had money, if not freedom, so she could afford to pay assorted indigents with literary pretensions to write the kind of books she liked. Given Eleanor's background it's understandable that she liked books about kings, knights in shining armor, pretty young fellows who played the lute and sang of love with throbbing emotion, and fair damsels cruelly imprisoned in towers. Her literary tastes gave rise to troubadour poetry, the courtly love tradition, and whole libraries of interminable French romances that concentrated heavily on 'The Matter of Britain' (King Arthur *et al*) and 'The Matter of France' (Charlemagne and Co.).

Now we jump forward three hundred years to the Wars of the Roses. There was a certain knight named Sir Thomas Malory (probably from Warwickshire) who sided with the Lancastrians. When the Yorkist faction gained the ascendancy, Sir Thomas was clapped into prison. He was not, strictly speaking, a political prisoner, however. He was in prison because he belonged there, since it appears that he was a career criminal more than a political partisan. There may have been some politics involved in the various charges leveled against him, of course, but the preponderance of evidence suggests that he was a sort of medieval Jesse James, leading a gang of outlaws on a rampage through southern England. He was imprisoned for sedition, murder, the attempted murder of the Duke of Buckingham, cattle-rustling, horse theft, the looting of monasteries, jail-breaking and not infrequently of rape. Sir Thomas seems to have been a very bad boy.

He was still a nobleman, however, and a sometime member of parliament, so he was able to persuade his jailors to let him visit a nearby library (under guard, of course). Sir Thomas was quite proud of his facility in the French language, and he whiled away the hours of his incarceration translating the endless French romances dealing with (what else?) King Arthur. The end result was the work we now know as *Le Morte d'Arthur*.

A technological break-through along about then ensured a wide distribution of Malory's work. William Caxton had a printing press, and he evidently grew tired of grinding out religious pamphlets, so, sensing a potential market, he took Malory's manuscript and edited it in preparation for a printing run. I think we underestimate Caxton's contribution to *Le Morte d'Arthur*. If we can believe most scholars, Malory's original manuscript was pretty much a hodge-podge of disconnected tales, and Caxton organized them into a coherent whole, giving us a story with a beginning, a middle, and an end.

Now we jump forward another four hundred years. Queen Victoria ascended the British throne at the age of seventeen. Queen

Victoria had opinions. Queen Victoria didn't approve of 'naughty stuff'. Queen Victoria had a resident poet, Alfred Lord Tennyson, and he cleaned up Malory for his queen to produce a work he called *Idylls of the King*. *Idylls of the King* is a fairly typical Victorian bowdlerization that accepted the prevailing attitude of the time that *Le Morte d'Arthur* was little more than 'bold bawdry and open manslaughter'. It glossed over such picky little details as the fact that Guinevere *was* an adulteress, that King Arthur *did* have an incestuous affair with his half-sister, Morgan le Fay, and other improprieties.

Another hundred years slip by and we come to Papa Tolkien, who was probably even prissier than Queen Victoria. Have you ever noticed that there aren't any girl Hobbits? There are matronly lady Hobbits and female Hobbit puppies, but no girls. The Victorians maintained the public fiction that females don't exist below the neck.

Contemporary fantasists all bow politely to Lord Tennyson and Papa Tolkien, then step around them to go back to the original texts for inspiration – and there are a *lot* of those texts. We have King Arthur and his gang in English; we've got Siegfried and Brunhild in German; Charlemagne and Roland in French; El Cid in Spanish; Sigurd the Volsung in Icelandic; and assorted 'myghtiest Knights on lyfe' in a half-dozen other cultures. Without shame, we pillage medieval romance for all we're worth.

Operating by trial and error mostly, we've evolved a tacitly agreed upon list of the elements that make for a good fantasy. The first decision the aspiring fantasist must make is theological. King Arthur and Charlemagne were Christians. Siegfried and Sigurd the Volsung were pagans. My personal view is that pagans write better stories. When a writer is having fun, it shows, and pagans have more fun than Christians. Let's scrape Horace's *Dulche et utile* off the plate before we even start the banquet. We're writing for fun, not to provide moral instruction. I had much more fun with the Belgariad/Malloreon than you did, because I know where all the jokes are.

All right, then, for item number one, I chose paganism. (Note that Papa Tolkien, a devout Anglo-Catholic, took the same route.)

Item number two on our interim list is 'The Quest'. If you don't have a quest, you don't have a story. The quest gives you an excuse to dash around and meet new people. Otherwise, you stay home and grow turnips or something.

Item number three is 'The Magic Thingamajig' – The Holy Grail, the Ring of Power, the Magic Sword, the Sacred Book, or (surprise, surprise) THE JEWEL. Everybody knows where I came down on that one. The Magic Thingamajig is usually, though not always, the object of the quest.

Item four is 'Our Hero' – Sir Galahad, Sir Gawaine, Sir Launcelot, or Sir Perceval. Galahad is saintly; Gawaine is loyal; Launcelot is the heavyweight champion of the world; and Perceval is dumb – at least right at first. I went with Perceval, because he's more fun. A dumb hero is the perfect hero, because he hasn't the faintest idea of what's going on, and in explaining things to *him*, the writer explains them to his reader. Don't get excited. I'm not putting Garion down. He's innocent more than stupid, in the same way Perceval was. Actually, he's fairly clever, but he's a country boy, so he hasn't been exposed to very much of the world. His Aunt Pol wanted him to be that way, and Polgara has ways to get what she wants.

Item number five is the resident 'Wizard' – Merlin, usually, or Gandalf – mighty, powerful, and mysterious. I scratched that one right away and went with Belgarath instead, and I think it was the right choice. I've got a seedy old tramp with bad habits – who just incidentally can rip the tops off mountains if he wants to. I chose to counter him with his daughter, Polgara, who doesn't really approve of him. That sorcerer/sorceress (and father/daughter) pairing broke some new ground, I think.

Item six is our heroine – usually a wispy blonde girl who spends most of her time mooning around in a tower. I chose not to go that route, obviously. Ce'Nedra is a spoiled brat, there's no question about that, but she *is* a little tiger when the chips are down. She turned out even better than I expected.

Item seven is a villain with diabolical connections. I invented Torak, and he served our purpose rather well. I even managed to give him a fairly believable motivation. Milton helped on that one. Torak isn't *exactly* Lucifer, but he comes close. As usual, he has a number of evil underlings to do his dirty-work for him.

(Stay with me. We're almost done.) Item eight is the obligatory group of 'companions', that supporting cast of assorted muscular types from various cultures who handle most of the killing and mayhem until the hero grows up to the point where he can do his own violence on the bad guys.

Item nine is the group of ladies who are attached to the bully-boys in item eight. Each of these ladies *also* needs to be well-defined, with idiosyncrasies and passions of her own.

And finally we come to item ten. Those are the kings, queens, emperors, courtiers, bureaucrats, *et al* who are the governments of the kingdoms of the world.

OK. End of list. If you've got those ten items, you're on your way toward a contemporary fantasy. (You're also on your way to a cast of thousands.)

All right then, now for a test: 'Write an epic fantasy in no less than three and no more than twelve volumes. Then sell it to a publisher. You have twenty years.' (*Don't* send it to me. I don't have a printing press, and I do *not* read in the field. It's a way to avoid contamination.)

STOP!! Do *not* uncover your typewriter, uncap your pen, or plug in your computer just yet. A certain amount of preparation might help. It's a good idea to learn how to drive an automobile *before* you hop into the family car and take off for Los Angeles, and it's probably an equally good idea to browse through a couple of medical texts *before* you saw off the top of Uncle Charlie's head in preparation for brain surgery.

Let me stress one thing at the outset. This is the way *we* did it. This is not the *only* way to do it. Our way worked out fairly well, but others, done differently, have worked just as well. If you don't like our way, we won't be offended.

Now, of necessity, we get into a bit of biography. This introduction is designed to provide enough biographical detail to answer students' questions and to provide a description of our preparations. I hope it satisfies you, because it's all you're going to get. My private life is just that – private – and it's going to stay that way. You don't really need to know what I had for breakfast.

I was born in Washington (the state, not the city) in 1931. (Go ahead. Start counting. Depressing, huh?) I graduated from high school in 1949, worked for a year, and then enrolled in a junior college, majoring in speech, drama, and English. I tore that junior college up. I won a state-wide oratorical contest and played the male lead in most of the drama presentations. Then I applied for and received a scholarship at Reed College in Portland, Oregon, and Reed turned out to be quite a bit more difficult. The college required a thesis for graduation, so I wrote a novel (what else?). Then I was drafted. The army sent me to Germany instead of Korea – where people were still shooting at each other. I'd studied German, so I got along fairly well, and when I wasn't playing soldier with my jeep and my submachine gun, I made the obligatory pilgrimages to Paris, London, Vienna, Naples, Rome, Florence, and Berlin (before the wall). It was all very educational, and I even got paid for being in Europe.

Then I came back to the States and was discharged. I had that GI Bill, so I went to the University of Washington for four years of graduate study. I've already told you about that, so I won't dwell on it. During my college years I worked part-time in grocery stores, a perfect job for a student, since the hours can be adjusted to fit in with the class schedule. Then I went to work for Boeing, building rocket ships. (I was a buyer, not an engineer.) I helped, in a small way, to put a man on the moon. I married a young lady whose history was even more interesting than mine. I was a little miffed when I discovered that her security clearance was higher than mine. I thought 'Top Secret' was the top of the line, but I was wrong. She'd *also* been to places I hadn't even heard of, since she'd been in the Air Force, while I'd been a ground-pounder. I soon discovered that she was a world-class cook, a highly skilled fisherwoman, and – after an argument about whether or not that was *really* a deer lying behind that log a hundred yards away late one snowy afternoon – she demonstrated that she was a dead shot with a deer rifle by shooting poor old Bambi right between the eyes.

I taught college for several years, and then one year the administrators all got a pay raise and the teaching faculty didn't. I told them what they could do with their job, and my wife and I moved to Denver, where I (we) wrote *High Hunt* in our spare time while I worked in a grocery store and my wife worked as a motel maid. We sold *High Hunt* to Putnam, and I was now a published author. We moved to Spokane, and I turned to grocery stores again to keep us eating regularly.

I was convinced that I was a 'serious novelist', and I labored long and hard over several unpublished (and unpublishable) novels that moped around the edges of mawkish contemporary tragedy. In the mid 1970s I was grinding out 'Hunsecker's Ascent', a story about mountain-climbing which was a piece of tripe so bad that it even bored me. (No, you can't see it. I burned it.) Then one morning before I went off to my day-job, I was so bored that I started doodling. My doodles produced a map of a place that never was (and is probably a geological impossibility). Then, feeling the call of duty, I put it away and went back to the tripe table.

Some years later I was in a bookstore going in the general direction of the 'serious fiction'. I passed the science-fiction rack and spotted one of the volumes of *The Lord of the Rings*. I muttered, 'Is this old turkey still floating around?' Then I picked it up and noticed that it was in its *seventy-eighth* printing!!! That got my immediate attention, and I went back home and dug out the aforementioned doodle. It seemed to have some possibilities. Then, methodical as always, I ticked off the above-listed necessities for a good medieval romance. I'd taken those courses in Middle English authors in graduate school, so I had a fair grip on the genre.

I realized that since I'd created this world, I was going to have to populate it, and that meant that I'd have to create the assorted 'ologies' as well before I could even begin to put together an outline. *The Rivan Codex* was the result. I reasoned that each culture had to have a different class-structure, a different mythology, a different theology, different costumes, different forms of address, different national character, and even different coinage and slightly different weights and measures. I might never come right out and *use* them in the books, but they had to be there. 'The Belgariad Preliminaries' took me most of 1978 and part of 1979. (I was still doing honest work in those days, so my time was limited.)

One of the major problems when you're dealing with wizards is the 'Superman Syndrome'. You've got this fellow who's faster than a speeding bullet and all that stuff. He can uproot mountains and stop the sun. Bullets bounce off him, and he can read your mind. Who's going to climb into the ring with this terror? I suppose I could have gone with incantations and spells, but to make that sort of thing believable you've got to invent at least *part* of the incantation, and sooner or later some nut is going to take you seriously, and, absolutely convinced that he can fly if he says the magic words, he'll jump off a building somewhere. *Or*, if he believes that the sacrifice of a virgin will make him Lord of the Universe, and some Girl-Scout knocks on his door – ??? I think it was a sense of social responsibility that steered me away from the 'hocus-pocus' routine.

Anyway, this was about the time when the ESP fakers were announcing that they could bend keys (or crowbars, for all I know) with the power of their minds. Bingo! The Will and the Word was born. And it also eliminated the Superman problem. The notion that doing things with your mind exhausts you as much as doing them with your back was my easiest way out. You *might* be able to pick up a mountain with your mind, but you won't be able to walk after you do it, I can guarantee that. It worked out quite well, and it made some interesting contributions to the story. We added the prohibition against 'unmaking things' later, and we had a workable form of magic with some nasty consequences attached if you broke the rules.

Now we had a story. Next came the question of how to tell it. My selection of Sir Perceval (Sir Dumb, if you prefer) sort of ruled out

'High Style'. I can write in 'High Style' if necessary (see Mandorallen with his 'thee's, thou's and foreasmuches), but Garion would have probably swallowed his tongue if he'd tried it. Moreover, magic, while not a commonplace, is present in our imaginary world, so I wanted to avoid all that 'Gee whiz! Would you look at that!' sort of reaction. I wanted language that was fairly colloquial (with a few cultural variations) to make the whole thing accessible to contemporary readers, but with just enough antique usages to give it a medieval flavor.

Among the literary theories I'd encountered in graduate school was Jung's notion of archetypal myth. The application of this theory usually involves a scholar laboring mightily to find correspondences between current (and not so current) fiction and drama to link them to Greek mythology. (Did Hamlet *really* lust after his mother the way Oedipus did?) It occurred to me that archetypal myth might not be very useful in the *evaluation* of a story, but might it not work in its *creation*? I tried it, and it works. I planted more mythic fishhooks in the first couple of books of the Belgariad than you'll find in any sporting goods store. I've said (too many times, probably) that if you read the first hundred pages of the Belgariad, *I gotcha*!! You won't be *able* to put it down. The use of archetypal myth in the creation of fiction is the literary equivalent of peddling dope.

The preliminaries to the Belgariad are actually out of sequence here. *The Personal History of Belgarath the Sorcerer* was written *after* the rest of the studies while I was trying to get a better grip on the old boy. You might want to compare that very early character sketch with the opening chapters of the more recent *Belgarath the Sorcerer*. Did you notice the similarities? I thought I noticed you noticing.

When I first tackled these studies, I began with *The Holy Books*, and the most important of these is *The Book of Alorn*. When you get right down to it, that one contains the germ of the whole story. After that, I added *The Book of Torak*. Fair is fair, after all, and 'equal time' sounds sort of fair, I guess. The *Testament of the Snake People* was an exercise in showing off. (A poem in the shape of a snake? Gee!) The *Hymn to Chaldan* was supposed to help explain the Arends. A war god isn't all *that* unusual.

The Marags are extinct, but that 'equal time' regulation was still in place, so I took a swing at the grief-stricken God Mara. I had fun with *The Proverbs of Nedra* – a sort of theological justification for pure greed. Maybe I'll make a deal with the New York Stock Exchange, and they can engrave those proverbs on the wall.

The Sermon of Aldur was a false start, since it speaks glowingly of 'Unmaking Things', which UL prohibited in the next section. That section, *The Book of Ulgo*, was rather obviously based on *The Book of Job*. Note that I'll even steal from the Bible. Gorim came off rather well, I thought. Incidentally, 'UL' was a typographical error the first time it appeared. I liked the way it looked on paper, so I kept it. (Would you prefer to have me claim 'Divine Inspiration?')

I'm going to disillusion some enthusiasts here, I'm afraid. Notice that the Mrin Codex and the Darine Codex aren't included here. They don't appear because they don't exist. They're a literary device and nothing more. (I once jokingly told Lester that I'd be willing to write the Mrin Codex *if* he'd agree to publish it on a scroll, but he declined.) I used the 'Mrin' as a form of exposition. Those periodic breakthroughs when Belkira and Beltira – or whoever else is handy – finally crack the code are the things that set off a new course of action. I catch hints of a religious yearning when people start pleading for copies of the 'Mrin'. Sorry gang, I'm not in the business of creating new religions. This is 'story', not 'revelation'. I'm a story-teller, not a Prophet of God. OK?

Once *The Holy Books* were out of the way, I was ready to tackle *The Histories*, and that's where all the 'ologies' started showing up – along with a chronology. When you've got a story that lasts for seven thousand years, you'd *better* have a chronology and pay close attention to it, or you're going to get lost somewhere in the 39th century. The histories of the Alorn Kingdoms are fairly central to the story, but it was the history of the Tolnedran Empire that filled in all the cracks. You'll probably notice how tedious the Tolnedran *History* is. If you think *reading* it was tedious, try *writing* it. It was absolutely essential, however, since much of the background material grew out of it.

Most of the similarities between the people of this world and our imaginary one should be fairly obvious. The Sendars correspond to rural Englishmen, the Arends to Norman French, the Tolnedrans to Romans, the Chereks to Vikings, the Algars to Cossacks, the Ulgos to Jews, and the Angaraks to Hunnish-Mongolian-Muslim-Visigoths out to convert the world by the sword. I didn't really have correspondences in mind for the Drasnians, Rivans, Marags, or Nyissans. They're story elements and don't need to derive from *this* world.

By the time we got to the histories of the Angarak Kingdoms, we were ready to dig into the story itself, so the Angaraks got fairly short shrift. I wanted to get on with it.

There were footnotes in the original of these studies, but they were included (with identifying single-spacing) in the body of the text. These are the mistaken perceptions of the scholars at the University of Tol Honeth. The footnotes I'm adding now are in their proper location (at the foot of the page, naturally). These later notes usually point out inconsistencies. Some of this material just didn't work when we got into the actual narrative, and I'm not one to mess up a good story just for the sake of sticking to an out-dated game-plan.

The addition of *The Battle of Vo Mimbre* was a sort of afterthought. I knew that epic fantasy derived from medieval romance, so just to re-enforce that point of origin, I wrote one. It has most of the elements of a good, rousing medieval romance – and all of its flaws. I'm still fairly sure that it would have made Eleanor of Aquitaine light up like a Christmas tree.

I wanted to use it in its original form as the Prologue for *Queen of Sorcery*, but Lester del Rey said, 'NO!' A twenty-seven page prologue didn't thrill him. That's when I learned one of the rules. A prologue does *not* exceed eight pages. Lester finally settled the argument by announcing that if I wrote an overly long prologue, he'd cut it down with a dull axe.

Oh, there was another argument a bit earlier. Lester didn't like 'Aloria'. He wanted to call it '*Alornia*'!!! I almost exploded, but my wife calmly took the telephone away from me and sweetly said, 'Lester, dear, "Alornia" sounds sort of like a cookie to me.' (Alornia Doone?) Lester thought about that for a moment. 'It does, sort of, doesn't it? OK, Aloria it is then.' Our side won that one big-time.

I'm not passing along these gossipy little tales for the fun of it, people. There's a point buried in most of them. The point to this one is the importance of the sound of names in High Fantasy. Would Launcelot impress you very much if his name were 'Charlie' or 'Wilbur'? The bride of my youth spends hours concocting names. It was – and still is – her specialty. (She's also very good at deleting junk and coming up with great endings.) I can manufacture names if I have to, but hers are better. Incidentally, that 'Gar' at the center of 'Belgarath', 'Polgara', and 'Garion' derives from proto-Indo European. Linguists have been amusing themselves for years backtracking their way to the original language spoken by the barbarians who came wandering off the steppes of Central Asia twelve thousand or so years ago. 'Gar' meant 'Spear' back in those days. Isn't that interesting?

When the preliminary studies were finished, my collaborator and I hammered together an outline, reviewed our character sketches, and we got started. When we had a first draft of what we thought was going to be Book I completed, I sent a proposal, complete with the overall outline, to Ballantine Books, and, naturally, the Post Office Department lost it. After six months, I sent a snippy note to Ballantine. 'At least you could have had the decency to say no.' They replied, 'Gee, we never got your proposal.' I had almost dumped the whole idea of the series because of the gross negligence of my government. I sent the proposal off again. Lester liked it, and we signed a contract. Now we were getting paid for this, so we started to concentrate.

Incidentally, my original proposal envisioned a trilogy – three books tentatively titled *Garion*, *Ce'Nedra*, and *Kal Torak*. That notion tumbled down around my ears when Lester explained the realities of the American publishing business to me. B. Dalton and Waldenbooks had limits on genre fiction, and those two chains ruled the world. At that time, they wanted genre fiction to be paperbacks priced at under three dollars, and thus no more than 300 pages.

'This is what we're going to do,' Lester told me. (Notice that 'we'. He didn't really mean 'we'; he meant *me*.) 'We're going to break it up into five books instead of three.' My original game plan went out the window. I choked and went on. The chess-piece titles, incidentally, were Lester's idea. I didn't like that one very much either. I wanted to call Book V *In the Tomb of the One Eyed God*. I thought that had a nice ring to it but Lester patiently explained that a title that long wouldn't leave any room for a cover illustration. I was losing a lot of arguments here. Lester favored the bulldozer approach to his writers, though, so he ran over me fairly often.

I *did* win one, though – I think. Lester had told me that 'Fantasy fiction is the prissiest of all art-forms.' I *knew* that he was wrong on that one. I've read the works from which contemporary fantasy has descended, and 'prissy' is a wildly inappropriate description (derived, no doubt, from Tennyson and Tolkien). I set out to delicately suggest that girls *did*, in fact, exist below the neck. I'll admit that I lost a few rounds, but I think I managed to present a story that suggested that there are some differences between boys and girls, and that most people find that sort of interesting.

All right, 'Time Out'. For those of you who intend to follow my path, here's what you should do. Get an education first. You're not qualified to write epic fantasy until you've been exposed to medieval romance. As I said earlier, there are all kinds of medieval literature. Look at the Norse stuff. Try the German stories. (If you don't want to read them, go see them on stage in Wagnerian operas.)

Look at Finland, Russia, Ireland, Iceland, Arabia – even China or India. The urge to write and read High Fantasy seems to be fairly universal.

Next comes the practice writing. I started on contemporary novels – *High Hunt* and *The Losers*. (The publication date of *The Losers* is June 1992, but I wrote it back in the 1970s. It's not strictly speaking a novel, but rather is an allegory, the one-eyed Indian is God, and Jake Flood is the Devil. Notice that I wrote it *before* we started the Belgariad.) If you're serious about this, you have to write *every* day, even if it's only for an hour. Scratch the words 'week-end' and 'holiday' out of your vocabulary. (If you've been *very* good, I *might* let you take a half-day off at Christmas.) Write a million or so words. Then burn them. Now you're almost ready to start.

This is what I was talking about earlier when I suggested that most aspiring fantasists will lose heart fairly early on. I was in my mid-teens when I discovered that I was a writer. Notice that I didn't say 'wanted to be a writer'. 'Want' has almost nothing to do with it. It's either there or it isn't. If you happen to be one, you're stuck with it. You'll write whether you get paid for it or not. You won't be able to help yourself. When it's going well, it's like reaching up into heaven and pulling down fire. It's better than any dope you can buy. When it's *not* going well, it's much like giving birth to a baby elephant. You'll probably notice the time lapse. I was forty before I wrote a publishable book. A twenty-five year long apprenticeship doesn't appeal to very many people.

The first thing a fantasist needs to do is to invent a world and draw a map. Do the map first. If you don't, you'll get lost, and picky readers with nothing better to do will gleefully point out your blunders.

Then do your preliminary studies and character sketches in great detail. Give yourself at least a year for this. Two would be better. Your 'Quest', your 'Hero', your form of magic, and your 'races' will probably grow out of these studies at some point. If you're worried about how much this will interfere with a normal life, take up something else. If you decide to be a writer, your life involves sitting at your desk. *This* is what you do to the exclusion of all else, and there aren't any guarantees. You can work on this religiously for fifty years and never get into print, so don't quit your day-job.

It was about the time that we finished Book III of the Belgariad that we met Lester and Judy-Lynn del Rey in person. We all had dinner together, and I told Lester that I thought there was more story than we could cram into five books, so we might want to think about a second set. Lester expressed some interest. Judy-Lynn wanted to write a contract on a napkin. How's *that* for acceptance?

We finished up the Belgariad, and then went back into 'preliminaries' mode. Our major problem with the Malloreon lay in the fact that we'd killed off the Devil at the end of the Belgariad. No villain; no story. The bad guys do have their uses, I suppose. Zandramas, in a rather obscure way, was a counter to Polgara. Pol, though central to the story as our mother figure, had been fairly subordinate in the Belgariad, and we wanted to move her to center stage. There are quite a few more significant female characters in the Malloreon than in the Belgariad. Zandramas (my wife's brilliant name) is Torak's heir as 'Child of Dark'. She yearns for elevation, but I don't think becoming a galaxy to replace the one that blew up was quite what she had in mind. The abduction of Prince Geran set off the obligatory quest, and abductions were commonplace in medieval romance (and in the real world of the Dark Ages as well), so we were still locked in our genre.

We had most of our main characters – good guys and bad guys – already in place, and I knew that Mallorea was somewhere off to the east, so I went back to the map-table and manufactured another continent and the bottom half of the one we already had. We got a lot of mileage out of Kal Zakath. That boy carried most of the Malloreon on his back. Then by way of thanks, we fed him to Cyradis, and she had him for lunch.

I'll confess that I got carried away with *The Mallorean Gospels*. I wanted the Dals to be mystical, so I pulled out all the stops and wrote something verging on Biblical, but without the inconveniences of Judaism, Christianity, or Mohammedanism. What it all boiled down to was that the Dals could see the future, but so could Belgarath, *if* he paid attention to the Mrin Codex. The whole story reeks of prophecy – but nobody can be really sure what it means.

My now publicly exposed co-conspiratress and I have recently finished the second prequel to this story, and now if you want to push it, we've got a classic twelve-book epic. If twelve books were good enough for Homer, Virgil, and Milton, twelve is surely good enough for us. We are *not* going to tack on our version of *The Odyssey* to our already completed *Iliad*. The story's complete as it stands. There aren't going to be any more Garion stories. Period. End of discussion.

All right, that should be enough for students, and it's probably enough to send those who'd like to try it for themselves screaming off into the woods in stark terror. I doubt that it'll satisfy those who are interested in an in-depth biography of their favorite author, but you can't win them all, I guess.

Are you up for some honesty here? Genre fiction is writing that's done for money. Great art doesn't do all that well in a commercial society. Nothing that Franz Kafka wrote ever appeared in print while he was alive. *Miss Lonelyhearts* sank without a ripple. Great literary art is difficult to read because you have to think when you read it, and most people would rather not.

Epic fantasy *can* be set in *this* world. You don't have to create a new universe just to write one. My original 'doodle', however, put us off-world immediately. It's probably that 'off-world' business in Tolkien that causes us to be lumped together with science fiction, and we have no business on the same rack with SF. SF writers are technology freaks who blithely ignore that footnote in Einstein's theory of relativity which clearly states that when an object approaches the speed of light, its mass becomes infinite. (So much for warp-drive.) If old Buck Rogers hits the gas-pedal a little too hard, he'll suddenly *become* the universe. Fantasists are magic and shining armor freaks who posit equally absurd notions with incantations, 'the Will and the Word', or other mumbo-jumbo. *They* want to build a better screwdriver, and *we* want to come up with a better incantation. They want to go into the future, and we want to go into the past. We write better stories than they do, though. They get all bogged down in telling you how the watch works; we just tell you what time it is and go on with the story. SF and fantasy shouldn't even speak to each other, but try explaining that to a book-store manager. Try explaining it to a publisher. Forget it.

One last gloomy note. If something doesn't work, dump it – even if it means that you have to rip up several hundred pages and a half-year's work. More stories are ruined by the writer's stubborn attachment to his own overwrought prose than by almost anything else. Let your stuff cool off for a month and then read it *critically*. Forget that *you* wrote it, and read it as if you didn't really like the guy who put it down in the first place. Then take a meat-axe to it. Let it cool down some more, and then read it again. If it still doesn't work, get rid of it. Revision is the soul of good writing. It's the story that counts, not your fondness for your own gushy prose. Accept your losses and move on.

All right, I'll let you go for right now. We'll talk some more later, but why don't we let Belgarath take over for a while?

PREFACE: THE PERSONAL HISTORY OF BELGARATH THE SORCERER[*]

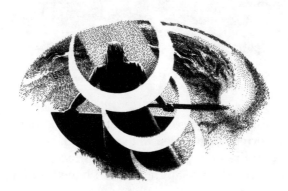

In the light of all that has happened, this is most certainly a mistake. It would be far better to leave things as they are, with event and cause alike half-buried in the dust of forgotten years. If it were up to me, I would so leave them. I have, however, been so importuned by an undutiful daughter, so implored by a great (and many times over) grandson, and so cajoled by that tiny and willful creature who is his wife – a burden he will have to endure for all his days – that I must, if only to have some peace, set down the origins of the titanic events which have so rocked the world.

Few will understand this, and fewer still will acknowledge its truth. I am accustomed to that. But, since I alone know the beginning, the middle, and the end of these events, it is upon me to commit to perishable parchment and to ink that begins to fade before it even dries some ephemeral account of what happened and why.

Thus, let me begin this story as all stories are begun, at the beginning.

[*] This first-person narrative was written to give us a grip on Belgarath's character and we wrote it almost twenty years ago. I always felt there was a story there. As it turned out, there were two, *Belgarath the Sorcerer* and *Polgara the Sorceress*. After we'd finished the Belgariad/Malloreon, we knew how the story ended, so we could then go back and write the beginning. Most of Part I of *Belgarath the Sorcerer* is an expansion of this ancient manuscript, which *also* dictated the first-person narrative approach.

I was born in a village so small that it had no name.* It lay, if I remember it correctly, on a pleasant green bank beside a small river that sparkled in the summer sun as if its surface were covered with jewels – and I would trade all the jewels I have ever owned or seen to sit beside that river again.

Our village was not rich, but in those days none were. The world was at peace, and our Gods walked among us and smiled upon us. We had enough to eat and huts to shelter us from the weather. I do not recall who our God was, nor his attributes, nor his totem. It was, after all, a very, very long time ago.

Like the other children, I played in the warm, dusty streets and ran through the long grass in the meadows and paddled in that sparkling river which was drowned by the eastern sea so many years ago that they are beyond counting.

My mother died when I was quite young. I remember that I cried about it for a very long time, though I must honestly admit that I can no longer even remember her face. I remember the gentleness of her hands and the warm smell of fresh-baked bread that came from her garments, but I can not remember her face – but then, there have been so many faces.

The people of my village cared for me and saw to it that I was fed and clothed and sheltered in one house or another, but I grew up

---

* The name of the village was added in *Belgarath the Sorcerer* to justify his name linguistically. 'Garath' could mean 'of the village of Gara' in the archaic form of several languages.

wild. I never knew my father, and my mother was dead, and I was not content with the simple, drowsy life of a small, unnamed village beside a sparkling river in a time when the world was very young. I began to wander out into the hills above my village, at first with only a stick and a sling, but later with more manly weapons – though I was still but a child.

And then came a day in early spring when the air was cool and the clouds raced overhead in the fresh, young wind, and I had climbed to the top of the highest hill to the west of our river. And I looked down at the tiny patch of dun-colored huts beside a small river that did not sparkle beneath the scudding clouds of spring. And then I turned and looked to the west at a vast grassland and white-topped mountains beyond and clouds roiling titanic in the grey sky. And I looked one last time at the village where I was born and where, had I not climbed that hill on just such a morning, I might well have died; and I turned my face to the west and I went from that place forever.

The summer was easy. The plain yielded food in plenty to a young adventurer with the legs to chase it and the appetite to eat it – no matter how tough or poorly cooked. And in the fall I came upon a vast encampment of people whitened as if by the touch of frost. They took me in and wept over me, and many came to touch me and to look at me, and they wept also. But one thing I found most strange. In the entire encampment there were no children, and to my young eyes the people seemed most terribly old. They spoke a language I did not understand, but they fed me and seemed to argue endlessly among themselves over who might have the privilege of keeping me in his tent or pavilion.

I passed the winter among these strange people, and, as is so frequently the case with the young, I learned nothing in that season. I can not remember even one word of the language they spoke.*

When the snow melted and the frost seeped up out of the ground and the wind of spring began to blow again, I knew it was time to leave. I took no joy in the pampering of a multitude of grandparents and had no desire to become the pet of a host of crotchety old people who could not even speak a civilized language.

---

* These old people are those Ulgos who chose not to follow Gorim to Prolgu. 'As the branch that is cut off, they are witheréd and dying.' (Because their women are barren.)

And so, early one spring morning, before the darkness had even slid off the sky, I sneaked from the camp and went south into a low range of hills where their creaky old limbs could not follow me. I moved very fast, for I was young and well-fed and quite strong, but it was not fast enough. As the sun rose I could hear the wails of unspeakable grief coming from the encampment behind me. I remember that sound very well.

I loitered that summer in the hills and in the upper reaches of the Vale to the south beyond them. It was in my mind that I might – if pursued by necessity – winter again in the camp of the old people. But, as it happened, an early storm caught me unprepared to the south of the hills, and the snow piled so deep that I could not make my way back across to my refuge. And my food was gone, and my shoes, mere bags of untanned hide, wore out, and I lost my knife, and it grew very cold.

In the end I huddled behind a pile of rock that seemed to reach up into the very heart of the snowstorm that swirled around me and tried to prepare myself for death. I thought of my village and of the grassy fields around it and of our small, sparkling river, and of my mother, and, because I was still really very young, I cried.

'Why weepest thou, boy?' The voice was very gentle. The snow was so thick that I could not see who spoke, but the tone made me angry.

'Because I'm cold and I'm hungry,' I said, 'and because I'm dying and I don't want to.'

'Why art thou dying? Art thou injured?'

'I'm lost,' I said, 'and it's snowing, and I have no place to go.'

'Is this reason enough to die amongst thy kind?'

'Isn't it enough?' I said, still angry.

'And how long dost thou expect this dying of thine will persist?' The voice seemed mildly curious.

'I don't know,' I said. 'I've never done it before.'

The wind howled and the snow swirled more thickly around me.

'Boy,' the voice said finally, 'come here to me.'

'Where are you?' I said. 'I can't see you.'

'Walk around the tower to thy left. Knowest thou thy left hand from thy right?'

I stumbled to my half-frozen feet angrier than I ever remember having been.

'Well, boy?'

I moved around what I had thought was a pile of rock, my hands on the stones.

'Thou shalt come to a smooth grey rock,' the voice said, 'somewhat taller than thy head and broad as thine arms may reach.'

'All right,' I said, my lips thick with the cold. 'Now what?'

'Tell it to open.'

'What?'

'Speak unto the rock,' the voice said patiently, ignoring the fact that I was congealing in the gale. 'Command it to open.'

'Command? Me?'

'Thou art a man. It is but a rock.'

'What do I say?'

'Tell it to open.'

'Open,' I commanded half-heartedly.

'Surely thou canst do better than that.'

'*Open!*' I thundered.

And the rock slid aside.

'Come in, boy,' the voice said. 'Stand not in the weather like some befuddled calf.'

The inside of the tower – for such indeed it was – was dimly lighted by stones that glowed with a pale, cold fire. I thought that was a fine thing, though I would have preferred it had they been warmer. Stone steps worn with countless centuries of footfalls ascended in a spiral into the gloom above my head. Other than that the chamber was empty.

'Close the door, boy,' the voice said, not unkindly.

'How?' I said.

'How didst thou open it?'

I turned to the gaping rock and quite proud of myself, I commanded, 'Close!'

And, at my voice, the rock slid shut with a grinding sound that chilled my blood even more than the fierce storm outside.

'Come up, boy,' the voice commanded.

And so I mounted the stairs, only a little bit afraid. The tower was very high, and the climbing took me a long time.

At the top was a chamber filled with wonders. I looked at things such as I had never seen even before I looked at him who had commanded me and had saved my life. I was very young, and I was not at the time above thoughts of theft. Larceny even before gratitude seethed in my grubby little soul.

Near a fire which burned, as I observed, without fuel sat a man (I thought) who seemed most incredibly ancient. His beard was long and full and white as the snow which had so nearly killed me – but his eyes – his eyes were eternally young.

'Well, boy,' he said, 'hast thou decided not to die?'

'Not if it isn't necessary,' I said bravely, still cataloguing the wonders of the chamber.

'Dost thou require anything?' he asked. 'I am unfamiliar with thy kind.'

'A little food,' I told him. 'I have not eaten in three days. And a warm place to sleep. I shall not be much trouble, Master, and I can make myself useful in payment.' I had learned a long time ago how to make myself agreeable to those who were in a position to do me favors.

'Master?' he said and laughed, a sound so cheerful that it made me almost want to dance. 'I am not thy master, boy.' He laughed again, and my heart sang with the splendor of his mirth. 'Let us see to this thing of food. What dost thou require?'

'A little bread perhaps,' I said, '– not too stale.'

'Bread?' he said. 'Only bread? Surely, boy, thy stomach is fit for more than bread. If thou wouldst make thyself useful – as thou hast promised – we must nourish thee properly. Consider, boy. Think of all the things thou hast eaten in thy life. What in all this world would most surely satisfy that vast hunger of thine?'

I could not even say it. Before my eyes swam the visions of plump, smoking roasts, of fat geese swimming in their own gravy, of heaps of fresh-baked bread and rich, golden butter, of pastries in thick cream, of cheese, and dark brown ale, of fruits and nuts and salt to savor it all.

And he who sat by the glowing fire that burned, it seemed, air alone laughed again, and again my heart sang. 'Turn, boy,' he said, 'and eat thy fill.'

And I turned, and there on a table which I had not even seen before lay everything which I had imagined.

A hungry young boy does not ask where food comes from – he eats. And so I ate. I ate until my stomach groaned. And through the sound of my eating I could hear the laughter of the aged one beside his fire, and my heart leapt within me at each laugh.

And when I had finished and drowsed over my plate, he spoke again. 'Wilt thou sleep now, boy?'

'A corner, Master,' I said. 'A little out-of-the-way place by the fire, if it be not too much trouble.'

He pointed. 'Sleep there, boy,' he said, and at once I saw a bed which I had seen no more than the table – a great bed with huge pillows and comforters of softest down. And I smiled my thanks and crept into the bed and, because I was young and very tired, I fell asleep almost at once. But in my sleep I knew that he who had brought me in from the storm and fed me and cared for me was watching through the long snowy night, and I felt even more secure in his care.

And that began my servitude. My Master never commanded in the way other masters commanded their servants, but rather suggested or asked. Amazingly, almost in spite of myself, I found myself leaping to do his bidding. The tasks, simple at first, grew harder and harder. I began to wish I had never come to this place. Sometimes my Master would stop what he was doing to watch my labors, a bemused expression on his face. Then he would sigh and return to the things which he did and which I did not understand.

The seasons turned, marching in their stately, ordered progression as I labored endlessly at impossible tasks. Then, perhaps three – or maybe it was five – years after I had come to the tower and begun my servitude, I was struggling one day to move a huge rock which my Master felt was in his way. It would not move though I heaved and pushed and strained until I thought my limbs would crack. Finally, in a fury, I concentrated all my strength and all my will upon the boulder and grunted one single word. 'Move,' I said.

And it moved – not grudgingly with its huge, inert weight sullenly resisting my strength – but quite easily, as if the touch of one finger would be sufficient to send it bounding across the plain.

'Well, boy,' my Master said, startling me by his nearness, 'I had wondered how long it might be before this day arrived.'

'Master,' I said, confused, 'what happened? How did the great rock move so easily?'

'It moved at thy command, boy. Thou art a man, and it is only a rock.'

'May other things be done so, Master?'

'*All* things may be done so, boy. Put but thy will to that which thou wouldst have come to pass and speak the word. It shall come to pass even as thou wouldst have it. I have marveled, boy, at thine insistence upon doing all things with thy back instead of thy will. I had begun to fear for thee, thinking that perhaps thou mightest be defective.'

I walked over to the rock and laid my hands on it again. 'Move,' I commanded, bringing my will to bear on it, and the rock moved as easily as before.

'Does it make thee more comfortable touching the rock when thou wouldst move it, boy?' my Master asked, a note of curiosity in his voice.

The question stunned me. I looked at the rock. 'Move,' I said tentatively. The rock did not move.

'Thou must command, boy, not entreat.'

'Move!' I roared, and the rock heaved and rolled off with nothing but my will and the word to make it do so.

'Much better, boy,' my Master said. 'Perhaps there is hope for thee yet. What is thy name, boy?'

'Garath,' I told him, and suddenly realized that he had never asked me before.

'An unseemly name, boy. I shall call thee Belgarath.'

'As it please thee, Master,' I said. I had never 'thee'd' him before, and I held my breath for fear that he might be displeased, but he showed no sign that he had noticed. Then, made bold by my success, I went further. 'And how may I call thee, Master?' I said.

'I am called Aldur,' he said, smiling.

I had heard the name before, and I immediately fell upon my face before him.

'Art thou ill, Belgarath?' he asked.

'Oh, great and powerful God,' I said, trembling, 'forgive mine ignorance. I should have known thee at once.'

'Don't do that,' he said irritably. 'I require no obeisance. Rise to thy feet, Belgarath. Stand up, boy. Thine action is unseemly.'

I scrambled up fearfully and clenched myself for the sudden shock of lightning. Gods, as all knew, could destroy at their whim those who displeased them.

'And what dost thou propose to do with thy life now, Belgarath?' he asked.

'I would stay and serve thee, Master,' I said, as humbly as I could.

'I require no service,' he said. 'What canst *thou* do for *me*?'

'May I worship thee, Master?' I pleaded. I had never met a God before, and was uncertain about the proprieties.

'I do not require thy worship either,' he said.

'May I not stay, Master?' I pleaded. 'I would be thy Disciple and learn from thee.'

'The desire to learn does thee credit, but it will not be easy,' he warned.

'I am quick to learn, Master,' I boasted. 'I shall make thee proud of me.'

And then he laughed, and my heart soared. 'Very well then, Belgarath, I shall make thee my pupil.'

'And thy Disciple also, Master?'

'That we will see in time, Belgarath.'

And then, because I was very young and very proud of myself and my new-found powers, I turned to a dried and brittle bush – it was mid-winter at the time – and I spoke to it fervently. 'Bloom,' I said, and the bush quite suddenly produced a single flower. I plucked it and offered it to him. 'For thee, Master,' I said. 'Because I love thee.'

And he took the flower and smiled and held it between his hands. 'I thank thee, my son,' he said. It was the first time he had ever called me that. 'And this flower shall be thy first lesson. I would have thee examine it most carefully and tell me all that thou canst perceive of it.'

And that task took me twenty years, as I recall. Each time I came to him with the flower that never wilted or faded – how I grew to hate that flower – and told him what else I had learned, he said, 'is that *all*, my son?' and, crushed, I went back to my studies.

And there were many other things as well that took at least as long. I examined trees and birds, fish and beasts, insects and vermin. I devoted forty-five years to the study of grass alone.

In time it occurred to me that I was not aging as other men aged.

'Master,' I said one night in our chamber high in the tower as we both labored with our studies, 'why is it that I do not grow old?'

'Wouldst thou grow old, my son?' he asked. 'I have never seen much advantage in it myself.'

'I don't really miss it all that much, Master,' I admitted, 'but isn't it customary?'

'Perhaps,' he said 'but not mandatory. Thou hast much yet to learn, and one or ten or even a hundred lifetimes are not enough. How old art thou, my son?'

'I think I am somewhat beyond three hundred years, Master.'

'A suitable age, my son, and thou hast persevered in thy studies. Should I forget myself and call thee "Boy" again, pray correct me. It is not seemly that the Disciple of a God should be called "Boy".'

'I shall remember that, Master,' I said, almost overcome with joy that he had finally called me his Disciple.

'I was certain that thou wouldst,' he said. 'And what is the object of thy present study, my son?'

'I would seek to learn why the stars fall, Master.'

'A proper study, my son,' he said, smiling.

'And thou, Master,' I asked. 'What is thy study – if I be not over-bold to ask.'

'I am concerned with this jewel,' he said, pointing at a moderate-sized grey stone on the table before him. 'It may be of some curiosity in the fullness of time.'*

'I am certain it shall, Master,' I assured him. 'If be worthy of thine attention, it shall surely be a curiosity at least.' And I turned back to my study of the inconstant stars.

In time, others came to us, some by accident, as I had come, and some by intent, seeking out my Master that they might learn from him. Such a one was Zedar. I came upon him one golden day in autumn near our tower. He had built a rude altar and was burning the carcass of a goat upon it. The greasy smoke from his offering was fouling the air, and he was prostrated before the altar, chanting some outlandish prayer.

'What are you doing?' I demanded, quite angry since his noise

---

* It was not until the Malloreon that we revealed the Orb's off-world origin. At first it was simply a rock Aldur had picked up in a riverbed and modified with the touch of his hand.

and the stink of his sacrifice distracted my mind from a problem I had been considering for fifteen years.

'Oh, puissant and all-knowing God,' he said, groveling in the dirt. 'I have come a thousand leagues to behold thy glory and to worship thee.'

'Puissant?' I said. 'Get up, man, and stop this caterwauling. I am not a God, but a man, just as you are.'

'Art thou not the great God, Aldur?' he asked.

'I am Belgarath,' I said, 'his Disciple. What is this foolishness?' I pointed at his altar and his smoking offering.

'It is to please the God,' he said, rising and dusting off his clothes. 'Dost thou think he will find it acceptable?'

I laughed, for I did not like this stranger much. 'I cannot think of a single thing you might have done which would offend him more,' I said.

The stranger looked stricken. He turned quickly and reached out as if he would seize the burning animal with his bare hands to hide it.

'Don't be an idiot,' I snapped. 'You'll burn yourself.'

'It must be hidden,' he said desperately. 'I would die rather than offend Mighty Aldur.'

'Stand out of the way,' I told him.

'What?'

'Get clear,' I said, irritably waving him off. Then I looked at his grotesque little altar, willed it away and said, 'Go away,' and it vanished, leaving only a few tatters of confused smoke hanging in the air.

He collapsed on his face again.

'You're going to wear out your clothes if you keep doing that,' I told him, 'and my Master will not be amused by it.'

'I pray thee,' he said, rising and dusting himself off again, 'mighty Disciple of the most high Aldur, instruct me so that I offend not the God.'

'Be truthful,' I told him, 'and do not seek to impress him with false show.'

'And how may I become his Disciple as thou art?'

'First you become his pupil,' I said, 'and that is not easy.'

'What must I do to become his pupil?' the stranger asked.

'You must become his servant,' I said, a bit smugly I must admit.

'And then his pupil?'

'In time,' I said, smiling, 'if he so wills.'

'And when may I meet the God?'

And so I took him to the tower.

'Will the God Aldur not wish to know my name?' the stranger asked.

'Not particularly.' I said. 'If you prove worthy, he will give you a name of his own choosing.' Then I turned to the grey stone in the wall and commanded it to open, and then we went inside.

My Master looked the stranger over and then turned to me. 'Why hast thou brought this man to me, my son?' he asked.

'He besought me, Master,' I said. 'I felt it was not my place to say him yea or nay. Thy will must decide such things. If it be that he please thee not, I shall take him outside and bid him be no more and so put an end to him and his interruption.'

'That is unkindly said, my son,' Aldur said sternly. 'The Will and the Word may not be used so.' *

'Forgive me, Master,' I said humbly.

'*Thou* shalt instruct him, Belgarath,' my Master said. 'If it should be that thou findest him apt, inform me.'

'I will, Master,' I promised.

'What is thy study currently?'

'I examine the reason for mountains, Master,' I said.

'Lay aside thy mountains, Belgarath, and study man instead. It may be that thou shalt find the study useful.'

'As my Master commands,' I said regretfully. I had almost found the secret of mountains, and I was not much enthused about allowing it to escape me. But that was the end of my leisure.

I instructed the stranger as my Master had bade me. I set him impossible tasks and waited. To my mortification, within six months he learned the secret of the Will and the Word. My Master named him Belzedar and accepted him as a pupil.

An then came the others. Kira and Tira were twin shepherd boys who had become lost and wandered to us one day – and stayed. Makor came from so far away that I could not conceive how he had even heard of my Master, and Din from so near that I wondered that his whole tribe did not come with him. Sambar simply appeared one day and sat down upon the earth in front of the tower and waited until we accepted him.

And to me it fell to instruct each of them until he found the secret of Will and the Word – which is not a secret, after all, but lies within every man. And in time each of them became my Master's pupil, and he named them even as he had named me. Zedar became

---

* An early indication of the prohibition against unmaking things.

Belzedar, Kira and Tira became Beltira and Belkira. Makor and Din and Sambar became Belmakor and Beldin and Belsambar. To each of our names our Master joined the symbol of the Will and the Word, and we became his Disciples.*

And we built other towers so that our labors and our studies should not interfere with our Master's work or each other's.

At first I was jealous that my Master spent time with these others, but, since time was meaningless to us anyway and I knew that my Master's love was infinite, so that his love for the others in no way diminished his love for me, I soon outgrew that particular childishness. And also, I grew to love the others as the bonds of our brotherhood grew. I could sense their minds as they worked, and I shared their joy at each new discovery they made. Because I was the first Disciple, they often came to me as to an older brother with those things they were embarrassed to lay before our Master, and I guided them as best I could.

Thus passed a period of perhaps a thousand years, and we were content. The world beyond our Vale changed and the people also, and no more pupils came to us. It was a question I always intended to pursue but never found the time to examine. Perhaps the other Gods grew jealous and forbade their people to seek us out, or

* A note here for the linguistically obsessed. 'Bel' may or may not be 'the symbol of the Will and the Word'. It is more likely that it means 'beloved'. 'Bel' is the masculine form, and 'Pol' is the feminine. Polgara's name derives directly from her father's name, since it's a patronymic like 'Ivan Ivanovitch' (Ivan son of Ivan) or 'Natasha Ivanova' (Natasha, daughter of Ivan) in Russian. Note that this principle does not apply to the name of Pol's sister, Beldaran, which perhaps indicates that Belgarath loved Beldaran more than he loved Pol.

perhaps it was that in their long passage through the endless generations, men somehow lost that tiny spark that is the source of the
power of Will and Word and is the lodestone that draws their spirits
inevitably to the spirit of Aldur. So it was that we were seven only
and were unlike any other men on earth.

And through all this time of study and learning, our Master,
Aldur, labored in infinite patience with that grey stone he had
shown me on the night he had accepted me as his Disciple. Once I
marveled to him that he should devote so much time to it, and he
laughed.

'Truly, my son,' he said, 'I labored once at least so long to create a
flower which is now so common that none take note of it. It blooms
beside every dusty path, and men pass it by without even looking at
it. But *I* know it is there, and I joy in its perfection.'

As I look back, I think I would give my life, which has stretched
over so many years, if my Master had never conceived the idea of
that grey stone which has brought so much woe into this world.

The stone, which he called a jewel, was grey (as I have said) and
quite round and perhaps the size of a man's heart. My Master found
it, I believe, in the bed of a stream. To me it appeared to be a very
ordinary stone, but things are concealed from me that Aldur in his
wisdom perceived quite easily. It may be that there was something
in the stone which he alone could see, or it may be that this ordinary
grey stone became what it became because of his efforts and his will
and his spirit with which he infused it. Whatever it may have been, I
wish with all my heart that he had never seen it, never stooped and
touched it, never picked it up.

At any rate, one day, a very long time ago, it was finished, and our
Master called us together so that he might show it to us.

'Behold this Orb,' he told us. 'In it lies the fate of the world.' And

the grey stone, so ordinary a thing, but which had been polished by the touch of our Master's hand for a thousand years and more, began to glow as if a tiny blue fire flickered deep within it.

And Belzedar, always quick, asked, 'How, Great Master, can so small a thing be so important?'

And our Master smiled, and the Orb grew brighter. Flickering dimly within it I seemed to see images. 'The past lies herein,' our Master said, 'and the present and the future also. This is but a small part of the virtue of this thing which I have made. With it may man – or the earth itself – be healed – or destroyed. Whatsoever one would do, even if it be beyond the power of the Will and the Word, with this may it come to pass.'

'Truly a wondrous thing, Master,' Belzedar said, and it seemed to me that his eyes glittered as he spoke, and his fingers seemed to twitch.

'But, Master,' I said, 'thou hast said that the fate of the world lies within this Orb of thine. How may that be?'

'It hath revealed the future unto me, my son,' my Master said sadly. 'The stone shall be the cause of much contention and great suffering and great destruction. Its power reaches from where it now sits to blow out the lives of men yet unborn as easily as thou wouldst snuff a candle.'

'It is an evil thing then, Master,' I said, and Belsambar and Belmakor agreed.

'Destroy it, Master,' Belsambar pleaded, 'before it can bring this evil to the world.'

'That may not be,' our Master said.

'Blessed is the wisdom of Aldur,' Belzedar said. 'With us to aid him, our Master may wield this wondrous jewel for good and not ill. Monstrous would it be to destroy so precious a thing.'*

'Destroy it, Master,' Belkira and Beltira said as in one voice, their minds as always linked into the same thought. 'We beseech thee, unmake this evil thing which thou hast made.'

'That may not be,' our Master said again. 'The unmaking of things is forbidden. Even I may not unmake that which I have made.'

'Who shall forbid anything to the God Aldur?' Belmakor asked.

'It is beyond thine understanding, my son,' our Master said. 'To thee and to other men it may seem that my brothers and I are limitless, but it is not so. And, I tell thee, my sons, I would not unmake the jewel even if it were permitted. Look about thee at the world in

---

* Notice that Belzedar's obsession with the Orb is introduced here.

its childhood and at man in his infancy. All living things must grow or they will die. Through this Orb shall the world be changed and shall man achieve that state for which he was made. This jewel which I have made is not of itself evil. Evil is a thing which lies only in the minds and hearts of men – and of Gods also.' And then my Master fell silent, and he sighed, and we went from him and left him in his sadness.

In the years which followed, we saw little of our Master. Alone in his tower he communed with the spirit of the jewel which he had made. We were saddened by his absence, and our work had little joy in it.

And then one day a stranger came into the Vale. He was beautiful as no being I have ever seen was or could be, and he walked as if his foot spurned the earth.

As was customary, we went to greet him.

'I would speak with my brother, thy Master,' he told us, and we knew we were in the presence of a God.

As the eldest, I stepped forward. 'I shall tell my Master you have come,' I said. I was not all that familiar with Gods, since Aldur was the only one I had ever met, but something about this over-pretty stranger did not sit quite well with me.

'That is not needful, Belgarath,' he told me in a tone that sat even less well than his manner. 'My brother knows I am here. Convey me to his tower.'

I turned and led the way without trusting myself to answer.

At the foot of the tower the stranger looked me full in the face. 'A bit of advice for thee, Belgarath, by way of thanks for thy service to me. Seek not to rise above thyself. It is not thy place to approve or disapprove of *me*. For thy sake when next we meet I hope thou wilt remember this and behave in a manner more seemly.' His eyes seemed to bore directly into me, and his voice chilled me.

But, because I was still who I was and even the two thousand years I had lived in the Vale had not entirely put the wild, rebellious boy in me to sleep, I answered him somewhat tartly. 'Thank you for the advice,' I said. 'Will you require anything else?' He was a God, after all, and didn't need *me* to tell him how to open the tower door. I waited watching closely for some hint of confusion.

'Thou art pert, Belgarath,' he told me. 'Perhaps one day I shall give myself leisure to instruct thee in proper behavior.'

'I'm always eager to learn,' I told him.

He turned and gestured negligently. The great stone in the wall of the tower opened, and he went inside.

We never knew exactly what passed between our Master and the strange, beautiful God who met with him. They spoke together for long hours, and then a summer storm broke above our heads, and we were forced to take shelter. We missed, therefore, the departure of the strange God.

When the storm had cleared, our Master called us to him, and we went up into his tower. He sat at the table where he had labored so long over the Orb. There was a great sadness in his face, and my heart wept to see it. There was also a reddened mark upon his cheek which I did not understand.

But Belzedar, ever quick, saw at once what I did not see. 'Master,' he said, and his voice had the sound of panic in it, 'where is the jewel? Where is the Orb of power which thou hast made?'

'Torak, my brother, hath taken it away with him,' my Master said, and his voice had almost the sound of weeping in it.

'Quickly,' Belzedar said, 'we must pursue him and reclaim it before he escapes us. We are many, and he is but one.'

'He is a God, my son,' Aldur said. 'Thy numbers would mean nothing to him.'

'But, Master,' Belzedar said most desperately, 'we *must* reclaim the Orb. It *must* be returned to us.'

'How did he obtain it from thee, Master?' the gentle Beltira asked.

'Torak conceived a desire for the thing,' Aldur said, 'and he besought me that I should give it to him. When I would not, he smote me and took the Orb and ran.'

A rage seized me at that. Though the jewel was wondrous, it was still only a stone. The fact that someone had struck my Master brought flames into my brain. I cast off my robe, bent my will into the air before me and forged a sword with a single word. I seized the sword and leapt to the window.

'No!' my Master said, and the word stopped me as though a wall had been placed before me.

'Open!' I commanded, slashing at the wall with the sword I had just made.

'No!' my Master said, and it would not let me through.

'He hath struck thee, Master,' I raged. 'For that I will slay him though he be ten times a God.'

'No,' my Master said again. 'Torak would crush thee as easily as thou would* crush a fly which annoyed thee. I love thee much, my eldest son, and I would not lose thee so.'

---

* This is grammatically incorrect. When using archaic language it is important to pay attention to the verb forms, which are *not* the same in second person familiar as they are in second person formal. The proper form here would be 'wouldst'.

'There must be war, Master,' Belmakor said. 'The blow and the theft must not go unpunished. We will forge weapons, and Belgarath shall lead us, and we shall make war upon this thief who calls himself a God.'

'My son,' our Master said to him, 'there will be war enough to glut thee of it before thy life ends. The Orb is as nothing. Gladly would I have given it unto my brother, Torak, were it not that the Orb itself had told me that one day it would destroy him. I would have spared him had I been able, but his lust for the thing was too great, and he would not listen.' He sighed and then straightened.

'There will be war,' he said. 'My brother, Torak, hath the Orb in his possession. It is of great power, and in his hands can do great mischief. We must reclaim it or alter it before Torak learns its full power.'

'Alter?' Belzedar said, aghast. 'Surely, Master, surely thou wouldst not *destroy* this precious thing?'

'No,' Aldur said. 'It may not be destroyed but will abide even unto the end of days; but if Torak can be pressed into haste, he will attempt to use it in a way that it *will* not be used. Such is its power.'

Belzedar stared at him.

'The world is inconstant, my son,' our Master explained, 'but good and evil are immutable and unchanging. The Orb is an object of good, and is not merely a bauble or a toy. It hath understanding – not such as thine – but understanding nonetheless – and it hath a will. Beware of it, for the will of the Orb is the will of a stone. It is, as I say, a thing of good. If it be raised to do evil, it will strike down whomever would so use it – be he man or be he God. Thus we must make haste. Go thou, my Disciples, unto my other brothers and tell them that I bid them come to me. I am the eldest, and they will come out of respect, if not love.'

And so we went down from our Master's tower and divided ourselves and went out of the Vale to seek out his brothers, the other Gods. Because the twins Beltira and Belkira could not be separated without perishing, they remained behind with our Master, but each of the rest of us went forth in search of one of the Gods.

Since haste was important, and I had perhaps the farthest to go in my search for the God, Belar, I travelled for a time in the form of an eagle. But my arms soon grew weary with flying, and heights have ever made me giddy. I also found my eyes frequently distracted by tiny movements on the ground, and I had fierce urges to swoop down and kill things. I came to earth, resumed my own form and sat for a time to regain my breath and consider.

I had not assumed other forms frequently. It was a simple trick without much advantage to it. I now discovered a major drawback involved in it. The longer I remained in the assumed form, the more the character of the form became interwoven with my own. The eagle, for all his splendor, is really a stupid bird, and I had no desire to be distracted from my mission by every mouse or rabbit on the ground beneath me.

I considered the horse. A horse can run very fast, but he soon grows tired and he is not very intelligent. An antelope can run for days without growing weary, but an antelope is a silly creature, and too many things upon the plain looked upon the antelope as food. I had not the time it would take to stop and persuade each of those things to seek food elsewhere. And then it occurred to me that of all the creatures of the plain and forest, the wolf was the most intelligent, the swiftest, and the most tireless.

It was a decision well-made. As soon as I became accustomed to going on all fours, I found the shape of the wolf most satisfactory and the mind of the wolf most compatible with my own. I quickly discovered that it is a fine thing to have a tail. It provides an excellent means of maintaining one's balance, and one may curl it about himself at night to ward off the chill. I grew very proud of my tail on my journey in search of Belar and his people.

I was stopped briefly by a young she-wolf who was feeling frolicsome. She had, as I recall, fine haunches and a comely muzzle.

'Why so great a hurry, friend?' she said to me coyly in the way of

wolves. Even in my haste I was amazed to discover that I could understand her quite easily. I stopped.

'What a splendid tail you have,' she complimented me, quickly following her advantage, 'and what excellent teeth.'

'Thank you,' I replied modestly. 'Your own tail is also quite fine, and your coat is truly magnificent.'

'Do you really think so?' she said, preening herself. Then she nipped playfully at my flank and dashed off a few yards, trying to get me to chase her.

'I would gladly stay a while so that we might get to know each other better,' I told her, 'but I have a most important errand.'

'An errand?' she laughed. 'Who ever heard of a wolf with any errand but his own desires?'

'I'm not really a wolf,' I told her.

'Really?' she said. 'How remarkable. You look like a wolf and you talk like a wolf and you certainly smell like a wolf, but you say you are not really a wolf. What are you, then?'

'I'm a man,' I said.

She sat, a look of amazement on her face. She had to accept what I said as the truth since wolves are incapable of lying. 'You have a tail,' she said. 'I've never seen a man with a tail before. You have a fine coat. You have four feet. You have long, pointed teeth, sharp ears and a black nose, and yet you tell me you are a man.'

'It's very complicated,' I told her.

'It must be,' she said. 'I think I will run with you for a while since you *must* attend to this errand. Perhaps we can discuss it as we go along and you can explain this complicated thing to me.'

'If you wish,' I said, since I rather liked her and was glad by then for any company, 'but I must warn you that I run very fast.'

'All wolves run very fast,' she sniffed.

And so, side by side, we ran off over the endless grassy plains in search of the God Belar.

'Do you intend to run both day and night?' she asked me after we had gone several miles.

'I will rest when it is needful,' I told her.

'I'm glad of that,' she said. Then she laughed, nipped at my shoulder and scampered off some distance.

I began to consider the morality of my situation. Though my companion looked quite delightful to me in my present form, I was almost positive she would be less so once I resumed my proper shape. Further, while it is undoubtedly a fine thing to be a father, I was almost certain that a litter of puppies would prove an embarrassment when I returned to my Master. Not only that, the puppies would not be entirely wolves, and I had no desire to father a race of monsters. But finally, since wolves mate for life, when I left her – as I would of necessity be compelled to do – my sweet companion would be abandoned, betrayed, left alone with a litter of fatherless puppies, subject to the scorn and ridicule of the other members of her pack. Propriety is a most important thing among wolves. Thus I resolved to resist her advances on our journey in search of Belar.

I would not have devoted so much time here to this incident were it not to help explain how insidiously the personality of the shapes we assume begin to take us over. Let any who would practice this art be cautious. To remain in a shape too long is to invite the very real possibility that when the time comes to resume our proper form, we will not desire to do so. I must quite candidly admit that by the time my companion and I reached the land of the Bear-God, I had begun to give long thoughts to the pleasures of the den and the hunt and the sweet nuzzlings of puppies and the true and steadfast companionship of a mate.

At length, we found a band of hunters near the edge of the forest where Belar, the Bear-God, dwelt with his people. To the amazement of my companion, I resumed my own shape and approached them.

'I have a message for Belar, thy God,' I told them.

'How may we know this to be true?' they asked me.

'Ye may know it to be true because I say it is true,' I told them. 'The message is important, and there is little time to delay.'

Then one of them saw my companion and cast his spear at her. I had no time to make what I did appear normal nor to conceal it from them. I stopped the spear in mid-flight.

They stood gaping at the spear stuck in the air as if in a tree. Irritated, I flexed my mind and broke the spear in two.

'Sorcery!' one of them gasped.

'The wolf is with me,' I told them sternly. 'Do not attempt to injure her again.' I beckoned to her and she came to my side, baring her fangs at them.

'And now convey me unto Belar,' I ordered them.

The God Belar appeared very young – scarcely more than a boy, though I knew he was much, much older than I. He was a fair-seeming, open-faced God, and the people who served him were a rowdy, undisciplined group, scarcely conscious of the dignity of their Master.

'Well-met, Belgarath,' he greeted me, though we had never met and I had told my name to no one. 'How does it go with my brother?'

'Not well, my Lord,' I told him. 'Thy brother, Torak, hath come unto my Master and smote him and hath borne away a particular jewel which he coveted.'

'What?' the young God roared, springing to his feet. 'Torak hath the Orb?'

'I greatly fear it is so, my Lord,' I told him. 'My Master bids me entreat thee to come to him with all possible speed.'

'I will, Belgarath,' Belar said. 'I will make preparations at once. Hath Torak used the Orb as yet?'

'We think not, my Lord,' I said. 'My Master says we must make haste, before thy brother, Torak, hath learned the full power of the jewel he hath stolen.'

'Truly,' the young God said. He glanced at the young she-wolf sitting at my feet. 'Greetings, little sister,' he said courteously, 'is it well with thee?'

'Most remarkable,' she said politely. 'It appears that I have fallen in with creatures of great importance.'

'Thy friend and I must make haste,' he told her. 'Otherwise I should make suitable arrangements for thy comfort. May I offer thee to eat?'

She glanced at the ox turning on the spit in his great hall. '*That* smells interesting,' she said.

'Of course,' he said, taking up a knife and carving off a generous portion for her.

'My thanks,' she said. 'This one –' she jerked her head at me '– was in so much hurry to reach this place that we scarce had time for a rabbit or two along the way.' Daintily she gulped the meat down in two great bites. 'Quite good,' she said, 'though one wonders why it was necessary to burn it.'

'A custom, little sister,' he laughed.

'Oh, well,' she said, 'if it's a custom.' Carefully she licked her whiskers clean.

'I will return in a moment, Belgarath,' Belar said and moved away.

'That one is nice,' my companion told me pointedly.

'He is a God,' I told her.

'That means nothing to me,' she said. 'Gods are the business of men. Wolves have little interest in such things.'

'Perhaps you would care to return to the place where we met?' I suggested.

'I will go along with you for a while longer,' she told me. 'I was ever curious, and I see that you are familiar with most remarkable things.' She yawned, stretched, and curled up at my feet.

The return to the Vale where my Master waited took far less time than had my journey to the country of the Bear-God. Though time is a matter of indifference to them normally, when there is a need for haste, the Gods can devour distance in ways that had not even occurred to me. We began walking with Belar asking me questions about my Master and our lives in the Vale and the young she-wolf padding along sedately between us. After several hours of this, my impatience finally made me bold.

'My Lord,' I said, 'forgive me, but at this rate it will take us almost a year to reach my Master's tower.'

'Not nearly so long, Belgarath,' he replied pleasantly. 'I believe it lies just beyond that next hilltop.'

I stared at him, not believing that a God could be so simple, but when we crested the hill, there lay the Vale spread before us with my Master's tower standing in the center.

'Most remarkable,' the wolf murmured, dropping onto her haunches and staring down into the Vale with her bright yellow eyes. I could only agree with her.

The other Gods were already with my Master in the tower, and Belar hastened to join them.

My brothers, the other Disciples of Aldur, awaited me at the foot of the tower. When they saw my companion, they were startled.

'Is it wise, Belgarath, to bring such a one here?' Belzedar asked me. 'Wolves are not the most trustworthy creatures.'

My companion bared her fangs at him for that.

'What is her name,' the gentle Beltira asked.

'Wolves do not require names,' I told him. 'They know who they are without such appendages.'

Belzedar shook his head and moved away from the wolf.

'Is she quite tame?' Belsambar asked me. 'I wonder that you had time for such business on your journey, and I know you would not loiter.'

'She is not tame at all,' I told him. 'We met by chance, and she chose to accompany me.'

'Most remarkable,' the wolf said to me. 'Are they always so full of questions?'

'It is the nature of man,' I told her.

'Curious creatures,' she said, shaking her head.

'What a wonder,' Belkira marveled. 'You have learned to converse with the beasts. Pray, dear brother, instruct me in this art.'

'It is not an art,' I said. 'I took the form of a wolf on my journey. The speech of the wolf came with the form and remained. It is no great thing.'

And then we sat, awaiting the decision of our Master and his brother Gods regarding the wayward Torak. When they came down, their faces were solemn, and the other Gods departed without speaking with us.

'There will be war,' our Master told us. 'My brothers have gone to gather their people. Mara and Issa will come upon Torak from the south; Nedra and Chaldan shall come upon him from the west; Belar and I will come upon him from the north. We will lay waste his people, the Angaraks, until he returns the Orb. It must be so.'

'Then so be it,' I said, speaking for us all.

And so we prepared for war. We were but seven, and feared that our Master might be held in low regard when our tiny number was revealed to the hosts of the other Gods, but it was not so. We labored to create the great engines of war and to cast illusions which confounded the minds of the Angarak peoples of the traitor, Torak.

And after a few battles did we and the hosts of the other peoples harry Torak and his people out onto that vast plain beyond Korim, which is no more.*

And then it was that Torak, knowing that the hosts of his brother Gods could destroy all of Angarak, raised up the jewel which my Master had wrought, and with it he let in the sea.

The sound was one such as I had never heard before. The earth shrieked and groaned as the power of the Orb and the will of Torak cracked open the fair plain; and, with a roar like ten thousand thunders, the sea came in to seethe in a broad, foaming band between us and the Angaraks. How many perished in that sudden drowning no one will ever know. The cracked land sank beneath our feet, and the mocking sea pursued us, swallowing the plain and the villages and the cities which lay upon it. Then it was that the village of my birth was lost forever, and that fair, sparkling river drowned beneath the endlessly rolling sea.

A great cry went up from the hosts of the other Gods, for indeed the lands of most of them were swallowed up by the sea which Torak had let in.

'How remarkable,' the young wolf at my side observed.

'You say that overmuch,' I told her, somewhat sharply.

'Do you not find it so?'

'I do,' I said, 'but one should not say it so often lest one be thought simple.'

---

* 'The high places of Korim, which are no more' are visited at the end of the Malloreon. This is misdirection from Belgarath.

'I will say as I wish to say,' she told me. 'You need not listen if it does not please you; and if you think me simple, that is your concern.'

Who can argue with a wolf? – and a she-wolf at that?

And now were we confounded. The broad sea stood between us and the Angaraks, and Torak stood upon one shore and we upon the other.

'And what now, Master?' I asked Aldur.

'It is finished,' he said. 'The war is done.'

'Never!' said the young God Belar. 'My people are Alorns. The ways of the sea are not strange to them. If it be not possible to come upon the traitor Torak by land, then my Alorns shall build a great fleet, and we shall come upon him by sea. The war is not done. He hath smote thee, my dear brother, and he hath stolen that which was thine, and now hath he drowned this fair land in the death-cold sea also. Our homes and our fields and forests are no more. This I say, and my words are true, between Alorn and Angarak shall there be endless war until the traitor Torak be punished for his iniquities – yea, even if it prevail so until the end of days.'

'Torak *is* punished,' my Master said quietly. 'He hath raised the Orb against the earth, and the Orb hath requited him for that. The pain of that requiting shall endure in our brother Torak all the days of his life. Moreover, now is the Orb awakened. It hath been used to commit a great evil, and it *will* not be used so again. Torak hath the

Orb, but small pleasure will he find in the having. He may not touch it, neither may he look upon it, lest it slay him.'

'Nonetheless,' said Belar, 'I will make war upon him until the Orb be returned to thee. To this I pledge all of Aloria.'

'As you would have it, my brother,' said Aldur. 'Now, however, must we raise some barrier against this encroaching sea lest it swallow up all the dry land that is left to us. Join, therefore, thy will with mine and let us do that which must be done.'

Until that day I had not fully realized to what degree the Gods differed from men. As I watched, Aldur and Belar joined their hands and looked out over the broad plain and the approaching sea.

'Stay,' Belar said to the sea. His voice was not loud, but the sea heard him and stopped. It built up, angry and tossing, behind the barrier of that single word.

'Rise up,' Aldur said as softly to the earth. My mind reeled as I perceived the immensity of that command. The earth, so newly wounded by the evil which Torak had done, groaned and heaved and swelled; and, before my eyes, it rose up. Higher and higher it rose as the rocks beneath cracked and shattered. Out of the plain there shouldered up mountains which had not been there before, and they shuddered away the loose earth as a dog shakes off water and stood as a stern and eternal barrier against the sea which Torak had let in.

Sullenly, the sea retreated.

'How remarkable,' the wolf said.

'Truly,' I could not but agree.

And the other Gods and their people came and beheld that which my Master and his brother Belar had done, and they marveled at it.

'Now is the time of sundering,' my Master said. 'The land which was once so fair is no more. That which remains here is harsh and will not support us. Take thou therefore, my brothers, each his own people and journey even unto the west. Beyond the western mountains lies a fair plain – not so broad perhaps nor so beautiful as that which Torak hath drowned this day – but it will sustain thee and thy people.'

'And what of thou, my brother?' asked Mara.

'I shall return to my labors,' said Aldur. 'This day hath evil been unleashed in the world, and its power is great. Care for thy people, my brothers, and sustain them. The evil hath come into the world as a result of that which I have forged. Upon me, therefore, falls the task of preparation for the day when good and evil shall meet in that final battle wherein shall be decided the fate of the world.'

'So be it, then,' said Mara. 'Hail and farewell, my brother,' and he turned and the other Gods with him, and they went away toward the west.

But the young God Belar lingered. 'My oath and my pledge bind me still,' he told my Master. 'I will take my Alorns to the north, and there we will seek a way by which we may come again upon the traitor Torak and his foul Angarak peoples. Thine Orb shall be returned unto thee. I shall not rest until it be so.' And then he turned and put his face to the north, and his tall warriors followed after him.

That day marked a great change in our lives in the Vale. Until then our days had been spent in learning and in labors of our own choosing. Now, however, our Master set tasks for us. Most of them were beyond our understanding, and no work is so tedious as to labor at something without knowing the reason for it. Our Master shut himself away in his tower, and often years passed without our seeing him.

It was a time of great trial to us, and our spirits often sank.

One day, as I labored, the she-wolf, who always watched, moved slightly or made some sound, and I stopped and looked at her. I could not remember how long it had been since I had noticed her.

'It must be tedious for you to simply sit and watch this way,' I said.

'It's not unpleasant,' she said. 'Now and then you do something curious or remarkable. There is entertainment enough for me here. I will go along with you yet for a while longer.'

I smiled, and then a strange thing occurred to me. 'How long has it been since you and I first met?' I asked her.

'What is time to a wolf?' she asked indifferently.

I consulted several documents and made a few calculations. 'As closely as I can determine, you have been with me somewhat in excess of a thousand years,' I told her.

'And?' she said in that infuriating manner of hers.

'Don't you find that a trifle remarkable?'

'Not particularly,' she said placidly.

'Do wolves normally live so long?'

'Wolves live as long as they choose to live,' she said, somewhat smugly, I thought.

One day soon after that I found it necessary to change my form in order to complete a task my Master had set me to.

'So *that's* how you do it,' the wolf marveled. 'What a simple thing.' And she promptly turned herself into a snowy owl.

'Stop that,' I told her.

'Why?' she said, carefully preening her feathers with her beak. 'It's not seemly.'

'What is "seemly" to a wolf – or an owl, I should say?' And with that she spread her soft, silent wings and soared out the window.

After that I knew little peace. I never knew when I turned around what might be staring at me – wolf or owl, bear or butterfly. She seemed to take great delight in startling me, but as time wore on, more and more she retained the shape of the owl.

'What is this thing about owls?' I growled one day.

'I like owls,' she explained as if it were the simplest thing in the world. 'During my first winter when I was a young and foolish thing, I was chasing a rabbit, floundering around in the snow like a puppy, and a great white owl swooped down and snatched my rabbit almost out of my jaws. She carried it to a nearby tree and ate it, dropping the scraps to me. I thought at the time that it would be a fine thing to be an owl.'

'Foolishness,' I snorted.

'Perhaps,' she replied blandly, preening her tail feathers, 'but it amuses me. It may be that one day a different shape will amuse me even more.'

I grunted and returned to my work.

Some time later – days or years or perhaps even longer – she came swooping through the window, as was her custom, perched sedately on a chair and resumed her proper wolf-shape.

'I think I will go away for a while,' she announced.

'Oh?' I said cautiously.

She stared at me, her golden eyes unblinking. 'I think I would like to look at the world again,' she said.

'I see,' I said.

'The world has changed much, I think.'

'It's possible.'

'I might come back some day.'

'As you wish,' I said.

'Goodbye, then,' she said, blurred into the form of an owl again, and with a single thrust of her great wings she was gone.

Strangely, I missed her. I found myself turning often to show her something. She had been a part of my life for so long that it somehow seemed that she would always be there. I was always a bit saddened not to see her in her usual place.

And then there came a time when, on an errand for my Master, I went some leagues to the north. On my way back I came across a small, neatly thatched cottage in a grove of giant trees near a small river. I had passed that way frequently, and the house had never been there before. Moreover, to my own certain knowledge, there was not another human habitation within five hundred leagues. In the house there lived a woman. She seemed young, and yet perhaps not young. Her hair was quite tawny, and her eyes were a curious golden color.

She stood in the doorway as I approached – almost as if she had been expecting me. She greeted me in a seemly manner and invited me to come in and sup with her. I accepted gratefully, for no sooner did she mention food than I found myself ravenously hungry.

The inside of her cottage was neat and cheery. A fire burned merrily upon her hearth, and a large kettle bubbled and hiccuped over it. From that kettle came wondrous smells. The woman seated me at the table, fetched me a stout earthenware plate and then set before me a meal such as I had not seen in hundreds of years. It consisted, as I recall, of every kind of food which I liked most.

When I had eaten – more than I should have probably, since as all who know me can attest, good food was ever a weakness of mine – we talked, the woman and I, and I found her to have most uncommon good sense. Though my errand was urgent, I found myself lingering, thinking of excuses not to go. Indeed, I felt quite as giddy as some adolescent in her presence.

Her name, she told me, was Poledra. 'And by what name are you known?' she asked.

'I am called Belgarath,' I told her, 'and I am a Disciple of the God Aldur.'

'How remarkable,' she said, and then she laughed. There was something hauntingly familiar in that laugh.

I never learned the truth about Poledra, though of course I had suspicions.

When the urgency of my errand compelled me to leave that fair grove and the small, neat cottage, Poledra said a most peculiar thing. 'I will go along with you,' she told me. 'I was ever curious.' And she closed the door of her house and returned with me to the Vale.

Strangely, my Master awaited us, and he greeted Poledra courteously. I can never be sure, but it seemed that some secret glance passed between them as if they knew each other and shared some knowledge that I was unaware of.

I had, as I say, some suspicions, but as time went on they became less and less important. After a while, I didn't even think about them any more.

That following spring Poledra and I married. My Master himself, burdened though he was with care and the great task of preparing for the day of the final struggle between good and evil, blessed our union.

There was joy in our marriage, and I never thought about those things which I had prudently decided not to think about; but that, of course, is another story.*

* That is not 'another story'. It's the core of *this* one.

·I·

THE HOLY BOOKS

THE BOOK OF ALORN[*]

Of the Beginnings

NOTE The myths of the Alorns describe a time when men and Gods lived together in harmony. This was the time before the world was cracked and the eastern sea rushed in to cover the land where they dwelt, a country which lay to the east of what is now Cthol Murgos and Mishrak ac Thull.

The cracking of the world is known in Alorn mythology as 'the sundering' or 'the dividing of the peoples', and their count of time begins then.

At the beginning of days made the Gods the world and the seas and the dry land also. And cast they the stars across the night sky and did set the sun and his wife, the moon, in the heavens to give light unto the world.

And the Gods caused the earth to bring forth the beasts, and the waters to bud with fish, and the skies to flower with birds.

And they made men also, and divided men into Peoples.

Now the Gods were seven in number and were all equal, and their names were Belar, and Chaldan, and Nedra, and Issa, and Mara, and Aldur, and Torak.

Now Belar was the God of the Alorns, and dwelt with them and loved them, and his totem is the bear.

And Chaldan was the God of the Arends, and he dwelt with them and was judge over them, and his totem is the bull.

And Nedra was God over the people who called themselves after

* This is a creation myth with resonances of the myths of several cultures on *this* world. It even has a flood. The flood myths on planet Earth were probably generated by the meltdown of the last ice age about 12,000 years ago. The flood on Garion's world was the result of a volcanic incident, which is described in some detail in the preliminary studies to the Malloreon.

his name, the Tolnedrans, and he cherished them and accepted their worship, and his totem is the lion.

And Issa was God over the snake people, and he accepted their dull-eyed worship, and his totem is the serpent.

And Mara was God over the Marags, which are no more, and his totem was the bat, but his temples are cast down and vacant, and the spirit of Mara weeps alone in the wilderness.

But Aldur was God over no people, and dwelt alone and considered the stars in his solitude. But some few of the people of the other Gods heard of his wisdom and journeyed unto him and besought him to allow them to stay with him and be his pupils. And he relented and allowed it to them, and they became his people and joined in brotherhood to learn at his feet, and his totem is the owl.

And Torak is God over the Angaraks, and sweet to him was their adulation and their worship and the smell of the burning of their sacrifices. And the Angaraks bowed down before Torak and called him Lord of Lords and God of Gods, and in the secret places of his heart Torak found the words sweet. And behold, he held himself apart from the fellowship of the Gods and dwelt alone in the worship of the Angaraks. And his totem is the dragon.

And Aldur caused to be made a jewel in the shape of a globe, and behold, it was very like unto the size of the heart of a man, and in the jewel was captured the light of certain stars that did glitter in the northern sky. And great was the enchantment upon the jewel which men called the Orb of Aldur for with the Orb could Aldur see that which had been, that which was, and that which was yet to be – yea, verily, even that which was concealed even though it were in the deepest bowels of earth or in darkness most impenetrable. Moreover, in the hand of Aldur could the jewel cause wonders no man or God had yet beheld.

And Torak coveted the Orb of Aldur for its beauty and its power, and in the deep-most crevasses of his soul resolved he to own it even if it came to pass that he must slay Aldur that it might be so. And in a dissembling guise went he even unto Aldur and spake unto him.

'My brother,' said he, 'it is not fit that thou absent thyself from the company and the counsel of thy brothers. I beseech thee that thou takest unto thyself a people and return to our company.'

And Aldur looked upon Torak his brother and rebuked him, saying, 'It is not I who have turned from the fellowship and sought lordship and dominion.'

And Torak was shamed by the words of Aldur, his brother, and was made sore wroth, and rose he up against his brother and smote him and reached forth his hand and took from his brother the jewel which he coveted, and then he fled.

And Aldur went unto the other Gods and spoke with them of what had come to pass, and the Gods rose up, and each of them besought Torak that he return the Orb to Aldur, but he in no wise would do it. And thus it came to pass that the Gods caused each his own people to gird themselves for war.

And behold, Torak did raise the Orb of Aldur and did cause the earth to split asunder, and the mountains were cast down, and the sea came in and did engulf the lands of the east where the people of the Gods dwelt. And the Gods took their people and fled from the great inrushing of the sea, but Aldur and Belar joined their hands and their wills and did cause mountains to rise up to set limits upon the sea which had come in. And the Gods were parted one from the other, and the people also. And men began to reckon time from the day in which Torak caused the seas to come in.

Now it came to pass that the six Gods went even unto the west with their people, but Torak took the Angaraks unto the east, and the sea that had rushed in separated the Angaraks from the other peoples.

Not without hurt, however, did Torak crack the earth, for such was the virtue of the Orb that in the day when Torak raised it against the earth and against the mountains did the Orb begin to glow. Faint at first, the fire of the Orb waxed stronger with each of the commands of Torak. And the blue fire of those distant stars seared the flesh of Torak. In pain did he cast down the mountains. In anguish did he crack the earth asunder. In agony did he let in the seas. And thus did the Orb of Aldur requite Torak for putting its virtue to evil purpose – Behold, the left hand of Torak was consumed utterly by the fire of the Orb, and like dry twigs did the fingers thereof flare and burn down to ashes. And the flesh on the left side of Torak's face did melt like wax in the holy fire of the Orb, and the eye of that side did boil in its socket.*

And Torak cried out a great cry and cast himself into the sea to still the burning which the Orb had caused, but it availed him not. Truly it is written that the pain of Torak which the Orb had caused in punishment will endure until the end of days.

And the Angaraks were dismayed by the anguish of their God,

---

* The maiming of a god has no obvious counterpoint in the mythologies of *this* world. Milton, however, *did* lock Lucifer permanently into the form of the serpent after he used that form in the temptation of Eve. The branding of Cain may also be an equivalent.

and they went unto him and asked what they might do to end his pain.

And Torak spake, calling the name of the Orb.

And they sought to bring the Orb unto him, but the fire which had awakened in the Orb consumed all who touched it, and they devised a great iron cask to bear it in.

And behold, when Torak opened the cask, the Orb burned with renewed fire, and Torak cried a great cry and cast it away from him.

And the Angaraks spake unto him, saying, 'Lord, wouldst thou have us destroy this thing or cast it even into the sea?'

And Torak cried a great cry again and spake, saying, 'No! Truly will I destroy utterly him who would raise his hand against the jewel. Though I may not touch it nor even behold it, I have dearly purchased it, and never will I relinquish it.'

And behold, Torak, who had once been the most beautiful of the Gods, arose from the waters. Fair still was his right side, but his left was burned and scarred by the fire of the Orb which had requited him thus for raising it against the earth and the other Gods with evil intent.

And Torak led his people away to the east and caused them to build a great city, and they called its name Cthol Mishrak, which is the City of Night, for Torak was ashamed that men saw him marred by the fire of the Orb, and the light of the sun caused him pain. And the Angaraks built for him a great iron tower that he might dwell therein and that their prayers and the smells of incense and the smoke of burning sacrifice might rise up unto him and ease his pain. And he caused the Iron Cask which contained the Orb to be placed in the top-most chamber thereof, and often went he and stood before the Iron Cask and stretched forth his remaining hand as he would touch the Orb. And his remaining eye yearned to behold its beauty, and then would he turn and flee weeping from the chamber lest his yearning become too great and he open the Iron Cask and perish.

And so it prevailed in the lands of the Angaraks which men called Mallorea for a thousand years and yet another thousand years. And the Angaraks began to call the maimed God KAL-TORAK – a name signifying at once King and God.

Of the six Gods who had with their people gone unto the west thus was their disposition. To the south and west to jungles dank and rivers sluggish went Issa, the serpent God and the snake people. And Nedra went even unto the fertile land to the north of jungle, and Chaldan took his people, the Arends, unto the northwest coast, and Mara sought the mountains above the Tolnedran plain.

But Aldur, in the pain of the loss of the Orb and the shame over what the jewel that he had made had wrought upon the world retreated even unto the Vale which lay at the headwaters of the river bearing his name, and shut himself away from the sight of men and of Gods – and none came nigh him but Belgarath, his first Disciple.

Now it came to pass that Belar, the youngest of the Gods and most dear to Aldur, took his people unto the north and sought they for a thousand years and yet another thousand years a way by which they might come upon the Angaraks and overthrow them and regain the Orb that Aldur might come forth again and men and Gods be rejoined in fellowship one with the other.

And the Alorns, the people of Belar the Bear-God, were a hardy people and warlike, and clad themselves in the skins of bears and wolves and shirts cunningly wrought of rings of steel, and terrible were the swords and axes of the Alorns. And they ranged the north – yea, even unto the land of eternal ice, to find the way they might follow into Mallorea to come upon their ancient foes and destroy them and to restore the Orb unto Aldur. And in his pride did each Alorn warrior upon his passage into manhood raise sword or axe unto the deathless stars and call forth his challenge even unto Torak himself. And in the iron tower of Cthol Mishrak did the maimed God hear the challenge of the Alorns and did see the cold light of the north flickering from their sword edges, and the pain of Kal-Torak did increase ten-fold, and his hatred of his youngest brother and of the rash people who followed him and cast their threats even in the teeth of the stars cankered in his soul.

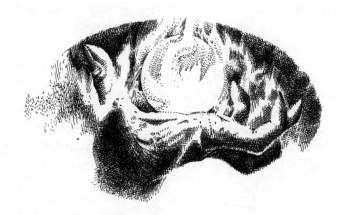

Now, of all the kings of the Alorns, the bravest and most crafty was Cherek of the broad shoulders, and went he even unto the Vale of Aldur and sought out Belgarath, Disciple of Aldur and spake unto him, saying, 'Now are the ways of the north open, and I have sons exceedingly bold. The signs and the auguries are propitious. The time is ripe to seek our way to the city of endless night and to regain the Orb from the usurper.'

But Belgarath was loath to go from the Vale of Aldur for behold, his wife Poledra was exceedingly great with child, and her time was nigh.

And yet did Cherek prevail upon him, and by night they stole away and were joined a thousand leagues to the north by the sons of Cherek.* And the eldest Dras was named and of great power and craftiness was he. And the second son Algar was named and fleet was he as the wind and bold. And the youngest was named Riva and pure was he and steadfast and his grip was as death, for naught upon which he set his hand could escape him.

And behold, the time of darkness was upon the north, and the season of snow and of ice and of mist, and the moors of the north glittered beneath the stars with rime-frost and steel-grey ice in the deathly cold. And Belgarath the Sorcerer took the shape of a great dark wolf, and on silent feet did he slink through the dark, snow-floored forests of the north where the trees cracked and shattered in the sundering cold.

And in those days were the ruff and shoulders of the great wolf Belgarath silvered by frost, and ever after was the Sorcerer Belgarath silver of hair and beard.

And it came to pass that the companions passed toward the south into Mallorea and even unto the City of Darkness which was Cthol Mishrak, wherein dwelt the maimed God who was king of the Angaraks. And ever were they guided by the wolf Belgarath who ran before them, his belly low to the ground and his shoulders and ruff touched with the silver of eternal frost.

And at last came they even unto the City of Night wherein dwelt Kal-Torak and his people, the Angaraks, and the wolf Belgarath slunk low to the ground and sought out the way and led them even into the dark city and yet unto the foot of the iron tower.

---

* We changed this in *Belgarath the Sorcerer*. That 'thousand leagues' looks great in a 'Holy Book', but it's too cumbersome in a story. Moreover, three thousand miles would have put them in the general vicinity of the north pole.

Then climbed they in crafty silence with muffled feet the rusted iron steps which had known no foot of man or God for twenty centuries. And Cherek of the broad shoulders, more like the Bear than the Bear-God himself, mounted first, and behind him Algar the fleet-footed and Riva the steadfast, and guarding the rear were Dras the bull-necked and the wolf Belgarath.

And mounted they the smoldering darkness of the tower and came even unto the iron-bound chamber of the maimed God where slept in pain-hunted slumber the titan Torak.

And he had caused his face to be bound up with iron to hide from men and Gods the melted flesh and burned eye which the Orb had wrought upon him.

And as they passed through the chamber of the maimed God, stirred he in his sleep and opened behind the iron binding the eye which the Orb had burned. And such was the power of the maimed God that the eye which *was not* glowed red, and the iron tower glowed likewise a smoldering and sooty red.

And passed they through in dreadful fear of the maimed and sleeping God who stirred ever in his sleep as the pain with which the Orb had touched him seared him.

And in the chamber beyond lay the Iron Cask in which had rested for a thousand years and yet for another thousand years the Orb of Aldur. And in fear looked they upon the Cask, knowing the power of the Orb.

And Cherek Bear-shoulders, King of the Alorns, spake unto

Belgarath the Sorcerer, saying, 'Take thou the Orb and return it unto thy Master, its rightful owner.'

And Belgarath, Disciple of Aldur, spake, saying, 'Nay, King of the Alorns. I may not touch it, neither may I look upon it, lest it destroy me. None may touch the Orb now unless he be without ill intent. Only him who would not use it may touch it now. Thus doth the Orb protect itself and the Gods and men and the very world – for behold, once was it used to crack open the earth and *will* not be used so again. If any here be without ill intent – if one of you be pure enough to take up the Orb and convey it at peril of his life and surrender it at the end of our journey with no thought of gain or of power or of dominion, let him stretch forth his hand now and take up the Orb of Aldur.'

And Cherek Bear-shoulders was troubled, and he spake, saying, 'What man is without ill intent in the deepest silences of his soul?' And he put forth his hand and as that hand came nigh unto the Iron Cask felt he even in his heart the great heat of the Orb that lay within and knew then his unworthiness. And bitter was that knowledge to him. And he turned away.

And Dras Bull-neck, his eldest son, came forward and stretched forth both his hands and put them upon the Cask. And then he withdrew them and turned his head and wept.

And Algar Fleet-foot came forward and stretched forth his hand. And he too withdrew his hand and turned away.

But Riva Iron-grip went even unto the Cask and opened it and did reach within and took up the Orb. And behold, the fire of the Orb shone through his fingers – yea, even through the flesh of his hand – and he was not burned.

'Behold,' spake Belgarath the Sorcerer unto Cherek Bear-shoulders, 'thy youngest son is pure and without ill intent. And his doom and the doom of all who follow after him shall be to bear the Orb and to protect it from evil.'

'So be it,' spake Cherek, King of the Alorns, 'and I and his brothers will sustain and protect him while this doom is upon him – even though it be until the end of days.'

And Riva muffled the Orb of Aldur in his cloak and hid it in his bosom, and the companions passed quickly out through the dreadful chamber wherein slept the maimed God, ever stirring and restless in his pain. And the eye that *was not* watched them. And Kal-Torak cried out in his sleep, but woke not.

And down they hurried even unto the foot of the tower. And then went they quickly unto the gates of the City of Darkness which was Cthol Mishrak and into the wasteland beyond.

And it came to pass when they had gone but three leagues did the maimed God awaken from his slumber and found the Iron Cask open and the Orb that he had so dearly purchased gone.

And horrible was the wrath of Kal-Torak. And girt he himself in black iron and took he up his great sword and his spear likewise, and went he then down from the iron tower and turned and smote it – and behold, the iron tower which had endured a thousand years and yet a thousand years more was cast down, and great was the ruin thereof.

And the maimed God spake unto the Angaraks in a great voice, saying, 'Because ye have permitted this thing to come to pass, shall ye dwell no more in cities. Because you have become unwatchful and indolent and have allowed a thief to steal that which I have purchased at such great cost, I will break your city and cast it down and drive you forth from this place, and ye shall be wanderers in the earth until ye return to me that which was stolen.' And he raised up his arms and broke the city and cast it down in ruin and drove forth the Angaraks into the wilderness, and Cthol Mishrak was no more.

And in the wasteland to the north* the companions heard the outcry from the city, and the Angaraks pursued them. And once the Angaraks came upon them, and Cherek Bear-shoulders and his sons Dras Bull-neck and Algar Fleet-foot did turn and withstand them, and the Angaraks fled. And again the Angaraks came upon them, and again did Cherek and his sons withstand them, though their numbers were greater.

---

* The account in *Belgarath the Sorcerer* differs. The pack ice of winter offered an alternative to that 'land bridge'.

And yet a third time did the Angaraks come upon them and with them strode Kal-Torak himself and the great hosts of the Angaraks.

And Riva Iron-grip saw that his father and his brothers were weary even unto death and that their wounds bled. And the bearer of the Orb did turn and did reach into his bosom and withdrew the Orb and held it forth that the maimed God and his hosts might behold it.

And great was the confusion of the host by reason of the Orb, and Kal-Torak cried out a great cry and did turn away, but drove he the Angaraks back again and commanded them to regain the Orb.

But Riva did raise again the Orb of Aldur, and it shone brighter even than before, and the eyes of the Angaraks were dazzled, and they turned away again, but the maimed God raised his hand against them and drave them yet once more against the companions.

And yet a third time did Riva raise the Orb, and the sky was lit by its fire, and behold, the front ranks of the host were consumed by it. And then did the hosts of the Angaraks flee from the Orb, and in no way could Kal-Torak drive them back again.

And so passed the companions again unto the north and returned they unto the west. And the spies of Torak did follow them, but Belgarath the Sorcerer assumed again the form of the wolf and waylaid the spies of Torak, and they followed no more.

And behold, the Gods of the west did hold council, and Aldur advised them. And he spake unto them, saying, 'It may not be that we ourselves make war upon our brother Torak, for in the warfare of Gods shall the world itself not be destroyed? Must we then absent ourselves from the world that our brother Torak not find us and make war upon us and thus destroy the world.'

And the other Gods were silent, each loath to leave the people he loved, but all knew that Aldur spoke truth, and that if they remained, would the world be destroyed.

And Belar, the youngest of the Gods, wept, for he loved deeply the Alorn people, and Aldur relented. And he spake unto them, saying, 'In *spirit* might each remain with his people, and guide them and protect them, but in no wise may Gods themselves remain, lest Torak find us and make war upon us and the world be unmade and our people perish utterly.'

'And wilt thou, my brother, bear away the Orb which is thy chiefest delight?' quoth Chaldan, God of the Arends.

'Nay, my brother,' quoth Aldur, and sad was his heart in the speaking. 'The Orb must remain, for only in the Orb lies that which will prevent our brother Torak from lordship of the world. So long as the Orb remains, Torak shall not prevail against it, and thy people will be safe from his enslavement.'

And so it came to pass that the Gods departed from the world which they had made, and in spirit only did they sojourn each with his people. And Torak only of the seven Gods did remain, but he was restrained by the Orb of Aldur from lordship over the world and prevented from the enslavement of all peoples of the world. And in the wastelands of Mallorea in the east did the maimed God know this, and the knowledge cankered in his soul.

And Belgarath spake unto Cherek and his sons, saying, 'Hearken unto the words of the Gods, for behold, this is their judgement and their doom* upon you. Here must we part and be sundered one from the other even as in the day wherein all men were sundered.'

And to Riva he spake, saying, 'Thy journey is longest, Iron-grip. Bear thou the Orb even unto the Isle of the Winds. Take with thee thy people and thy goods and thy cattle, for thou shalt not return. Build there a fortress and a sanctuary and maintain it and defend the Orb with thy life and with the lives of thy people, for know ye that the Orb alone hinders Torak from Lordship and Dominion – even over the whole world.'

And to Dras he spake, saying, 'Turn thou aside here, Bull-neck, and maintain the marches of the north against the Angaraks and against Kal-Torak. Take thy people and thy goods and thy cattle also and return no more, lest the marches be unguarded.'

And to Algar he spake, saying, 'Turn thou also aside here, Fleet-

---

* 'Doom' originates in Scandinavian mythology, and the word in contemporary English derives from the Scandinavian 'dom'. It does *not* mean 'preordained death', but rather 'destiny' or 'fate'.

foot, and maintain the plains to the south against the enemy. Take thy people and thy goods and thy cattle also and return no more lest the plains be unguarded.'

And to Cherek he spake, saying, 'Upon thee, Bear-shoulders, lies the doom of the sea. Go thou onward even unto the peninsula of the north that is named for the Alorns. And build thou thereon a sea-port and a fleet of swift ships and tall, and maintain the seas that the enemy come not by water against Riva, thy son. And maintain there thy people and thy goods and thy cattle. And teach unto thy people the ways of the sea that none upon the waters may prevail against them.'

And he raised up his face and spake in a great voice, saying, 'Hear me, Torak-One-eye. Thus is the Orb defended and made secure against thee. And thou shalt not prevail against it. I, Belgarath, first Disciple of Aldur, proclaim it. In the day that thou comest against the west shall I raise war upon thee, and I shall destroy thee utterly. And I will maintain watch upon thee by day and by night. And I will abide against thy coming – yea, verily, be it even unto the end of days.'

And in the wastelands of Mallorea Kal-Torak heard the voice of Belgarath and was wroth and smote about him in his fury, destroying even the very rocks, for he knew that in the day when he went against the kingdoms of the west, in that day would he surely perish.

And then did Cherek Bear-shoulders embrace his sons and turned away and saw them no more.

And Dras Bull-neck turned aside and abode in the lands drained by the Mrin River, from Aldurfens north to the steppes and beyond, and from the coast to the mountains of Nadrak. And he builded a city at Boktor east of the junction of Mrin and Atun. And men called this northern land the country of Dras, or, in the language of the Alorns, Drasnia. And for a thousand years and yet another thousand years dwelt the descendants of Dras Bull-neck in the north and stood they athwart the northern marches and denied them unto the enemy. And tamed they the vast herds of reindeer, and the horned beast became as cat or dog unto them, and they took from the rivers and marshes furs and skins most luxuriant; and bright gold they found and silver also and did commerce with the kingdoms of the west and with the strange-faced merchants of the east also. And Drasnia prospered, and Kotu at Mrin-mouth was a city of wealth and power.

And Algar Fleet-foot turned aside and went to the south with his people and his goods and his cattle. And horses were there on the broad plains drained by the Aldur river, and Algar Fleet-foot and his people caught horses and tamed them, and for the first time in the world men rode upon horses. And the people of Algar named their country for their leader and called its name Algaria. And they became nomads, following after their herds and ever keeping watch that the enemy not come upon them. And they builded a fortress to the south of Algaria and called it The Stronghold, and they garrisoned it but they dwelt not there, preferring to remain with their herds. And for twenty centuries they dwelt in these lands and traded horses to other kingdoms.

And Cherek Bear-shoulders returned even unto Aloria which is to the north and west, and because he had been divided from his sons and the Alorn people were no longer one, he called the name of the country with his own name, and ever after for a score of centuries was the land known as Cherek. And he builded a great city at Val Alorn and a seaport there at the mouth of the Alorn River, and ships caused he to be built unlike the ships of other nations – for behold, the ships of others were for commerce and the carrying of goods, but the ships of Cherek were for war. And the people of Cherek became sea warriors and patrolled they the seas that the enemy not come across the dark water unto the Isle of the Winds. And it was rumored that the people of Cherek were pirates and brigands of the sea, but none could say for sure.

And Riva Iron-grip went forth even unto the west coast of Sendaria and took ship and did sail with his people and his goods and his cattle across the Sea of the Winds unto the Isle that lay therein. And many days did he search the coast until he found the spot where he might land. And upon all the Isle of the Winds there is but one place to land a ship and he did alight there and took his people and his goods and his cattle and placed them on the strand, and then burned he the ships which had borne him thence that none might return. And he caused to be built a fortress and a walled city around it. And they called the name of the city Riva and nought that was builded therein was for commerce or for display, but for war only.

And within the fortress in the most heavily defended spot caused Riva to be built a throne-room and carved he a great throne therein of black rock. And high was the back thereof.

And it came to pass that a deep sleep fell upon Riva, and Belar, Bear-God of the Alorns, came to him in a dream. And Belar spake unto him, saying, 'Behold, Guardian of the Orb, I will cause two

stars to fall down from out the sky, and I will show thee where they lie, and thou shalt take up the two stars and shall place them in a great fire and shall forge them. And the one star shall be a blade, and the other a hilt, and it shall be a sword that shall guard the Orb of my brother Aldur.'

And Riva awoke, and behold, two stars did fall from out the sky, and Riva sought them, and the spirit of the Bear-God was with him and showed him where the stars that had fallen had come to earth. And Riva took them up and bore them back to the city and forged them even as Belar had instructed.

But behold, when it was done, the blade and the hilt could in no way be joined together.

And Riva lifted his face and cried out unto Belar. 'Behold, I have marred the work, for the blade will not be joined unto the hilts, and the sword will not become one.'

And a fox which had sat near, watching the work, spake unto Riva, saying, 'The work is not marred, Iron-grip. Take up the hilt and place the Orb thereon even as a pommel-stone.'

And Riva knew that he was in the presence of an enchantment and did even that which the fox had commanded. And behold, the Orb became as one with the hilts which Riva had forged from the star Belar had caused to fall. And even the strength of Riva's hand could not sunder them one from the other.

And Riva spake, saying, 'Still is the work marred, for the blade and the hilts still remain unjoined.'

And the fox spake again, saying, 'Take the blade in thy left hand, Iron-grip, and the hilts in thy right and join them.'

'It may not be,' quoth Riva, 'for they will not join.'

And the fox laughed, saying, 'How is it that thou knowest that they will not join when thou hast not yet attempted it?'

And Riva was ashamed, and took up the blade in his left hand and the hilts in his right and did set them together, and behold, the blade passed into the hilts even as a stick into water, and the sword was joined and even the strength of Riva's hand could not unjoin it.

And the fox laughed again, saying, 'Take up the sword, Iron-grip, and go forth with it and smite with it the great rock which doth stand upon the highest mountain upon this Isle.'

And Riva took up the sword and went unto the mountain and raised up the sword against the great rock which stood thereon.

And he smote once and clave the rock in twain, and the water gushed forth therefrom and formed a river which flowed down even unto the city of Riva.

And the fox laughed again and ran away, but stopped once and looked back, and Riva beheld that the fox was a fox no longer, but the great silver wolf, Belgarath, whom he had known before.

And men called the river that flowed from the rock which Riva had clave The River of Veils by reason of the mists which ever surrounded it as it descended into the valley where lay the city of Riva.

And Riva caused the sword to be placed upon the great black rock that stood at the back of his throne. And it did hang point downward with the Orb which was now the pommel-stone at the highest point, and did the sword cleave itself unto the rock, and none save Riva could remove it therefrom. And such was the virtue of the Orb that it did burn with cold fire when Riva sat upon the throne. And when he took down the sword and raised it did the sword itself become as a great tongue of blue flame, and all who beheld this great wonder were amazed and understood it not.

And thus was wrought the Hall of the Rivan King, and thus his throne and thus was forged his sword. And ever after were the descendants of Riva marked with the mark of the Orb upon the palm of their hands, and the manchild who would become king was borne at his birth unto the throne-chamber and the hand that was so marked was placed upon the Orb that it might know him and destroy him not when he came into his inheritance.

And with each such joining did the bond between the Orb of Aldur and the line of Riva become stronger. And the Orb waxed

in brilliance with each infant touch as if it rejoiced that the line remained unbroken.

And so it endured in the City of Riva for a thousand years and for yet another thousand years.

And with the sundering of the companions and the departure of Cherek and his sons, hastened Belgarath southward for a thousand leagues even unto the Vale of Aldur that he might behold his children, the fruit of the womb of Poledra, his wife. And came he even unto the Vale of Aldur and found that his wife had been delivered of twin daughters, and then had she died.

And his eldest daughter was named Polgara, and even as an infant were her eyes steely and her face grim. And dark was her hair as wing of raven, and because she was his eldest, even in the fashion of the Sorcerers, stretched he forth his hand and laid it upon her brow – and behold, her mother, Poledra, had in her final hour, divided her anger from her love. And in Polgara, the dark-haired twin, resided her anger that Belgarath her husband, had gone from her when her time was nigh. And thus it was that when Belgarath, her father, laid his hand upon Polgara's brow did the hair thereof turn white, and ever after was the raven hair of Polgara touched at the brow with the same silver which marked the ruff of the dark, frost-touched wolf.

And his second daughter Beldaran was called, because the mark of the Sorcerers was not upon her. And fair was she, and her hair was like gold. And dearly was she beloved by her father and equally by her dark-haired sister. And they contended one with the other for her affection. But it came to pass that when his daughters had reached their sixteenth year did Belgarath fall into a deep sleep, and in a dream did the spirit of Aldur come unto him and spake, saying, 'My beloved disciple, I would have thy house joined with the house of the guardian of the Orb. Choose thou, therefore, which of thy daughters wilt thou give to the Rivan King to wife, for in the joining of thy house with the house of Riva shall a line invincible be forged that will join my will with the will of my brother Belar, and Torak himself may not prevail against us.'

And in the deep silences of his soul was Belgarath tempted. Thus might he rid himself of his spiteful daughter whose tongue seared like acid and whose white lock was ever a rebuke unto him. But, knowing the burden upon the Rivan King, sent he instead Beldaran, his fair daughter to be the mother of the Rivan line – and wept when she was gone.

And Polgara wept also with the departure of her sister, knowing in her soul that the beloved Beldaran would fade and that her love for Riva would age her and that like a flower would she wither and drop away. But in time Polgara dried her tears and went even unto her father.

And she spake unto her father, saying, 'Behold, Old Grey Wolf, thus are we alone, and now mayest thou reveal unto me the secrets of our line that I may succeed thee and care for thee in thy dotage.'

And then was Belgarath mightily provoked and raised up his hand against his spiteful daughter, but she smiled upon him sweetly, and his hand faltered, and he turned and fled from her.

And she called after him, saying, 'Father, still hast thou not instructed me in our art.'

And Belgarath fled. And, laughing, did his daughter, Polgara, pursue him.*

* An abbreviated version of this became the prologue for Book One of the Belgariad, *Pawn of Prophecy*, and Belgarath repeated it at Faldor's farm to give Garion a reference point. It also recurs in *Belgarath the Sorcerer*.

THE BOOK OF TORAK

BEHOLD,

I am Torak, King of Kings, Lord of Lords. I *was* before aught else was. I will *be* when all that has been made is unmade, yea, even beyond the end of days. I *was* when the world was englobed and the vast seas contained and the mountains heaved up out of reeking slime to claw at the vault of heaven. I will *be* when the mountains crumble into sand and are carried away as dust on the endless wind and the seas dwindle down into stagnant pools and the rounded world shrivels and is no more.

Seven were we, and joined our hands and *made* all that is made.

---

* The University of Tol Honeth has its origins in this headnote: a group who were meticulous about details, but who had no idea what was *really* going on.

And separated we the sea from the land and set the moon and the sun in their courses and covered the world with forests and grasses. Beasts we made and fowls, and lastly Man, to be the servant and the instrument of our will. And we divided the men we had made into peoples, and each of us took unto himself a people to mold and shape to his own purposes – all save Aldur, who was ever contrary and discontented in that we would not grant him dominion over all the world and lordship over us as well. And he withdrew himself from us and sought to entice our servants away from us with his enchantments.

And the people who were *mine* called themselves Angarak, and offered they burnt sacrifice and worship unto me. And I blessed them, and they prospered and grew numerous. And in their gratitude raised they up an altar unto me in the high places of Korim which are no more. And to test and prove their love of me, I required at certain seasons the sacrifice of a score of their fairest maidens and another score of their bravest youths. And it was done gladly, so great was their love of me, and was it deemed honor to be chosen for the knife and the altar-fire. And I was well-pleased and blessed them even more, and they prospered above all men and multiplied exceedingly.

And it came to pass that my brother, Aldur, who had despite unto me in that I had a numerous people who loved and worshiped me, conspired in the secret places of his soul and created in my despite a thing with which he might thwart my purposes, and a thing whereby he might gain Lordship and Dominion.

Went I then unto Aldur and besought him that he give up this thing and return to the fellowship of the Gods. But he had despite unto me and spake slightingly to me in a manner unfit, and I saw that this thing which he had made had such power over him that it twisted his soul and raised enmity between him and his brothers. And so it was that to save my brother took *I* the burden of the thing itself upon me.

But Aldur was wroth and went unto our brothers and beguiled them into enmity toward me, and each of them came to me and spake slightingly unto me, commanding me to return to Aldur the thing that had twisted his soul and which I had taken that he might be freed of the enchantment of it. But I resisted them, and would in no wise do it.

Then girded they for war, and the sky was made black with the stinking smoke of their forges as their people beat out weapons with which to rend and maim my people.

But I would not permit it – that the blood of men be spilt and the

Gods make war upon each other, and raised I the cursed thing which Aldur had made and with it divided I the land that the seas might come in and separate the peoples one from the other that they might not come upon each other and their blood be spilt.

But such was the malice which Aldur had wrought into the thing accurséd that in the day that I raised it to divide the world that men's blood not be spilt did it smite me with fire. Even as I spake the commands unto it did it sear my flesh. And the malice of Aldur consumed the hand with which I held the thing accurséd and blinded the eye with which I beheld it and marred one half of my face with its burning.

And I caused it to be bound up in a cask of iron that it might injure none other, and named it CTHRAG-YASKA, the burning stone, that men and Gods might be wary of it and its evil never again be unleashed to destroy flesh with the malice of Aldur. And upon myself I took the burden of guarding CTHRAG-YASKA that it be bound in iron until the end of days and all its mischief with it.

And I bore my people away to the east in Mallorea, and on a sheltered plain did they build a great city and called its name Cthol Mishrak in remembrance of my suffering. And I concealed their city with clouds so that men might not find them to despoil them for their love of me.

Then labored I for a thousand years and yet another thousand to raise the curse which Aldur in his malice had laid on the stone, CTHRAG-YASKA. Well I knew that in the day of the lifting of the curse would men and Gods be rejoined in brotherhood and fellowship, and the malice of Aldur unto me would be broken, and I would be restored and made whole to greet my brothers unmarred.

Great were the enchantments and words of power which I cast at the obdurate stone, but still its evil fire burned, and its curse was upon the world by reason of the malice of Aldur.

And Belar, the youngest of my brethren, conspired with Aldur against me and raised up his uncouth people against me and caused each of them to curse me and have despite unto even me who had suffered so greatly that men's blood not be spilt.

And behold, it came to pass that the evil sorcerer, Belgarath, who had ever sat at the right hand of Aldur, whispering the fell counsel of malice and enmity unto him, came with four others as a thief and bore away CTHRAG-YASKA. And one of them, the youngest, had been so woven about with spells and enchantments that he took up CTHRAG-YASKA and was not burned, and they bore it away.

Bravely did my warriors pursue them, and many were slain, and even I strode with them that we might regain CTHRAG-YASKA and so prevent the evil which it would bring to the world. But behold, the young man raised the thing accurséd and cast about its evil fire, and my people were consumed by it, and the thieves escaped, bearing CTHRAG-YASKA with them. And then was evil loosed in the world. And pulled I down the city of the Angaraks, and mighty *Cthol Mishrak* was laid waste that the enemies of my people not come upon them and destroy them utterly. And divided I the Angaraks into five tribes. The Nadraks made I hardy and bold and set them in the north to guard the ways by which the thieves had come. And the Thulls made I enduring and broad of back that they might bear burdens without tiring, and set them in the middle lands. And the Murgos made I the fiercest and most numerous and set them in the south that they might multiply greatly against the evil that had been unloosed in the world. And the most of my people kept I with me in Mallorea, which hath no limits, to serve me and to multiply against the day when war would be raised by the kingdoms of the west. And lastly made I the Grolims and instructed them in enchantments and wizardry and raised them as a priesthood before me and caused them to keep watch over all my people wheresoever they might be.

And I raised up a mighty people and set them to labor that we might undo the evil that had beset the world and regain CTHRAG-YASKA that the malice of Aldur had made and thus hold and keep the world from the destruction which no man or God might forestall.

And behold, my brothers feared my wrath in that they had conspired against me and sent thieves to steal CTHRAG-YASKA. And they did flee from me – yea, and departed from the world and remained but in spirit each with his own people.

And for a thousand years and yet another thousand and three hundred more[*] did I send Nadraks and Murgos against the savage and barbarian Alorns with Thulls to bear their burdens and Grolims to guide them in my service. And it availed not, for the sons of the great thief Cherek, aided by the wicked sorcery of Belgarath, chief disciple of Aldur, did fall upon my people and destroy them.

In the west did the sons of Algar bestride strange beasts, swift and cruel, and harried my people back even unto the black mountains. And to the north did the sons of Dras the thick-witted, eldest son of Cherek, the thief, lie in wait and savagely ambush the brave

---

[*] The chronology was revised.

Nadraks I had sent and foully destroyed them – yea, so utterly that a thousand years passed ere their numbers were restored. And call the Angaraks this battle the Battle of the Grief-Place, and each year upon the day of the Battle of the Grief-Place are a thousand Thullish maidens sacrificed and a thousand Thullish young men also. And also are sacrificed a hundred Murgo maidens and a hundred Murgo warriors and ten Nadrak maidens and ten Nadrak champions and a Grolim priestess and a new-born Grolim man-child, borne in her arms. And this is done that my people not forget the Battle of the Grief-Place and it will be so until CTHRAG-YASKA be returned unto me or until the end of days.

And it came to pass that my brother Issa slept, and I knew of this by reason of the counsel of Zedar,* a wise and just man who had abjured the malice of Aldur and the evil dominion of the wicked sorcerer Belgarath and had come unto me with offer of service and respect. Now Zedar had been a Disciple of Aldur and was well-taught in enchantments and sorceries, and after the fashion of sorcerers had his name been called Belzedar. But he had abjured this unseemly name upon the day when he had come into my service. And he brought forth a vision, and behold, my brother Issa, ever sluggish and indolent, had fallen into a deep slumber which had endured for a hundred years, and his priests could not rouse him nor the queen of his people either. And sent I Zedar unto the land of the snake people who worship my brother Issa, and he spake unto their queen and offered unto her wealth and power and Dominion over many lands if she would fall down and worship me and do my bidding. And behold, she consented to it, and in secret sent she her emissaries unto a certain place and did break the power of CTHRAG-YASKA which had by reason of the malice of Aldur and the sorceries of Belgarath raised a barrier against me. And once the sons of Riva, youngest son of Cherek, were no more, the enchantment was broken, and then might I come against the kingdoms of the west and demand the return of CTHRAG-YASKA that I might undo its evil sorceries.

And now are my people made ready, and will we now come against the kingdoms of the west which have hearkened unto the counsel and beguilements of wicked Gods and evil sorcerers and have sought to deny me that which is *mine*. And I will smite them

---

* This passage establishes the apostasy of Belzedar. In actuality, Zedar is a tragic hero. When he originally went to Mallorea, he thought he was clever enough to deceive Torak. He was wrong, and, like Urvon and Ctuchik, he is more a slave than a disciple.

with my wrath and harry them and multiply their sufferings enormously. And behold, I will cause them all to fall down and worship me, forasmuch as my brothers have all fled, I *only* remain, and I *only* am God in the world. And all men shall worship me and raise the sweet odor of sacrifice to me and I shall have Lordship and Dominion over all things, and the world shall be *mine* –

(The copy of the manuscript breaks off here.)

TESTAMENT OF THE SNAKE PEOPLE

NOTE   This strange fragment was discovered in the ruins of a Nyissan temple
during an exploratory expedition by the twenty-third Imperial legion
into northern Nyissa following the Alorn invasion of the land of the
Snake People during the early forty-first century. The antiquity of the
fragment and the general condition of the ruins of the temple in which
it was found indicate that both more probably date back to the time of
the invasion of the Marags rather than the more recent Alorn incursion.

1. *Once*
> lived we in caves,
>> beside still brooks
>>> and in mossy dells,
>>>> and
>>>>> ISSA
>>>>>> was with us,
>> (dull-eyed ISSA with cold skin)
>>>> – Praise the glory of ISSA's name –

2. *Content*
> were we to bask in sun
>> on warm rocks
>>> and to slither at night
>>>> into dens cool and dry
>>>>> beneath the rocks,
>>>>> and
>>>> ISSA
>>> moved among us –

(Slow
> the movements,
>> sinuous and subtle)
>>> and touched our faces
>>>> with dry cold hand,
>>> and lapped
>> our scent from

out of air

with

flickering

tongue

– Praise the glory of ISSA's name –

3. *Solitary*

watched we

the turn

of seasons,

years, light as dust

lay upon us,

and uncaring we watched

and ISSA

Instructed us

(sibilant the

voice

of beloved

ISSA

and wise).

– Glory to the wisdom of ISSA –

4. *Coiled*

we with our

brothers,

the serpents,

and kissed

the

sweet

venom

from

their lipless smiles

while

ISSA

watched

and guarded

our

childlike play

– Praise the watchfulness of mighty ISSA –

5. *But*

Other Gods made war, and we knew not why.

Some trifle

that had no use or value was the cause of their contention.
> Still lay we in timeless drowse, basking in sun's
> Warmth and the glory of ISSA's gaze
> > – Adore the beauty of the scaled face of ISSA –

6. *And*

Shattered then the other Gods the earth herself, and the rocks of our dens fell in upon us, crushing the people of ISSA as they slept, and the seas rushed in, drowning the caves and the mossy dells, stilling forever the soft sibilance of our brooks and streams, engulfing the sweet land which ISSA had given us.
> – Oh weep for the precious land of ISSA –

7. *Journeyed*

We then toward those lands where the sun makes his bed, and ISSA led us. Found we there a fair land of swamp and tangled thicket and sluggish rivers, dark beneath the trees. And our brothers, the serpents, dwelt there in abundance. And ISSA commanded us that we raise a city beside the holy River of the Serpent, and called we the name of the city *Sthiss Tor* in honor of the holy wisdom of ISSA.
> – All praise to ISSA, cold and fair –

8. *And yet*

There came a time when ISSA called us to him and spake unto us, saying:

'Behold, it has come to pass that I must depart from thee. The Gods have warred, and the earth may no longer sustain us.'

Loud were our lamentations at ISSA's words, and we cried out unto him, saying:

'We beseech thee, oh mighty God, absent thyself not from us, for who will lead and guide us if thou depart?'

And ISSA wept.
> – Revere the tears of sorrowing ISSA –

9. *Again*

Spake ISSA unto us, saying:

'Behold, I am thy God, and I love thee. In spirit shall I abide with thee, and from thy number will I select the one through whom shall I speak. Thou shalt hear and obey the one – even as it were me.'
> – Hear and obey the word of ISSA –

10. *Now*

Of all the servants of ISSA, most beloved was Salmissra, the Priestess, and ISSA touched her and exalted her and spake unto the people again, saying:

'Behold my handmaiden, Salmissra. Her have I touched and exalted. And she shall be queen over thee and have dominion, and her voice shall be *my* voice, and thou shall call her name eternal, for I am with her – even as with thee unto the end of days.'

– All praise to eternal Salmissra, handmaiden of ISSA –

11. *Spake*

Then eternal Salmissra, Queen of the Serpent People, saying:

(The remainder of the fragment has been lost.)*

---

* This is typical of the Nyissan character, and the addition of the hundreds of narcotics available to them enabled us to posit an alien culture with no correspondence to any on *this* world. It is reasonable for them to be the way they are. Their society has echoes of the Egyptian, but only slight ones.

HYMN TO CHALDAN

NOTE: This is the famous War-hymn of the Asturian Arends believed to have been composed sometime early in the second millennium. While there exist Mimbrate and Wacite hymns of similar tenor, this particular piece most universally captures the spirit of Arendia, and despite its Asturian origin it is widely sung in Mimbrate chapels even to this day. Historical research indicates that it was also popular in Wacune before those people were obliterated during the Arendian Civil Wars.

Honor, Glory and Dominion be thine, O Chaldan.
Grant, Divine Lord, Victory unto thy Servants.
See, O our God, how we adore Thee.
Smite, Great Judge, the Wicked and Unjust.
Chastise our Foes. Consume them with Fire.
Scourge him who has despite unto us.
Blessed be the Name of Chaldan

Power, Might, and Empire be thine, O Chaldan.
Bless, Warrior God, the Weapons of thy Children.
Gird us, Great One, in Armor impenetrable.
Hear, Blessed Chaldan, our Lament for the Fallen.
Comfort us in our Bereavement.
Revenge us upon our Enemies.
Blessed be the name of Chaldan.

Wisdom, Honor, Eternal Worship be thine, O Chaldan.
Give, O our God, courage for the battle.
Hearken, Divinity, unto our War-Prayer.
Sustain, Magnificence, our just Cause.
Punish him who speaks slightingly to us.
Blessed be the name of Chaldan.

There are, of course, some four hundred and eighteen more verses, but the quality definitely deteriorates beyond this point, and the descriptions of the punishments invoked upon enemies are too graphic to repeat in a text which might inadvertently fall into the hands of women or children.

THE LAMENT OF MARA

NOTE FROM THE IMPERIAL LIBRARIAN OF TOL HONETH:

This peculiar piece was produced by a melancholy monk at Mar-Terin in the late 27th century. Though he steadfastly maintained until his death that these were the actual words of the grieving God, Mara, it is easily evident that this mournful work is rather the product of a mind diseased by solitude, racial guilt and the continual wail of the wind in the barren trees near the monastery.

The unfortunate history of the destruction of Maragor and the extermination of its people is a moral burden which the Tolnedran Empire must bear. We must not, however, lapse into hysteria as a result of our sense of guilt. Rather we must resolve never again to turn to such savagery in our quest for advantage and profit.

Truly, the spirit of the God Mara stands as a continual remonstrance to us; and, balanced against the proverbs of our own beloved Nedra, provides every decent and right-thinking Tolnedran with those bounds against which he may measure his conduct.

EEEE – AAAAY!
> EEEE – AAAAY!
Oh Weep for Mara whose people are no more.
> Sorrow,
>> Sorrow,

Grief and Woe
> The people are destroyed, the elders and the children.
The men are cut down, and the women, fountainhead
> of race and blood and kind
>> are slain.
> The people of Mara are no more.

EEEE-AAAAY!

EEEE-AAAAY!

Sorrow

and

Sorrow

The people of Mara are no more.
Cursed then is the land.
Betrayed am I by my brothers.
Betrayed land of the Marags shall be forever

Accursed.
My hand shall be raised against it.
No fruit shall it bear to outlanders.
No rest or sleep shall they find there.
Madness only shall they reap
among my empty cities.
And I will raise an army of the dead
against all who come into this land.
Blood and death to all who profane my sacred altars.
EEEE – AAAAY!
EEEE – AAAAY!
Sorrow!

Sorrow!

Sorrow!

O, weep for Mara, whose people are no more.[*]

---

[*] This was written to explain the haunting of Maragor. Note that we now have *two* insane gods (Torak being the other). Mara recovers, however, when Taiba appears. Note also the hints of a matriarchal society.

THE PROVERBS OF NEDRA

NOTE There are some 1800 proverbs of Nedra. The few presented here are a random sampling containing the general spirit of the advice of Nedra to his people. The fact that Tolnedra is the dominant power in the west is silent testimony to the efficacy of Nedra's advice.

1. Kill not. Dead men cannot buy from thee.

2. Steal not. Give full measure, and thy customer shall return.

3. Covet not. Keep thy mind unto thine own business and thou shalt prosper.

4. Store up thy goods against thine old age. Prepare for adversity, and be prudent in thine expenditures.

5. Be bountiful unto thy children and unto thy brother's children so that they will be bountiful unto thee when thy vigor is diminished.

6. Bribe not the tax-collector. If he will betray the throne, will he not betray thee also?

7. Adulterate not the coinage nor shave away fragments therefrom. The coin thou sendest away today shall return unto thee tomorrow, and then whom hast thou robbed?

8. Dabble not. Select thy wares and become conversant with them. Who can know both shoes and jewels at the same time?

9. Deal in the very best thou canst afford. Who will buy from one who hath no faith in his own goods?

10. Be patient in thy dealings. Courtesy and wit are gold. Anger and spite are brass.

11. Cheat not. Thy customer will remember thee and shall never return.

12. Revenge thyself not on him who hath dealt falsely with thee. No profit is to be found in revenge.

13. Be ever watchful of the servant with ambition. If he is stupid, he will steal from thee. If he is clever, he will supplant thee.

14. Traffic only in tangible things. Who can weigh the wind or measure a promise?

15. Store up gold. Time cannot tarnish it, nor fashion cheapen. Trade thy gold only in the certainty of bringing in more.*

---

* The merchant class has been greatly neglected in fantasy, but wrongly. This Tolnedran 'greed' added an interesting side-light to the character of our heroine. Ce'Nedra *loves* money.

THE SERMON OF ALDUR

Unto his Disciples[*]

Unto his Disciples*

TRULY

I say unto thee that the world was made with a word. For the Seven joined together and spake the one word – Be –

And the world was.

I say again, in the speaking of the word was the world made, and all that is in the world was made thus. And Truly, I say unto thee also, thus may the world be unmade.† For in the day that my brothers and I join again and speak the words – Be Not – in that day shall the world perish.

Infinite is the power of the word, for the word is the breath and soul of the mind, and as I have taught thee it is in the mind that all power lies. If thy mind have power, put that power into the word, and that which thou dost desire shall come to pass. But if thy mind be untutored or if it should be that thou falter or fear or doubt, the greatest words of power shall avail thee not – for with thy mind and with the word must be joined the will. And thus has it ever been.

It has come to pass that I must now go from thee and our paths must part. There is discontent and turmoil abroad in the land, and if it should come to pass that my brothers and I were drawn in to this conflict, our contention would destroy the world. Thus, that we might preserve the world and that we never again be forced to raise

---

* As mentioned in the Introduction this was a false start. We were still groping around the edges of 'the Will and the Word' when it was written, and this was an attempt to define it and to set some limits, the most important being that you have to believe that it is going to work. This 'power' is essentially Godlike. (And God said, 'Let there BE light!' And there WAS light.') The King James version is poetic, but some of its translations are highly questionable. The West Saxon translation (eighth century) uses the word 'Geworcht' ('Make' or 'construct') instead of that oversimplification 'BE'. This suggests that there's a certain amount of effort involved in the process.

† This is that 'unmaking' business that we finally prohibited.

our hands against our beloved brother who has been maddened by his afflictions must we go from this world.

In sorrow I go from thee, but know that my spirit will be with thee always to aid thee and to comfort thee.

As I leave thee, I charge thee with a duty and lay upon thee a heavy burden. Verily, my beloved Disciples, thou art not as other men. Together have we sought out wisdom that we might more perfectly understand the meaning of the power of the word. That power is with thee, and thy minds have been bent to its use. Upon thee therefore falls the duty of preserving the world now that I and my brothers must depart. Some will remain here in this Vale to seek out further the meaning of the power of the word; others must go forth into the lands of strangers and use the power of the word to preserve the world and to stand as a barrier against my brother until the appointed one shall appear who will do that which must be done.

It will come to pass that some among thee will sicken of this endless burden, and with will and mind and the power of the word will they cause themselves to no longer be – for it is a simple thing to say 'be not' and to perish. For them I grieve, knowing that which is to come to pass.

And behold, one among thee shall bend his mind and will and the power of the word to exalt himself above all men, and he too shall perish, and I grieve for him as well.

In parting I abjure thee, seek not to pit thy will and thy mind and the power of the word against my brother Torak. Know that he is a God, and though thy mind be as strong as his and thine understanding of the power of the word be as perfect, his will is to thine as is thine to that of a child. Know that this it is that makes him a God. In the invincibility of his will is Torak a God, and in that only. In the day that thou seekest to raise thy will against the will of Torak, in that day shalt thou surely perish. But more than this – if it should come to pass that the power of the word be raised against Torak, no power that exists in the endless starry reaches of the Universe can save the world. For I say unto thee, if Torak in his madness turn mind and will and the power of the word against thee, shall the world be shattered, and the shards thereof scattered like dust among the stars.

Lest ye grow fearful and disconsolate at the enormity of thy task, know that the Orb which I have made hath the power to curb the will of Torak. For it hath confounded him, and not without cost hath he raised it against the world.

And it shall come to pass that in a certain day shall come the One who is to use the Orb, and if he be brave and pure, shall Torak be overthrown. But if he falter or be tempted by the power of the Orb, shall Torak overcome him and recapture the Orb, and then shall the world be Torak's forever.

But behold, the madness of my brother Torak is a disease and a canker unto the Universe, and if it should come to pass that he prevails in this, it must be that my brothers and I raise our hands against him, for the madness of Torak unchecked shall rend the Universe even as he hath cracked this world which we made and which we love. And thus will we come against him with the most fearful power. In sorrow shall we pronounce the dread words – 'Be Not' – and our brother Torak shall be no more, and, as it must needs be, this lovely world also shall be no more.

Guide well therefore the child and the man who is to be the Appointed One and prepare him for his great task. Know that if he fail, Torak shall conquer, and my voice must be joined with the voices of my Brethren to speak that final – 'Be Not' – which will unmake all that we have made. And, though it will grieve me beyond thy power to understand, I will bend all of my mind and all of my will into that fateful word, and this world will shimmer and vanish as morning mist beneath the weight of the noon sun.

Thus I leave the world in thy keeping, my sons. Fail not in thy duty to me and to the world.

I will go now to seek pleasant fields among the stars and shaded pathways to strange suns; and, if all passeth well, shalt thou join me there when thy task is done.

– And, so saying, did Aldur turn and ascend into the star-strewn skies, and no man hath seen him more –

THE BOOK OF ULGO[*]

NOTE This is the famous southern copy of this disputed work. It differs in certain crucial details from the seven other fragmentary copies, and is considered by certain scholars to be a corrupt, third-hand copy with no historical or theological value. It is, however, the only complete copy we have, and provides the only clues we have to the understanding of the enigmatic Ulgos. How it came to be in the possession of the Dryads in southern Tolnedra is, of course, a mystery.

At the Beginning of Days when the world was spun out of Darkness by the wayward Gods, dwelt there in the silences of the heavens a spirit known only as UL. Mighty was he, but withheld his power as the younger Gods combined to bring forth the world and the sun and the moon also. Old was he and wise, but withheld his wisdom from them, and what they wrought was not perfect by reason of that. And they had despite unto him that he would not join with them, and turned they their backs upon him.

And it came to pass that the younger Gods wrought beasts and fowls, serpents and fishes, and lastly, Man. But by reason of the withholding of the power and the wisdom of UL, it was not perfect and was marred. Many creatures were wrought which were unseemly and strange, and the younger Gods repented their making and tried they to unmake that which they had wrought so that all things upon the world which they had made might be fair and seemly. But the Spirit of UL stretched forth his hand and prevented them, and they could not unmake that which they had wrought, no matter how monstrous or ill-shapen. And he spake unto the younger Gods, saying: 'Behold, what thou hast wrought thou mayest in no wise unmake, for in thy folly hast thou torn asunder the fabric of the heavens and the peace thereof that thou might bring forth this world of thine to be a plaything and an entertainment. Know, however, that whatsoever ye make, be it ever so monstrous or unseemly, it will

---

[*] Once we started on this particular Holy Book we began to see all kinds of possibilities beyond the original intention of providing background for Relg. And when we expanded the Ulgos into the Dals, the Melcenes, the Morindim, and the Karands, we had constructed much of the non-Angarak population of Mallorea.

abide and be a rebuke unto thee for thy folly. For in the day that one thing which is made is unmade, in that day shall *all* that is made be unmade.'*

And the younger Gods were wroth, and in despite spake they unto each monstrous or unseemly thing they made, saying, 'Go thou even unto UL, and he shall be thy God.' And UL spake not.

And the younger Gods wrought men, and each selected that people which pleased him to be God over them. And it came to pass that when each had chosen, there were peoples yet who had no God. And the younger Gods drave them out, saying, 'Go thou even unto UL, and he shall be thy God.'

Now these were the generations of the wanderings of the Godless ones. Long and bitter were the years when they wandered in the wastelands and the wilderness of the west.

And it came to pass that among their number was a just and righteous man named Gorim, and he spake unto the multitudes of the Godless ones, saying, 'Stay thou and rest from thy wanderings here upon this plain. I will take upon myself the search for the God named UL that we might worship him and find thereby a place in the world. For verily, we wither and fall as leaves by the wayside by reason of the rigors of our wanderings. The children die and the old men also. Better it is that one only die. Abide here against my return.'

* Here is that prohibition, but this isn't the final word. It was ultimately refined so that 'Be not' wouldn't obliterate the entire world, but only the person foolish enough to say it. Primitive mythologies seethed with 'forbidden words' ('Jehovah' is probably the most prominent). We tampered with that idea and made the obliteration the result of a *command* rather than a mere word. Sin doth lie in the intent.

And lo, Gorim went out from the multitude alone and sought the God named UL that his people might find a God to worship and a place in the world.

Twenty years sought he the God named UL in the wilderness and found him not. And things monstrous and gross assailed him in the wilderness, but he prevailed and was not slain.

And yet he wearied in his wanderings, and his hair grew grey as the years dropped like leaves upon his head. And upon a certain day Gorim despaired and went up unto a high mountain and spake unto the sky in a great voice, saying, 'No more! I will search no longer. The Gods are a mockery and a deception; the world is a barren void; there is no UL; and I am sick of my life which is a curse and an affliction unto me.'

And behold, the Spirit of UL spake unto him, saying, 'Wherefore art thou wroth with me, Gorim? Thy making and thy casting out were not of my doing.'

And Gorim was sore afraid and fell down upon his face before the Spirit of UL.

And UL spake unto him, saying, 'Rise, Gorim, for I am not thy God.'

But Gorim rose not. 'Oh, my God,' quoth he, 'hide not thy face from thy people who are sorely afflicted by reason that they are outcast and have no God to protect them.'

And again UL spake unto him, saying, 'Rise, Gorim. Seek thou a God elsewhere, for I am God unto no people. I made thee not, and am incurious as to thy fate.'

But still Gorim rose not. 'Oh, my God,' quoth he again, 'thy people are outcast and they perish as leaves before the cold winds of winter. The children die and the old men also, and there is no place in the broad world where they might find rest.'

And the Spirit of UL was troubled by the words of Gorim, the just and righteous man, and he rose up in wrath saying, 'Rise, Gorim, and quit this place. Cease thy drasty complaining, and leave me in peace. Seek thou elsewhere a God, and trouble me no more, for I am not thy God.'

And still Gorim rose not. 'Oh, my God,' quoth he, 'yet will I abide. Thy people hunger and they thirst also. They seek only thy blessing and a place wherein they might dwell.'

And UL spake, saying, 'Then will I depart from here, for thy speech wearies me.'

And yet did Gorim abide in that place and went not away. And, behold, the beasts of the fields brought him to eat, and the fowls of the air brought him to drink by reason of his holiness. And did he abide there a year and more.

And the Spirit of UL was sore troubled.

And came unto that place the things monstrous and unseemly that the Gods had made and that the Spirit of UL forbade them to destroy, and sat they at the feet of Gorim. Chimeras and Unicorns were there and Basilisks and Winged Serpents also, and they abode there watching Gorim.

And UL came unto Gorim and he spake, saying, 'Abidest thou still?'

And Gorim fell upon his face, saying, 'Oh, my God, thy people cry unto thee in their affliction.'

And the Spirit of UL fled.

And there did Gorim abide and was brought meat by dragons and water to drink by creatures unnamed. And the days and months did rain down, and another year passed.

And again came UL unto Gorim and spake, saying, 'Abidest thou still?'

And again Gorim fell upon his face, saying, 'Oh, my God, thy people perish in the absence of thy care.'

And again did the spirit of UL flee from the righteous man.

And there still did Gorim abide, and food and drink were brought unto him as an offering unto his holiness and his righteousness by things that have no name and things that are unseen. And passed yet another year.

And the Spirit of UL came again unto the high mountain where Gorim abode, and the creatures monstrous, named and unnamed, seen and unseen, made great moan.

And UL spake, saying, 'Rise, Gorim.'

And Gorim fell upon his face and spake, saying, 'Oh, my God, have mercy.'

And UL spake, saying, 'Rise, Gorim. I am UL – thy God, and I command thee to rise and stand before me.' And reached he down and lifted Gorim up with his hands.

'Then wilt thou be my God?' Gorim asked of UL, 'and God unto my people also?'

And UL spake, saying, 'I am thy God and the God of thy people also.'

And Gorim looked down from the high place whereon he had abode and beheld the unseemly creatures which had fed him and comforted him during his travail, and he spake unto the God UL, saying, 'And what of these, oh, my God? Who will be God unto the Basilisk and the Minotaur, the Dragon and the Chimera, the Unicorn and the Thing Unnamed, the Winged Serpent and the Thing Unseen?'

And the Spirit of UL spake not and was wroth.

'For also are these outcast, oh, my God,' quoth Gorim. 'The younger Gods cast them out in thy despite because they were monstrous and unseemly. Yet is there beauty in each. The scales of the Basilisk are like jewels. The head of the Chimera is lofty and noble. The Unicorn is of exceeding beauty, and its single horn is intricately twisted and graceful. The wings of the Dragon are majestic, and the body of the Minotaur magnificent. Behold them, oh, my God. Turn not thy face from them, for in them is great beauty and delight unto the eye if thou be but willing to look. Unto thee was each sent by the younger Gods and was told to seek thee out to be their God. Who *will* be their God if thou turnest thy face from them?'

'It was done in my despite,' quoth UL, 'and these monstrous beings sent unto me to bring shame upon me that I had rebuked the younger Gods. I am not God unto monsters.'

And Gorim looked upon his God and spake, saying, 'Oh, my God, mayhap the space of a little time will give thee leisure to reconsider. Yet will I abide here a little while, trusting in thy justice and thine infinite mercy.' And so saying, he sat himself again upon the earth.

And the God UL spake unto Gorim, saying, 'Tempt not the patience of thy God, Gorim. I have consented to be God unto thee and thy people, but in no wise will I be God unto monstrous things.'

And the creatures who sat at the feet of Gorim made great moan.

'Yet will I abide, oh, my God,' Gorim said and rose not from the earth.

'Abide if it please thee,' quoth UL and departed from that place.

And it was even as before. Gorim abode, and the creatures sustained him, and UL was troubled.

And it came to pass that the Great God UL relented even as before by reason of the holiness of the righteous man, Gorim, and he came unto Gorim and spake, saying, 'Rise, Gorim, that thou mayest serve thy God.' And he reached down and lifted up Gorim with his hands, and commanded him, saying, 'Bring unto me in turn each of the creatures who sit before thee that I might consider them, for if it is as thou sayest and each hath beauty and worthiness, then will I consent to be their God also.'

And Gorim brought each creature before his God, and UL marveled at the beauty of each and that he had not seen it before. And the creatures prostrated themselves before the Great God UL and made great moan and besought his blessing.

And the Spirit of UL raised up his hands and blessed them, saying, 'Behold, I am UL, and I find great beauty and worthiness in each of you, in the Dragon and the Minotaur, in the Dwarf and the Basilisk, in the Unicorn and the Chimera, in the Dryad and the Troll, in the Centaur and in the Thing Unnamed, and even find I beauty in the Thing Unseen. And I will be thy God, and thou shalt prosper, and peace shall prevail among you.'

And the heart of Gorim was made glad, and he called the name of the high place where all of this had come to pass 'Prolgu', which is 'holy place'. And he departed from that place and returned he unto the plain to bring his people unto UL, their God. And behold, they recognized him not, for the hands of UL had touched him, and all color had fled from the touch of UL, and the body and the hair of Gorim were as white as new snow. And his people feared him and drave him from their midst with stones.

And Gorim cried out unto UL, saying, 'Oh, my God, thy touch hath changed me, and my people know me not.'

And the Spirit of UL raised his hand, and behold, the people were all made even as Gorim. And the Spirit of UL spake unto the people in a great voice, saying, 'Hearken unto the words of thy God. This is he whom ye have called Gorim. He it was who came unto me and by reason of his great holiness prevailed upon me to accept ye as my people, and watch over thee and provide for thee and to be God over thee. And henceforth shall this man be called UL-GO in remembrance of me and in token of his holiness. In him am I well-pleased. Thou shalt do even as he commands thee, and thou shalt go even where he leads. And behold, any who fail to obey him or to

follow him will I cut off even as the limb is cut from the tree, and they shall wither and perish and be no more.'

And he who had been Gorim and was now called UL-GO spake unto the people and commanded them to take up their goods and their cattle and to follow him into the mountains before them.

And behold, the elders of the people believed him not, nor that the Voice which they had heard had been the Voice of UL, and they spake unto him in great despite, saying, 'If thou be the servant of the God UL, perform thou a wonder in proof thereof.'

And UL-GO answered them, saying, 'Behold thy skin and thy hair. Is this not wonder enough for thee?'

And they were troubled and went away. And again they came unto him, saying, 'Lo, the mark upon us is by reason of a pestilence which hath fallen upon us and which *thou* hast brought unto us from some unclean place. Still see we no wonder in proof of the favor of the God UL.'

And UL-GO grew weary of them and spake in a great voice, saying, 'Verily I say unto the people, ye have heard the Voice of the Great God UL. Much have I suffered in thy behalf, and now will I return even unto Prolgu, the holy place. Let him who would follow me do; let him who would not, remain.' And he spake no more, but turned and went even toward the mountains. And some few of the people took up their goods and their cattle and followed him. But behold, the greater part of the people remained, and they reviled UL-GO and those who followed him, saying, 'Where is this wonder which proves the favor of UL? We defy the Voice which spake unto us. We *will* not follow UL-GO, neither will we obey him, and behold, we wither not, neither do we perish.'

And UL-GO looked upon them with a great sadness and spake unto them for the last time, saying, 'Verily, ye have besought a wonder from me. Behold, then, the wonder. Even as the Voice of UL hath said are ye witherèd as the limb of the tree which is cut off. In this day have ye perished.' And he led the few who would follow him up into the mountains even unto Prolgu.

And the multitude of the people mocked him and then returned they unto their tents and laughed at the folly of those who had followed UL-GO.

'Behold,' they said, 'howso are we witherèd, and by what token might we know that we have perished?' And they laughed at this great folly for the space of a year, and then laughed no more, for behold, their women were barren and bore no more, and the people witherèd as the limb that is cut off, and, in time, they perished and were no more.

But the people who followed UL-GO came with him unto Prolgu, the holy place, and built there a city, and the Spirit of UL was with them, and they dwelt in peace with all the creatures who had sustained UL-GO.

And the peace of UL was with them for a thousand years, and yet another thousand, and they were troubled not. And they deemed that the Peace of UL should abide forever, but it was not so, for lo, the younger Gods quarreled over a stone that one had made, and in their quarrel was the earth broken asunder and the seas did come in. And the earth was maddened by reason of her wounding. And behold, the creatures which had dwelt in peace with the people of UL-GO were maddened also by the wounding of the earth, and rose they up against the fellowship of UL and cast down their cities and slew the people, and few only escaped.

And these were the years of the troubling. The creatures which had been the friends of the people of UL-GO hunted them and slew them, and the people fled even unto Prolgu, the holy place, there they durst not come for fear of the wrath of UL. And loud were the cries and the lamentations of the people unto UL. And the Spirit of UL was troubled by reason of their sufferings, and behold, he revealed unto them the caves that lay under Prolgu, the holy place, and went the people then into the sacred caves of UL and dwelt there.

And the people of the other Gods came because their lands had been broken by the war of the Gods, and they took lands and called them by strange names. But held the people of UL to the caverns and galleries beneath the holy place at Prolgu and had no dealings with them. And UL protected his people and hid them from the strangers, and the strangers knew not that the people were there.

And behold, the unseemly creatures which had broken the peace of UL by reason of their maddening fed upon the flesh of the strangers, and the strangers feared the mountains of UL and shunned them. But the people of UL abode and were safe.

– The manuscript breaks off here.

❧II❧

the histories

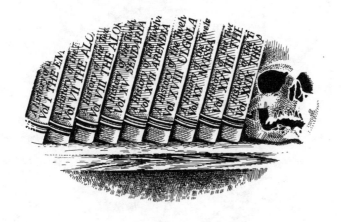

Sea of the Winds
Jarviksholm
CHEREK
R. DUSED
Val Alorn
Gulf of Cherek
Kotu
THE FEN
Aldurford
THE BORE
Darine
R. OF VEKS
Riva
ISLE of the WINDS
Sendar
SENDARIA
GREAT NORTH ROAD
Muros
CAMAAR R.
Camaar
ARENDISH FOREST
ASTUR R.
PROLGU
ULGOLAND
THE STRONGHO
ARENDIA
Great Western Sea
Vo Mimbre
R. AREND
FOREST OF VORDUE
Tol Vordue
TOLNEDRA
CARAVAN ROUTE
Tol Horb
NEDRANE R.
Tol Honeth
Tol Borune
Tol Rane
THE KINGDOMS OF THE WEST AND THE ANGARAKS
WOOD OF THE DRYADS
R. of the WOODS
NYISSA
MARAGOR
R. of the SERPENT
Sthiss Tor

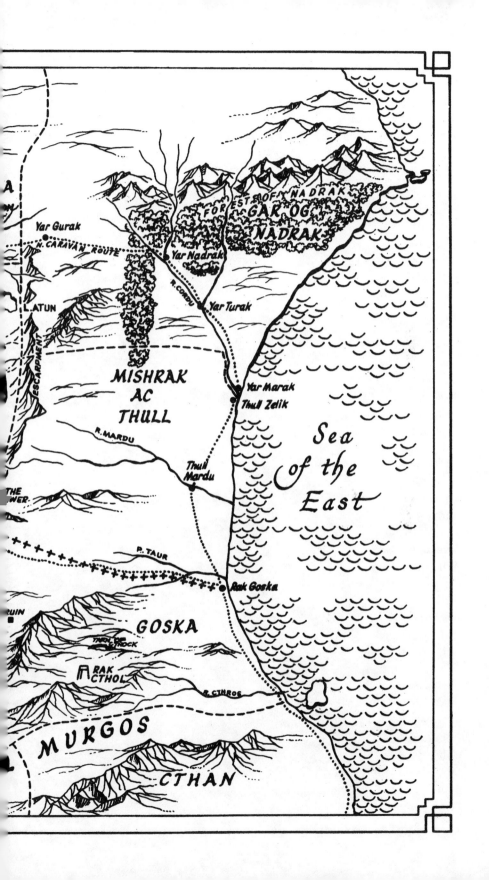

At Tol Honeth 5368 *

NOTE Excerpted from **A History of the Twelve Kingdoms of the West –**
Being an account of their past, their development, their geography,
their principal commerce and the character of their people. Compiled by
the Imperial Historical Society at the command of his Imperial Majesty,
Ran Borune XXIII.

A NOTE ON DATING: By general consensus of the Council of
Tol Vordue, the eight kingdoms agreed to make the Alorn
mode of dating the standard for trade, commerce, diplomacy and all
other dealings among themselves. It was generally agreed that this
mode provided a more coherent and continuous numbering system
than the Tolnedran mode which numbers the years of a Tolnedran
Dynasty or the Arendish mode which starts over again with each
new king (a system made trebly confusing by the fact that there
have, on occasion, been as many as three self-proclaimed Kings of
Arendia), or the Mode of the Ulgos who do not number years at all
but name them.

Thus the Tolnedran year 347 was the Arendish year 5 (or 9, or 3)
and was in turn the Ulgo year Marag. The Alorn year 3480 was more
to the liking of merchants and traders, since it was a more stable
form.

The reckoning of Alorn years dates back to some mythic event in
the Alorn past – apparently some catastrophe which they commem-
orate – but no reputable scholar has ever been able to obtain verifiable information about the event from Alorn priests or storytellers.

---

* This date is not a coincidence. Garion was born in 5354, so he is fourteen at this point
(and so is Ce'Nedra). This is the year when the quest begins with Garion, Polgara and
Belgarath leaving Faldor's farm to join Silk and Barak.

GENERAL BACKGROUND AND GEOGRAPHY *

The western kingdoms comprise a large, rather heavily mountained area lying between the Great Western Sea and the Sea of the East and extending from the tropical jungles south of the Kingdom of Nyissa northward all the way to the polar ice in the northern-most reaches of Cherek, Drasnia and Gar og Nadrak. The area is roughly two thousand leagues† from north to south and perhaps fifteen hundred leagues from east to west.

Competent geographers generally agree that the mountains which form the central spine of the continent are one chain running from south to north and dividing at the headwaters of the Aldur River to embrace the high Algarian plains and further to the north the steppes of Drasnia. The contending view that the mountains are two ranges running north to south and intersecting at the headwaters of the Aldur is generally discredited.‡

The western coastline of the continent is a moist, fertile plain extending inland for varying distances ranging from one hundred leagues in Sendaria to three hundred at the widest point in Arendia. The average, however, would be closer to two hundred leagues. From this plain rise quite gradually the western foothills to the mountain range which bisects the continent. Portions of this coastal plain are heavily forested – for example, the great forest in the north of Arendia, the Forest of Vordue in northern Tolnedra, the romantically named Wood of the Dryads in southern Tolnedra and the extensive forests – more properly jungles – in Nyissa.

To the south the mountains dominate the entire land mass, ranging perhaps thirteen hundred leagues from the eastern coastline of southern Cthol Murgos westward to the headwaters of the river of the Serpent in Nyissa.

Lying in the mountains of southern Tolnedra is a large, fertile basin roughly one hundred and fifty leagues by forty leagues. This basin is dotted by the ruins of the Marag culture, and is, unfortunately, totally uninhabitable.

Another interesting feature of the southern mountains is the

---

* This brief section is really no more than a verbalization of the map cast in the fictionalized voice of the scholars at the University of Tol Honeth. Note that we describe only half a continent at this stage.

† We used the 'league' (three miles) fairly consistently.

‡ This is an absurdity, of course. Fun, though.

wasteland of Murgos, a vast arid plain which appears to be a dry lake bed or sea bottom.

The eastern coast of the continent is significantly less fertile than is the west. The coastlines of Cthol Murgos, Mishrak ac Thull and Gar og Nadrak are rocky and tend to be backed by rolling steppes only sparsely covered by rough grasses. The eastern foothills are but lightly timbered with the exception of the vast forest of Nadrak in the north.

In the central part of the continent, the mountains divide at the Vale of Aldur and the division between them widens out into the plains of Algaria, a vast grassland five hundred leagues square and watered by the Aldur River which runs for eight hundred leagues north to empty into the Gulf of Cherek through the marshes, known as Aldurfens, at its mouth.

North of the Algarian plains, the Mrin river runs westward out of the Drasnian hills to join with the River Atun to the west of Boktor.

Across the Gulf of Cherek from Drasnia lies the Cherek peninsula, hereditary home of the Alorn people. With the exception of a fertile, though hilly, basin south of Val Alorn, the peninsula is largely mountainous, being an extension of the western range which lies to the south of the Gulf of Cherek.

One distinctive feature of the Gulf of Cherek is the tidal bore between the southern tip of Cherek and the northern-most tip of Sendaria. This narrow place in the straits of Sendaria is known as the Cherek Bore. Currents through the bore are so fierce that only the most experienced navigators will attempt passage.

Westward, a hundred leagues off the coast lies the Isle of the Winds, a rocky, inhospitable island beaten by endless gales from the vast open ocean beyond and approachable only at the port of Riva. The island is perhaps a hundred leagues wide by three hundred leagues long. It is a tribute to the human spirit that this most inhospitable place in all the world is in fact inhabited, however sparsely.

THE EMPIRE OF TOLNEDRA

NOTE TO THE IMPERIAL STUDENT*:

Since this, your Highness, is likely to be your first exposure to the plain truth about your country, it might be well to explain our motives in presenting what is – at times – so unflattering a picture. Our study of history has proved that he rules best who rules without illusions, and it is the desire of the entire faculty to make your Highness the best ruler possible. In the next several years your Highness will study statecraft, diplomacy, politics, foreign relations and economic theory. As your education proceeds, your Highness will routinely receive copies of all but the most sensitive reports presented to your father, the Emperor. Your Highness will, in the classroom, make Imperial decisions which will then be compared with the actual decisions of the Emperor himself, and extensive critiques will be conducted to evaluate those decisions. It is therefore essential that now, at the very beginning of your studies, you receive the clearest possible understanding of the genuine realities which obtain in Tolnedra as well as in other kingdoms. This survey, which is periodically updated, is designed to provide those realities.

---

* The University of Tol Honeth supposedly exists for the sole purpose of educating the crown prince. Also, we decided to distinguish between 'your Highness' and 'your Majesty'. ('Highness' for a prince or princess; 'Majesty' for a king or queen.) This is *not* consistently followed in the royal courts of *this* world.

GEOGRAPHY

Tolnedra, to state the obvious, is one of the larger of the western kingdoms. Its northern border is formed by the lower reaches of the River Arend and proceeds easterly thence around the southern tip of Ulgoland, then southeasterly along the rim of the western Algarian escarpment at the Vale of Aldur to the by-and-large indistinct frontier with Cthol Murgos in the east. The border then proceeds southward to the lower reaches of the district of the Marags – that area once referred to as Maragor which was assimilated by Tolnedra early in the third millennium. Thence the border runs generally westerly, fronting still on Cthol Murgos to the northeastern tip of Nyissa, then to the lower reaches of the River of the Woods and finally to the shores of the Great Western Sea.

While it is a commonplace to speak in public pronouncements of the 'sacred and inviolable borders of Imperial Tolnedra', it must be understood that any boundary not marked by some natural feature – such as a river – is only an approximation. This is particularly true in mountainous country where lack of human habitation (as well as lack of interest) makes efforts to demarcate precisely a useless pastime.

At any rate, fully two thirds of Tolnedra is wasteland of rock and ice and gloomy, endless forests sighing in the chill mountain winds.

The significant portion of Tolnedra is the western third, a fertile coastal plain lying between the River Arend to the north and the River of the Woods to the south. It is upon this plain that Tolnedra in fact exists. Four of the five major cities lie there as well as the bulk of agriculture and commerce. In antiquity, the central portions of this plain were periodically inundated by the vast floods of the Nedrane River. It was the labor of two early dynasties to dike the Nedrane from Tol Honeth to Tol Horb, providing not only the necessary flood-control but also that broad waterway that makes Tol Honeth, despite the fact that it lies a hundred leagues inland, one of the major ports of the world.

In the north, along the Arendish border, lies the forest of Vordue where extensive logging operations provide sufficient hardwood lumber for the fine furnishings of which Tolnedrans are so fond. Softer woods, for construction, are taken from the mountains to the east, but the wood of the Dryads to the south remains inviolate for reasons which will become clear later. While there were extensive mines in the south central mountains around Tol Rane, the deposits of gold, silver, copper, iron and tin have been exploited to the point where the depth of the mines makes the extraction of these useful and ornamental metals both difficult and dangerous.

Tolnedra's two seaports of Tol Horb at the mouth of the Nedrane and Tol Vordue at the mouth of the Arend conduct between them a major portion of the world's commerce. Tol Borune on the south plain is the center of an enormous agricultural empire. Tol Honeth, the Imperial capital, has been justly called 'the hub of the world'.

THE PEOPLE

Tolnedrans are shorter and somewhat darker in complexion than the blond, rangy Alorns of the north. Racially, they are akin to the Arends, the Nyissans and the now-defunct Marags. Thus we observe three broad racial groupings in the twelve kingdoms – Alorns, Angaraks and the southern peoples. The racial background of the Ulgos is, of course, a mystery.*

Our people, through long habituation and perhaps by native inclination, are the most politically-minded and acquisitive of any people in the twelve kingdoms. Commerce is the very soul and blood of Tolnedra. Because, from time immemorial, we have engaged in trade and bargaining, Tolnedrans instinctively turn to policy in preference to war as a means of gaining our national objectives. As Nedra, in his wisdom, said, 'Where is the profit in making war on a customer?' and again, 'An enemy may be pillaged once, but a customer is an endless resource.'

Perhaps because of this, Tolnedrans deal a bit sharper than other peoples, and a Tolnedran Emperor must be eternally watchful lest he be misled by the (and let us be honest) greed of his advisors and the merchant barons who habitually besiege the Imperial Throne with petitions designed almost inevitably to line their own purses.

Lest this be construed as an unbridled condemnation of our people, let us hasten to point out the innumerable advantages which have accrued to our empire as a result of our single-minded pursuit of profit. Tolnedran society was never fractioned by the existence of clans such as we observe in the Alorn Kingdoms. Adherence to clan is a symptom of a morbid fear of strangers, and Tolnedrans have ever

* The use of the word 'race' is somewhat archaic. The Alorns are clearly Scandinavian; the Tolnedrans, Marags, Arends, and Nyissans are Mediterranean. The Angaraks, with their 'angular eyes' were intended to suggest the Mongols of Genghis Khan or the Huns of Attila.

welcomed contact with strangers as an opportunity to open new avenues for commerce. Similarly, we have never been burdened with the institution of serfdom which has blighted the development of Arendia. As a wise Tolnedran noble once said, 'Far better to pay a man for a job and wish him well than to feed him eternally in idleness.' Nor are we obsessed with the kind of religious fanaticism which so dominates the lives of the Nyissans, the Angaraks and the Ulgos. Our Nedra is a tolerant God who is content with a few formalities on ceremonial occasions. The sole exception to this generalization is the monastic community which lies in the western reaches of the area that was once Maragor. These gentle souls devote their lives in poverty and humility to the expiation of our national crime, the destruction of the Marags. While many of our people find the mendicant members of this fraternity an aggravation, it must be pointed out that their continual propitiation of the wronged and sorrowful spirit of the God Mara in all probability averts his vengeance.

One other anomaly exists in southern Tolnedra. This anomaly is, of course, the Dryads. Like the Ulgos, the Dryads predate the western migration of civilized men into the west. Their numbers have always been very small, and they are seldom seen out of the wood of the Dryads which lies along our southern border. A secretive people, they have managed to remain aloof from the main stream of Tolnedran society. Their sole contribution to our culture perhaps was the marriage of a Dryad princess to a noble of the House of Borune. In exchange for this woman the Dryads extracted a promise from the Borunes that their woods would remain eternally inviolate. This promise was formalized by the Imperial Decree of Ran Borune I, the son of the Dryad woman and the Borune noble and the founder of the FIRST BORUNE DYNASTY. While uncounted generations of timber barons have cursed the decree while eyeing the enormous oaks of the Dryad forest with unconcealed greed, it must be conceded that Tolnedra has benefited tremendously from the unlikely merging of this strange people and one of our noblest houses. The Borune Dynasties have been among the most stable and enlightened in our history, and Borune Emperors seem possessed of uncommon good sense. The common people have a saying, 'Blessed be the name of Nedra that he has given us the Borunes,' which perhaps sums it up best.*

One curious characteristic of the House of Borune has been

---

* The emperor who commissioned this study was a member of the Borune family, so the scholar who wrote this was evidently trying to ingratiate himself.

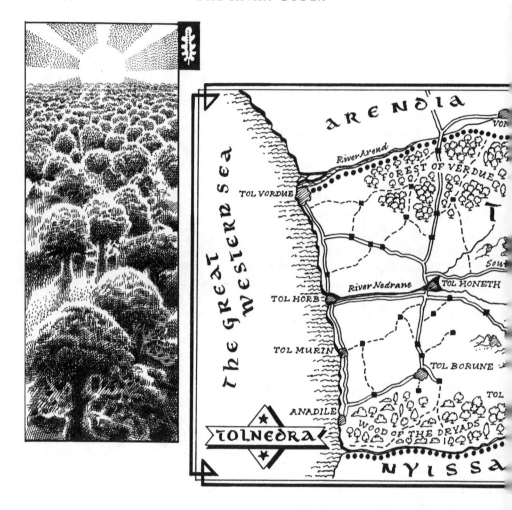

observed down the centuries. While the male children of the house show little physical difference from ordinary Tolnedrans, the female children always differ markedly from the other women of our race. They are all quite tiny, and their hair is inevitably a deep, flaming red – a color which poets have rather extravagantly compared to that of the leaves of the oak tree in autumn. Their complexions are also significantly fairer than the olive skin of other Tolnedran women, and in certain light appear to have almost a faint greenish hue. Borune princesses, delicate and vibrant, may be justly considered the true jewels of the Empire.

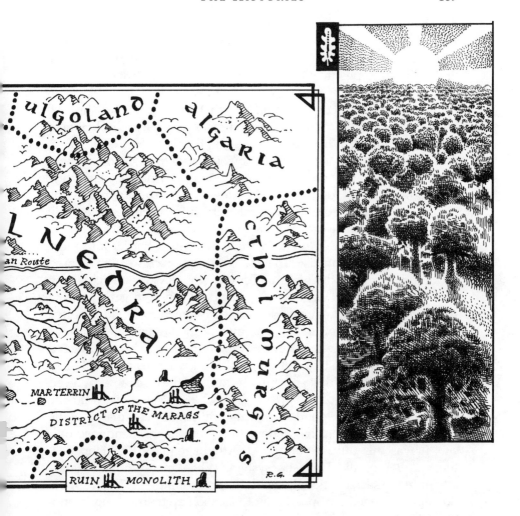

PRE-DYNASTIC HISTORY

As did the other peoples of the west, the Tolnedrans migrated from the east during the early centuries of the first millennium. They established themselves on the central plain and began construction of their first city, Tol Honeth, on the large island in the Nedrane River. The present glory of Tol Honeth belies the crude log and mud fortress which first stood on the site. Written records of the pre-Dynastic era are tantalizingly brief, and few have survived down to the present. The documents of the FIRST HONETHITE DYNASTY, however, provide us with some insight into what life must have been like in prehistoric Tolnedra by virtue of those subjects which were of major concern to our first Emperors. Fire, flood, pestilence and civil war appear to have been endemic in those dark early years.

It is perhaps not an exaggeration to state that the Tolnedran Empire was born out of fire – or at least that it rose from the ashes. All wooden structures are susceptible to fire, and the city of Tol Honeth was no exception. Whatever the cause, in the first years of the ninth century a great conflagration broke out, and the island city was consumed from one end to the other. A minor city official, surveying the damage, concluded that stone does not burn and began the reconstruction of the city in that material while the embers were still smoldering. While a gang of wood-cutters may construct a log palisade in short order, work in stone is a much harder and more time-consuming enterprise. The vast construction crews who labored for decades to raise the walls of Tol Honeth provided the core as it were of the Imperial Legions. The standard ten-man gang used to transport large single stones became the elemental squad. The ten gangs of ten – the hundred – who moved the larger stones became the company, and the ten hundreds – the thousand – who dragged the vast foundation stones of the walls and wharves of Tol Honeth became the legions. The co-operative effort and the discipline involved in the construction of the city welded these work-gangs into the strong units which responded quite naturally to the commands of the overseer of the entire construction effort – the above-mentioned offi-cial. It was this official who became the legendary Ran Honeth I, the founder of the Dynastic system. When marauding brigands attempted to sack the fledgling city, the work-gangs, under the direc-tion of Ran Honeth, dropped their tools, took up their weapons, and, because of their superior discipline, easily drove them off. Thus the idea of Empire was born. Once the work-gangs had tasted victory, the rest was simple. In a series of lightning moves, Ran Honeth consolidated his control over the entire Tolnedran people and estab-lished order, peace and security throughout the entire central plain.

THE FIRST HONETHITE DYNASTY 815–1373
(558 years, 23 Emperors)*

The major efforts of the FIRST HONETHITE DYNASTY were directed at the extension of the northern boundary of Tolnedra to the River Arend, the establishment of the port-fortresses at Tol Vordue and Tol Horb, and, of course, the building of the north dike on the Nedrane River. When the last Emperor, Ran Honeth XXIII, died without issue, the Empire was thrown into consternation.

THE FIRST VORDUVIAN DYNASTY 1373–1692
(319 years, 16 Emperors)

By the sheerest good fortune, the commander of the Imperial garrison at Tol Vordue – and, incidentally, the primary civil official as well – was a strong-minded, talented man who, less from ambition than from a powerful sense of personal responsibility, marched to Tol Honeth at the head of his legions to assume the Throne. It was at that time that the procedure for orderly Dynastic succession was established, thus saving the Empire from disintegration.

The Council of Advisors, a broad-based group of representatives from all districts of the Empire, gathered in emergency session and concluded that the commander of the Tol Vordue garrison was *going* to be the next Emperor with or without their consent, and they therefore carried his name to the Temple of Nedra where the priests consulted with the God himself.

NOTE Popular superstition has it that in the early years of the Empire Nedra was **physically** present in the temple, sustained and served by the priesthood. Modern theologians, however, have discounted this and hold the more rational view that, while Nedra has always been with us in **Spirit**, his **physical** presence at any time in our long history is incapable of substantiation.

When the priests emerged from the temple with the blessings of Nedra upon Ran Vordue I, the FIRST VORDUVIAN DYNASTY was established, and the orderly succession was preserved.

The Vorduvians were vigorous and energetic Emperors, and they

---

* The dynasties provided a convenient, methodical way to establish the chronology. That was their main purpose, but the frictions between the great families also proved very useful.

soon turned their attention to the lands south of Nedrane. Early in the Dynasty, our southern border was pushed to the banks of the River of the Woods, and the essential part of the Empire was complete.

Tol Borune was constructed in the center of the southern plain, and the remainder of the Dynasty devoted its efforts to the construction of the south dike on the Nedrane River.

THE SECOND HONETHITE DYNASTY
1692–2112 (420 years, 19 Emperors)

The years of this Dynasty were a period of consolidation and development. It was also a period of our first significant contacts with other nations. As so frequently is the case in Tolnedran history, it was the merchants who led the way. The initial contacts with the Arends and Nyissans were peaceful and profitable, but the Marags steadfastly refused to permit the entry of strangers into Maragor. The Emperor Ran Honeth XVII attempted to solve this problem by the construction of Tol Rane on Maragor's western border. The purpose of Tol Rane was to provide a commercial center where the Marags could come to trade, but it soon had another, grimmer purpose. It quickly became evident that the Marags had considerable quantities of fine gold, and the accidental discovery of free gold in the streams of the border region set off a stampede of fortune-hunters to Tol Rane.

Creeping across the border into Maragor by night, these adventurers sought gold in every stream-bed until the Marags became aware of their presence. It was only then that we learned the horrid truth about our eastern neighbors.

It was in 2115 that a survivor of one of those groups of gold-seekers stumbled back to Tol Rane with his tale of horror. His

companions had been taken by a band of Marags and, one by one, they had been ritualistically killed and then eaten.

While human sacrifice in one form or another was not uncommon in certain religions, the cult of Mara was the only one we have ever encountered which practiced ritual cannibalism. The news spread throughout Tolnedra like a grassfire, growing with each telling, until the entire nation was aflame with it. Speeches by officials fanned the fury of the populace, and there were soon deputations in Tol Honeth demanding war.

The Emperor, Ran Vordue I of the SECOND VORDUVIAN DYNASTY, still only three years from the investiture of his reign and the beginning of his Dynasty, submitted finally to the importunings of the people and began preparations for war.

THE SECOND VORDUVIAN DYNASTY
2112–2537 (425 years, 20 Emperors)

It is to the eternal shame of the Vorduvians that it was during one of their Dynasties that the extirpation of the Marags occurred. Although the fact that the Marags were cannibals was undeniably true, that fact might well have been ignored had it not been for the presence of gold in Maragor. The border could easily have been sealed and other means taken to persuade the Marags to abandon their revolting practice; but the war party in Tolnedra, thinking only of the gold, pushed the inexperienced Emperor into the ultimate sanction of war.

The campaign in Maragor lasted for four years and was marked with the kind of savagery seldom seen in the west. Tolnedran legions operating out of Tol Rane quickly encircled the relatively small nation, then turned and struck inward at the heart of Maragor. The Marags, still weakened after their disastrous expedition in Nyissa, were no match for the might of the legions. The commanders of those legions, imbued with a kind of religious fervor, systematically slaughtered the entire populace as they went, and only at the last when the remnants of the Marags had been harried into a single valley in central Maragor were they persuaded to relent. Unfortunately, it was not humanity which moved the Tolnedrans to mercy, but once again our national vice – greed. The surviving Marags were spared in order that they might be sold to Nyissan slavers, who, like vultures, hovered on the outskirts of the battle.

Thus perished Maragor and with it no small measure of Tolnedran pride.

The horde of Tolnedran gold-seekers and commoners greedy for land which had hovered on the border awaiting the conclusion of the war swept into Maragor like a wave, frantic lest some other find more gold or take more land. But, as we learned to our sorrow, the grief-stricken spirit of Mara, God of the Marags, still abode in the land. The wave which had descended broke and recoiled back as Mara took his vengeance upon the adventurers. The tales which returned from that haunted land have fed nightmares in Tolnedra for over three millennia. The wailing of Mara is heard from one end of Maragor to the other by day, and by night, the fearful shades of slaughtered Marags stalk the land shrieking, their blood-smeared faces glowing with a ghastly light.

The weaker among the treasure-seekers soon went mad and cast themselves into rivers or hurled themselves off precipices; the stronger returned, shaken and ashen-faced to Tolnedra without gold, without land, and often only marginally with their sanity.

It was one of these survivors who devoted his fortune and the remainder of his life to the establishment of the great monastery at Mar-Terin where the monks for three thousand years have sought to propitiate Mara and to comfort the spirits of the slain Marags. The simple courage of the monks of Mar-Terin in the face of unspeakable horror is a testament to all that is best in the Tolnedran character.

The remainder of the Dynasty was uneventful until the reigns of the last four emperors. Trade was expanded with the Arends to the north and to a lesser degree with the Nyissans to the south, and the great ship-yards at Tol Vordue and Tol Horb were erected. Tolnedran vessels began to ply coastal waters in search of trade, and by 2400 had reached as far north as the Sea of the Winds off the northwest coast of what is now Sendaria.

It was at that point that we first encountered the Chereks. In 2411 a Tolnedran commercial flotilla was set upon by a Cherek fleet which emerged from the Cherek Bore. Tolnedran vessels, slow and wide, are built to carry cargo, and have never been a match for the swift, narrow war-boats of the Chereks. The battle was short, and the loss of lives and goods appalling.

Emperor Ran Vordue XVI quickly armed every available vessel and mounted a punitive expedition against Cherek. The results, of course, were lamentably predictable. Like wolves, the Chereks cut the fleet to pieces and sank every single ship.

Advised of Tolnedra's presence by these two unfortunate encounters, Cherek pirates soon began to appear off the west coast of Arendia and Tolnedra.* The city of Tol Vordue was sacked and burned eight times in those bloody centuries, and Cherek vessels, groaning under the weight of Tolnedran treasure, wallowed back to the north like some great sea-caravan.

Finally, in the first years of the 26th century, Ran Vordue XIX fortified Tol Vordue, building high walls to the seaward and increasing the garrison of his ancestral city ten-fold. Three expeditions of Chereks were beaten off, and they soon turned to easier prey. Tol Horb was sacked twice, and only the great iron chain across the Nedrane River prevented the Cherek fleet from ascending the river to the gates of Tol Honeth itself.

At about this time the last Emperor of the SECOND VORDU-VIAN DYNASTY died without issue, and, in addition to its troubles with the pirates from Cherek, the nation was thrown into the turmoil which always accompanies Dynastic succession.

THE FIRST BORUNE DYNASTY 2537–3155
(618 years, 24 Emperors)

It had been generally assumed during the closing years of the reign of Ran Vordue XX that the Throne would once again pass to the Honethite family, and several worthy members of that numerous

---

* This was significantly modified in *Belgarath the Sorcerer*. The notion that a race of pirates had never heard of the richest place on earth before is obviously absurd. As an aside here, note that in 'Beowulf', the original King of the Spear-Danes (Gar-Dena) is referred to as 'the Sheaf Child', an obvious derivation from the Story of Moses. The people of the dark ages *did* have contacts with each other, and some Viking stole the idea and shamelessly used it in 'Beowulf'.

clan had already begun the expensive but necessary task of bribing various members of the Council of Advisors (which body incidentally had increasingly assumed certain legislative functions to relieve the Emperor of that tedious task in the increasingly complex Tolnedran society). But by that very maneuvering, the Honethites effectively barred themselves from the Throne when Ran Vordue XX died, since the Council found itself deadlocked with no one noble of the Honethite Family receiving a clear majority. After eleven months of bickering, the Council was finally forced to turn elsewhere.

When the name of a young Borune noble was put forward by those members of the Council elected from his district, the Vorduvian and Horbite factions in the Council quickly swung their votes in his favor, since it is unfortunately true that the Honethites have never been extremely popular with the nobility of other cities, given their propensity to be a bit over-proud and their habit of dispensing Imperial largesse preponderantly to the citizens of Tol Honeth.

The Honethites reacted with a vigorous campaign against the young Borune noble, making a very large issue of his questionable background. (His mother was a Dryad.) But in the end the coalition of Vorduvians, Borunes and Horbites pushed the vote through the Council, and the name of the young Borune was carried to the Temple and presented to the Priests of Nedra. Following the confirmation by the priests, Emperor Ran Borune I was crowned and assumed the golden Throne in Tol Honeth.

The young Emperor soon proved to be a happy choice. After examining the problem of Cherek depredations along the coast, he set the legions to work constructing a highway along the coast between Tol Vordue and Tol Horb. There was much grumbling among the legions about this, for the men had grown accustomed to garrison life in the cities and were unhappy at being forced to lay aside their dress uniforms and the abundance of young (and not so young) women who always find soldiers attractive. Powerful friends of legion officers protested to the Emperor about this unseemly disruption of the social lives of the soldiers, but Ran Borune remained firm.

The import of his plan soon became evident. The legions were spaced at intervals along the entire northwest coastline with each legion assigned its own section of road to complete. Thus, wherever the Cherek freebooters came ashore there was a legion awaiting them. The benefits to the nation achieved by this single plan were enormous. A fine highway was constructed, the legions (softened by garrison life) were restored to fitness, the Chereks were persuaded to seek entertainment elsewhere, and the unhealthy influence of idle soldiery on the political, social and moral life of the cities was removed. Following a wave of resignations by young officers and private soldiers who no longer found military life attractive, a new and tougher breed entered the legions, and the service was much improved. Since the benefits obtained from putting the legions to work were so obvious, the Borune Emperors laid out a vast network of highways reaching to all parts of Tolnedra which was to occupy the military for a thousand years.

It was also during the FIRST BORUNE DYNASTY that the Diplomatic Service was instituted. At first the Service consisted mainly of merchants who regularly visited foreign nations, but they were soon replaced by genuine professionals whose skill in handling relations between Tolnedra and frequently difficult and much less civilized nations is legendary. Evidence of that skill is to be found in the fact that there was a full diplomatic mission in Vo Mimbre during the later years of the lengthy border dispute between the Mimbrate Arends, who sought control of the forest of Vordue, and the Empire, which insisted that its northern border was at the River Arend. Further proof of the brilliance of the Service is found in the fact that Tolnedra maintained full diplomatic relations with all three Arendish factions throughout the entire Arendish Civil War with missions to Vo Mimbre, Vo Astur and Vo Wacune.

The major thrust of Tolnedran policy (which is to say Borune policy) throughout the period of the Arendish Civil War was to maintain, insofar as possible, a balance of power between the three contending duchies. So long as Arendia remained divided, Tolnedra's northern border remained secure. When a philosopher delivered a formal remonstrance to Emperor Ran Borune XXII about the immorality of fomenting war and untold human suffering in Arendia simply for Tolnedran advantage, the Emperor replied blandly, 'But this is politics, dear fellow, and has nothing to do with morality. One would always be wise to keep the two completely separate. Morality deals with what we might like to do, but politics deals with what we must do. There's no connection between them at all.'

The diplomats of the Borunes also made their way to the north and established relations with the Chereks and Drasnians at Val Alorn and at Boktor. The Chereks were eventually persuaded to cease their attacks on Tolnedran shipping in the Sea of the Winds, and a healthy three-way commerce soon developed as goods from

Drasnia moved in Cherek vessels from Kotu through the Gulf of Cherek and the Cherek Bore to the port of Camaar in what is now Sendaria for transshipment to Tolnedran vessels. Profits to all three nations were enormous as a result of this arrangement, and the Chereks soon discovered that more could be made in honest trade than could be reaped by piracy.

The question of trade with the Isle of the Winds, however, was much more difficult to settle. The Chereks continued their blockade of the port of Riva unabated for reasons which are largely unclear. It was generally assumed that the Isle was either a Cherek colony or a Cherek protectorate, but neither assumption now appears to be correct. Though the Rivans are Alorns as are the Chereks, the Drasnians and the Algars, it would appear that they are a separate people independent of Cherek. The blockade, which frustrated generations of Tolnedran and Sendarian merchants seems to have had some religious significance which was incomprehensible to Tolnedran diplomats. Finally, in the Accords of Val Alorn in 3097 as a part of the brilliantly wrought treaty which normalized relations between Cherek and Tolnedra, the blockade was lifted and Tolnedran vessels began to call on the port of Riva.

It had generally been assumed that the Rivans had been a tacit party to the Accords of Val Alorn, but this quickly proved not to be the case. Merchants landed on the rocky strand of that inhospitable isle only to be faced with the grim and unscalable walls of the Fortress of Riva itself. The gates of the fortress remained closed, and the Rivans refused to even acknowledge the presence of the merchants.

It was the last Borune Emperor who mounted the disastrous assault on the city, proving perhaps that even the noblest line deteriorates in time. Five legions were dispatched to Riva to force the gates of the city, and a horde of merchant vessels hovered in the bay, awaiting the opening of the gates. There is, it may be observed at this point, something decidedly unhealthy in the Tolnedran character. While he is normally a solid, sensible man, the average Tolnedran grows positively frantic when his impulse to trade is frustrated. There have been occasions when Imperial forces have been used to open relations with stubborn people, and it has been observed that some merchants, driven beyond sanity by their eagerness to be first, have actually dashed ahead of the forefront of the legions waving their wares and importuning the startled opposing warriors. This impulse – this greed, if you will – is what raised the disaster at Riva to such colossal proportions.

At the first assault of the legions upon the gates of the city, the

Rivans emerged and systematically destroyed not only the five legions, but every vessel in the harbor as well. The loss of life and goods was incalculable.

When the news was brought to Ran Borune XXIV in Tol Honeth, the last Borune Emperor, in a fury, prepared to launch the full might of the Empire against the Rivans. He was, however, brought abruptly to his senses by a curtly-worded note from the Cherek ambassador.

'Majesty,' it read.

'Know that Aloria will permit no attack upon Riva. The fleets of Cherek, whose masts rise as thick as the trees of the forest, will fall upon your flotilla, and the legions of Tolnedra will feed the fish from the hook of Arendia to the furthest reaches of the Sea of the Winds. The battalions of Drasnia will march south, crushing all in their paths and lay siege to your cities. The horsemen of Algaria shall sweep across the mountains and shall lay waste your Empire from end to end with fire and sword.

'Know that in the day that you attack Riva, in that day will the Alorns make war upon you, and you shall surely perish, and your Empire also.'

Shaken by the awful finality of the note, Ran Borune reconsidered. A hasty reading of the document which had laid down the stipulations of the Accords of Val Alorn revealed a clause which had previously seemed mere ritualistic gibberish, but the import of which now became horrifyingly clear. The clause, 'but Aloria shall maintain Riva and keep it whole', revealed the fact that the Alorn Kingdoms were bound into a kind of confederation or Over-nation. Thus, a treaty with Cherek was not a treaty with Aloria; and while Cherek had agreed not to make war on Tolnedra, Aloria had made no such promise. With difficulty the legions might successfully pursue war against any one of the Alorn Kingdoms, but if those kingdoms joined together, they would be invincible.

Thus it was that the project of a punitive expedition against the Rivans was quickly dropped.

In time the Rivans relented and permitted the construction of a commercial enclave outside the walls of their city, and, though they grumbled about it, the merchants of the west were forced to be content with that single concession.

Thus the FIRST BORUNE DYNASTY drew to a close. Its accomplishments were literally staggering, and, though it ended on a somewhat humiliating note, it is nonetheless one of the most towering Dynasties in the entire history of the Empire.

THE THIRD HONETHITE DYNASTY
3155–3497 (342 years, 17 Emperors)

The scramble for the Throne at the end of the FIRST BORUNE DYNASTY marked the nadir of Tolnedran politics. Simple bribery was no longer sufficient, and the contending candidates openly purchased the votes of the Council. Further, it is widely suspected (and generally held to be true) that they even stooped to assassination as a means of achieving their goal. The votes in the Council swung back and forth as members whose votes had been purchased by one or the other of the candidates sickened quite suddenly and died for no apparent reason and their replacements were shamelessly bought as soon as they reached Tol Honeth. The introduction of Nyissan poisons into Tolnedran politics was gruesomely evident.

In the end, the Honethites prevailed – not through any particular virtue, but rather because they were the wealthiest family and could afford to buy more votes.

Perhaps the most telling indication of how incompetent the Honethites had become is revealed in the fact that during the entire period of the THIRD HONETHITE DYNASTY there was not one single treaty or agreement with a foreign power to improve the position of the Empire. Indeed, in view of the Northern Accords between Drasnia and Gar og Nadrak which established the North Caravan Route with a virtual Drasnian monopoly at its western terminus, it might be convincingly argued that the position of the Empire actually deteriorated during the reign of the Dynasty.

Instead of devoting themselves to foreign affairs and the improvement of domestic conditions in Tolnedra as had the Borune Emperors, the Honethites instead turned to shamelessly looting the Imperial Treasury and to selling positions of power to the highest bidder.

Abroad, the Arendish Civil War ground on interminably, and negotiations with Drasnia and Algaria proceeded at a snail's pace, due in large measure to the unbridled greed of a long succession of Honethite Emperors who inevitably sought *personal* advantage in any treaty proposal.

THE SECOND BORUNE DYNASTY 3497–3761
(264 years, 12 Emperors)

Thus, when Ran Honeth XVII died childless in 3497, the people of Tolnedra turned almost universally to the Borunes. When certain

Council members, recalling the vast fortunes which had been made during the unseemly struggle that had accompanied the previous Dynastic turnover, advertised that their votes were for sale, they were promptly mobbed by the citizenry of Tol Honeth itself.

A vast rabble gathered outside the Council chamber and took up a thunderous chant, 'Bor-une, Bor-une, Bor-une,' which gave the Council a grim hint as to what would be its fate if any other name were carried to the Temple of Nedra. It was the first time in history that the common people had ever taken an active part in the selection of an Emperor.

True to their reputations, the Borunes immediately set about repairing the damage which had been done by the Honethites. Once again the legions were put to work on roads and walls and upon long-overdue repairs to wharves, jetties and dikes. The usual grumbling came to an abrupt halt when seven legion commanders were summarily executed for refusing to obey direct Imperial orders to move out of their garrisons to the construction camps.

Abroad, the Borunes brought the negotiations with the Drasnians to a speedy conclusion, and the Agreement of Boktor was signed in 3527. Though it did not provide the advantage many had wished, it nonetheless gave Tolnedran Merchants access to the thriving northern trade.

In a move unheard of previously, the Borunes dispatched twenty legions to Sendaria to construct 'as a gesture of goodwill' the network of highways which linked Sendar and Camaar with Darine

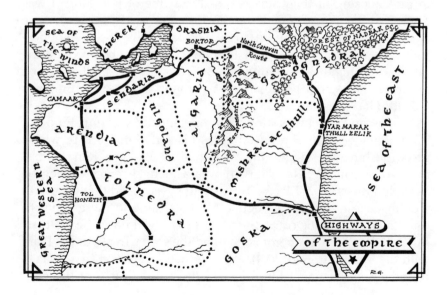

on the northeast coast which faces on the Gulf of Cherek. This action produced glum faces in Val Alorn, but the King of Cherek (which country nominally held Sendaria at that time) quickly perceived that the improvements in Sendaria would enormously increase the tax-base in that district at no cost to the Cherek treasury. The legion-built highways effectively broke the Cherek monopoly in the transport of goods from Boktor to Camaar. The fact that Cherek vessels were the only ships in the world at that time able to negotiate the savage and treacherous currents of the Cherek Bore was no longer the dominating reality of the northern trade. It was now possible for Sendarian merchantmen to ply the coastal route from Kotu to Darine and then to transship overland to Camaar on the new highway. The increase in trade and the lowering of prices resulting from the development of healthy competition gave an enormous boost to the economies of all nations involved.

THE FIRST HORBITE DYNASTY 3761–3911
(150 years, 6 Emperors)

It is a tribute to the wisdom of the aged Ran Borune XII, the childless last Emperor of the SECOND BORUNE DYNASTY, that the transition of power to the Horbites at the end of his reign was so smooth. Always innovators, the Borunes for the first time took a direct hand in the choosing of their successors. The name of Ran Horb I was carried to the Temple *before* the old Emperor died. Although once again certain members of the Council bewailed the loss of an opportunity to sell their votes, Ran Borune XII was so beloved by the people that none dared oppose him. Thus, in no small measure, we have the Borunes to thank for perhaps the greatest Emperor Tolnedra has ever had.

While Ran Horb I was surely a competent and vigorous Emperor in the manner of the Borunes, it was his son, Ran Horb II, whose accomplishments stagger the imagination. Because Ran Horb I married late in life, Ran Horb II was a mere seventeen when he ascended the golden Throne. It was widely assumed that his youth would make him easy to beguile by the older and more sophisticated members of the court. Such quickly proved not to be the case. In 3793, the young Emperor concluded the secret Treaty of the Plain with the Mimbrate Arends. Perceiving that the endless Civil War in Arendia had become a hindrance to the development of the west and a disruption of trade and commerce, the Emperor sided with the weaker faction, the Mimbrates, and joined in the final destruction of the Asturian Arends. The Emperor let it be known in Cherek and Algaria that the legions stationed in Sendaria for the maintenance of the highways built there by the Borunes would no longer hinder the movement of raiders upon northern Arendia. Thus, with their forces divided, the Asturians were no match for the assault by the Mimbrate Knights across the southern frontier of Asturia and the diversionary movement of a Tolnedran column along the coast. Then began in Arendia a war of attrition against the Asturians which lasted for almost twenty years.

Meanwhile, Imperial negotiators, urged on by the Emperor, concluded the Algarian agreement with Cho-Dorn the Old, Chief of the Clan-chiefs of the Horse People. The agreement caused a wave of consternation among the merchant princes of Tolnedra, since virtually no trade advantage was gained. Although it was widely denounced in commercial circles, the one concession the Emperor gained which made the treaty perhaps more valuable than any other was permission to construct the Great North Road across Algaria to the southern border of Drasnia. Thus, for the first time, a land route directly to Boktor was possible. The legions were permitted to enter Algaria for the purpose of constructing the road. As the Emperor observed to one grumbling merchant, 'I would trade off the Horse People – even if they were ten times more numerous – for overland access to Boktor.' When one balances the volume of trade coming out of the east into Drasnia, one can only agree with the wisdom of our most splendid Emperor.

In 3822, Vo Astur, seat of the Asturian Arendia, fell before the onslaughts of the Mimbrates, and, like Vo Wacune, the city was destroyed. The Mimbrates, however, though they had won the victory and crowned their Duke the first unchallenged King of Arendia, were exhausted by the final struggle. The restrictions imposed by the Emperor in return for Tolnedran assistance in the destruction of the Asturians in many respects made the Arends virtually a subject people. Though it rankled the proud Mimbrates, they were too weak to protest, and the new King had other problems. Though they had been defeated and Vo Astur had been laid waste, there were still Asturian Arends in the north. They retreated into the trackless reaches of the Arendish forest and began the guerilla warfare which was to sap the strength of the Mimbrate Kings for over a thousand years.

Nothing, of course, could have suited Tolnedran purposes better.

The open battles and extensive military campaigns which had made travel through Arendia so hazardous were at an end, replaced by the hit and run tactics of the Asturians and the futile expeditions of the Mimbrates into the dark forest in pursuit. The Emperor reached a secret agreement with the Asturians which guaranteed freedom of movement along the Great West Road which the legions were constructing southward through their forest. At the same time, in accordance with the Treaty of Tol Vordue, other legions were constructing the southern leg of the highway north from the River Arend.

Although the Great West Road and the Great North Road were not to be completed for over a century, the concept was now clear. When these colossal projects were finished, it would be possible to travel overland from Tol Honeth to Camaar, from Camaar to Boktor, and – along the North Caravan Routes – from Boktor to Yar Marak and Thull Zelik in the Kingdoms of the Angaraks.

This was the zenith of Tolnedran power. Ran Horb II was quite literally the most powerful man in the world. By Imperial Decree in 3827 he created the Kingdom of Sendaria on the northwest coast. When certain northern merchants protested, he pointed out that it was more efficient and far less costly to allow the Sendars to govern themselves than it was to attempt to administer a country five hundred leagues beyond our northern border. 'Let the Sendars enjoy the aggravation of administering their own country,' he said. 'So long as we have the right trade agreements with them, we will lose little by our generosity.'

In the twilight of his life, Ran Horb II, then well over eighty, concluded the Agreement of Sthiss Tor, formalizing trade relations with Nyissa; and, in one of his most stunning moves, signed the Accords of Rak Goska which established the South Caravan Route through the mountains of Cthol Murgos. It would soon be possible for a man on a good horse to depart from Tol Honeth, ride north to Boktor, cross to the Eastern Sea at Yar Marak, then go south to Rak Goska and cross the mountains to return to Tol Honeth. In his dying words to his son, Ran Horb II said, 'Keep the roads. So long as the roads are kept, Tolnedra rules the world.'

And so it was. The remainder of the HORBITE DYNASTY was devoted to the completion of the system of highways which was to make Tolnedra supreme in the west. There was little else to be done.

THE FIRST RANITE DYNASTY 3911–4001
(90 years, 7 Emperors)

The ill-fated FIRST RANITE DYNASTY ascended to power follow-ing the death of the last Horbite Emperor. The verdict of history is perhaps unkind to these unfortunates. A hereditary ailment in their line struck them down inevitably in their prime. So it was that no one Ranite Emperor lived long enough to achieve anything of any significance. History quite correctly regards the Ranites simply as caretakers.

THE THIRD VORDUVIAN DYNASTY
4001–4133 (132 years, 3 Emperors)

At the turn of the fifth millennium, the Vorduvians once again gained control of the Imperial Throne. Since Tol Vordue is a major sea-port, the Vorduvians have always felt that sea-commerce is much preferable to overland trade, and during the century and more of their reign, the roads of Ran Horb II fell into disrepair, and the power of the Empire declined.

No sooner had the Vorduvians been installed in Tol Honeth than one of the cataclysmic events in the history of the west occurred. The Rivan King, Gorek the Wise, was assassinated at Riva by a contin-gent of Nyissan merchants acting on the orders of Queen Salmissra of Nyissa. Ran Vordue I stood by helplessly while the world quite literally collapsed around his ears. The horrid suspicion that had hovered in the most secret councils in Tol Honeth since the days of the last of the Borunes became a dreadful reality – the Alorns joined together to make war. Aloria did, in fact, exist. The campaign of the Alorns against Nyissa was short and savage. Viewing the ugly temper of our northern friends, Ran Vordue wisely chose not to object to the technical violation of Tolnedran territory by the south-ward-moving columns of Algars and Drasnians nor the presence in our territorial waters of huge fleets of Cherek warships.

When the war was over and Nyissa had for all real purposes ceased to exist, all Tolnedra quite literally held its breath. The temper of the Alorns was ugly, and they had demonstrated a capa-bility for a sustained and coordinated military campaign none had ever suspected. If they had chosen to turn north from ravaged Nyissa, all the might of the Empire would not have been sufficient to stop them. The entire fate of the civilized world hung on the whim of the barbaric Kings of Aloria.

It was with enormous relief that Tolnedra watched the return of the Drasnian and Algarian columns through the mountains toward the Vale of Aldur and the swift passage of the lean, black warships of Cherek northbound along our coast.

In the years following the war of the Alorns upon Nyissa, there was turmoil in the west. The Alorn Kings seemed preoccupied and gathered frequently for council at Riva. Without the firm hands of their kings to control them, the rowdy Alorns frequently violated the provisions of many of their treaties and agreements with Tolnedra. Imperial Ambassadors attempting to protest were frequently ignored or curtly dismissed. The Vorduvian Emperors seemed powerless to regain control of the situation.

THE SECOND HORBITE DYNASTY 4133–4483
(350 years, 16 Emperors)

It was during the SECOND HORBITE DYNASTY that the full impact of the South Caravan Route began to be felt in Tolnedran commerce. With an apparent sudden change of heart, the laconic Murgos became almost overnight keenly interested in trade with the west, and caravans soon were moving in both directions along the South Caravan Route. Murgos, Thulls and even occasional Nadraks became common sights in the streets of Tol Honeth. They also began to appear in Vo Mimbre, Camaar and Sendar.

This healthy expansion of east-west contact by way of the South Caravan Route offset the decline in commerce resulting from the turmoil in the Alorn Kingdoms.

The outstanding diplomatic achievement of the SECOND HORBITE DYNASTY was the mission to Ulgoland and the ultimate concluding of the Treaty of Prolgu – although, to be candid, there has been only small commercial advantage in the severely limited trade with the Ulgos. The achievement can be measured more in terms of increased knowledge than in profit.

It was, incidentally, the opening of contact with the mysterious Ulgos that sparked the theological debate which has raged throughout the west for centuries. (See the History of the Ulgos for further discussion.)

THE SECOND RANITE DYNASTY 4483–4742
(259 years, 17 Emperors)

The SECOND DYNASTY of the short-lived RANITES saw enormous increases in trade between Tolnedra and Cthol Murgos. Indeed, one merchant observed sourly, 'You can't look anywhere anymore without seeing a Murgo.' While this is perhaps an exaggeration, it is certainly true that Murgo merchants were to be seen on virtually all roads in the Empire, and it was not uncommon to encounter them in Arendia and even the remotest village in Sendaria. One curious fact was that no Murgo, insofar as we can tell, ever visited an Alorn Kingdom and that none even attempted to penetrate Ulgoland.

Gradually the situation to the north began to stabilize, and commerce once again proceeded normally.

These perhaps were the golden days of the west. With the exception of the bickering of the Arends in the north of their country, conflict was almost non-existent. Trade flowed smoothly east and west along both the North and South Caravan Routes, and Tolnedra profited in almost every transaction. The Ranite Emperors were too preoccupied with their own health problems to engage in any Imperial adventures, and an able and conscientious bureaucracy developed to maintain roads and ports, standardize fees and bribes and generally see to the day-to-day ordering of the thousand details upon which the stability of the Empire rests.

THE THIRD BORUNE DYNASTY 4742 to date
(626 years, 23 Emperors)

When the last Ranite Emperor died, Tolnedra turned once again to the Borunes. One can only conclude that, while in *some* of His choices for Emperor, Nedra may have drowsed, in His choice of the Borunes to guide the Empire through the troubled times of the last years of the fifth millennium our God was surely with us.

Through the reigns of the first three Borune Emperors, the world proceeded normally, much as it had during the Ranite period. Ran Borune IV was crowned, and for ten years all seemed well. Then, quite suddenly in 4864, without explanation, the Murgos closed the South Caravan Route and the Nadraks severely curtailed eastward movement along the North Route. The following year the reasons became painfully obvious.

In the spring of 4865 the Angaraks invaded Drasnia. In the forefront of their assault were Nadraks, Thulls and Murgos, and behind them in a human sea that stretched from horizon to horizon came the hordes of the Malloreans. In the center of the host, borne upon the shoulders of literally thousands, was the huge black iron pavilion in which rode the dreaded Kal-Torak himself.

History is unclear concerning the precise relationship between Kal-Torak and other Angarak Kings, but there can be no question that Kal-Torak of Mallorea ruled over them with almost god-like authority.

The civilized world stood aghast at the destruction of Drasnia. Though the other Alorn nations attempted to aid their cousins, their efforts were fruitless. It quickly became evident that Kal-Torak came, not as a conqueror, but as a destroyer. The cities of Boktor and Kotu were literally pulled down, and the smaller Drasnian towns and villages were put to the torch. Worse still, the population of this prosperous northern nation was systematically exterminated, and what few captives were taken were turned over to the dark-robed, steel-masked Grolim Priests for the unspeakable human sacrifices which are such an integral part of the Angarak religion.

A few battered and bloody elements of the superb Drasnian Army escaped southward into Algaria, and a few others were taken off the islands at the mouth of the Aldur River by Cherek warships, but the bulk of the army was simply smothered by the uncounted hordes of Malloreans who swept across the land. Members of the general populace who were not slain or captured fled northwest into the empty reaches of the Drasnian steppes or into the vast marshes at the mouth of the Mrin River. Some few survivors who fled to the north eventually made their way across the River Dused in the far north and thence down the coast to Val Alorn in Cherek. For those who sought refuge in the fens and marshes, however, there was scant hope for survival.

Once Drasnia had been crushed, the Angaraks turned southward and struck into Algaria. Here, of course, they met a different foe. Algar horsemen, the finest cavalry on earth, continually savaged the flanks of the horde, littering the Algarian grasslands with Angarak dead. In retaliation – or perhaps as a part of a preconceived plan – the Angaraks slaughtered the Algarian herds, both horses and cattle, and glutted themselves on the meat. Finally, fed to the point of satiety, they simply killed the animals and left them to rot where they fell. The sky over Algaria grew black with vultures and ravens as the Angaraks passed.

The occupation of Drasnia was one thing, but the occupation of Algaria was quite another. With the exception of the reindeer herders of the far north, the Drasnians live in cities and towns like other civilized people. The Algars, on the other hand, are nomadic horsemen. The central Algarian plain is a vast, empty grassland. To speak of occupying such an expanse is much like speaking of occupying the ocean. The Algars simply permitted the hordes of Kal-Torak to pass and then fell upon their rear in the vicious hit and run attacks which are so famous in Algarian legend and song.

Although the horde suffered hideous casualties in their march southward, Kal-Torak did not falter. He laid siege to the Stronghold, the traditional seat of the Algarian King and the closest thing to a city in all Algaria. The Stronghold of the Algars is one of the most unassailable land fortresses in the world, not because of any particular difficulty of the surrounding terrain, but quite simply because of the unbelievable height and thickness of its walls. Because those walls reach higher than the tallest tree, scaling ladders cannot be built to permit assault over the top of them, and because the walls are thirty feet thick, no siege engine can breach them.

The Angaraks hurled themselves at this man-made mountain for six months until they realized the futility of their attacks and settled down for a protracted siege.

That siege was to last for eight years (4867–4875). The impregnability of the Algarian Stronghold gave the west the time needed to mobilize.

In the late spring of 4875, disgusted by the futility of his efforts against the Stronghold, Kal-Torak turned west and began his march toward the sea. Once again he was pursued by Algar horsemen and vengeful Drasnian Infantry units. In the mountains he encountered yet another problem. By night the Ulgos came forth from their caverns and butchered the sleeping Angaraks by the thousands. It was a diminished horde that came down upon the plains of Arendia, but a horde nonetheless. It has been estimated by reliable witnesses that Kal-Torak mounted his attack upon Vo Mimbre with at least 250,000 men. If the reports from Drasnia during the early days of the Angarak invasion may be believed, the horde numbered in excess of a half-million. If these figures are at all accurate, then we may assume that the campaigns in Drasnia and Algaria and the trek across Ulgoland cost Kal-Torak nearly half his army. (This of course does not take into account occupying forces left behind in Drasnia and the substantial number of Malloreans who were to maintain the siege of the Algarian Stronghold.)

Thus the stage was set for the titanic and bloody struggle which men have come to call the Battle of Vo Mimbre.

Stopping only briefly to rest and regroup after the perilous passage through the mountains of Ulgoland, Kal-Torak proceeded immediately down the River Arend to the city of Vo Mimbre. It was immediately apparent that his intention in Arendia was the same as it had been in Drasnia – the total destruction of the nation and its peoples. Horrid evidence of this marked his trail down the River Arend. Atrocities too ghastly to describe here were his common practice.

As the horde drew near the city of Vo Mimbre, the west prepared to close with the Angaraks in the ultimate battle.

The preparations had been long and difficult and had been accompanied by grave doubts as to the eventual outcome. Kal-Torak seemed invincible. Moreover, though it was assumed that his intent was to strike south toward Tol Honeth, no one could be certain exactly where he would emerge from the mountains. Thus it was necessary for the forces of the west to hold themselves in readiness until Kal-Torak committed himself to battle.

During the eight years of the siege of the Stronghold of the Algarians, the generals of the west had studied a hundred possible battlefields and prepared a strategy for each. It was during these preparations at the Imperial military college in Tol Honeth that it became evident that Brand, the Warder of Riva, was a tactical genius. Assisted by the oddly assorted pair who advised him, he devised tactics that took advantage not only of terrain features, but also of the contrasting strengths of the widely varied armies of the west.

NOTE: At the time certain discreet inquiries were made as to the identity of Brand's advisors, but without success. The man appeared to be aged but vigorous and had an almost encyclopedic knowledge of not only the west but of the Angarak Kingdoms as well. The woman, a strikingly handsome lady with a silver lock at her brow, had the uncanny gift of instantly perceiving the weaknesses and strengths of any given situation. Although her imperious manner offended many of the generals, they soon came to respect her intuition in such matters. It has been widely assumed that the two were Rivan nobles, but sketches of them made surreptitiously during the extensive meetings reveal that they have none of the racial characteristics of Rivans. Unfortunately, their identities are forever locked in the vault of time.*

---

* This is one of those 'internal footnotes' I mentioned earlier.

In the early summer of 4875 the Angaraks deployed for the assault on Vo Mimbre. This was the commitment for which Brand and his armies had waited. Though Tolnedran strategists had long believed that a second Angarak force would strike west along the South Caravan Route out of Cthol Murgos and had built a line of fortifications in the mountains to meet that threat, their fears proved groundless. As the woman who advised Brand pointed out, 'Vast armies cannot fight in the mountains – they require open spaces. And Torak is too arrogant for subterfuge. He will smash you, not trick you.' Thus, virtually at the last moment, Emperor Ran Borune IV withdrew the bulk of his forces from the eastern mountains of Tolnedra and returned his legions to Tol Honeth.*

Then it was that, for the first time in history, a huge land army was transported by water to the scene of a battle. A huge Cherek fleet arrived at Tol Honeth, and the legions embarked. The swift Cherek vessels conveyed the legions down the Nedrane, north along the coast and thence up the River Arend to a point some ten leagues west of Vo Mimbre. The two-hundred league forced march from Tol Honeth to Vo Mimbre would have taken more than a week, and the legions would have arrived exhausted on the battlefield. The Chereks deposited fresh troops on the north bank of the River Arend almost within sight of the battle in two days.

On the morning of the third day of the battle, the forces of the west closed with the Angaraks. The Battle of Vo Mimbre has been analysed in great detail, and the study of the moves, countermoves, deployment and so forth will, of course, be presented by the faculty of the Department of Military Arts and Sciences. For Historians, a rough sketch is adequate.

Upon a pre-arranged signal, the Mimbrate Knights issued from the city and attacked the Angarak horde from the front. Then, when the Angaraks were concentrating on this direction, Algarian Cavalry, Drasnian Infantry and the Ulgo irregulars attacked Kal-Torak's left; the Tolnedran legions, accompanied by Cherek Berserks, assaulted his right. Attacked on three sides, Kal-Torak committed his reserves. Then it was that the Rivans, the Sendars, and the Asturian archers came upon him from the rear.

The battle raged for hours, and the issue was still in doubt when Brand issued his challenge to Kal-Torak to meet him in a single

---

† This was modified later. Kal-Torak (Torak himself) *did* have a second army, but it came from the south, not the east, and it was bogged down in the Desert of Araga by that unnatural blizzard.

combat. This duel was the decisive incident in the battle. The loss of either leader would so confound and demoralize his army that the victory would fall easily to the survivor. In the end, though he seemed the stronger of the two, Kal-Torak faltered, and Brand, taking advantage of his foe's momentary confusion, struck him down.

The leaderless Angaraks, surrounded and demoralized, were then systematically cut to pieces by the combined armies of the west. The few elements which escaped fled back across the mountains, raised the siege of the Algarian Stronghold and struggled into the wilderness of the mountain range which marks the boundary between Algaria and Mishrak at Thull. The occupation forces in Drasnia withdrew back into Gar og Nadrak, and the war was over. The Malloreans had been destroyed in the battle, and the Nadraks, Thulls and Murgos were so decimated that they would never again pose a threat to the west.

It was at this point that Tolnedra's greatest peril arose. The other nations of the west, overwhelmed by the enormous victory Brand had given them, hovered for a time on the verge of crowning the Rivan general Emperor of the west. It was only through the extraordinary efforts of Mergon, Tolnedran ambassador to the court at Vo Mimbre, that this disaster was averted. At length he restored the balance of good sense, and the proposal was dropped.

In return, however, the western kings imposed a humiliating condition upon the Empire. While Brand himself indicated no desire for such a fortuitous marriage, the assembled kings decreed that the Rivan King should have the hand of an Imperial Princess in marriage. This, of course, is an absurdity, since the line of the Rivan Kings died with Gorek the Wise when he was assassinated in 4002, but the kings were adamant. Thus it is necessary for every Tolnedran Princess to make the arduous and often dangerous journey to the fortress at Riva upon her sixteenth birthday and to await there for three days a bridegroom who will never come.

Ran Borune was infuriated by this humiliation, but Mergon pointed out that the combination of Alorns, Ulgos, Arends and Sendars could easily overthrow the legions and impose their will on Tolnedra from the throne-room in Tol Honeth itself if they chose.

In his last act as overgeneral of the west, Brand directed that the lines of Asturia and Mimbre be joined by marriage to bring the Arendish Civil War to a final conclusion. It was impossible for even the brilliant Mergon to head off this wedding, and Tolnedran policy in Arendia took a disastrous defeat. Since that policy for two millennia had been to keep Arendia divided and therefore weak, one can well imagine how the news of the unification of the houses of Mimbre and Astur was greeted in Tol Honeth. Mergon, however, advised the Emperor that the Alorns were feeling burly following the battle, and that wisdom would seem to indicate that graceful acquiescence might be a course preferable to forced acceptance.

Ran Borune agreed and wryly observed that a united Arendia *might* prove troublesome at some future date, but a united Aloria with an army in the field not two hundred leagues from the gates of Tol Honeth was all the trouble that *he* needed at that particular moment.

The years following the Battle of Vo Mimbre ushered in a period of economic disaster in the west. The destruction of the Algarian herds by marauding Angaraks forced the Algars to suspend their customary annual cattle-drive to Muros in Sendaria for the decades required to rebuild their herds. The vengeful Drasnians closed the North Caravan Route against Nadrak merchants, and the Murgos sealed their border, cutting off all trade along the South Caravan Route. Thus, in addition to a meat famine in the west, trade with the east became impossible except along those secret trails far to the south known only to Nyissan slave-traders. And so it was that, while it was distasteful, Tolnedra had no alternative but to increase its trade with the snake people. By virtue of her monopoly of eastern trade, the unwholesome influence of Queen Salmissra increased enormously in the west. Dull-eyed Nyissan merchants began to appear in the major ports along the west coast, and their dealings, always deceitful, began to color virtually all aspects of commerce in the west. Nyissa prospered enormously, and the luxury – even opulence – of Sthiss Tor soon began to rival even that of Tol Honeth itself.

The recovery from the years of economic depression which followed the Angarak war was slow and painful. It took the efforts of three Borune Emperors to finally persuade the Drasnians to reopen the North Caravan Route, and in the first years the resulting trade was disappointingly meager. The Algarian herds began to arrive at Muros again, but in nothing like their former numbers, since the Algars steadfastly held back their finest animals for breeding stock. The reduction in the supply of beef, however, provided an opportunity for the development of a new industry in Sendaria. The raising of hogs became a national preoccupation. The hog, of course, has one enormous advantage over the cow in terms of trade – his meat may be cured. Thus, while cattle must be driven enormous distances to their ultimate markets, hogs may be slaughtered and cured on the farms of their origin and the tasty hams and succulent bacon may be shipped quite easily without fear of spoilage. Fortunes were made in Sendaria, and many a Sendar noble began his upward climb to position and respectability as a hog-baron.

And then, perhaps a hundred years ago, the grim-faced Murgos suddenly relented and reopened the South Caravan Route. Amazingly, these harsh and war-like people seemed to have developed an almost insatiable urge to trade. The caravans from the east were long and literally piled high with those very goods for which the rapacious Nyissans demanded their highest prices – silks, spices, curious tapestries and the fine Mallorean carpets that are almost never seen in the west.

The resumption of trade along the South Caravan Route has begun the recovery of the Tolnedran economy. Gone, however, are the days of absolute dominance in commerce. The merchants of other nations have increasingly come to demand their share of the markets that were formerly exclusive Tolnedran preserves, and kings and their governments have more and more realized that the strength of a nation is measured more in the health of its commerce than in the size of its army. Governments, therefore, have increasingly become involved in trade negotiations. Those fine old days when the kings of the west played their childish games of war and conquest while the Empire alone concentrated on the serious business of commerce are forever gone. The other nations have, in a very real sense, grown up; and, while we may lament our loss of advantage, we must welcome them into the market-place and cheer the tremendous growth of healthy competition from which all mankind must benefit.

Today, in the great commercial centers, Tol Honeth, Camaar, Muros and Boktor, the market-places literally seethe with merchants from all parts of the known world. Sendar and Tolnedran, Murgo and Drasnian, Nadrak and Arend, Nyissan and Cherek, an occasional Algar, brutish Thulls, and even of late grey-cloaked Rivans vie with each other for the customer's attention and bargain endlessly with each other.

Tolnedra currently faces the inevitable turmoil of Dynastic succession. Our present Emperor, Ran Borune XXIII, a vigorous man in his fifties, is a widower with only one female child of thirteen and has quite firmly stated his intention not to remarry. The contending families have already begun maneuvering in the Council of Advisors in their quest for the Throne. We must hope that Nedra in His wisdom will guide us in the selection of a Dynasty to lead us through the years ahead which, while they may be fraught with uncertainties, are likely also to be rich with opportunities.*

* This 'history' is a scant 40 pages (or so) in length, but it gave a grand overview of about 5000 years of history which proved to be invaluable.

UNIVERSAL WEIGHTS AND MEASURES[*]

DISTANCE

1 League	3 Miles
½ League	1½ Miles
Inch	Standard
Span	9 Inches
Yard or Pace	3 Feet
Chain	66 Feet
Fathom	6 Feet

FLUID MEASURE

Ounce	
Pint	
Gill	¼ Pint – 4 ounces

Try to avoid using 'gallon' and 'quart'.

DRY MEASURE

Ounces	
Pounds	16oz = 1 Pint
Peck	16 pounds
Bushel	164 pounds
Stone	14 pounds
Hundredweight	100 pounds

[*] These little details add the necessary sense of reality to a story. Note that most of them are the same as they are here in the 'real' world.

Tolnedra

COINAGE*

All coins and bars are marked with the Emperor's likeness. Because of her dominance in trade, Tolnedra's coinage is the standard by which other currency is measured. The basic unit is the Mark. A Mark is a half a pound of metal.

GOLD
1. *Gold Mark*: 8 ounce bar worth approximately $1,000
2. *Half Gold Mark*: 4 ounce bar worth approximately $500
3. *Quarter Gold Mark*: 2 ounce gold coin worth approximately $250 (called an *Imperial*)
4. *Noble*: 1 ounce gold coin worth approximately $125
5. *Crown*: ½ ounce gold coin worth approximately $62.50
(The names of gold coins include the word 'Gold'. Thus, 'A Gold Noble'.)

SILVER
Silver is worth ⅟₂₀ the value of gold. Thus:
1. *Silver Mark* = $50
2. *Silver Half-Mark* = $25
3. *Silver Imperial* = $12.50
4. *Silver Noble* = $6.25
5. *Silver Crown* = $3.12
6. *Half-Crown*: The half-crown is a 1 ounce brass coin worth $1.56
7. *Penny*: Copper. 100 pennies make a half-crown.

* These values are arbitrary, and have little relationship to the current value of precious metals.

Questionable coins or bars are taken to the temple for verification by the priests of Nedra. Each temple has a set of verified scales.

The priests charge a 1% fee.

COSTUME

MEN
The upper classes wear a toga-like 'Mantle'. These garments are color-coded to show rank.

The military uniform is Roman.

Merchants wear belted gowns with deep, wide pockets. They are also color-coded to show rank.

Menials and craftsmen wear tunics – just below the knees and sleeves to the elbows. Leggings in winter. Leather aprons.

WOMEN
Gowns of a Grecian cut. Color-coding is legally required, but the law is largely ignored except on formal occasions. The hair is worn in the Grecian manner.

Tolnedrans customarily wear daggers (the sign of a free man) but the daggers are largely ornamental.

WEAPONRY
The short-sword – about 2 feet long – lances, javelins, the short bow.

Heavy siege weapons – catapults, etc.

RANK

Title	Addressed as	Color code *
The Emperor	Your Majesty	Gold
The Imperial Family	Your Highness	Silver with Gold Trim
Grand Dukes	Your Grace	Blue with Gold Trim

The heads of the Major families – Borunes, Ranites, etc.:

Members of his family	Varied	Blue with Silver Trim
Count	My Lord John	Green Trim
Baron	Baron John	White Trim
Noble	Sir John Brown	No Trim

COMMERCIAL RANK
(Commercial rank is based on yearly income)

Title	Income	Color code
Grand Master Merchant	1 Million Gold Marks	Red Gown
Master Merchant	½ Million Gold Marks	Blue Gown
Grand High Merchant	100,000 Gold Marks	Green Gown
High Merchant	50,000 Gold Marks	White Gown
Merchant	10,000 Gold Marks	Brown Gown

* The color coding to indicate rank is largely implicit in the books.

THE COMMONS
Artisans are identified by color-code on their tunics

Grand Master carpenter, cobbler, etc.	Red Trim
Master Cobbler, etc.	Blue Trim
Grand High Cobbler, etc.	Green Trim
High Cobbler, etc.	White Trim
Cobbler (usually a one-man shop)	Brown Trim

FREEMEN (WORKERS)
They wear no trim
Wages are standardized; about $800 per year
Slightly less for farm-workers
Prices of staples are fixed by law

Note: Rank in the priesthood is equivalent to rank in the nobility.
Rank in the bureaucracy is equivalent to commercial rank.
Academics rank with Artisans.
Doctors and Lawyers have the equivalent of commercial rank.

POPULATIONS

Tol Honeth	250,000
Tol Vordue	100,000
Tol Horb	90,000
Tol Rane	40,000
Tol Borune	10,000

7 – 8 Million Tolnedrans, mostly in villages or on farmsteads

MAJOR HOLIDAYS

Midwinter – Erastide – (the world's birthday). Feasting, jollity, parties, gifts

Midsummer – The Festival of Nedra. Prayers, religious observances

Various – The current Emperor's birthday

Early Fall – Ran Horb's Day. Celebration of the birthday of the greatest emperor. Military parades; patriotic speeches

Late Fall – Mara's Day. A day of guilt. Offerings to Mara. Pay all debts. Processions of penitents

RELIGIOUS OBSERVANCES

The priesthood is comfortable and not very devout. Religion is formal and perfunctory. Prayers are largely for luck and profit.
The Monastery at Mar-Terin – cloistered
Mendicant Monks – beggars
Most Tolnedrans aren't very religious

Appendix on Maragor

The kingdom of the Marags which once lay in that pleasant vale in the southeast quarter of what is now Tolnedra is, as all men know, no longer in existence. The destruction of Maragor is, of course, our national shame. This is not stated out of some desperate need for guilt which we observe among some of our less stable colleagues, but is, rather, a cold and incontrovertible fact. The Marags were not by any means an admirable people, but their annihilation, as we now know, was an unnecessarily extreme response to a cultural aberration which might have rather easily been rechanneled.

GEOGRAPHY

The vale which was once Maragor is a mountain-surrounded and fertile valley at the headwaters of the River of the Woods measuring one hundred leagues by twenty-five leagues. It is dotted with lakes and watered by the sparkling rivers which form the upper tributaries of the River of the Woods. Those hardy souls who have traversed it report that it is truly one of the loveliest spots in the known world. The horror which dwells there, of course, makes Maragor totally uninhabitable. It is also, unfortunately, non-exploitable for precisely the same reason. The free gold still glitters on the bottoms of the streams, but none dare risk their sanity to claim it.

THE PEOPLE

The Marags were a short, olive-skinned people of the same racial stock as Tolnedrans, Nyissans and Arends. The single characteristic which all the world thinks of when the Marags are mentioned is, of course, the fact that they were cannibals. How extensive this practice was is the subject of much debate among scholars. The savagery with which the Tolnedran legions extirpated the Marag culture left little in the way of documentary evidence behind; and one may be certain that if no Tolnedran willingly would now enter Maragor for *gold*, he would be much less likely to go there in search of records or fragments of parchment.

The archives in the monastery at Mar-Terin, however, *do* contain some few fragments which provide a sketch outline of the Marag culture.

They were, it appears, a secretive people with little desire for contact with outsiders. They were also, insofar as we are able to determine, largely matriarchal, and the institution of marriage among them was strangely under-developed. No stigma seems to have been attached to out-of-wedlock birth, and casual liaisons appear to have been commonplace. Beyond these few tantalizing hints, little is known of the Marags.

HISTORY

We must assume that the Marags migrated to the west during the first millennium as did the other peoples of the west, although there is no way to substantiate this. Cities and temples of stone were erected in the Vale, but when they were constructed and by whose order, we have no way of knowing, only that the legions which destroyed the country did attest to their existence. The cities appear to have been oddly-constructed assortments of stone buildings without protective walls around them, and the temples, standing alone on the plain, were vast constructions of enormous stones erected with incredible amounts of primitive labor.

The only body of historical documents we have relate to the nineteenth-century war between Maragor and Nyissa. The causes of that war are unclear, but the Marags mounted an invasion of the jungle-country of the snake people and pressed rapidly on to the Nyissan capital at Sthiss Tor. The reports of the field commanders of this invasion provide certain chilling hints about the nature of Marag religious practices. The conclusion of each report of the capture of a Nyissan city or town lists – by name – those luckless inhabitants who were 'assumed' for the greater glory of Mara. We can only shudder at the thinly veiled meaning of that term.

The Marag invasion, of course, came to grief after the occupation of Sthiss Tor. The cunning Nyissans had, before evacuating the city, poisoned everything edible in the vicinity. Marag soldiery sickened and died in appalling numbers, and the desperate field commanders frantically appealed to their superiors back in Maragor for food. Ultimately, they were forced to abandon the city and flee back through the jungles to the mountains and thence across to Maragor. The trail of dead and dying soldiers they left behind them gives mute testimony to the virulence of Nyissan poisons.

The only other contact between the Marags and outsiders came just prior to the destruction of the entire people. Tolnedran merchants attempting to enter Maragor in search of trade were driven out of the country. No amount of official remonstrance on the part of the Imperial Court could persuade the Marags to relent, and eventually the city of Tol Rane was constructed on Maragor's western boundary to provide a suitable site for trade. The few Marags who took advantage of this commercial opportunity paid handsomely for the wares they purchased in fine gold. It was the discovery of this gold which sealed the fate of Maragor.

The events leading up to the Tolnedran invasion and the details of that ruthless campaign have already been discussed and need not be repeated here.

When the campaign was over, the few pitiful survivors were sold to Nyissan slave-traders who promptly chained them together and drove them in long columns across the mountains into the jungles of Nyissa. Their ultimate fate is mercifully hidden from us.

Thus perished Maragor – the living Maragor at any rate. The horrid reality of the dead Maragor remains to haunt us fully three millennia after our ill-advised adventure there.

Reports of the exact nature of the shades which haunt the vale which was once Maragor are hardly verifiable, since most who have been there and survived hover on the verge of madness. All confirm that the Spirit of Mara shrieks and wails throughout the land, but reports of the hideous phantoms who haunt the land vary widely. Curiously, all the more coherent accounts indicate that the ghosts are *female*, which seems to make their mutilated shades that much more horrifying. This latter observation is confirmed in part by the monks of Mar-Terin who (though madness stalks *their* ranks also) provide us with the most authoritative accounts of the ghosts who have made Maragor not only uninhabitable but unapproachable as well.

Let Imperial Tolnedra resolve most firmly that never again will we allow ourselves to be pushed by our greed into such shameful acts, and let perished Maragor – an eternal rebuke – stand forever between Tolnedra and a repetition of this most monstrous crime.

COINAGE

No coinage. Marags had a barter economy. The costume was Greek. Men – short tunics and sandals. Women – short silk dresses.

SOCIAL ORGANIZATION*

Houses and land belonged to the women. Men were athletes, hunters and soldiers. The society was very loose and considered immoral by other races. The men lived in semi-military dormitories – when they weren't 'guests' in the house of this or that woman. Men had no property. The Marags were very enthusiastic about athletic tournaments. Religious observances were orgiastic in nature. The society tended toward a lot of nudity because the Marags had a great admiration for the human body. Their temples doubled as athletic stadiums.

---

* In *Belgarath the Sorcerer* Belgarath spends some time in Maragor after Poledra's apparent death. This paragraph on Marag social organization served as the basis for that sojourn.

THE CANNIBALISM

This came about as the result of a mis-reading of one of their sacred texts. It was ritualistic in nature, and those consumed were all non-Marags.

MANNERS

Marags were good-natured and happy-go-lucky. The men were not interested in trade (which made the Tolnedrans crazy). The Marags were total Pagans with virtually no inhibitions. The women were very generous with both their property and their personal favors.

There were probably no more than a million Marags.

THE ALORN KINGDOMS

NOTE The four kingdoms of the Alorn peoples, Cherek, Drasnia, Algaria, and the Isle of the Winds are a direct outgrowth of the Kingdom of Aloria which existed in antiquity and which was divided during the reign of the legendary Cherek Bear-shoulders at about the end of the second millennium.

The Isle of the Winds

GEOGRAPHY

The northwest-most of the twelve kingdoms, the Isle of the Winds is a rocky, almost uninhabitable island to the west of Sendaria and Cherek and to the north of Arendia. Perpetual, gale-force winds sweep off the ocean to beat against the island's west coast. Because of reefs and high cliffs, the island is totally unapproachable except at Riva, the island's only city. A limited fishery exists at Riva, and there appears to be some mining in the mountains of the island – mostly in useful metals such as iron and copper, although there do appear to be deposits of gold and silver which do not seem to be extensively exploited.

THE PEOPLE

Although they call themselves Rivans (after their legendary first king) the inhabitants of the island are basically Alorn and descendants of a fairly substantial migration which appears to have occurred at about the beginning of the third millennium. Curiously enough, the migration to the island by the Rivans seems to have occurred as one single expedition, significantly unlike the customary migratory pattern of other peoples which is characterized by succeeding waves and periods of consolidation. The Rivans are markedly different from their Alorn cousins in Cherek, Drasnia and Algaria. They are generally called the Grey-Cloaks (from their national costume) by the common people of other kingdoms, although until recently they were seldom seen off the island. The Rivans are sober, even grim, and close-mouthed to the point of rudeness. Reported to be savage warriors, they are fanatically loyal to their ruler (called simply the Rivan Warder) and wholly committed to the defense of their capital at Riva.

THE HISTORY OF THE RIVANS

As previously discussed, the Rivans migrated to the Isle sometime in the early years of the third millennium. Amazingly, the line of Rivan royalty appears to have descended in one unbroken line from the legendary Riva Iron-grip to the last Rivan King, Gorek the Wise, who was assassinated in 4002 by agents of the Nyissan Queen. This unbroken succession marks the longest dynasty in the history of all the twelve kingdoms, apparently enduring for nearly two thousand years.

Perhaps in keeping with their national character, the Rivans have formed no alliances with any of the other kingdoms, and have steadfastly refused to sign even the most rudimentary trade agreement with the representatives of the Tolnedran Emperor. This rigid stubbornness was a source of unending frustration to whole generations of Tolnedran diplomats and a continuous irritation to two complete Tolnedran Dynasties.

Following the Accords of Val Alorn in 3097, efforts were made to establish normal trade relations with the Rivans but without success, and finally, in 3137, Ran Borune XXIV mounted the disastrous expedition to the Isle to force the gates of Riva. The adventure, of course, was an unmitigated disaster. Preparations were then made for a full-scale invasion of the Isle, until the now-famous note from the Cherek ambassador persuaded the Emperor to abandon the entire project.

In time the Rivans grudgingly consented to the construction of a commercial enclave outside the city walls, and visiting merchants were forced to be content with that single concession.

By custom, no merchant or emissary is ever permitted inside the walls of the city itself, and most certainly not within the fortress at the center of the city.*

There are but two exceptions to this. The first is the Alorn Council which occurs once each ten years and during which the kings of Algaria, Drasnia, Cherek and sometimes of Sendaria (when the King of Sendaria chances to be an Alorn) journey to Riva and are conveyed – alone – to the Rivan throne-room where, it is rumored, they report to the Rivan Warder concerning the search for the heir to the Rivan Throne. The other exception to this rule is in accordance with the humiliating agreement of Vo Mimbre which requires that each Tolnedran Imperial Princess present herself in her wedding gown before a Rivan Throne for a three-day period on her sixteenth birthday.

NOTE Tolnedran Princesses for the past five hundred years since the great Battle at Vo Mimbre have reported that the entire city of Riva is little more than a walled defensive position with individual houses forming salients, redoubts, bastions and the like, and that the streets are laid out in such fashion that they are overlooked by and exposed to overhead

---

* This xenophobic restriction was significantly relaxed during the actual writing.

attack by each succeeding row of thick-walled houses. Moreover, the roofs of Rivan houses are all of slate, and there is nothing exposed within the city which will burn. The Fortress is a sheer tower with enormously thick walls and but one very narrow iron door. The throne-room is reported to be a very large chamber, musty and unused, in which sits the Rivan Throne, a large seat of black basalt with a rusted sword embedded, point downward in the back and having a large greyish-colored pommel-stone – possibly some artifact or souvenir out of the dim reaches of the Rivan past.

For the first thousand years of its history, the Isle of the Winds was deliberately isolated, cut off from all contact with the civilized world. For reasons which are largely unclear, Cherek warships maintained a continual blockade of the port of Riva, allowing no vessels of any nation to land there. Convinced that there was enormous wealth on the island, Tolnedran and Sendarian merchants pressured the Emperor at Tol Honeth for several generations to force the Cherek Alorns to lift their blockade. This was finally accomplished in the Accords of Val Alorn of 3097, and a horde of Tolnedran and Sendarian ships descended on the harbor at Riva only to be met by unscalable walls and a silent, locked gate. The details of the efforts to persuade the Rivans to trade were discussed elsewhere (see The History of Tolnedra).

The controversy ultimately was resolved peacefully, although for a time the west hovered perilously near the brink of open and general war.

The single most significant event in Rivan history was the assassination of King Gorek the Wise by a party of Nyissan merchants, apparently upon the instruction of the Nyissan Queen in 4002. The incident is marked by confusion, and a factual, detailed account of what actually took place has never been forthcoming. It appears that the royal family was invited to the commercial enclave to receive a special gift from the Queen of Nyissa. Upon their arrival at the Nyissan compound, they were attacked by seven Nyissan merchants armed with the traditional poisoned knives of their race. The king, the queen, the crown prince and his wife and two of their three children were killed, but no trace of the remaining prince was ever found. Two of the Nyissan merchants survived the assault by the Rivan guards and were at length persuaded to reveal their connection to the Nyissan Queen.

The resulting war between the Alorn Kingdoms and Nyissa was perhaps one of the most brilliant military campaigns in the history of the west, which fact raises serious doubts about the customary dismissal of the Alorns as barbarian Berserks. A series of hit and run raids on the Nyissan coast by Cherek raiders diverted the attention of the snake people while a vast force of Drasnian Infantry and Algarian Cavalry made the seemingly impossible trek across the mountains of western Tolnedra and attacked down the upper reaches of the River of the Serpent. An expeditionary force of Rivans ascended the River of the Woods and made a swift overland attack on the Nyissan capital of Sthiss Tor, entering the city while a majority of the Nyissan army was in the east attempting to hold off the invading Algarians and Drasnians and the remainder of their force was trying to repel a major landing of the Cherek fleet at the mouths of the River of the Serpent.

Before she died, Queen Salmissra XXCVII was persuaded to reveal to the leader of the Rivan force precisely what had been behind the assassination, but the leader, Brand (who was later chosen to the post of Warder of Riva) did not reveal that information to anyone but the Alorn Kings.*

The Tolnedran Emperor attempted to intercede, but the Alorns proceeded to systematically destroy the entire kingdom of Nyissa, pulling down the city of Sthiss Tor, burning towns and villages and driving the inhabitants into the jungles. So savage was this Alorn extermination that for five hundred years the entire country appeared depopulated, and only after that length of time were the frightened Nyissans persuaded to come out of the trees and begin the process of rebuilding their capital.

In some measure due to the enormous volume of trade which was being destroyed and the tremendous loss of revenue resulting, a Tolnedran force moved south to restrain the Alorn barbarians, but they were met at the River of the Woods by an overwhelming force of Drasnians, Algarians and Cherek Berserks. It was not until that point that it was fully realized in Tol Honeth the actual size of the Alorn army on our southern border. The commander of the Tolnedran Legions prudently decided not to interfere with the Alorns but merely positioned his force along the north bank of the River of the Woods to protect the integrity of Tolnedran territory.

The twelve hundred years which followed the destruction of Nyissa was spent by the Rivans in their endless (and futile) quest for the heir to the Rivan Throne. Persistent rumors based on the sketchy and confused testimony of witnesses to the assassination

---

* This account differs markedly from the one in *Belgarath the Sorcerer*.

maintained that the youngest son of the Crown Prince, a boy of nine,* escaped the knives of the Nyissans by plunging into the sea. Had this in fact been the case, the child would surely have perished, for the Sea of the Winds at Riva is bitterly cold throughout the year. Rumors persist, however, long after reason despairs, and the Rivans have painstakingly tracked down each vague hint or clue. Scores of impostors have emerged over the centuries, but the Rivans would appear to have some ultimate test which none yet has passed.

The quest for the heir to the Rivan Throne was interrupted only by the Angarak invasion of the west under Kal-Torak in 4865. It was the thirty-first Warder of Riva who was the overgeneral of the western forces and who led the assault upon the rear of the main force of Kal-Torak before the walls of Vo Mimbre in 4875, and it was this same thirty-first warder (traditionally named Brand – although the Warder is *selected* rather than ascending to his position by birth) who met and defeated Kal-Torak in single combat. (See the prose epic 'The Battle of Vo Mimbre' for a colorful though basically accurate description of that duel.)

Following this amazing display of prowess, the assembled rulers of the west pledged allegiance to the Rivan Throne in an outburst of enthusiasm over the crushing of Kal-Torak, and only the presence of mind of Mergon, the Tolnedran ambassador to the court at Vo Mimbre forestalled the immediate installation of Brand XXXI as Emperor of the West. The concession wrung from Mergon in exchange was the aforementioned Agreement of Vo Mimbre, which specified that upon his return the Rivan King will be given to wife an Imperial Tolnedran Princess.

Upon the completion of the battle, Brand XXXI returned to Riva, and since that time Rivan traders have been seen throughout the known world. Although they are shrewd bargainers, it is commonly believed in the highest governmental circles at Tol Honeth that these 'merchants' are in fact agents of the Rivan Warder engaged in that centuries-long and obviously futile search for the heir to the Rivan Throne.

Whatever their motives, the Grey-Cloaks are a welcome addition to the world of commerce, and it is to be hoped that in time the Rivans will outgrow their secretive ways and assume their proper place in the family of nations.

---

* Geran becomes a boy of six in *Belgarath the Sorcerer* and *Polgara the Sorceress*.

Riva

COINAGE

GOLD

1. A 1 ounce gold coin called a 'Rivan Gold Penny' equal to a Tolnedran 'Noble'.
2. ½ ounce gold coin called a 'Rivan Gold Half-Penny' equal to a Tolnedran 'Crown'.

SILVER

1. A 2 oz. silver coin called a 'Rivan Silver Double-Penny'. 10 Double-Pennies = a Gold Penny = a Silver 'Imperial'.
2. A 1 oz. silver coin, a 'Silver Penny'. 20 = 1 Gold Penny.
3. A ½ oz. silver coin called a 'Silver Half-Penny' = a Tolnedran Silver Crown.

BRASS OR COPPER

Called a 'brass' or a 'copper'
Theoretically equal, but in practice a brass is worth 2 coppers
100 brass = a Silver Half-Penny
200 coppers = a Silver Half-Penny

COSTUME

There are no class distinctions in Rivan costume, but the nobles and the wealthy wear slightly finer clothing. The standard is a tunic, long-sleeved, belted and reaching to mid-thigh. Long, fairly wide sleeves. Also leggings (wrappings) laced around with thongs or cord. The standard grey cloak is a heavy, sleeveless mantle with a hood.

Rivan clothing is grey – undyed wool. Rivan sheep have a curious grey color and extremely fine, thick wool.

On state or formal occasions a blue linen tunic with discreet silver embroidery is worn by all ranks.

SHOES
A soft leather half-boot (felt in the winter)

ARMOR
Chain mail and pointed steel helmets

RANK
The distinction between noble and commons is generally indicated in the weaponry. The customary weapons of the Rivans are a four-foot broadsword and an 18 inch dagger. The sword-belts of the nobility are gold or silver-studded. Those of the commons are plain.

WOMEN
Wear linen gowns, long sleeved and sober and decorous. Belting is a concession to vanity and the gowns are cross-tied to accentuate the bosom. The hair (usually blonde) is worn long and flowing with elaborate braiding around the temples to give a coronet effect.

COMMERCE

Bread, again a standard, costs slightly more in Riva than in Tolnedra, but the Rivans are thrifty and industrious so there is virtually no poverty on the island. Fairs are held in the meadows along the River of Veils behind the city of Riva and there is a great deal of barter as opposed to cash transactions. Trade items – wool, sheep, a few cattle, hogs, produce. Useful goods, shoes, pots, pans, etc.

RANK

THE WARDER
Selected by the nobility in conclave at Riva. Invested with the name Brand and wears an iron circlet on state occasions.

THE BARONS

20 only. Each represents a district in the city of Riva and is responsible for its maintenance and defense. The residents of a district are the Baron's men. Some Rivans live in the outlands – a few shepherds, some farmers, etc. This is a largely self-contained society with a remarkably stable population.

MODES OF ADDRESS

'My Lord Brand' to the Warder.
'Sir John' to the Barons.
'Friend John' to the commons – not unusual for a lower class Rivan to
    call a Baron 'Friend John' as well.

POPULATION

The population of the city of Riva is about 100,000; another half million or so in villages and on farmsteads.

RELIGIOUS OBSERVANCES

Temple of Belar in the city of Riva
Religious observances standard Alorn (See Cherek)
Honor is also paid to Aldur
Religion: see Cherek

MAJOR HOLIDAYS

Erastide – The world's birthday – a week-long celebration in mid-
    winter.
Riva's Birthday – Early summer – Patriotic rededication to the
    defense of the Orb.
Gorek's Day – Or a day of national mourning over the death of Gorek
    the Wise – early September.

Festival of Belar – Spring. A religious holiday. Feasting, some drinking.
Brand's Day – Celebration of the victory at the Battle of Vo Mimbre.
    Military games. Midsummer.

Cherek

Cherek is a mountainous peninsula on the northwest coast, extending northward to the polar ice. With the exception of the valley of the Alorn River and the fertile basin south of Val Alorn, Cherek is too mountainous to be arable. There is some fishery in the Gulf of Cherek, and fairly extensive mineral deposits in the mountains – iron, copper, gold, silver, tin, certain gem-stones. The capital city at Val Alorn is a town of some 40,000, walled, stone-constructed, with narrow streets and high-pitched roofs.

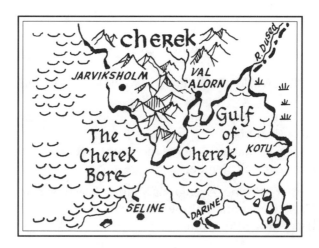

THE PEOPLE

The Chereks are, of course, the elemental, archetypal Alorns. They are a noisy, boisterous, hard-drinking, rowdy race with little reverence for proprieties and little patience for subtlety. They are master ship-builders and superb seamen, but unfortunately have always had little taste for honest commerce, preferring piracy on the high seas to legitimate trade. It has been observed that frequently even the most stable merchant among the Chereks will fall back upon this predilection when the opportunity presents itself, and Tolnedran vessels are therefore always wary when meeting a Cherek vessel at sea.

Perhaps because their stock is more undiluted than that of their cousins in Drasnia and Algaria, the Chereks are a taller, somewhat blonder people. Their social structure is clannish, but the clans all pay homage to the Throne at Val Alorn. Such feuds and disputes as periodically erupt are either settled by the King or decided in ritualized single combat.

THE HISTORY OF THE CHEREKS

It is evident that the Alorns have occupied the Cherek peninsula for at least four millennia. The great Temple of Belar, the Bear-God of the Alorns, at Val Alorn has been reliably dated to the eleventh century and is a truly remarkable example of prehistoric architecture. It appears that the Alorns were a fairly extensive tribe of northern nomads who settled in Cherek sometime early in the first millennium, and, although artifacts of the primitive Alorn culture have been found in northern Drasnia and in the mountains of Gar og Nadrak, it is quite evident that the Cherek peninsula is their ancestral home.

Runes dating back into antiquity have indeed identified the country as Aloria, but this name appears to have been changed to Cherek in honor of Cherek Bear-shoulders, a great king who reigned over the Alorns at the end of the second millennium. Apparently a man of enormous power, King Cherek held sway over a vast northern empire extending from the Vale of Aldur to the polar ice and from the west coast to the far eastern reaches of what is now Gar og Nadrak, encompassing all of Algaria, Drasnia, Gar og Nadrak and northern Sendaria as well as the Cherek peninsula.

The exact cause is unclear, but during the later years of his reign the empire of King Cherek was broken up into four separate Alorn Kingdoms, and the Alorns withdrew from the east to the borders of Drasnia.

The first contacts between Cherek and the Tolnedran Empire came during the 25th and 26th centuries when Cherek pirates began systematically destroying all Tolnedran vessels which strayed into the Sea of Winds, and Cherek Berserks made landings all up and down the west coast, sacking and burning cities in Sendaria, Arendia, Tolnedra and Nyissa. The City of Tol Vordue at the mouth of the River Arend was burned to the ground eight times during those two centuries.

By the beginning of the fourth millennium, Tolnedran emissaries had concluded a series of treaties and trade agreements with the Chereks, and relations began to assume some semblance of normalcy. In 3097 the Accords of Val Alorn opened the sea lanes to the city of Riva with certain provisos. (See the history of the Isle of the Winds.) Following the eventual opening of the Rivan commercial enclave, the city of Val Alorn began a modest trade with the Isle of the Winds and with Drasnia to the east. The bulk of Cherek commerce, however, derives from the sea transport of goods from the Drasnian port of Kotu through the Gulf of Cherek and the Cherek Bore in the Straits of Sendaria around the hook of Arendia to the southern ports. Despite the splendid system of highways constructed by Emperor Ran Horb II (see the History of Tolnedra), Cherek vessels, modeled on the long, narrow Cherek warships, move much more rapidly than the caravans of other merchants traveling the thousand leagues from Boktor at the western terminus of the North Caravan Route to the Sendarian port of Camaar. Thus Cherek merchants can easily put their goods on the docks at Tol Vordue or Tol Horb or even on the wharves of Tol Honeth months before similar goods can arrive via the overland route. The Chereks are also able to avoid the innumerable tolls, taxes, duties, port fees, bribes, gratuities and gifts which are the lifeblood of commerce, and this more than makes up for the occasional vessel lost to weather, uncharted reefs, or bad luck in those occasional encounters at sea of which the Chereks are so fond. Tolnedran merchants have bitterly complained about this advantage to the whole succession of Tolnedran Emperors for two thousand years without notable success, since the wily Cherek negotiators agreed in the Accords of Val Alorn to a tax of ten percent of their net upon any goods sold in Tolnedra to be paid directly into the personal treasury of the Emperor.

In 4002, apparently in accord with a secret treaty with the Rivans, the entire Cherek fleet sailed southward and participated in the assault upon Nyissa. Since that time it has been no secret that there exists an Alorn confederation – an illegal arrangement in direct violation of numerous treaties with Tolnedra, all of which contain a clause of exclusivity forbidding the signatory nation from concluding treaties or agreements with any other power without Tolnedran consent.

It must be conceded, however, that these secret agreements were invaluable during the war against the Angarak hordes of Kal-Torak (4865–75) when the Alorns arose as one people in response to the near-destruction of Drasnia and the wasting of the Algarian herds.

It was in 4875 that Cherek warships appeared for the first time at Tol Honeth and conveyed virtually the entire Imperial Garrison north to the River Arend and thence up that river to the vast plain to the west of Vo Mimbre that they might fall upon the Angarak right flank. Further, it must be conceded that it was the presence of the Rivan Warder which mobilized the entire west against the Angarak threat. His leadership of that unlikely force of Rivans, Chereks, Sendars and northern Arends who assaulted the rear of the Mallorean Horde was the final blow upon that bloody field, since Algar cavalry, the remnants of Drasnian infantry and Ulgo irregulars had already begun the assault upon the Angarak left. This three-pronged attack, the most concentrated effort in military history, is generally conceded to have been the only thing that could have stemmed the Angarak tide.

Cherek has prospered in the years since the defeat of the Angaraks, gaining advantage by assisting the Drasnians in the rebuilding of Boktor and Kotu and in the repair of the causeway across the Aldurfens on the Great North Road.

The present King of Cherek is Anheg IX (called by some Anheg the sly). He has been on the Throne in Val Alorn for nine years. He is a large, dark-haired man with a brutish face. Though he appears to share the Alorn fondness for rowdy drinking and boastful swagger, he is in fact, a highly educated man and a shrewd politician. He is fully aware of the complex politics of the southern nations as well as the more elemental alliances of the Alorn Kingdoms. He spends much time in study, and is generally held by those who know him to be the equal at least of the Tolnedran Emperor, who has had the benefit of instruction by an entire university. The King of Cherek, however, conducts his own studies, and, it is rumored, has even learned old Angarak so that he might read in the original the forbidden BOOK OF TORAK, a work accursed by all civilized nations and religions.

The palace of Anheg is a vast warren of unused chambers and dank corridors – befitting, perhaps, a building that has been three thousand years in construction. His private chambers are given over to study and to obscure experimentation.

Anheg's closest friend and advisor is his cousin Barak, a giant Alorn warrior with the temper of a Berserker and the subtlety of a Tolnedran ambassador. Barak has, it is reliably reported, been entrusted with a number of highly delicate missions for his cousin. Our informants in Val Alorn, however, report that he is generally believed by Cherek nobility to suffer from some obscure stigmata or 'Doom', as our northern friends call it, and is periodically morose and even melancholic. What the nature of this 'Doom' might be is a matter which causes tight lips and white knuckles on the sword-hands of our Cherek friends and an absolute refusal to discuss Barak's affliction – even under the most skillful prodding.[*]

Cherek

COINAGE

GOLD
1. A 1½ oz. gold coin called a 'shield' equals about $200
2. A ¾ oz. gold coin called a 'half shield' equals about $100
Cherek gold coins are octagonal and the weights are not very exact. They are usually hoarded and are seldom seen in trade.

---

[*] This description of Barak derives from an earlier character sketch.

SILVER

The standard of trade in Cherek

1. A one pound silver bar milled on the edges and stamped with the King's rune. Called a 'Silver King' equals $100.
2. A ½ lb. silver bar called a 'Silver Queen' equals $50.
3. A 4 oz. silver coin (very big) called a 'Silver Prince' equals $25.
4. A one oz. silver coin called a 'Silver Princess' equals $6.50 (Tolnedran silver Noble)

COPPER

1. A copper penny 1 oz. octagonal equals 6.5¢
2. A copper half-penny round equals 3.25¢

Note: Copper is slightly more valuable in Cherek because of its scarcity in that country. (No brass coins in Cherek.)

COSTUME

MEN

Basically Viking – lots of furs. Linen tunics. Leggings. Shoes are very crude. Cherek men are armed almost all of the time. Swords, axes, spears, like a boar-spear, javelins, daggers. Helmet – various shapes decorated usually with the clan totem on top – no horn on helmets. Chain-mail shirts or heavy bull-hide with steel plates sewn on. Beards common.

WOMEN

Linen gowns. Belted. Cross-tied bodice to accentuate the bosom. (Cherek women are busty and quite proud of that fact.) Hair is braided and frequently bound up into elaborate headdresses.

COMMERCE

Extensive bartering. Market-place in most towns and villages. Ship building is a major industry around Val Alorn.

RANK

THE KING
Hereditary. Always wears his crown. (Has a crown built onto his helmet for wars.) State robes are very fine and trimmed with ermine.

THE EARLS
Actually Clan-chiefs. Some 30-40 of them.

LORDS
The hereditary nobility. Associated with land. Can be invested at the King's whim.

WARRIORS
Not exactly noble, but treated with more respect than commoners.

COMMONERS
Unlanded men – farm workers, dock-hands, etc. largely drawn from the descendants of Thralls (Thralldom was abolished at the end of the 2nd millennium).* The social structure of Cherek is quite fluid and upward mobility is very common. Any man with a sword or axe can rise to warrior status and can in time be made a Lord by the King. Chereks are quite concerned with proprieties of such things.

MODES OF ADDRESS

The King is called 'Your Majesty' on formal occasions but is often called by his first name even by commoners. Nobles are called 'Lord John' on formal occasions but again often called just 'John'.

---

* We chose not to follow the institution of thralldom (slavery). It *was* present in Europe during the Dark Ages, but it would have served no purpose in this story.

MANNERS

Much care is taken to avoid offense. Chereks are touchy and quarrel-some. Boasting is permitted but no insult. Chereks sing a great deal but not very well (loud). A lot of feasting and drinking in the winter. Fights are common but the tendency is to use clubs or staves rather than swords to hold down the fatalities. Adultery is not uncommon but is severely punished when caught.

HOLIDAYS

Erastide – Midwinter
Festival of Belar – Spring
King's Birthday – Varies. Now midsummer
Cherek's Birthday – Fall
Victory Celebration – For Battle of Vo Mimbre – Midsummer

POPULATION

Probably 2 million total*

RELIGIOUS OBSERVANCES

Priests are muscular and war-like. Bonfires on the Altar. Choral singing. Sermons are biting attacks on personal sinfulness. (Like the Scottish Dominie.) Incantations for luck.

THE CULT OF THE BEAR
A group of warrior monks (like Templars) dedicated to the service of Belar – chapters in Drasnia, Algaria, Riva and Sendaria. These form the core of the armies of those nations – fundamentally an Anti Angarak society – arch conservative.†

---

* These population numbers were low throughout. We had the Dark Ages in mind, but the societies that developed in the story were noticeably more advanced.
† The Bear-cult makes its first appearance here. At the time we had no idea how important it would turn out to be.

Drasnia

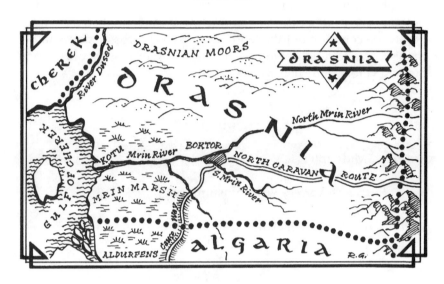

GEOGRAPHY

Drasnia is a large northern country lying between the mountains of the east and the Gulf of Cherek. It is, by and large, a plain extending from Aldurfens up through Mrin Marsh and thence to the Drasnian Moors which extend northward to the polar ice. The principal Drasnian preoccupation is with the vast herds of reindeer which provide the mainstay of Drasnian economy.* Drasnia's strategic position astride the North Caravan Route has provided a vast wealth from time immemorial. The two major cities, the capital at Boktor, northern terminus of the Great North Road and western terminus of the North Caravan Route out of Gar og Nadrak, and the island seaport of Kotu at the mouth of the Mrin River have been important commercial centers since before the dawn of recorded history.

---

*The reindeer were later eliminated.

THE DRASNIANS

With the possible exception of the sphinx-like Rivans, the Drasnians are the most enigmatic of the Alorns. Perhaps because of their isolated frontier situation and the brute savagery of the Drasnian winter with its winds howling down across the Drasnian Moors, they are at once openly friendly but with a certain reserve, seeming to draw a line beyond which a stranger is not invited. They are hard traders, but are scrupulously honest. Their profits are gained from certain advantageous trade laws and toll arrangements. Like all Alorns, they are warlike, and warriors from the northern reaches of Drasnia – as a result of their life-long following of the reindeer herds – are the finest infantry in the world, easily able to keep pace with cavalry units on long marches. Like all infantry units, their weapon of choice is the long spear.

The Drasnians are not as clannish as other Alorns, their culture appearing to have progressed to the stage where district and regional loyalties are at least on a par with blood ties.

THE HISTORY OF DRASNIA

Like the Rivans and Algars, Drasnians were separated from the main body of Alorns at the time of the break-up of the empire of King Cherek Bear-shoulders at the end of the second millennium. For the first thousand years of their history, the Drasnians appear to have been nomadic herdsmen following the yearly migrations of the reindeer herds. One curious feature of their early history was the existence of a series of fortified camps along the western reaches of the mountain range which marks their border with Gar og Nadrak.

The camps seem not to have been continuously occupied, but rather to have been periodically used by any one of a dozen Drasnian tribes. Evidence exists in the form of artifacts and large quantities of skeletal remains that a major battle took place in a narrow valley just before one of these camps. The invading force appears to have been Angarak, judging from the artifacts and the distinctive skull-shape of the majority of the remains, and it does appear that the Drasnians won a decisive victory and stemmed what might have been a prelude to a major invasion of the west by a highly organized Angarak force. The event can be roughly dated to the 25th century and appears to have been a major effort by the Angaraks to penetrate the west – unlike the continuous probes sent down into Algaria throughout the third millennium. Thus it is that all the kingdoms of the west owe a profound debt of gratitude to those unknown Drasnian warriors for stopping an invasion which, given the unorganized state of the west in the third millennium, must certainly have resulted in all of us growing up under an Angarak dictatorship.[*]

Once the aggressive push of the Angaraks was quelled by this great but unnamed battle and by a number of similar, though smaller, engagements in Algaria, trade began with the east, and the Drasnians began construction of their capital at Boktor and their seaport at Kotu.

Boktor grew rather naturally at the western end of the North Caravan Route which existed long before it was formalized in the agreement reached in 3219 between the Kings of Drasnia and Gar og Nadrak. Boktor became a major commercial center in the north long before the other Alorn cities had even begun to consider the advantages of trade. Kotu, meanwhile, flourished as the major seaport of the north. By the middle of the fourth millennium, trade agreements had brought Drasnia into the commercial empire of Tolnedra, although the hard-bargaining Drasnians had so twisted the standard agreements that it is difficult to say where the advantage actually lay. Suffice to say that the stipulation that all merchandise transfers at Boktor take place through the agency of a Drasnian intermediary brought tears of chagrin to the eyes of Tolnedran merchants, since it effectively prevented direct trading with eastern merchants at the terminus of the North Caravan Route.

Drasnia prospered throughout the fourth millennium, and by the early years of the fifth stood as a commercial power rivaling Tolnedra.

---

[*] We chose not to follow up on this battle.

When the Rivan King was assassinated in 4002, the massed
Drasnian infantry made one of the most astounding treks in history,
covering the thousand leagues from Boktor to the Vale of Aldur in
sixty days* to join forces with the Algar cavalry for the overland
assault on Nyissa. Drasnian infantry was particularly effective
against Nyissan soldiery, since Nyissans traditionally took to the
trees when assaulted, and the long Drasnian spears were able to
quite easily reach them in the lower branches where they normally
took refuge. Indeed, in certain areas of the jungles of eastern Nyissa
the trees are festooned with human skeletons to this very day.

For all their power and courage, the Drasnians were the first to
fall when the savage Angarak hordes of Kal-Torak spilled down out
of the mountains of Nadrak and onto the plains in the spring of
4865. Although they resisted valiantly, the Drasnians were largely
destroyed. Their cities were pulled down, and those who were not
killed were enslaved. Upon command of the King, a few crack units
of the southern Drasnian army escaped into northern Algaria and
evaded the southward march of the main body of the Angarak
hordes southwestward toward Arendia.

These infantry units accompanied the Algarian cavalry across the
southern tip of Ulgoland and fell upon the Angarak left flank with
particular savagery during the decisive Battle of Vo Mimbre.

The units effected the release of the surviving Drasnian captives
from the retreating Nadraks, and these sorry remnants formed the
basis for the rebirth of the Drasnian nation. Assisted by Chereks and
Algars, the new monarch at Boktor, Rhodar I (the general who had
commanded Drasnian forces during the war) rebuilt the city of
Boktor, cleared the rubble and sunken vessels from the harbor at
Kotu, and rebuilt the great causeway across the northeastern reaches
of Aldurfens.

For a century following the Angarak invasion, Drasnian border
guards systematically and routinely killed all travelers from the east
until continued remonstrances from Tolnedra persuaded them to
abandon the practice and to restore normal trade along the North
Caravan Route. In some measure the decline of Tolnedra can be
directly traced to this drying up of northern commerce.

The present King of Drasnia, Rhodar XVIII, is an immensely fat,
jolly man in his mid-sixties who appears to be somewhat simple but
is, in fact, a shrewd and clever man who is ever watchful. Drasnian

---

* This was written before the scale was established. It is in fact 80 leagues from Boktor to
the Vale, and crack infantry could make that far in eight days.

merchants are found throughout the known world, and through their agency the Drasnian intelligence system is probably the finest in the world.

It is said – probably with some measure of truth – that the Tolnedran Emperor cannot change his tunic without word of it being delivered to Boktor within the hour.

Drasnia

COINAGE

GOLD

1. A 2 oz. gold plaque (rectangular) called a 'Gold Bull' – equals about $250.00
2. A 1 oz. gold coin (square) called a 'Gold Cow' – equals about $125.00
3. A ½oz. gold coin (also square) called a 'Gold Calf' – equals about $62.50

SILVER

1. A 2 oz. silver plaque shaped into an open rectangle called a 'silver link' (can be hooked together into chains)
2. 10 links make a 'chain' – equals about $125.00
3. A 1 oz. square silver coin called a 'Token' – equals about $6.25

BRASS AND COPPER

Coins in these metals are, of course, the basis of trade among the common people and are struck in each district. Called 'coppers' or 'brass'.

All are exactly 1 oz. Copper has one fifth the value of brass.

Brass has one fifth the value of silver.

Weights of Drasnian coins are extremely precise and the metals are very pure.

In addition, the Drasnians have developed a rudimentary banking system involving sight drafts between members of the same family using complicated codes. i.e. 'John gave me 100 chains here in Boktor. You give him 100 chains in Yar Marak' (less 10% of course).

COSTUME[*]

MEN

Somewhat Russian. Heavy into furs. Linen tunics belted, leggings, soft leather boots with heavy soles – felt boots in winter and huge fur capes – like blankets.

Armor – steel plates sewn to leather. Helmets squared on top and long nose guard.

Merchants wear fur-trimmed gowns – unbelted – and close-fitting caps. Gowns are usually colored to indicate the area of trade. The color-coding is quite elaborate. All Drasnian men carry broad daggers, but they are concealed under their clothes.

WOMEN

Linen in summer, wool in winter. Gowns very full and not excessively ornamented. Drasnian women wear their hair long and straight down the back.

---

* Quite frequently the costumes proved irrelevant.

COMMERCE

Highly developed. Lots of local shops in each neighborhood. Major commercial centers along the docks in Boktor and Kotu. Huge amounts of money change hands daily. Keep track on slates and settle at the end of the day. Each major merchant has his own strong room – heavily guarded. (Drasnian blacksmiths have devised elaborate locks.)

RANK

THE KING
Hereditary

THE PRINCES
These are Clan-chiefs. All are related – distantly – to the King. 20–30 in the country.

LORDS
Hereditary nobility associated with land. Similar to Cherek.

CHIEFS
These are the owners of the reindeer herds and the clan-leaders of the tribes which tend them. They are very primitive groups, and the chiefs are to varying degrees powerful particularly in the north. Each tribe has its own huge pasturelands. The authority of the King is far from absolute in the north.*

COMMONERS
All others. All Drasnian men are bearers of arms.

MILITARY
Units organized on the family-tribe basis.

MODES OF ADDRESS

Addressed by Rank, thus 'King John', 'Prince Fred'. Commoners called 'Worthy John' or 'Friend John'.

* This was not retained.

MANNERS

Drasnians are polite and have a great sense of humor. The transition from calling someone 'Worthy John' to calling him 'Friend John' is extremely elaborate, and Drasnians are amused when outsiders attempt to go through the stages of the process.

Note – Drasnians have developed an elaborate 'finger language' consisting of barely perceptible gestures. Can hold entire conversations with each other even while talking to some foreign merchant. Highly useful in trade negotiations and in their espionage work.*

HOLIDAYS

Erastide
Festival of Belar
Dras's Birthday
Day of Sorrow (when Angaraks invaded) early June (Lent here)
Day of Victory (Battle of Vo Mimbre) late June

POPULATION

Population approximately 1½ million

Algaria

GEOGRAPHY

With the exception of the Aldurfens to the north and the area south of the low range of hills that mark the upper reaches of the Aldur River, Algaria is a vast, rolling grassland lying between the two arms of the mountain range that forms the spine of the continent. The land is fertile and well-watered by the Aldur and could be profitably

*The 'secret language' proved to be very useful, although it was just an aside in the Preliminaries.

farmed, but the Algars prefer instead to remain semi-primitive herdsmen. Virgin gold occasionally appears in transactions with the Algars, but no hint of its source can be found.

The Algarian herds are the finest in the known world and provide meat for most of the kingdoms of the west. The yearly cattle-drive to Muros in Sendaria along the Great North Road is one of the genuinely magnificent spectacles one may behold. Centuries of carefully controlled breeding have made Algar horses un-surpassed.

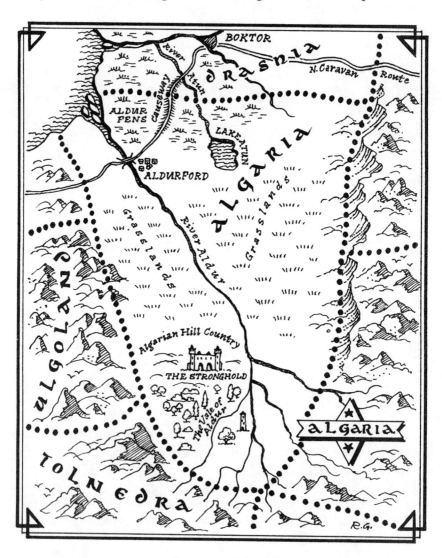

THE PEOPLE

The Algars, of course, are merely another branch of the numerous Alorn people and are similar to their northern cousins. They are tall, fair and generally an open people, honest in their dealings and firm in their friendships and alliances. They dwell for the most part in large wagons in which they follow the wanderings of their herds. An Algarian city can rise in the space of an hour – a well-ordered city of tents and pavilions, neatly laid out on streets, and the whole surrounded by a wall of poles which are carried under their wagons.

Each of these moveable cities represents an entire Algarian clan – usually numbering up to a thousand armed and mounted men and their families. The herds of each clan are vast and are owned in common. As with most Alorns, feuds among them are not uncommon, but the last clan-war took place at about the end of the third millennium. Since that time disputes have been settled by ritualized single combat.

There are two major peculiarities about Algarian society. The first is the presence in the hill country at the south of the grassland of a vast stone fortress known simply as 'The Stronghold' which is garrisoned but not actually occupied. The second is the continuous mounted patrols maintained around the perimeters of the Vale of Aldur, a beautiful but uninhabited area in the extreme south of the kingdom. Both the garrison at the Stronghold and the patrols in the Vale are comprised of contingents from all of the clans.

THE HISTORY OF THE ALGARS

Once again we see an Alorn people who were separated from their fellows at the time of the disintegration of the empire of Cherek Bear-shoulders. The legendary founder of the nation was Algar Fleet-foot, second son of old King Cherek. Like Drasnia and Riva, Algaria was populated at the end of the second millennium. There appear to have been large herds of wild horses and cattle on the Algarian plains, and the people were soon mounted upon the horses and their own herds had mingled with the wild cattle, creating a new breed much sturdier than the somewhat scrubby Alorn cattle they had brought with them, while not so totally unmanageable as the wild cattle indigenous to the plains.

There is evidence that a prolonged series of skirmishes with Angarak raiding parties took place along the eastern escarpment of Algaria with always the same predictable results. The Angarak columns were, naturally, on foot and were quite simply cut to pieces by the mounted Algars. The ability of the Algars to move rapidly and to call upon other clans for reinforcements as required made the Angarak penetration suicidal. No hint of motive can be discovered to explain why the Angaraks continued these hopeless expeditions for a thousand years.

During the fourth millennium Tolnedran emissaries attempted to conclude treaties with the Algars as they had with the other kingdoms of the west, but suffered a full five hundred years of frustration, since they were unable even to *identify* the Algarian King – often negotiating for years with a man who turned out to be a mere clan-chief. When they finally did manage to single out the true king of the Algars, the venerable Cho-Dorn the old, the wily old bandit came to the negotiation pavilion armed with copies of every treaty the emissaries had hammered out over half a millennium of negotiation and insisted that every concession granted in every treaty be honored, slyly reminding the emissaries that *he* was the king and asking them how they could presume to offer him less than they had offered a mere Clan-chief.

The result was one of the more humiliating treaties ever concluded by the Empire. No Tolnedran garrisons were permitted within the borders of Algaria. No commerce was allowed within the country except for certain limited trade at Aldurford in certain precisely specified items – mostly tools and necessities rather than the high-profit luxury items. There was not even the most-favored status customarily accorded Tolnedran merchants. This made it necessary for Tolnedran cattle-buyers to appear at Muros in Sendaria and to actually vie with others in the purchase of Algarian cattle rather than to select, at their own price, the cream of the herd as was their practice elsewhere. They were also forced to bid their lowest prices on items the Algarian clans purchased in quantity (Algars seldom purchase items individually) invariably in competition with other merchants from other nations. All of this has made the great fair at Muros in Sendaria one of the major commercial events of the year. Tolnedran merchants have complained bitterly about the treaty with the Algars, but Emperor Ran Horb II had, at the time of its signing, eyes only for the vision of the Great North Road, and each of the concessions granted the Algars forged more miles of that splendid dream.

When word reached Algaria in 4002 that the Rivan King had been assassinated, an event took place which had never before been witnessed. The Tolnedran ambassador, Dravor, reported in secret dispatches to Tol Honeth that the entire population gathered at the Stronghold leaving the herds only sparsely attended. There was a great conference of the Clan-chiefs with King Cho-Ram IV, and an army of the finest warriors was conscripted from the assembled clans. Ambassador Dravor reported further that other elements of Algar cavalry were set to patrolling the borders. Then, at the end of sixty days, the multitudes of Drasnian infantry appeared and joined with the Algar cavalry in their trek across the mountains to attack the eastern borders of Nyissa. While this horde was technically in violation of Tolnedran territory, the Emperor, Ran Vordue I, prudently chose not to intercept them.

Algar cavalry struck terror into the hearts of the Nyissans, and King Cho-Ram IV and King Radek XVII of Drasnia developed a series of tactical alternatives involving the cooperation between infantry and cavalry units which remain classics to this day.

Following the destruction of Nyissa, Algaria prospered, although there appears to have been a significant tightening of security along the eastern border.

With the invasion of Drasnia by the Angaraks, the Algars attempted to aid their northern cousins but were repulsed by the sheer numbers of the Angaraks and Mallorean hordes – estimated by some to number as many as a half-million warriors. For the second time the Algars gathered at the Stronghold and the population – with the exception of the finest cavalry units, entered the fortress and sealed the gates.

Following the destruction of Drasnia, the main body of Angaraks marched southward, systematically destroying Algarian herds as they went. In 4867 began the siege of the Algarian Stronghold – a siege that continued for eight years. With the possible exceptions of Prolgu in Ulgoland and Rak Cthol in Cthol Murgos, the Algarian Stronghold is probably the most unassailable land fortress in the world.

The Angaraks were continually harassed by hit and run attacks of nomadic Algar cavalry units. Even when some Angaraks (mostly Murgos) mounted themselves on Algar horses, they were no match for the Algars.

In 4874, Kal-Torak apparently decided to abandon his effort to reduce the Stronghold and, leaving a token force to maintain the siege, he turned westward across Ulgoland to begin his Arendian campaign.

The units of Algar cavalry continued to harass his flanks, but withdrew once his main force had entered the mountains.

It is uncertain why Kal-Torak chose to expend the time and effort in the prolonged siege at the Stronghold rather than strike immediately along the route of the Great North Road into Sendaria and thence southward into Arendia and Tolnedra. It may be that he felt that his rear would never be secure so long as an intact Algar nation remained behind him, or possibly two thousand years of humiliating defeats at the hands of the Algars had made the destruction of the horse-people one of the paramount goals of the Angarak race.

Whatever his motives, the giant Kal-Torak was soundly defeated at the Battle of Vo Mimbre when Algar cavalry units, accompanied by the survivors of the annihilation of Drasnia, crossed the southern tip of Ulgoland by way of passes known only to the Ulgos and attacked the Angarak left flank in the concerted effort of the third day of the battle. It is generally conceded that the Algar cavalry charge directed against the Murgos was instrumental in the victory.

Following the victory at Vo Mimbre, the Algars harassed the retreating Angaraks and succeeded in raising the siege of The Stronghold. They also pursued the remnants of the Nadrak and Thullish Angaraks to the north and forced them finally to evacuate all their garrisons in Drasnia.

When peace was restored in 4880, the Algars found that their herds had been decimated and scattered, and the rounding up of their livestock and the taking of an accurate count of their losses took the better part of ten years. During this period they refused to sell *any* of their cattle, causing what amounted to a meat-famine in the west, and the virtual bankruptcy of the merchants who had depended on the Fair at Muros for their livelihood.

As the herds were gradually rebuilt, trade was again resumed, but has still not been fully restored to its former volume.

The current King of the Algars is Cho-Hag VII, a man of forty who appears to be an able ruler, though the council of the clans is reserving its judgement until he has reigned longer than the three years he has sat upon the horse-hide throne.

Appendix on the Vale of Aldur

NOTE: Information concerning the Vale of Aldur is limited and largely speculative. The reader should always be aware of this fact, and the information contained herein should never be used as the **sole** basis for policy decisions related to this area.

GEOGRAPHY

The Vale of Aldur is an area of forests and meadows lying along the upper reaches of the west fork of the Aldur River, nestling as it were in the fork or juncture of the eastern and western arms of the vast mountain range which forms the spine of the continent. It lies at a somewhat greater elevation than the grasslands to the north and receives more rainfall. It is, therefore, more heavily vegetated. It appears to be a pleasant, well-watered area, but is, so far as our investigators have been able to determine, uninhabited.

From time immemorial certain reports have come back from the area – usually from travelers who have lost their way, since the Algars steadfastly refuse to permit anyone to cross the Vale. Our informants advise us that there are in fact structures of various kinds in the Vale – structures of enormous antiquity. One Sendarian merchant who had wandered away from the South Caravan Route found himself in the Vale and discovered several moss-grown ruins in the Vale and, on the third day of his wanderings, came upon a huge stone tower with no visible door and reaching very high into the air – higher perhaps than the tallest tree. He was discovered there by a mounted Algar patrol who quickly escorted him back to the Caravan Route but refused to discuss the tower.

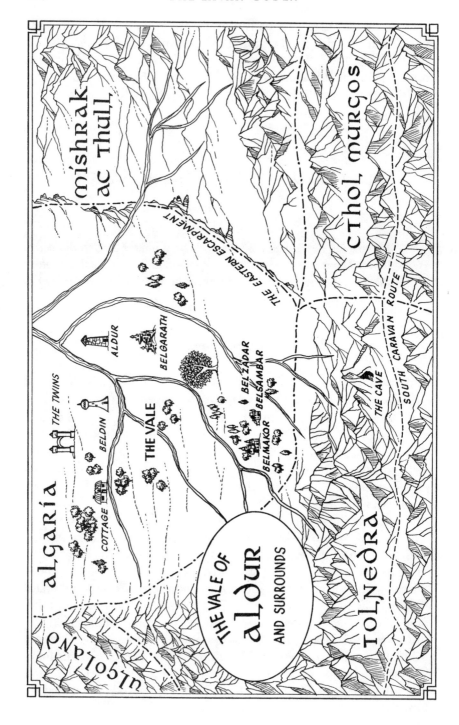

The folk-lore of certain rude and unlettered people makes mention of a 'Brotherhood of Sorcerers' which is supposedly headquartered in the Vale, but this can probably be discounted. The so-called Sorcerers, Wizards, Magicians and the like whom we have all seen either as solitary mendicant vagabonds or associated with traveling circuses are, of course, all charlatans whose 'magic' consists of a few crude sleight-of-hand tricks and a few common chemicals for altering the color of water. These tricks, while a source of amusement to the common people, hardly elevate their practitioners to the exalted status to which this folk-lore would assign them.

Since there is no hard evidence that the Vale is inhabited by a separate people, Tolnedra has long taken the position that the Vale is simply an integral part of Algaria. This is particularly evident since Algar horsemen patrol its borders. The ruins which supposedly dot the Vale cannot really be taken to represent the work of a non-Alorn culture, but rather must be viewed as a tantalizing archeological curiosity.

The University has frequently petitioned the Emperor to raise the question of permission for an archeological expedition into the Vale, but the Algars refuse to discuss it or even to admit that the Vale exists.

Algaria

COINAGE

Algars do not have coins.
Their standards are based on livestock
A horse (standard) is worth about $50
(good horses are more expensive)
3 cows make a horse
5 cow hides = 1 cow
Algars *do*, however, trade, using coins of other nations and free gold (nuggets and dust) panned from rivers and streams in the foothills.

COSTUME

MEN

All Algar outer garments are leather. Soft boots, baggy-legged trousers. Metal-studded vests (much like Tartars or Mongols) add in winter wool shirts, socks and under trousers. Also heavy wool capes.

Swords are curved (scimitars or sabers) lances and a short bow. Ropes are used (in conjunction with a lance-like pole – no lariats).

Armor – steel-plated leather coats, pot-like helmets with a chain-mail head and neck cover. Men's heads are shaved except for a long scalp-lock. Moustaches but no beards.

WOMEN

Same clothes as men. Hair worn in a pony-tail style.

COMMERCE

Strictly barter. Items needed by the clans are purchased by the Clan-chief and *bestowed* as gifts. Lively trade between clans in weapons, livestock (breeding stock usually) and useful items.

RANK

KING

Chief of the Clan-chiefs.

CLAN-CHIEFS

Tribal leaders members of the council of clans. 20 in all.

HERD-MASTERS
Heads of subclans, responsible for segments of the herd. Five or six to a clan.

WARRIORS
All Algar men are warriors. Even the women are war-like.

MODE OF ADDRESS

To the King 'Cho' an Algar word signifying chief of chiefs. Except for the King, all others are addressed by name and most courteously.

MANNERS

Algars tend to be a bit more formal than other Alorns. Elaborate etiquette about who eats first, seating, etc. Very touchy about insults. Gifts are the very heart of Algar social relations. Everybody gives gifts to everybody.

POPULATION

Scarcely more than 100,000 living in their wagon-cities.

HOLIDAYS

Erastide
Festival of Belar
Breeding time – Fall – gathering of clans for mingling herds
Dropping time – Spring – the calving and foaling
Algar's birthday

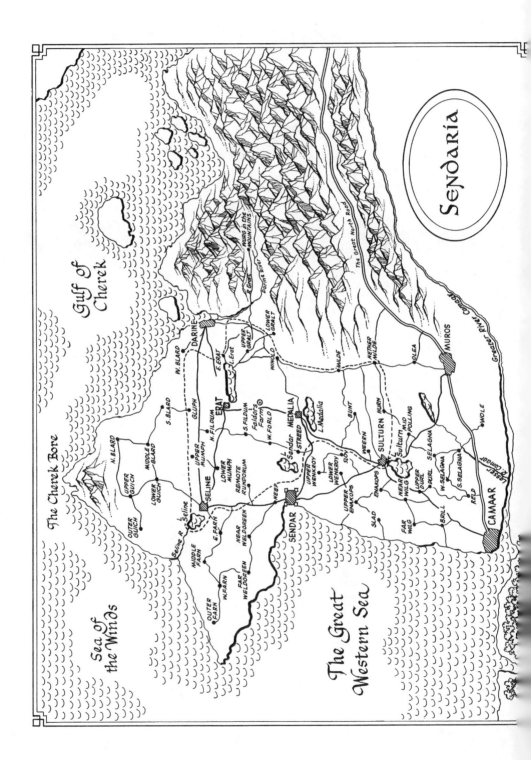

SENDARIA[*]

GEOGRAPHY

Sendaria, or the lake country, is one of the smallest of the twelve kingdoms. It lies on the northwest coast and encompasses those lands to the west of the Algarian grasslands and north of the Greater Camaar River. It is bordered by Arendia and Ulgoland to the south, Algaria to the east, the Gulf of Cherek to the north and the Sea of the Winds to the west. Although there are mountains along Sendaria's eastern side, they are largely uninhabited, and the bulk of the population lives on the fertile plain extending from their western slopes to the Sea of the Winds.

Because of the abundant rainfall and rich soil, Sendaria is the breadbasket of the western kingdoms, and her agricultural exports provide one of the pillars of commerce. Sendaria is also one of the more thickly-populated kingdoms. It is, above all, a tidy nation, with neat farms and well-scrubbed cities.

The population is largely dispersed, and there are more towns and villages in Sendaria than in the other kingdoms. The roads are well-maintained and provide a useful network for the rapid movement of farm produce to market.

The two major cities are Camaar, the major seaport of the north, located on the southern border at the mouth of the Camaar River, and Sendar, the capital, located on the coast just below the westward jut of the Seline Peninsula. Like most seaports, Camaar is a brawling, rowdy town, but Sendar is prim and proper and has a great respect for the civilities.

There are fairly extensive gold deposits in the mountains which have drawn generations of fortune-hunters who have added to the melting-pot nature of Sendaria.

---

[*] This section is more detailed because 'Our Hero' is raised in Sendaria and believes that he's a Sendar.

THE PEOPLE

Perhaps the best way to describe a Sendar is to repeat the old joke wherein one man asks another, 'What is a Sendar?' and the other replies by asking, 'Indeed, what is he not?' In truth, Sendaria, the crossroads of the north, is home to virtually every racial stock to be found in the west. Because of the enormous fertility of the land, settlers from every kingdom have found their way there. It is even possible in certain remote villages to find certain strikingly pure Angarak strains. The land is settled by Alorns from the northern king- doms, Arends and Tolnedrans from the south, and even an occasional Nyissan. To prevent the kind of bickering and even open bloodshed such a volatile mixture might very well engender, the Sendars have developed an elaborate and strictly-observed etiquette. No mention is ever made of a person's race or religion, and the open proselytizing on behalf of one's God is considered the worst form of bad manners. Sendars will discuss crops, weather, taxes and other practical matters, but will *never* discuss race or religion. They are hard-headed, practical, and their kingdom operates at a profit so that taxation (which they all complain about) is extraordinarily light. By some happy chance, the mingling of the peoples in Sendaria has produced a people with the best features of all races and few of the unpleasant characteristics. Like the Alorns, they are hardy and strong, but unlike them they are not quarrelsome or unduly boisterous. They have the bravery of the Arends, but not their melancholy or their touchy, stiff-necked pride. They have the business acumen of we Tolnedrans, but not (and let us be honest) our all-consuming urge to maximize profit which occasion- ally causes *some* Tolnedran merchants to enter into practices which are not – strictly speaking – ethical. Sendars, like Drasnians, are scrupu- lously honest, knowing that their fortuitous geographical location gives them tremendous advantage.

THE HISTORY OF SENDARIA

Unlike the other kingdoms of the west, Sendarian history does not begin in the dim and uncertain stretches of the distant past. Although the region has been inhabited since time immemorial and has been claimed at times by Arendia, Algaria, Cherek and even Tolnedra, the modern nation was *created*, if you will, by Emperor Ran Horb II of the first Horbite Dynasty in the year 3827 as an extension of Tolnedran policy in the north. By creating Sendaria, the Emperor established a buffer state between Algaria and Arendia, thus preventing the commercial advantage which would have accrued to the burgeoning Mimbrate mercantile families following the destruction of the Asturian Arends.

Without any genuine hereditary nobility dwelling in the area, the Sendars were compelled to hold an election, the first ever held in known history which involved *universal* suffrage. After tremendously long and involved arguments about property qualifications and the like for participating in the voting, the ever-practical Sendars decided to let everyone vote. When the question of women voting was raised, community leaders simply extended the vote to *everyone*. It is generally conceded that parents cast the ballots of their infant children, but this unique experiment appears to have come off with a minimum of election fraud.

Unfortunately, the first ballot produced 743 viable candidates with vote tallies ranging from eight for a northern farmer named Olrach to several thousand for a number of the more prosperous landholders around Lake Sulturn.

The balloting continued for six years and became a sort of national picnic. With enormous good humor, the Sendars continued to cast ballot after ballot until exhausted candidates began to withdraw their names in disgust.

Finally, on the twenty-third ballot in the spring of 3833 everyone was stunned by the fact that someone had actually received a slim majority. National leaders, election officials and a number of people who hoped for positions in the new court donned their finest garb and journeyed to a small farming village on the east side of Lake Erat in northern Sendaria. There they found their elected King, a rutabaga farmer named Fundor, vigorously fertilizing his fields.

The troop of notables trudged across the fields toward their new monarch, and when they reached him they greeted him with a great cry, 'Hail, Fundor the Magnificent, King of Sendaria,' and fell upon their knees in his August presence.

History mercilessly records the first words of the new King. They were as follows: 'I pray you, your eminences, have a care for your finery. I have just well-manured the bed you are kneeling in.'

The assembled notables, it is reported, rose quickly to their feet.

They discovered that Fundor's name had been placed in candidacy by his neighbors before the first ballot in order that they might have *some* recognition of their district in the tremendous proceedings. Fundor had believed that his name was no longer on the ballot after the first vote and was overcome to learn of his election. To cover his confusion, he invited the whole party into his kitchen for cakes and ale.

History reports that Mrs Fundor (who was to become Queen Anhelda) was none too gracious about a group of manure-smeared strangers in her kitchen.

A sooth-sayer who accompanied the throng pressed the new King for a prediction, believing as they all did that each word the King spoke that day would be of tremendous significance.

And the King spake thusly: 'I believe it's going to be a good year for rutabagas – if we don't get too much rain.'

The King and his family were rushed to the capital at Sendar where he was duly coronated and installed in the Royal Palace.

The rutabaga harvest that year, incidentally, failed miserably.

From that date no one has ever taken the Sendarian monarchy seriously – least of all the Sendarian monarchs. Remarkably enough, however, they are actually very good kings. They are just, even-handed and open, caring more for the welfare of the people than they do for their own pomp and prestige. They seem to all be possessed of a wry good humor that makes the court at Sendar a delight to visit.

Sendaria avoided the upheaval which shook the world at the time of the assassination of the Rivan King and continued her existence in uninterrupted tranquility and prosperity until the invasion of Kal-Torak in 4865. The Sendarian monarch at that time, Ormik the Warlike, raised an army of Sendars, a mismatched and motley crowd, neither infantry nor cavalry, with an odd assortment of weapons, and joined the forces marching south under the generalship of the Rivan Warder. They fought bravely, however, holding the center against repeated onslaughts of Malloreans at the Battle of Vo Mimbre.

Following the defeat of the Angaraks, Sendaria suffered a temporary economic decline as a result of the closing of the North Caravan
Route and the cessation of the cattle drives from Algaria to Muros
for the years which were required to restore the Algarian herds. The
decline of the Sendarian economy, however, was only temporary
and did not have the permanent and disastrous effects we witnessed
in Tolnedra.

The present monarch of the Sendars is Fulrach the Splendid, a
short, rather dumpy man in his mid-fifties who is, like his predecessors, an able administrator, but who has made no truly notable
achievement in the twenty years since he ascended the throne. He is
good-natured and soft-spoken and wears a short brown beard.

Sendaria

COINAGE

Because their kingdom was established by Imperial decree at a time
when Sendaria was dominated by Tolnedra, Sendarian coins are the
same as Tolnedran *except* the King's likeness is on the coins, and
Sendarian coins suffer a 5–7% discount due to impurities in the
metal. The term 'Sendarian' is a prefix to their coinage to distinguish
between their coins and Tolnedran.

Extensive presence of other coins in circulation.

COSTUME

Standard medieval. Jerkins, tabards, leggings, hose, caps, toques, shoes of soft leather. Hooded jackets, etc. among commoners. Stout capes for foul weather.

Women wear short-sleeved dresses. Headdresses for formal occasions. Kerchiefs for informal. Broad aprons.

All wear wooden shoes in muddy fields.

MERCANTILE CLASSES AND TRADESMEN
Wear clothing associated with their trade or long gowns and bag hats. Their women wear fine gowns, if they can. Young men tend to be a bit foppish – doublets, hose, fancy shoes and the long visored cap.

MEMBERS OF THE NOBILITY
Wear gowns trimmed with fur, hose, surcoats, woolen or linen shirts. On very formal occasions the chain-mail suit with surcoat, helmet and sword.

YOUNG MEN
Are quite foppish, hose, doublets, soft shoes or boots, small-swords (less than the broadsword but more than a rapier) similar to sons of tradesmen or merchants but richer, and the sword distinguishes them.

WOMEN
Wear the gown and the wimple. The high pointed hat. A great deal of bosom is displayed. A great deal of fancy cloth used. Hair is generally worn long in Sendaria. Variously coiffed. Women's garb is more likely to reflect the national heritage of the family than that of the men.

Except for the nobility, it is *not* standard practice in Sendaria to go about armed. Not illegal, but not customary.

SOCIAL ORGANIZATION

Status goes thus: Nobility, Mercantile, tradesmen, farmers, laborers.

It is considered bad manners to snub those of lower rank. Sendars are very polite to each other. The bulk of the land consists of free-holdings – privately owned farms. The large farmers (equivalent to an 18th century squire) have certain legal duties as well (as magistrates). They are called free-holders, a term of respect.

Sendaria is divided into Districts. Some are almost exclusively occupied by members of one racial grouping; others more homogeneous. Many towns and villages. Districts administered by an Earl (chief magistrate). Districts divided into Ridings. Ridings into Townships. These divisions are usually each associated with a town or village. Townsmen and villagers *tend* to look down on farmers.

Sendarian farmsteads are usually constructed in the central European defensive style (all walls facing out around a courtyard). Crofts are small, rented farms. Villagers often farm the nearby fields.

Churches are used in common by all religions – careful scheduling.

RANK

THE KING AND QUEEN
At the court in Sendar. By custom, they rule jointly.

THE EARLS
Chief administrators of Districts.

THE COUNTS
Chief administrators of Ridings.

BARONS
Chief administrators of a Township (sometimes) – not all Townships have Barons.

ASSORTED
Lords, Marquis, Viscounts, Baronets, Margraves, Knights, Dukes, etc. These are titles bestowed by the King for service or to honor excellent men. Some are hereditary, some are not. No one is quite sure which ranks higher, and Sendars are too polite to push it. These titles are usually bestowed on court functionaries. The work loaded on them far outweighs the honor of the title.

MODES OF ADDRESS

To the King and Queen – Your Highness, Your Majesty, Your Royal Highness.

To all other nobles – 'My Lord' or 'your Grace'. 'My Lord' used among nobles, 'your Grace' by commoners. The Unlettered sometimes say 'your Honor' not knowing what else to say.

To Burgers, Merchants or Free-holders – Title 'Merchant John', 'Free-holder Fred' or simply 'your honor'.

All other – 'Goodman'.

MANNERS

Sendars are extremely polite. (They are, after all, elemental Englishmen.) They have a great deal of interest in local affairs but are extremely provincial. They are hospitable. They treat their employees well. Wages and prices are set on all goods and services in the kingdom. They are watchful of strangers but are friendly.

The nobility is not haughty and, like the King, look upon their rank as a responsibility rather than a privilege. More father figures than masters.

They are hard-working and thrifty. The 'Free-holding' is a large (usually 100 acres or more) farm, neatly kept, and the farm buildings around the central court are extensive – a rabbit-warren of single rooms. Huge kitchens and a vast dining hall. *Many* workers on such a farm. Since room and board is part of the pay, not *too* much cash is involved in hiring a worker. There is an effort to have all useful arts represented on the free-holding – blacksmith, cobbler, cooper, wheelwright, carpenter etc. Married couples *usually* rent a croft and save up to buy their own free-holding.

Marketing is well-organized. Customary practice is for buyers to visit the town and village market places and some of the larger free-holdings. They bring their own wagons or rent those of independent wagoneers – a rowdy bunch. Hauled quickly to a major market, re-sold for delivery to places all up and down the west coast. Tend *not* to deal in extremely perishable goods – root crops, beans and moist-land grains – because of transit-time.

HOLIDAYS

Erastide – A *really* big thing in Sendaria – a two week orgy of gifts, feasts, dancing, jollity and sentimental good fellowship. Midwinter.

Sendaria Day – The date of the coronation of the first King. A big midsummer holiday. (4th of July.)

Blessing Day – A spring ritual. The blessing of the fields. Priests of most of the Gods go about with a big procession/following and bless the fields prior to planting.

Harvest Day – Celebration in the fall at the conclusion of the harvest (Thanksgiving).

RELIGIOUS OBSERVANCES

Priests of most religions in most communities (no Grolims). Observances are civilized and engender good-feeling. Friends will wait for each other to finish in the church before usual Sabbath frolics. (In actuality three Gods in Sendaria – Belar, Chaldan and Nedra. Very few Angaraks, no Marags – of course – and no Nyissans.)

POPULATION

Population about 3-4 million.

ARENDIA

GEOGRAPHY

Arendia is the heavily forested area lying between Sendaria to the north and Tolnedra to the south and stretching from the mountains, where it borders Ulgoland, to the Great Western sea. Vast fertile plains extend for hundreds of leagues in the southern and western reaches of the kingdom, and those plains are largely given over to the production of wheat. The mineral deposits in the eastern highlands have been largely undeveloped, but there is a thriving cottage industry in weaving and the inevitable black-smithery. There are – or rather *were* – three major cities in Arendia, Vo Mimbre, Vo Astur, and Vo Wacune. The latter two cities are uninhabited ruins now as a result of the savagery of the Civil Wars. Vo Mimbre is a grim fortress still bearing the scars of the vast battle fought there against the Angaraks of Kal-Torak. Of all the kingdoms of the west Arendia is certainly the most blessed by nature. Her dark and bloody history, however, proves that tragedy is possible even in the brightest of settings.

THE PEOPLE *

The Arends are the most stiff-necked people of the twelve kingdoms, intensely proud and with a vast sense of honor. While the common people appear to have normal sense, the nobility (as one

---

* Mandorallen and Lelldorin grew out of this segment.

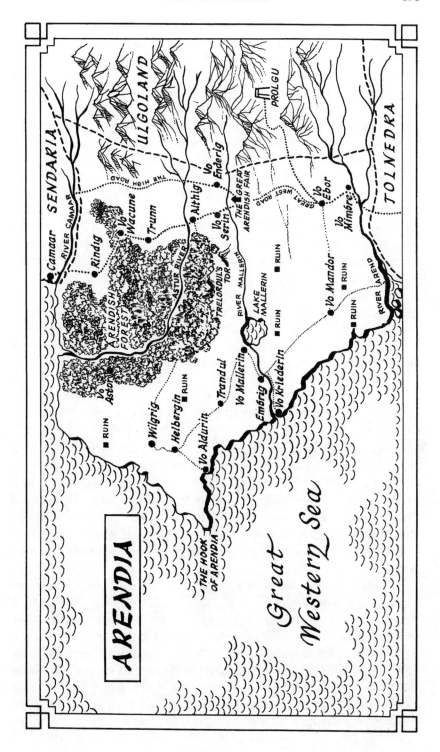

Tolnedran ambassador was wont to say) have minds unviolated by thought. The culture is the most fundamentally feudal and conservative in the west. The Arends are shorter and darker than the rangy blond Alorns to the north and show certain racial similarities to Tolnedrans and Nyissans. They are a humorless people with strong tendencies toward melancholy. Their songs are lugubrious accounts of lost battles and hopeless last stands against overwhelming odds – complete with lengthy casualty lists which include the genealogy of each of the slain. If the songs are to be believed, Arendish maidens are rampantly suicidal, casting themselves off towers or into rivers or plunging a variety of sharp instruments into themselves on the slightest pretext. Arendish men are savage warriors, but the Knights consider the most elemental tactics or strategy beneath their dignity. They are masters of the frontal attack and the last stand. The charge of the Mimbrate Knights at the Battle of Vo Mimbre was truly awe-inspiring, although its purpose was largely diversionary.

Cautionary note: Arends are *extremely* proud and sensitive. The tiniest slight, real or imaginary, will evoke anything from a blow to the side of the head up to and including a formal challenge to single combat – always fought to the death in Arendia. Only the most skilled diplomats should ever have dealings with these people.

THE HISTORY OF ARENDIA

Like the other peoples of the western kingdoms, the Arends migrated out of the east during the early centuries of the first millennium. By the year 2000, the three major cities, Vo Mimbre, Vo Wacune and Vo Astur existed in their present locations, and were the seats of three more or less rival Duchies. The Mimbrate house controlled the southern reaches, the Asturians the west, the Wacites the north. (The Wacite holdings were located primarily in what is now Sendaria.)

The institution of Knighthood among the Arends has always been a hindrance to the development of the kingdom. By the 23rd century, Arendia was dotted with castles, keeps, forts and strongholds. The entire energy of the nation has been devoted to war and the preparation for war, and Arendish Knights live in an almost perpetual state of armed conflict. The struggles between the contending Duchies is duplicated at the local level. A dispute over a pig or a broken fence can set neighbors at each other's throats, and because of the interlocking relationships between the various barons, earls, viscounts etc., these disputes spread rapidly and can, if unchecked, flare into open civil war.

The third millennium marked the period of Arendish expansionism. The Asturians solidified their hold on the west and, in a surprise move, fortified the southern bank of the Astur River against the Wacites and the southern edge of the great Arendish Forest against the Mimbrates, effectively cutting Arendia in two by extending a band of control from the borders of Ulgoland on the east to the sea on the west. The Mimbrates and Wacites naturally both declared war at that point, but the hastily-erected wooden blockhouses of the Asturians proved to be substantial enough to repel them. In point of fact, neither of the other Duchies could bring their full forces to bear on the Asturians since the Wacites were engaged in a war against Cherek in the northern reaches of Sendaria as a part of their grand plan to extend their power to the north and the Mimbrates were engaged in their centuries-long dispute with Tolnedra in *their* attempt to extend their influence to the south.

The Duke of Asturia then proclaimed himself King of Arendia (2618) and called upon his fellow Dukes to come to Vo Astur to pay him homage. It is difficult to determine if this maneuver by the Duke of Asturia was a clever ploy designed to infuriate the other two Dukes into a precipitous withdrawal from their foreign wars in order to attack him or if it was the result of sheer, arrogant stupidity. One is always tempted to believe the worst of an Arend, but we must look at the results rather than the appearance.

The war of the three kingdoms followed, lasting for approximately eleven hundred years. The Wacite and the Mimbrate Dukes each proclaimed *themselves* King of Arendia and issued royal commands similar to that made by the Asturian. Thus there were three kings in Arendia, all contending.

The Chereks quite naturally took advantage of the preoccupation of the Wacite Duke and bit off large pieces of northern Sendaria. Similarly, Tolnedran generals took the opportunity to push seriously weakened Mimbrate forces back beyond the River Arend, eliminating for the time the threat of Arendish invasion.

The war of the three kingdoms was one of the darkest periods in Arendish history. It was a time of alliances broken, of betrayal, of surprise attack, of assassination and ambush. One example should serve to illustrate. In 2890 the Asturians and Mimbrates had formed an alliance against the Wacites, who were dominant at that time. The expedition into Wacune was highly successful, and the Wacite nobility was virtually wiped out. In the latter days of the campaign in what is now south-central Sendaria, the Asturians suddenly turned on their Mimbrate allies and annihilated them. Thus, with one stroke, the Asturians had very nearly destroyed Wacune and had wiped out a major part of the Mimbrate Army. To defend themselves and to prevent the Asturian Duke from achieving the monarchy, the Mimbrates immediately formed an alliance with the remnants of the Wacites and concluded treaties with certain Cherek chieftains and some of the western clans in Algaria. These freebooters assaulted Asturia from the seaward and the landward side while the Mimbrates attacked her southern borders and the Wacites struck from the north. Asturia quite naturally collapsed and immediately formed an alliance with Wacune to attack the now-dominant Mimbrates.

As a result of constant attrition, the effect not only of the civil war but also of the ceaseless attacks by Cherek seafarers and Algar horsemen, the Wacite Duchy was finally so weakened that it was possible in 2943 for the Asturians to move decisively against their northern cousins at a time when the Mimbrates were preoccupied by a border war against Tolnedra. The campaign was short and brutal. Wacune was crushed, never to rise again. Vo Wacune was torn down, and all surviving members of the Wacite nobility were sold to Nyissan slavers, who carried them off to the south.

The savage destruction of Wacune by Asturia shocked the civilized world, and the weight of sympathy of other nations was firmly on the side of the Mimbrate Arends. The consolidation made possible, however, by the elimination of the Wacite nobility and the absorption of the Wacite serfs into the Asturian feudal system, made Asturia virtually impregnable for centuries.*

It must be candidly admitted, however, that through the closing centuries of the third millennium and throughout most of the fourth, it was a basic tenet of Tolnedran policy to maintain the balance of power between the contending Duchies of Mimbre and Asturia. From a practical standpoint, it was to the enormous advantage of the Empire to encourage the friction between the two contending houses, since a strong and unified Arendia would have made the development of the Tolnedran Empire an impossibility. It is of course a truism that the Arendish Knights are one of the most awesome forces in the west. Had the Arends been united at any time during the third or fourth millennia, the Empire would never have been, and the whole history of the west would have changed. The

---

* We expanded on the destruction of Vo Wacune at the beginning of *Queen of Sorcery* and during *Polgara the Sorceress*.

stalemate between Mimbre and Asturia lasted until 3793 when the
Mimbrates concluded a secret treaty with Tolnedra. In return for
certain military assistance from the Empire (largely the removal of
restrictions upon Cherek freebooters and Algar raiders and the
northward march of a column of ten legions from Tol Vordue toward
Asturia's southern border) the Mimbrates pledged a *limited* allegiance to the Tolnedran Emperor. This opportunity arose when the
continual warfare in Arendia had become a nuisance hindering the
construction of the Great West Road and an interference with
normal commerce.

The four-pronged attack against her so stretched the defensive
capability of the Asturians that their supply of manpower dried up,
and the nation collapsed into that most useless (and most typically
Arendish) defense – the retreat into fortified strongholds. The details
are gloomy and need not be repeated. The results were inevitable.
Asturia fell. Vo Astur was laid waste. The last Duke of Astur fell in
battle, and his family was all but exterminated. Asturia as a recog-
nizable nation was no more. It was, however, a weakened Mimbrate
Duke who was crowned the first unchallenged King of Arendia, and
the Tolnedran design in the west was complete. Arendia was no
longer a threat.

Although a Mimbrate King sat on the throne at Vo Mimbre, he was
in many respects a puppet-king – albeit a dangerous one. The most
elemental of the rights of sovereignty, that of conducting one's own
relations with other nations, was severely curtailed by the provisions of the Treaty of Tol Vordue. Arendish merchants were severely
limited in terms of what commodities and goods they could import
or export, and Tolnedra profited hugely from the arrangement.

The Kings at Vo Mimbre had other problems, however, which
did not give them time to brood about the possible injustices implicit
in their treaty with Tolnedra. Although the cities and strongholds

of the Asturians had been destroyed, the Asturian nobility and yeomanry remained intact – although greatly diminished. The nobles simply retreated into the vast reaches of the Arendish Forest, taking the always-loyal peasantry with them. What they could not carry off, they burned. Thus the Mimbrate King fell heir to a smoking wasteland, empty and unpeopled. The fiefdoms granted his loyal followers became a punishment instead of a reward, since land without the people to work it is a burden. Whole villages in the Duchy of the Mimbrates were uprooted and transplanted into the north to work the holdings of their feudal lords, and their efforts were largely to no avail since Asturian brigands crept from the forests by night, burning crops and villages with abandon. It was also observed that Asturian bowmen routinely used Mimbrate peasants for target-practice. This quite naturally caused the peasants to avoid the edges of those fields which abutted on the forest, and in time this grisly game developed in the Asturian bowman a capability of phenomenal accuracy at unbelievable ranges.

The activities of the Asturian outlaws provided the Emperor at Tol Honeth with the pretext for the formation of the Kingdom of Sendaria in the north, which stripped the Arendish King of a little more than a third of his nation. As the Emperor explained, 'Sendaria will close the northern door to these outlaws. You may hunt them down now without fear that they will escape to the north.' The King of the Arends received this with a glum face, since 'hunting down' well-armed men in a forest which stretches three hundred leagues in each direction is rather like hunting down fish in the ocean.

For a thousand years, however, Arendish Kings mounted expeditions against the Asturian brigands in the north. Whole generations were swallowed up in the dim, silent stretches of the forest, and old men woke screaming as they remembered the horror of the expeditions of their youth. The forest became a labyrinth of caves and tunnels and hiding holes. Dead-falls and pit-traps made the roads impassable. (The sole exception being the Great West Road which was patrolled by Tolnedran Legionaries and which the Asturians in a secret treaty with Tol Honeth had agreed to leave open.) Asturian archers, already the finest in the world, became even more proficient, and the floor of the forest was littered with mossy bones and rusting armor. Transplanted Mimbrate peasants plowed and planted, and the Asturians came out of the forest and reaped and gathered. Paradoxically, it was frequently necessary to import food into one of the most fertile places on earth.

The situation in Arendia remained unchanged until 4875 when

Kal-Torak came across the mountains of Ulgoland and down onto the Arendish plain. While it might have been expected that the Asturian Arends would simply hide in their forest and watch the destruction of the Mimbrates, such was not the case. Apparently the persuasive powers of the Rivan Warder were sufficient to move the Asturians to join with the Rivans and Sendars on their great march southward to the Battle of Vo Mimbre.

NOTE The battle of Vo Mimbre is the most celebrated event in the history of the twelve kingdoms. The details of the strategy, tactics and the individual heroism of various participants are too well-known to make their repetition here necessary. Elsewhere in these studies is a portion of the Arendish epic which deals with the battle. While the work is a bit overpoetic for Tolnedran tastes, it is nonetheless, a fairly straightforward account. In this respect it is unlike certain bardic productions which literally seethe with enchantments, magic and unseen monstrosities, all of which may be very well for the entertainment of children and illiterate peasants, but has no place in a work which strives to some seriousness.

At the conclusion of the Battle of Vo Mimbre, by unspoken mutual agreement, the Mimbrate King and the Baron who had led the Asturians through the final years of their endless war with the Mimbrates adjourned to a quiet dell just east of the city, and there, without preamble, they fell upon each other with their swords. By the time they were discovered, both were dying from innumerable wounds. The Mimbrate Knights and the Asturian Foresters would undoubtedly have resumed the eons-old bloodshed between them on the spot had it not been for the timely intervention of Brand XXXI, the towering Warder of Riva, who had just overthrown the mighty Kal-Torak. The enthusiasm of all the kingdoms of the west over his victory gave his word virtually the weight of law. Summoning both the Mimbrate and Asturian Barons before him, he quickly determined that the heir to the Mimbrate throne was a strong young man, and that the last descendant of the Asturian Duchy was a young maiden. He thereupon ordered that the two be married, thus joining the two houses in a unified monarchy and ending the war that had lasted for eons. When it was pointed out to him that a marriage between an Asturian and a Mimbrate was more likely to *cause* a war than end one, he instructed that the two young people be imprisoned alone together in a tower for the space of one year. This was done, and for the first several months the shouts of the two as they wrangled and argued could be heard for some distance. In time, however, the shouts subsided, and upon their emergence from the tower, the couple seemed quite content to marry and to rule jointly.

It is strongly suspected that this ploy was the invention of the two advisers of the Rivan Warder, a strange pair whom history has never identified. Both wore the traditional grey cloaks of the Rivans, but no distinguishing badges or crests. The man was grizzled and grey, and seemed quite fond of sharing a bottle or two with the common soldiery. The woman was strikingly handsome with an imperious presence. As one Tolnedran General remarked, 'She carries herself more like an Emperor than the Emperor himself.'

Following the unification of the two houses by the marriage of the Mimbrate Prince Korodullin and the Asturian Princess Mayaserana, the nation lived in peace and outward harmony. The Asturians returned to their lands and lived in relative peace with their Mimbrate neighbors. It was during this period that a rather intricate dueling code was developed whereby disputes could be settled directly between two contending parties without plunging entire districts into war.

The time of peace which followed unification profited Arendia enormously. Fortunes have been made from the abundant wheat harvests, and there has been a greater supply of good bread in the nations of the west than ever before. It is, however, characteristic of the people that much of this wealth has been poured into fortifications and arms. Apparently, Arendish nobles believe in their hearts that the peace is only temporary and, as always, they prepare for war.

The present King of Arendia, Korodullin XXIII, is a somewhat sickly young man who has sat upon the throne at Vo Mimbre for little more than a year.

NOTE It has been observed by certain breeders of livestock that a strain is severely weakened by too much inbreeding. It is unfortunately true that the touchy political situation in Arendia makes it mandatory that all members of the Royal Family of Arendia marry as closely within the blood-line as possible without violating the universal laws forbidding incest. The centuries of cousin-marriage have undoubtedly accentuated defects which would have been quite easily washed-out by the influx of new blood.

Arendia

COINAGE

Large numbers of gold and silver coins from the period of the civil wars of varying weights and purity. Practice is to weigh them and check extensive tables for value.

One of the provisions of the Treaty of Tol Vordue was that Arendia would use Tolnedran coins, which they do.

COSTUME

SOLIDLY MEDIEVAL
Because of the nature of the country, Arendish noblemen *never* leave home without being fully armed and at least partially armored – chain mail and surcoats inside wool or linen or fancier fabrics, elaborate robes, crowns etc.

ARMOR
Arends are a little heavier into plate armor than other nations – not quite the free-standing suit, but breastplates and strap-on guards over upper arm, forearm, thigh, shin, front of throat. Full visored helmets (not hinged). Weapons: swords, axes, maces, lances, etc., etc.

WOMEN

Very medieval. High waist. Pointed cap, etc. Lots of brocades, etc. *Heavy* cloth.

BURGERS

(Townsmen) Merchants. Guild-type hose, jackets baggy, tam-o'-shanters. Cloaks, robes, very elaborate marks of rank on robes etc.

SERFS

Usual serf-stuff, burlap, rags. Arendish serfs are badly downtrodden.

FORESTERS

(Asturians) Robin-Hood stuff. Nobles encumbered by their mail but they wear it.

COMMERCE

The Burgers *try*, but Arendish nobility is so stupid that they keep putting obstacles in the way. Needless embargoes, prohibitions on the removal of gold from the fiefdom, etc. Taxation is brutal in Arendia. Lots of smuggling and tax-evasion. Tax-collectors are frequently bushwhacked. (Standard item of apparel for tax-collectors is a thick, close-grained, and well-fitting plank under the mail to protect the back from arrows – not uncommon to see a tax-collector ignoring the two or three arrows stuck in his back.)

SOCIAL ORGANIZATION

Strictly feudal – vassals, serfs etc. Arch conservative. Nobility *very* uppity. Tremendous importance of HONOR. Code of dueling to avoid warfare. Formal meeting of Knights – charge with lances. The fight on foot afterward. (Considered bad form for a mounted man to attack a man on foot.) Usual King Arthur stuff.

Some degree of courtly love – all pretty formal.

Political marriages. Women bored to tears. Certain amount of fooling around. Poetry and romance have left Arendish women pretty senseless. Lots of suicides.

RANK

The King	Hereditary from the marriage of Korodullin and Mayaserana
The Dukes	The King's brothers and cousins
The Earls	Other members of the Royal Family
The Barons	Heads of other noble houses
The Viscounts	Their brothers and cousins
The Counts	Other members of those families
Lords	Feudal Lords of specific manors
Knights	Unlanded nobility
Burgers	Town dwellers with *some* substance
Freemen	Usually town laborers or craftsmen
Serfs	Bound to the land

MODES OF ADDRESS

King	'Your Majesty' (even the Queen calls the King this)
Queen	'Your Highness' (same – King calls her this)
Dukes and Earls	'Your Grace'
Barons	'Your Magnificence'
Viscounts and Counts	'Your Eminence'
Lords	'Your Lordship'
Knight	'Sir John'

MANNERS

Arends are formal to the point of being socially incapacitated. Their lives are so circumscribed by custom and the rigid social structure that their entire lives seem to be a kind of stately dance. Lots of bowing and formal address. Honor, which is to say good name, is everything and almost anything can be considered an affront. The period of the Civil War proves that they can be extremely treacherous, however. The major concern of the monarchy is to head off the Arendish tendency toward civil violence – no private wars. The King's time is taken up adjudicating disputes between the various nobles.

Vassals are suitably subservient *but* very proud, nonetheless. The commoners are servile, knowing that their masters have life or death power over them. Arendish justice is capricious and savage. Serfs are treated badly.

HOLIDAYS

Erastide – Formal banquets
Festival of Chaldan – Late Spring – the most religious holiday
Festival of Korodullin and Mayaserana – A combination of the celebration of the victory at Vo Mimbre and the unification of the nation
King's Birthday – A patriotic holiday – formal jousting
The Lord's Birthday – Local celebrations on each estate

RELIGIOUS OBSERVANCES

Pretty much medieval Catholic. Religious orders abound, supported by the nobility and providing an escape for the serfs. Usually established to provide perpetual prayer for victory of some lord. Three major orders – Mimbrate, Asturian and Wacite monks. (The monks are *never* molested in war – bad luck.)*

Female orders formed for similar purposes. Severely cloistered. They provide an outlet for surplus female children of the nobility.

Priests, Bishops and the head of the church, the Archbishop of Vo Mimbre.

---

* We largely ignored the Arendish church in the story. There were occasional references to monks and monasteries, but we saw no real purpose in getting too deeply involved in the intricacies of a religion resembling medieval Catholicism.

ULGOLAND*

GEOGRAPHY

Ulgoland (or simply Ulgo as the Ulgos themselves call it) is mountainous – indeed it consists solely of mountains. It is bounded on the east by Algaria, on the west by Arendia, on the north by Sendaria and on the south by Tolnedra. There are no known passes through the country, and the only road to the capital at Prolgu was built following the war against the Angaraks at the end of the fifth millennium. There appear to be large amounts of mineral wealth in Ulgoland, but the Ulgos steadfastly refuse to permit mining within their boundaries; and, since time immemorial, expeditions of adventurers into the country have vanished without a trace.

THE ULGOS

These are perhaps the strangest of all the peoples of the west. Not only do they worship a strange God, live in caves deep in the earth and speak a language unrelated to the civilized tongues of the north or the west, but they are also *physically* different from any other known race. They are significantly shorter than Alorn or Arend, and their skin is markedly pale – perhaps as a result of generations of cave-dwelling. Their hair is without color, and their eyes are quite

*This is almost entirely misconception – something on the order of those late medieval geographies which announced (in all seriousness) that the natives of Madagascar had a foot growing out of the tops of their heads.

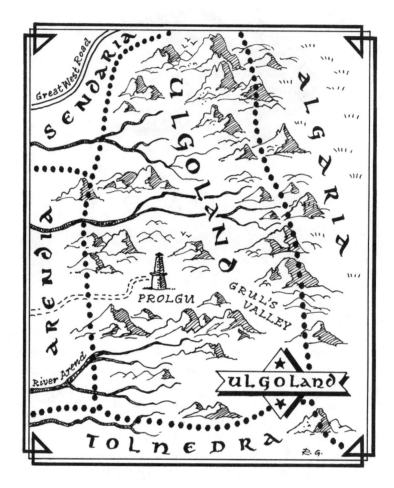

large and sensitive to light. The extent of their numbers is unknown since their habitations are below ground and no outsider has been able to determine the extent of the caverns and galleries beneath their mountains. They are a suspicious and secretive people and appear to be totally uninterested in commerce or trade.

THE HISTORY OF THE ULGOS

It is speculated that the Ulgos are the original inhabitants of the continent, although no known document records the first meeting between a civilized man and an Ulgo. It is generally agreed that civilized men migrated to this continent from the east sometime during the first millennium, at which time the original five kingdoms

(Aloria, Arendia, Tolnedra, Nyissa and Maragor) were established. It appears that the presence of the Ulgos predates that migration. Their secretive ways, however, makes it impossible to pinpoint specifics.

Because of the inhospitable nature of their country, few travelers entered their land during the first four millennia of the present era. Superstitious tales of hideous monsters who attacked travelers without warning were undoubtedly the result of systematic Ulgo terrorism designed to keep their country inviolate.

In more modern times a limited trade has been established, and following the battle of Vo Mimbre, a road was pushed through to Prolgu.

The first contacts with the Ulgos came about through the efforts of the Tolnedran trade negotiator, Horban, who was the personal representative and cousin of Emperor Ran Horb XVI during the decade of the 4420s. It was Horban who braved the legendary terrors of the Ulgo mountains and made his way to the forbidden city of Prolgu with only a small detachment of cavalry as an escort.

At first the Ulgos not only refused to negotiate but even refused to reveal themselves to him. For eight months he camped inside the walls of what appeared to be an abandoned city. He wandered about the moss-grown streets observing with amazement the incredible antiquity of the place.

Late one afternoon in the fall of 4421, Horban was astounded to find himself quite suddenly surrounded by a group of heavily cloaked and hooded men who took him prisoner and spirited him into a nearby vacant house. He was then taken into a cellar under that house, and a door in the floor was opened to reveal the vast, dimly lighted caverns beneath where the Ulgos reside.

Horban attempted to speak with his captors but without any success. The languages of the west are, of course, all members of the same linguistic family. Thus a Tolnedran may speak with an Alorn

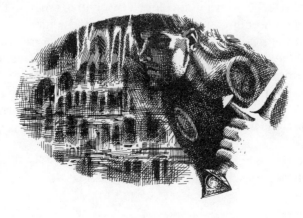

or an Arend or a Nyissan without significant difficulty; and, with great patience on each side, may even converse rudimentarily with an Angarak; but the language of the Ulgos is totally alien.

He was placed in a fairly comfortable chamber, given food and drink, and in time was visited by three very old men who attempted to converse with him. When they discovered that he could not understand them, they set about teaching him their language.

After two years of instruction, Horban was taken before the King, who by tradition is named UL-GO or given the title 'Gorim', apparently a term of respect.

The conversation between Horban and the Gorim of the Ulgos is remarkable not merely for what it reveals, but also for that it tantalizingly conceals. In his report to the Emperor, Horban provided the following summary:

The Gorim first demanded of the emissary what business he had in the land of the Ulgos and why he had desecrated their holy place at Prolgu.

Horban replied as diplomatically as possible that since the Ulgos chose to live beneath the ground, it was impossible for outsiders to even know that they existed. He described himself as an investigator sent to confirm or disprove persistent rumors about a people living in the mountains.

Then the Gorim asked how Horban had escaped 'the monsters', and would not elaborate on his cryptic question when Horban professed ignorance of any such creatures.*

And then, in open violation of the most fundamental tenet of good manners, the Gorim asked Horbin the name of his God. The question was so startling that Horban was able to quote it verbatim.

'And who is your God?' the Gorim said, his face stern. 'Is it he who cracked the world?'

Horban quickly realized that the Ulgos could not be held to an etiquette which had been developed by civilized men to forestall the inevitable wrangling and probable bloodshed which would accompany theological disputation and chose, therefore, not to take offense. He replied, as formally as possible, 'I have the honor, exalted one, to be a disciple of the Great God Nedra.'

The Gorim nodded. 'We know of him,' he said. 'The eldest save Aldur. A serviceable God, though a bit too stiff and formal for my liking. It is the third God, Torak, the maimed one, who is our enemy.

---

* Obviously, the Algroths, Hrulgin, and Eldrakyn, among others.

He it was who cracked the earth and unloosed the evil that bestrides the world above. Truly, had you confessed to the worship of Torak, would you have been carried to a pit and cast down into the sea of endless fire that lies infinitely far below.'

A shaken Horban had then inquired of the Gorim how it was that he appeared to have such intimate knowledge of the seven Gods. The response of the Gorim sparked a theological debate which has lasted for over 900 years. He said: 'We know of the seven Gods because UL has revealed them to us, and UL knows them better than any, since he is older than they.'

This simple statement was, of course, a thunderbolt which galvanized the theologians of all the western nations. They were immediately roused from their involuted efforts to each prove the superiority of *his* God and plunged into the most significant debate in five millennia. The fundamental question, of course, was: 'Are there seven Gods as we have always believed or are there eight?' If there are seven, then the Ulgos in heathen idolatry worship a false God and should be converted or exterminated. If there are eight and this mysterious 'UL' is *also* a God, then has he not been excluded from ceremonial offerings for over 5000 years? and ought we not propitiate him? And if there are eight, might there not be nine – or nine-hundred? Alorn theologians confirmed from *their* sacred writings that the God of the Angaraks, Torak, indeed *did* crack the world and that he *was* maimed. Fascinating as these questions are, it is not our purpose here to expound upon them. It is sufficient to note that the Ulgos are the source of the dispute.

At the conclusion of his discussion with the Gorim, Horban concluded a limited trade agreement which allowed two caravans per year to make the journey to Prolgu and to encamp in the valley beneath the city – a valley known by an Ulgo word which, translated, means 'where the monsters waited', a quaint term related to their mythology. At that time, the Gorim stated that those of his people who had the inclination might go there and view the goods of the merchants. When Horban pressed for more frequent caravans or even a permanent commercial community in the valley, the Gorim denied permission, saying, 'The limitation is for your own protection,' and refused to elaborate.

For the first hundred years, the trade with the Ulgos was woefully unprofitable. Many times Tolnedran merchants made the long and arduous caravan journey to Prolgu and waited the appointed three weeks without a single customer coming up from the depths of the earth to view their goods. Appeals to the Emperor to dispatch a military expedition to force the Ulgos up out of their caves so that the merchants might tempt them with their goods were largely ineffectual, since there was nothing in the treaty *requiring* the Ulgos to buy, and the city at Prolgu, situated as it is on the top of a sheer mountain, is perhaps one of the most totally unassailable places in the world. As one Ranite Emperor said, 'I could pour the wealth and young manhood of the Empire into those barren mountains and gain nothing thereby.'

In time our caravans grew smaller and were frequently unaccompanied by troops, and occasionally they disappeared without a trace. The Ulgos vaguely mentioned 'monsters', but refused to elaborate.

During the invasion of the Angaraks in the 4860s and 70s, the Algar cavalry and Drasnian infantry elements which closed in behind the enemy on the way to the battleground before the Arendish city of Vo Mimbre were startled by the sudden emergence from their caverns of thousands of curiously armed Ulgos, all, as usual, hooded and with their faces and eyes veiled against the light.

It is evident that there is some eons-old dispute between the Ulgos and the Angaraks, the origins of which are lost in antiquity. The Algars and Drasnians soon had no difficulty in following the Hordes of Kal-Torak, since the trail was littered with the bodies of the unfortunates whom the Ulgos systematically ambushed. Because of the sensitivity of their eyes to the light, Ulgos function best at night, and the toll they took of the sleeping Angaraks was ghastly.

At the Battle of Vo Mimbre, the Ulgos participated in the assault upon the Angarak left with the Algars and the Drasnians. When they shed their robes and hoods for battle, they revealed the traditional armor of the Ulgos, a curious leaf-mail, shaped much like the scales of a serpent and overlapping in such fashion that it is virtually impenetrable. The armor is colorfully referred to as 'dragon-skin'. During the battle, the Ulgos displayed uncommon valor, closing savagely with the much larger Murgo warriors who held the left flank; and after the battle when darkness had fallen, Ulgo warriors roamed the battlefield making certain that no wounded Angarak escaped.

When things had returned somewhat to normal following the war, limited trade was resumed, but the Ulgos have retained their secretive ways.

The current Gorim of the Ulgos appears to be extremely ancient, though the dimness of the light in their caverns makes such fine distinctions difficult. The mode by which the Ulgos choose their Gorim or how far back into the dim reaches of the past the line extends are questions, of course, which are likely never to be answered.

Ulgoland

COINAGE

Ulgos do not use coins, but rather barter for items both useful and ornamental. Ulgo jewelry is so exquisite and so finely wrought that it is nearly priceless in the west. They will also trade in raw gold and silver and in cut and uncut gems.

COSTUME

Standard garments – linen pajama-like affair. Hooded cloaks of the coarse cloth. All dyed quite dark.
Linen – cloth (wild flax gathered near cave-mouths).
A coarse cloth woven from the fiber of a tree bark similarly gathered.
Soft leather – deer-hide taken by nocturnal Ulgo hunters.

Personages wear robes – quite heavy – one solid piece. White.

Armor – overlapping, diamond-shaped steel scales sewn to leather. *Weapon* – the knife – designed and perfected by Ulgo craftsmen – quite ornamental with lots of hooks and saw edges. Long ice-pick. Short-handled picks with needle points, etc. *Women* wear soft robes. Hair is elaborately plaited. Jeweled head-bands.

COMMERCE

Strictly barter in useful goods or in services. Ulgos *do* have fields, planted and harvested at night. Planted at random so as to be unde-tectable. They also hunt meat – meat is a rarity in the Ulgo diet. Lots of root vegetables, grains and nuts.

SOCIAL ORGANIZATION

Ulgo society is a theocracy. The Gorim is a Moses figure, a lawgiver and a judge. People divided into tribes. Elders of the tribes advise the Gorim. Scholars study the writings of the original Gorim – a very Jewish society in that respect.

Ordinary people live in chambers cut out of the stone along the various galleries in the vast limestone caves.

Note: The caves of the Ulgos are naturally heated by geothermal forces. Cooking is with small coal fires. Smoke and fumes are carried off in cunningly constructed vents. Light provided by tiny oil lamps or by refracted surface light (through glass prisms).

Ulgo society is totally involved with religion. Much time is taken up with prayer. Prophecy and the casting of Auguries is enormously important. Upon special dates certain special openings with special glass prisms allow the light of certain stars to enter the caverns, colors and shadows are then interpreted. (Ulgos are masters of primitive optics because of their work in glass.)

They also have extensive knowledge of 'the monsters' and know how to deal with most of them.

They are not prolific. Many restraints on population. Infant mortality is quite high among them. A static, unmoving society with no real hope of growth. Philosophical, somewhat melancholy. Much emphasis on scholarship, study and attaining holiness or righteousness – a mass effort at attaining sainthood – Essene, possibly. Religious ecstasy or religious excess common. Hermits in the farthest caverns. (Ulgo artifacts are so beautiful because they are the work of zealots.)

The Ulgo Holy Books are the Journals of Gorim kept on his quest in search of the God UL. These rather pedestrian daybooks have been elevated into something mystical. Holiness is often predicated on some new and unusual interpretation of a quite ordinary event. *The Book of UL-GO* is a much later poetic version of the original *Daybooks of Gorim*. There have been internecine wars in the caverns of the Ulgos over interpretation of certain obscure and delirious passages from Gorim's journals. A totally closed and inward-looking society EXCEPT for their universal hatred of Torak, the one whose action condemned them to the caverns.

UL-GO theology is split rather violently. One branch holds that the caves are what UL intended. The others that a deliverer shall come and destroy Torak and the Ulgos will be allowed to return to the surface.

RANK

The Gorim – High priest and King.
Oldmen – Leaders of each tribe.
Tribal Elders – Seven in each tribe. Seven tribes of Ulgos – fairly significant racial differences between them.
The priests of UL – very numerous.

The selection of Gorim, Oldmen and Elders is a process that is part election, part prophecy, part lottery and part gut-feel. The Gorim is *not* hereditary. No one but an Ulgo can understand the process. Age is very important in the selection.

MODES OF ADDRESS

To the Gorim – 'My Gorim', 'Holy One', rarely, 'Holy UL-GO'
To the Oldmen –'Beloved of UL', 'Wisdom'
To the Elders – 'Righteousness', 'Selected of UL'
To the Priests – 'Master'
To the Scholars – 'Learned One'
To the Commoners – 'ULGORIM John' – meaning approximately 'Just
  and righteous in the sight of UL'

MANNERS

Quite formal modes of address. A great deal of formula recitatif
and response in conversation. 'Great is the power of UL' – 'All praise
the name of UL'. Entire conversations can consist of stereotyped
phrases. Personal chambers are *absolutely* private. Temples are
huge chambers. Ulgos attend religious services daily. Work in open
galleries on studies, art-work, crafts, etc.

People are strangely apart from each other.

HOLIDAYS

The Day of Acceptance – The day UL accepted Gorim – the Holiest
  Day
The Day of Despair – When Gorim went to Prolgu and cursed his life
The Day of Following – The day the few followed Gorim.
Also some 130 other observances of key dates in the Journals of
  Gorim

POPULATION

Population – perhaps 750,000 total

NYISSA

GEOGRAPHY

The kingdom of Nyissa lies on the southern boundary of Tolnedra, below the River of the Woods. It is bounded on the west by the waters of the Great Western Sea and on the east by the low range of mountains which mark the doorstep of the vast, uninhabited wilderness of western Cthol Murgos. The southern boundaries of the kingdom are quite indistinct, since there are only trackless jungles in that quarter. It is the claim of the Nyissan court at Sthiss Tor that Nyissa *has* no southern boundary but continues on to the southern edge of the world, but few take such grandiose claims seriously, since no kingdom can with any authority claim lands which it cannot occupy.

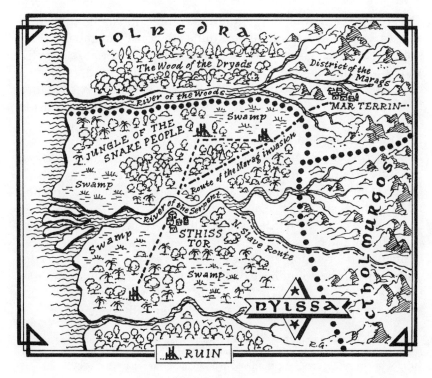

For the most part, Nyissa is densely forested, enveloped as it were in a vast, trackless, sub-tropical jungle. The land is marshy and the soil extremely fertile. Despite this, farming in the land of the snake people is minimal. The vast effort required to clear and maintain fields appears to be beyond the capabilities of the somewhat sluggish inhabitants.

The capital at Sthiss Tor would seem to be the only city of any size in the entire kingdom, although it is difficult to verify this, since the Nyissans, always secretive, forbid travel by foreigners into the hinterlands. Casual observation, however, indicates that the bulk of the citizenry reside in small villages usually located on or near the major river system of the country, aptly named the River of the Serpent. No hard evidence exists of any significant mineral deposits in the kingdom, but again, this is impossible of verification.

Sthiss Tor itself is a large, well-fortified stone city some eighty leagues up the River of the Serpent. It is considered a hardship post by members of the Tolnedran diplomatic corps because of the pestilential climate.

THE PEOPLE

The Nyissans are similar in stature and complexion to the Tolnedrans and Arends, and are, therefore, quite obviously members of the same broad racial group. As observed previously, they are a secretive and somewhat indolent people, difficult to know and even more difficult to like. Their worship of the Serpent-God, Issa, has led them to adopt certain reptilian mannerisms which most outsiders consider repugnant.

While the nation is referred to as a kingdom in conformity with the practice in other western countries, this designation is not precisely accurate, since the ruler of the Nyissans has always been a Queen. The traditional name, Salmissra, appears to have no particular hereditary significance, and the process by which successors are chosen is a closely guarded secret intimately involved in the religious life of the Nyissans, since the Queen is also the high priestess of the national religion.[*]

Because of the abundance of strange flora in the Nyissan jungles, the snake people have developed a vast lore having to do with herbal compounds and drugs, and it is generally believed, though

---

[*] Salmissra is modeled in part on Cleopatra, obviously, and Nyissan society is to a degree Egyptian, though not entirely. In the Belgariad the Nyissans are incomprehensible villains, but in the Malloreon Sadi proved to be an important character, as did Zeth.

probably erroneously, that the entire nation is addicted to one or the other of these compounds. The drugs *do*, however, play a significant part in Nyissan religious observances. It is also unfortunately true that one of the sidelines of Nyissan pharmaceutical experiments has been the development of a vast range of poisons and toxins which have intruded upon occasion into the politics of Tolnedra. The removal of a political adversary in Tolnedra has always been too simple a matter largely because of the lamentable proximity of the Nyissan border.

Sadly, the basic industry of Nyissa has always been the slave-trade. The battlefields of the wars and insurrections of the west have for thousands of years been haunted by Nyissan slavers. They are indeed sometimes as prevalent as ravens. Although the trade is generally condemned, captives without the means to afford ransom all too frequently end up in chains on Nyissan slave ships. The fate of these unfortunates is unknown, but since the Nyissan slavers almost invariably pay for their goods and supplies with Angarak gold (which has a distinctive reddish cast by reason of the iron deposits in the vicinity of the mines of Gar og Nadrak and Cthol Murgos), it is generally assumed that the ultimate destinations of the slaves are the Angarak Kingdoms to the east. One shudders at the thought of what may happen to them once they fall into the hands of the Grolim priests in those dark lands.

THE HISTORY OF THE SNAKE PEOPLE

Because of the secretive nature of the Nyissans, attempts to gather historical data about them are extraordinarily frustrating. Indeed, beyond a few cursory facts, most of which came to light during the Alorn invasion of 4002-3, little is actually known about the country's history.

Generally it is assumed that the Nyissans were a part of the vast westward migration which took place during the first millennium, at which time were also established the kingdoms of Aloria, Arendia, Maragor and the Empire of Tolnedra.

It is a commonplace to observe that history is a by-product of war, and with the exception of the Alorn invasion mentioned above and a legendary conflict between Nyissa and Maragor late in the second millennium, the Nyissans have had almost no conflicts with the other kingdoms of the west.

The causes of the Maragor–Nyissa war are shrouded in the mists of antiquity, and what few actual records we have of the conflict are at best fragmentary as a result of the excessive zeal of Tolnedran soldiery during the extirpation of the Marags in the third millennium. What remains is a sketchy body of reports, requisitions, diaries and the like which provide a shadowy outline of the conflict and little else.

Whatever the unknown cause was, it appears that the Marags considered themselves the offended side, and the mounting of their expeditionary force was something in the nature of a holy crusade.

At any rate, during the mid-nineteenth century, Marag columns struck down across the northeastern frontier of Nyissa and plunged toward Sthiss Tor, 250 leagues to the west. Field commanders reported the existence of broad highways through the jungles and mighty cities which were besieged and pulled down. While some of this may be shrugged off as primitive exaggeration, it must be conceded that there may indeed be some grain of truth in those reports. Tolnedran expeditions into northern Nyissa following the Alorn invasion of the fifth millennium noted the existence of vast, jungle-choked ruins* and barely perceptible highways through the dense growth. Whatever the truth may be, the Marags pressed on, pausing only to violate Nyissan temples and to perform their own disgusting rites upon the altars of the Snake God.

* An obvious reference to the ruins of Angkor Wat in Cambodia.

At the approach of the Marag columns, Queen Salmissra and her retinue fled the city of Sthiss Tor and sought refuge in the jungles to the south. The Marags found that they had conquered an empty city surrounded by unpeopled fields.

At that time occurred one of the most monstrous incidents in the history of warfare. After the Marags had occupied the city for perhaps ten days, the soldiers began to sicken and die in alarming numbers. The frantic pleas for food sent back to Maragor by field commanders camped in the midst of a fertile plain burgeoning with unharvested crops provide poignant substantiation to what had taken place. Before their evacuation of the city, the Nyissans had systematically poisoned every scrap of edible food in the vicinity of the capital. They had even, by means known only to them, poisoned fruits and vegetables while they still hung from trees or nestled in the fields. Such cattle as were left for the Marags had, with a technique that staggers the imagination, been poisoned in such a way that, while the cattle remained healthy, all who ate their flesh died.

A decimated and delirious column of the few pitiful survivors stumbled out of the jungles and back to Maragor, leaving their trail littered with the bodies of their dead.

While it is conjecture only, it is fairly safe to assume that the lessons of the Marag invasion were not lost on the Nyissans. The highways (if indeed they were highways) provided easy passage through the jungles for invading troops, so they were permitted to fall into disuse, and the jungles reclaimed them. Since the Nyissans are not a prolific people (their use of drugs inhibits reproductive activity severely), large cities simply provide larger concentrations of people to fall victim to surprise attack, and the limited population can be severely depleted by only a few such attacks. Thus, it became in all probability a matter of state policy to disperse the population broadly in small cities and towns and even villages – except for the capital, of course.

And so it is that we see the truth of the adage; history *is* the product of war. Had there been no Marag invasion, Nyissa might well have developed along entirely different lines. Cities might have arisen and the jungle been cleared, but it was not to be. The motto which appears above the door of the throne-room of Queen Salmissra in Sthiss Tor speaks volumes: 'The Serpent and the Forest are one.' The jungles of Nyissa are the refuge and the defense of the snake people, and we must not expect that they will ever be cleared.

During the reign of Ran Horb II of the First Horbite Dynasty (sometimes referred to as the architect of Empire), a sustained effort was made to conclude the customary trade agreements with the Nyissans. Vordal, a noble of the Vordue line of the Imperial Family was entrusted with the delicate task of negotiating with Queen Salmissra. His reports provide graphic and chilling details of the lethal intrigues which prevail in the Nyissan Court. Each noble, functionary or priest normally employs a sizeable staff of herbologists and chemists whose sole purpose is the distillation, compounding and mixing of new poisons and antidotes. A break-through by one of these professional poisoners is usually marked by the sudden and frequently ghastly deaths of all members of an opposing faction. Since most Nyissan politicians are able, as a result of heavy preventive dosing with all known antidotes and a brutal regimen of desensitization involving the eating of gradually increased amounts of the toxins themselves, to ingest quantities of poisons sufficient to fell a legion, the new poisons which are developed are of terrifying potency.

Vordal reports that Queen Salmissra watched these lethal games with a reptilian amusement, not even turning a hair when her most trusted advisor quite suddenly turned black in the face, fell to the floor in violent convulsions and died frothing at the mouth like a mad dog. Nyissan Queens learn quite early to develop no permanent attachments. Their training is so rigorously bound by eons-old tradition and their lives so circumscribed by ritual that there is very little in the way of appearance or personality that distinguishes one Queen from her predecessors or her successors.

At long length Vordal was able to conclude the treaty with the Nyissans, a difficult task since frequently the negotiator with whom he was dealing died quite suddenly in the midst of the most sensitive negotiations. The treaty provided for a commercial compound near the docks at Sthiss Tor, and Tolnedran merchants were rigidly restricted to that compound. While it is certainly not the best treaty ever concluded, the Nyissans' seemingly inexhaustible supply of good red Angarak gold makes it easier to put up with the restrictions. Further, the Nyissans' phlegmatic turn of mind renders them indifferent to the intricacies of bargaining, and they will generally pay without question any price that is asked. Thus it is that trade with the snake people is highly profitable, but few if any Tolnedran merchants are ever comfortable in Sthiss Tor. Most will limit themselves to two or three voyages up the River of the Serpent. The profits are enormous, but there is something about the Nyissans that compels even the greediest to soon depart.

The most celebrated event in the history of Nyissa was the Alorn invasion in 4002–3 as a result of the Nyissan assassination of the Rivan King, Gorek the Wise. The motivation behind this apparently senseless act has never been fully disclosed, although the Alorn Kings were able to extract it in detail from Queen Salmissra XXXIII before she died. It is generally assumed that there was Angarak involvement in the plot, but why the Angaraks would hold such enmity toward the monarch of a remote island is unclear. Beyond this, one wonders what could conceivably have been offered to a Nyissan Queen to purchase her cooperation.

Whatever Salmissra's motives, the act was indisputably hers, and the Alorn retribution was swift and terrible. As previously discussed, the combined forces of Cherek, Drasnia, Algaria and the Isle of the Winds made quick work of the Nyissans. Following their victory, the Alorns systematically and savagely destroyed the entire nation, tearing down the towns and burning the villages. All Nyissans who fell into their hands were ruthlessly put to the sword. Once again it was only the jungles that prevented the snake people from being totally exterminated.

So brutal had been the destruction of Nyissa by the Alorns that for five hundred years and despite frequent searches by Tolnedran expeditions, no sign was visible that any Nyissans survived the holocaust. Then, and only gradually, did the snake people emerge from the jungles to begin timidly rebuilding the capital at Sthiss Tor. Amazingly, it appears that the Queen continued to dominate Nyissan life even though her people had been scattered to the winds. Queen Salmissra LXXIII emerged from the jungles as imperious as had been her predecessors and so closely resembling the face on ancient coinage that many had the eerie feeling that she was the same woman.

The cause for this resemblance, however, had come to light during one of the Tolnedran expeditions into Nyissa following the Alorn invasion. In the vicinity of the capital were discovered several stately houses, each identical to the others, and in the sealed central hall of each house were discovered the skeletal remains of nineteen youthful females. Remnants of clothing indicated that all were identically dressed, and the remains were all precisely the same height. In the surrounding rooms were the remains of numerous other Nyissans as well – some in the garb of servants, others in the robes of priests. The reason for the unbroken line and the uncanny resemblance of each Queen to all who had passed before her became abundantly clear. At a certain stage in the life of a Queen, a search was made of the country to discover twenty young women who closely resembled her. At the time of the old Queen's death, one of the twenty was chosen to succeed her. The rest were summarily put to death, along with their servants, teachers and priests, in order to prevent any effort to supplant the chosen one. In this manner, the Queen is made secure, and the line of succession is guaranteed.

Since their one excursion into the realm of international affairs ended so disastrously, the Nyissans have remained steadfastly neutral. Much concern existed in the Imperial court at Tol Honeth during the invasion of the Angaraks under Kal-Torak in the 49th century over the possibility that a second column of Angaraks and Malloreans might be proceeding secretly through the jungles of the snake people to strike across Tolnedra's southern border and thus crush the west in a vast pincer movement. Given the proximity of Nyissa to the western reaches of Cthol Murgos and the peculiar relationship of the snake people with the Angaraks, this possibility was all too real. As a result, Imperial legions fortified the northern banks of the River of the Woods, and the bulk of Tolnedra's forces were moved to the south and garrisoned at Tol Borune and at Tol Rane in order to counter any such attack. Despite fearful casualties, continuous patrols probed northern Nyissa for any evidence of the expected Angarak approach.

Queen Salmissra vigorously protested the Tolnedran violation of the territorial integrity of her realm, but was put off with a series of diplomatically worded notes from the Emperor himself.

In the end, of course, the expected second front failed to materialize, and we must concede that the diversion of the thirty-seven legions to the south weakened Tolnedra's ability to participate in the decisive Battle of Vo Mimbre and may in some measure have contributed to the humiliation of the Empire in the infamous accords which followed that battle.

Following the Angarak war, Nyissans have again resumed the slave-trade, although the relative peace which has prevailed in the west since that upheaval has severely limited the number of captives available to them. A few years after the war, Nyissan merchants began buying up foodstuffs in the west, always paying the highest prices. This sudden change contributed noticeably to the food shortage resulting from the destruction of the Algarian herds. It is suspected that the Nyissans were acting as agents for the Murgos, and that the food shortage had spread virtually across the entire continent.

In recent years, Nyissan traders and merchants have been much in evidence in all parts of the west even more so than during the short period of Nyissan commercial dominance as a result of the closing of both the North and the South Caravan Routes. As always, the motives of the Serpent Queen in Sthiss Tor are a mystery.

The present Queen, Salmissra XCIX, appears to be a somewhat more strong-minded ruler than have been many of her precursors who were merely pawns in the control of various court functionaries. Her age, of course, is indeterminate as a result of the use of certain closely guarded herbal compounds reserved for her alone which have the apparent capability of retarding or halting entirely the more visible ravages of the aging process.

N O T E From time immemorial there have been rumors, myths, legends, folklore and a good deal of just plain nonsense circulated about the Nyissan Queen. Many of these are too ludicrous or grotesque to bear repeating. One story has her the same original Salmissra who is restored every so many years to youth and beauty by feeding, vampire-like upon various sacrificial victims. There is often gross speculation about her sex-life – one group contending she is a virgin, another contending that she is driven by the drugs she uses into abnormal sexual voracity, yet a third contending that as high priestess of snake cult she couples only with serpents.

Quite obviously, most of this is too ridiculous to merit refutation. These facts we know: The Nyissan Queen has never been observed to have had children. The Nyissan Queen has never been observed to have had a husband. From this we must conclude that she is required to maintain the **appearance** at least of celibacy during her reign. Any other speculation is sheer waste of time and quite certainly is no area of investigation for any proper scholar.[*]

Nyissa

COINAGE

Nyissan coins are triangular, and their weights are not exact (Nyissans routinely shave the edges of coins)

---

[*] So much for 'prissy'.

GOLD

'The Golden Queen' a 5 oz. double triangle with a likeness of
　Salmissra in each quarter worth about $625.00
'Golden Half Queen' 2½ oz. triangle worth about $312.50
'Golden Quarter Queen' 1¼ oz. triangle worth about $156.25

SILVER

Silver Queen – 5 oz., worth about $31.25
Silver Half Queen – 2 ½ oz., worth about $15.62
Silver Quarter Queen – 1¼ oz., worth about $7.81

COPPER

A large triangular piece worth about 50 cents

COSTUME

Nyissan city dwellers wear loose robes of lightweight silk embroi-
　dered and decorated. In the country, shorter robes.
Nyissan men shave their heads.
Nyissan women wear elaborate and somewhat revealing gowns, lots
　of jewelry and a serpent crown. The fabric of her gown is almost
　transparent. Hair worn Egyptian-style. All body hair removed.
Armor – such as it is – chain-mail vest.
Weapons – short, poisoned knives, short bows with poisoned arrows.
Ceremonial swords and long-handled axes like Halberd.

COMMERCE

Nyissans are much into commerce. A great deal of profit is made in
slaves and in trade. They seem indifferent to the finer points of
haggling because the Angaraks pay so much for slaves (a form of life

insurance). Nyissans are deceitful and not above giving short-weight and adulterating the product. They don't trust each other much.

SOCIAL ORGANIZATION

Again a theocracy. Salmissra is not only Queen, but also is high priestess. She is supreme, but the court functionaries wield a great deal of power. Court is rather like a cross between Egyptian and Chinese. Many functionaries are eunuchs. The Queen's whim is law, thus everyone tries to stay on her good side to protect himself. Very political, very conniving, Byzantine.

Commoners are simply laborers, but slaves do all the heavy work. (Slaves have their tongues removed.)

RANK

THE QUEEN
Supreme Queen and High Priestess.

THE HIGH PRIESTS
Pretty heavy in the temple but not so much at court.

THE HIGH CHAMBERLAIN
The Queen's chief Advisor – depending on the Queen, this is the one who more or less runs the country. Most Queens are preoccupied with their own diversions and he has full rein. A few, however, have been strong-minded enough to run things themselves.

ASSORTED FUNCTIONARIES OF THE COURT
These are, in effect, bureaucrats who handle various aspects of government. Much jealousy and bickering and so forth.

MODES OF ADDRESS

The Queen – 'Eternal Salmissra', 'Beloved of Issa'
The High Priests – 'Most High'
The High Chamberlain – 'My Lord High Chamberlain'
Others at Court – My Lord this or that (Title)
Commoners – Called by name only
Slaves – 'You' or 'Slave'

Note on the Queen: The drug she takes to keep her perpetually young is also a powerful aphrodisiac, and since she must dose with it daily, the Queen is in a perpetual state of sexual arousal. (It also inhibits – prevents – pregnancy.) It is this that makes most Queens docile. They are too busy satisfying their lusts to have time for government. Part of the duties of court functionaries are to service the Queen. She also keeps a stable of slaves for this purpose. Other drugs make them unnaturally potent.

Note on Drugs: The antidotes to the various poisons are usually addictive. Thus most Nyissans are addicts – euphoric and some-times half-asleep. These addictions are what hold down the Nyissan birth-rate. The men are too doped-up to be much interested in sex. Nyissan women frequently turn to slaves for satisfaction, and lesbianism is quite common.

MANNERS

Elaborately formal. No open hostility. Hissing is considered a sign of respect.

HOLIDAYS

Erastide – Not all that important in Nyissa
Day of the Serpent – Issa's Birthday
Day of Salmissra – Traditional birthday of the Queen
Festival of the Poison Ones – The day when Salmissra kisses a cobra –
   (a special drug she takes makes her odor pleasing to the snake so
   that he will not bite).

RELIGIOUS OBSERVANCES

Lots of snake-stuff – snake handling, etc. Day of the Serpent – a naked group-grope in the temple in company with a lot of non-venomous snakes. Pet snakes are household gods. Etc., etc.

POPULATION

About 2 million Nyissans. 250,000 in Sthiss Tor.

THE ANGARAK KINGDOMS

NOTE Because their history is so completely interwoven, it would be largely impractical and repetitious to deal with each of the Angarak Kingdoms separately. Indeed, while there are slight cultural differences between Nadraks, Thulls and Murgos, they are hardly more than those differences one might distinguish between the inhabitants of Tol Rane, Tol Honeth and Tol Vordue in Tolnedra. Further, because of the unity of their policy, it is perhaps useful to consider these kingdoms as little more than administrative districts of one single national entity.

GEOGRAPHY

The Angarak Kingdoms, consisting of Gar og Nadrak, Mishrak ac Thull and Cthol Murgos, lie along the eastern edge of the continent. The most notable features of the kingdoms are the vast stretches of inhospitable mountains, barren steppes and dreary wastelands. While their lands are rich in mineral wealth, the Angaraks have never fully exploited those riches.

Gar Og Nadrak

The northern-most of the kingdoms is covered with vast forests in its central and north central portions and with the inevitable and towering mountains to the west and north. To the east and south, moor-lands stretch to the shores of the Eastern Sea. Two major rivers, the Cordu and the Drak on Du flow generally southeasterly, joining at Yar Turak in the central moors to form the Greater River Cordu which empties into the sea at the site of the twin cities of Yar Marak and Thull Zelik, the eastern termini of the North Caravan Route. The only other population center of any significance in

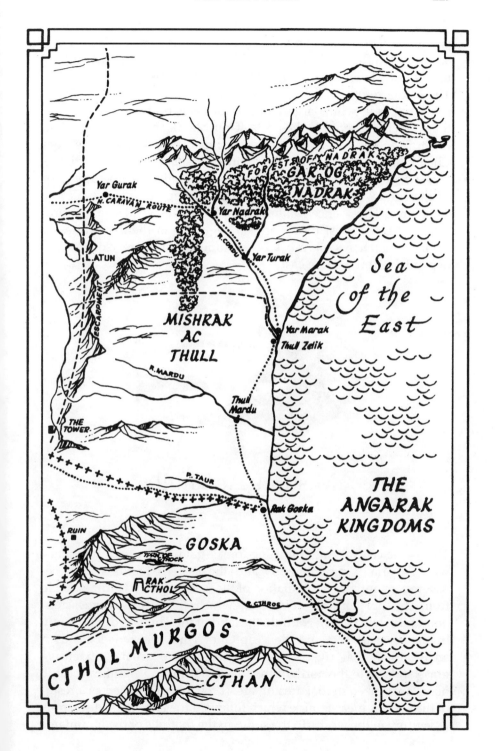

Gar og Nadrak, aside from the capital of Yar Nadrak, is the fortified city of Yar Gorak on the northwest border with Drasnia. It is generally believed that to the northeast lies the land bridge to the endless reaches of Mallorea, although the Nadraks refuse to confirm this. The evidence of this bridge and the possibility of another caravan route across it, while largely presumptive, is borne out by the fact that vessels observed in the ports at Yar Marak and in Thull Zelik in Mishrak ac Thull are coastal scows incapable (or so observers from Cherek have informed us) of sustained ocean voyages. Our friends from Cherek further advise us that the Angaraks are woefully poor seamen and would be unable to sustain any significant transoceanic commerce. Thus, since Mallorean trade articles – silks, spices and jewelry for the most part – appear regularly in the inventories of Nadrak merchants, it must be assumed that there exists some dependable route to the east.

Mishrak Ac Thull

This is the central Angarak Kingdom. Again, its western boundary with Algaria is mountainous and the eastern foothills are tree-covered, a southern continuation of the vast forests of Nadrak. Aside from the northern River Cordu, which forms the northeastern boundary with Gar og Nadrak, the land of the Thulls is drained only by the River Mardu, and their capital of Thull Mardu is located on an island in that river some hundred leagues inland. Extensive grasslands lie to the north of the River Mardu, and significant cattle herds are grazed in that area of late. (Probably developed as a result of the serious meat-famine which followed the Angaraks' disastrous adventure in the west.) To the south in the foothills of the mountains a sparsely timbered belt exists which soon gives way to the empty reaches of the wastes of Murgos. The southern boundary of Mishrak ac Thull is the Taur River.

Cthol Murgos

This southern Angarak Kingdom is the most bleak and uninviting. The seaport of Rak Goska at the mouth of the Taur is the only city of any size in Cthol Murgos, aside from the theological capital at Rak Cthol, and forms the eastern terminus of the South Caravan Route.

Cthol Murgos is, by any civilized standard, an uninhabitable wasteland. Because of the aridity of the country, agriculture is minimal, and the Murgos must import virtually all their foodstuffs. The bleak coastline is backed for a hundred leagues with the bleak wastes of Murgos; there is again, as in Mishrak ac Thull, a narrow belt of stunted trees; and then there is only the endless barren waste of the southern mountains.*

The only geographic feature worthy of note in those mountains is the vast, flat Wasteland of Murgos just to the west of the first range of mountains. The area, perhaps a hundred leagues wide and three hundred long, appears to have been a huge inland sea at some time in the dim reaches of the pre-historic past. Either the sea was drained during some cataclysmic geological upheaval, or a drastic change in climate to the present aridity caused it to gradually dry up. Whatever the reason, only the sea-bed remains. Enormous stretches of barren salt-flats are interspersed with endless expanses of black sand and ridges of tumbled basalt slabs. Somewhere near the center of the wasteland is the Tarn of Cthok, a foul-smelling lake seething with chemical salts and so noxious that even the vultures of Cthol Murgos are frequently overcome by the fumes as they fly over it and fall into the water and perish. The marge of the lake is a bubbling quagmire, forever churned by stinking gasses rising from the very bowels of the earth.

Somewhat to the west of the tarn rises the solitary peak which is the site of Rak Cthol, the forbidden theological capital of the Murgos. The sides of the peak are smooth basalt, and the only approach to the city is by way of a narrow, inclined causeway, built

* The Tolnedrans didn't know about southern Cthol Murgos at this point.

in the distant past by unspeakable amounts of human labor. One is sickened at the thought of whole generations of slaves toiling away their lives to lay this pathway to Rak Cthol. The walls of the city are as high as the peak itself. What lies within the city is a mystery, since no outsider is permitted to enter.

As is the case with Nyissa, which forms the northwestern boundary of this bleak country, the southern border of Cthol Murgos is indistinct. The western reaches of the land of the Murgos are arid mountains, bleak and uninhabited.

THE PEOPLE

While they are all Angaraks, there are subtle distinctions between the inhabitants of the three eastern kingdoms and between them and the Malloreans (also Angarak) who dwell in unnumbered hordes in the uncharted lands beyond the Eastern Sea.

THE NADRAKS

These northern-most Angaraks are more volatile than their brothers to the south. While all Angaraks are war-like, it was the Nadraks who conducted the centuries-long campaign which continually probed the borders of Drasnia and Algaria during the third millennium. Fortunately, the Nadraks are also acquisitive, and it was this characteristic which made possible the opening of the North Caravan Route from Boktor to Yar Marak. With the growth of trade, there has also been a growth of information, and as a result of more frequent contact, we know more about the Nadraks than we do of Thulls or Murgos or Grolims. Nadrak hunters range the vast forests of the north, providing the luxuriant furs for which Gar og Nadrak is so justly famous. Nadrak miners, unlike the Murgos to the south, scorn the use of slave labor and hack gold and gems from the living rock with their own hands. A rowdy group, these foresters, hunters and miners are susceptible to the pleasures of keg and flagon, and Drasnian agents, posing as merchants, have for centuries used this susceptibility to their own advantage. Much information can be gained concerning concentrations of troops, movements and even the temper of officials in Yar Nadrak, the capital, for the minor investment in a few kegs of ale in wayside camps and villages.

The present King of the Nadraks is Drosta lek Thun, an excitable man in his early forties who has made some effort to make the court at Yar Nadrak a more courtly and civilized one, but the ambassadors of the western kingdoms realize that beneath his shrill charm, Drosta is a treacherous and dangerous ruler.

THE THULLS

These central Angaraks are bulkier than the Nadraks to the north, who tend to be nearly as rangy as Alorns. Thulls tend to be broad of shoulder, wide-backed, thick-hipped and somewhat slow-witted. In battle we have observed that the Thulls are more likely to rely on brute strength rather than on any degree of skill or tactics.

While it might appear that such people would be easy to best in any kind of trade, merchants renowned throughout the west for their canniness and the sharpness of their dealings have been frustrated by the Thulls who display that suspicion that is frequently a characteristic of the less-intelligent. Further, dealing with the Thulls is a dangerous business since they tend in the direction of homicidal rages at the first hint of chicanery – real or imagined.

Perhaps the fairest indication of the Thullish character is the fact that the favorite sport at village fairs in the back-country of Mishrak ac Thull is the head-butting contest – a form of competition that is not infrequently fatal to both participants.

The Thulls are prolific, perhaps as a result of the legendary appetite of the generously proportioned Thullish women.

The aged King of the Thulls, Clota Hrok, still sits firmly on his throne in Thull Mardu, despite the efforts of his eldest son Gethel to persuade him to retire.*

THE MURGOS

These are the most savage of the Angaraks. All Murgo men are warriors and habitually wear armor as casually as civilized men wear wool or linen. They are stockier than the Nadraks, but not so bulky as the Thulls.

---

* Gethel was elevated to the throne in the Belgariad.

The Murgos are close-mouthed to the point of rudeness, which makes trade with them extremely difficult. The bleakness of their homeland has perhaps infected their character. It is not uncommon for a Murgo merchant to conduct negotiations without ever speaking. He will examine the merchandise offered, lay a certain amount of gold on the table, and, if the trader objects to the sum, he will simply pick up his gold and depart. For the trader, for whom haggling is often more important than profit, this can be frustrating in the extreme.

Murgos will not discuss their theological capital at Rak Cthol (or even admit that it exists), and large portions of their uninhabitable country are absolutely forbidden to outsiders.

It has been persistently rumored that the Murgo population is much more extensive than the scanty numbers which are evident along the South Caravan Route or in the streets of Rak Goska would indicate, and many have suspected the existence of vast Murgo cities lying in the southern mountains of Cthol Murgos below the river Cthrog. Since those areas are strictly closed, however, the rumors are impossible to substantiate.

One note of caution must be sounded in any discussion of the Murgos. Murgo women are kept closely confined and are never seen in public – not even the youngest female children. To the casual observer it might appear that Cthol Murgos is inhabited entirely by males. This, however, is not the case, and travelers and merchants who visit would be well-advised to avoid those portions of Murgo houses normally marked by black doors, for to violate the sanctity of the women's quarters in any Murgo household is to invite instant death.

The King of the Murgos is Taur Urgas, a man of uncertain sanity, who holds the country in an iron grip.

THE MALLOREANS

Little is known in the west of these strange people. Occasionally, by chance, Mallorean merchants are encountered in Yar Marak, Thull Zelik or Rak Goska. Since they speak an Angarak dialect that is virtually unintelligible to westerners, direct communication with them is almost impossible. The extent of the Mallorean Empire is unknown, but the traditional words, 'limitless', 'boundless', 'vast', and so forth indicate lands of staggering dimensions.

Agents of the Drasnian Kings, who from the time of the establishment of the North Caravan Route, have probed the Angarak kingdoms in the guise of merchants, have devoted centuries to the unraveling of the mystery of the Malloreans, but with only small success. What little we do know of them, however, is a tribute to the patience and perseverance of these Drasnian agents.

Physically, the Malloreans appear to be the archetypical Angaraks, neither as tall as the Nadraks nor as thick-bodied as the Thulls, nor are they quite as muscular as the typical Murgo. Their dispositions would seem to be more open, but the keen-eyed Drasnians have noted a tendency among them to be – if not precisely fearful – at least apprehensive in the presence of Grolim priests. Drasnian intelligence speculates that Mallorea is in all probability a theocracy dominated by Grolims who rule by terror in the service of Torak, the Angarak God.

NOTE The only Mallorean who has played any significant part in the history of the west was the 49th century conqueror, Kal-Torak, who led the invasion of the Malloreans and western Angaraks and who was defeated at the famous Battle of Vo Mimbre. The prefix 'Kal' is untranslatable, but would seem to signify that the meaning of the name was 'Arm of Torak' or possibly 'Spirit of Torak'. The popular superstition that it was the God Torak himself is, of course, nonsense.

THE GROLIMS

These are the ubiquitous Angarak priests who are seen in all parts of the Angarak kingdoms. Little can be known of them except by implication, since they steadfastly refuse to even speak to non-Angaraks. No hints can be gathered as to their physical appearance due to the shrouding, hooded black robes they customarily wear and the soul-chilling steel facemasks which are the marks of their priesthood. These masks, supposedly replicas of the face of the God Torak, conceal the entire face and help to explain the awe with which the Grolims are regarded.

It is unknown whether the Grolims are an order, selected from the body of the Angarak populace, or if they are a separate tribe. Drasnian agents have attempted for millennia to unravel this mystery, but without success, since not even the most drunken Nadrak miner will ever discuss the Grolims.

Fragmentary reports from the battlefield at Vo Mimbre hint at the possibility that the Grolims are not exclusively male, but that there were also priestesses among the bodies on that field, but the necessity for rapid disposal of the dead to avoid the possibility of pestilence made verification of this impossible.

Whatever their origins and true nature, however, the Grolims dominate Angarak life. The hideous orgies of human sacrifice which characterize the Angarak religion are presided over by Grolims, and the sacrificial victims, despite popular belief in the west, are not drawn exclusively from the ranks of slaves. Even the remotest villages of Nadraks and Thulls have the traditional black altar of Torak, stained with the blood of the unnumbered victims who for millennia have gone screaming under the knife.

No information exists, of course, about the nature of the organization of the Grolim priesthood. One suspects that there exists somewhere – either in Mallorea or perhaps at Rak Cthol or some other inaccessible place – some high priest or chief priest or some such figure, but this is sheer speculation.

THE HISTORY OF THE ANGARAKS

Little is known of the early millennia of these people. It appears that their migration across the northern land bridge from Mallorea took place at the end of the second or the beginning of the third millennium, much later than the western migration of the other peoples of the west.

The first western contact with them came, as is almost always the case with primitive peoples, in the form of war. It was the Nadraks who led the probing attacks against Drasnia and Algaria during the third millennium until the time of the great unnamed battle in eastern Drasnia which has been roughly dated to the 25th century. It was at that time that a major Angarak penetration occurred. The decisive defeat of the Nadraks at this battle quelled Angarak expansionism in the north until the time of Kal-Torak.

As relations between Gar og Nadrak and Drasnia normalized (roughly by the end of the third millennium) trade between the two nations began – tentatively at first and with great suspicion on each side – but gradually growing until the North Caravan Route was established, more by custom than by any formal agreement between the two kingdoms.

It was in 3219 that the Kings of the two nations met at a great border encampment astride the Caravan Route to formalize what had simply grown as a result of the human need to trade. Kings Reldik III of Drasnia and Yar grel Hrun of Gar og Nadrak ultimately concluded the treaty that has been the despair of Tolnedran commercial barons for over two thousand years. Under the terms of the agreement, only Drasnian caravans are permitted access to the Nadrak portions of the North Caravan Route and conversely only Nadrak caravans may enter Drasnia. Thus, even as Drasnia dominates all western commerce generated by the Caravan Route, so Gar og Nadrak dominates all trade with the other Angarak states. Thus, it is as rare to see a Murgo or a Thull in Boktor as it is to see a Sendar or a Tolnedran in Yar Marak, since the fees charged by the rapacious caravan masters of both states quite literally eat up any possible profit.

Efforts by Tolnedran negotiators to break the stranglehold Drasnia held over the northern trade at the time of the conferences which brought Drasnia into the Tolnedran commercial Empire were totally without success, and at that time Tolnedra began to look for another route to the east.

Enlisting the aid of Nyissan slavers, who had regular contact with the Murgos, Tolnedran commercial envoys were able to finally institute talks at Rak Goska. The difficulties involved in dealing with the grimly laconic Murgos can not be exaggerated. The talks – if they could be called such – continued intermittently for seventy years. Infuriatingly, the Murgos appeared indifferent to the fact that between them the Drasnians and Nadraks had a virtual monopoly on all east-west trade. Finally, however, in 3853 an agreement was finally reached which established the South Caravan Route between Tol Honeth and Rak Goska. This is a brutal route, and fully half of all caravans which attempt it are lost. The Murgos scrupulously patrol the route, and, while they respect the protected status of the Route itself, they regard all who stray from this often poorly-marked trail as invaders and fall upon them with great savagery.

The only possible alternative route is forever closed since it would involve crossing the Vale of Aldur on a direct line from Tol Honeth to the borders of Mishrak ac Thull, and the stubborn Algars steadfastly refuse even to discuss the matter or to permit any contact with the Angaraks across their eastern frontier.

Thus it is that most of the traditional sources of information concerning the history of a people are denied to us in our study of the Angaraks. The merchant has ever been the truest friend of the historian, and in a situation where trade is so severely limited, information is so scanty that much of our understanding of the Angaraks is the result of speculation and guess-work.

In essence, then, we have three tribes (or four – if one counts the Grolims as a separate people) who migrated out of the dim reaches of western Mallorea sometime at the end of the second millennium. Some ancient and unknown enmity existed between them and the Alorn peoples of the north, and for a thousand years they attempted to penetrate Drasnia and Algaria but were steadfastly repulsed by the legendary warriors of those lands. In time, those hostilities were reduced sufficiently to permit a certain minimal contact between the Angaraks and the peoples of the west.

In the fifth millennium, the Mallorean hordes under Kal-Torak moved across the land bridge in northeastern Gor og Nadrak and were joined by the Nadraks, Thulls and Murgos in the invasion of the west. Defeated finally at the Battle of Vo Mimbre, the surviving western Angaraks fled back to their kingdoms along the shores of the Great Eastern Sea.

For a century following the invasion, there existed a state of virtual war along the borders between the Angaraks and the west. Skirmishes and ambushes between the opposing sides made those frontiers the most dangerous places in the known world.

Gradually, once again, relations began to normalize, and trade – though severely limited – was resumed along the North Caravan Route. Almost five hundred years, however, were to pass before the stiff-necked Murgos permitted the reopening of the South Caravan Route. Then, almost overnight, they quite suddenly relented – indeed seemed to welcome the resumption of commerce. Oddly, for the first time, there has been significant caravan traffic from the *east*, and the sight of mailed Murgo merchants and their Thullish porters in the streets and along the quays of Tol Honeth have become commonplace.

Alarmists have contended that these Angaraks are in fact spies probing the west in preparation for yet another invasion, but these are the counsels of timidity. Our own merchants in the south and those of the Drasnians in the north have witnessed no unusual military activity, and the numbers of the western Angaraks are so limited that without the aid of Mallorea they could not hope to mount a sustained campaign against the west. Kal-Torak is dead. His like will never appear again, and without such a leader to spur them on there is little likelihood that the hordes of Mallorea would ever again join with the western Angaraks in those desperate adventures which so nearly exterminated them in the past.

Gar Og Nadrak

COINAGE

All coins have the likeness of Torak on the face, and all coins – even though stamped in either Gar og Nadrak or Cthol Murgos are universal among the Angaraks. (Coinage originated in Mallorea.)

GOLD
Angaraks use large gold bars or ingots for major transactions.
10 lb. bar called a gold tenweight, worth about $20,000

5 lb. bar called a gold fiveweight, worth about $10,000
1 lb. bar called gold pound, worth about $2,000
½ lb. bar called goldmark, worth about $1000

GOLD COINS
4 oz. coin called a goldpiece, worth about $500
2 oz. coin called a half goldpiece, worth about $250
1 oz. coin called quarter goldpiece, worth about $125
½ oz. coin called gold token, worth about $62.50

SILVER
4 oz. coin, worth about $25
2 oz. coin, worth about $12.50
1 oz. coin, worth about $6.25
½ oz. coin, worth about $3.125

COPPER
Coins called 'Coppers', worth one hundredth of a silver token

COSTUME

Nadraks wear a lot of fur.

MEN
Pants, jackets of leather, mid-calf boots, fur caps (pretty Hunnish or Mongolian). Felt overcoats, belted and ankle-length. Fur robes in bitter weather. Leather vests in summer. Dress clothing for indoors is wool, linen or silk.

ARMOR
Breastplates and pointed helmets. Leather jackets with steel plates sewn on cover arms and shoulders. Same with pants. Long, slightly curved swords. Daggers. Nadrak clothing is usually black.

WOMEN
Gowns of fairly heavy material – richly ornamented and pretty concealing.

SOCIAL ORGANIZATION

Freer than other Angarak societies. Hunters, woodsmen and miners tend to be free spirits – their own men, subject directly to the King. Others are in clans, subject to chieftains. Reverse dowries for women you *pay* a man for his daughter – hence the interest in trade and in profit.

    Note on slaves[*]– Among the Nadraks, slaves exist only for insurance purposes. Slaves are substitutes for Nadraks chosen for sacrifice. If you're chosen, buy a slave and send him (or her) instead. Thus, slaves are worked but not seriously mistreated. The freemen – miners, woodsmen, hunters, etc. are for the most part exempt because sacrifices are chosen from the clans (so many each).

RANK

The King – Still subservient to Torak and must obey orders brought
  to him by Grolims from Mallorea.

* This was significantly modified as the character Vella was developed.

The Jarls (Earls) – The Clan-chiefs subservient to the King.

The Warlords – Keepers of castles and leaders of groups of warriors – subservient to the Jarls.

The Warriors – Next in line.

The Peasantry – Farm workers. Not exactly serfs. They are used as soldiers.

Freemen – Merchants, woodsmen, hunters, miners. Can be quite wealthy. Mostly town dwellers.

MODES OF ADDRESS

The King – August Majesty
Other Nobles – My Lord
Warriors – Brave John or Mighty John
Freemen – Miner John, Merchant John, etc.
Peasants – John
Slaves – You or Slave. Never called by name

MANNERS

Nadraks are bold, war-like and rowdy. They are the most likeable of the Angaraks. They like to drink and they like to make money. They are somewhat less fearful of the Grolims than are other Angaraks.

All Angarak societies are cruel, and public executions (as well as the sacrifices) are a common entertainment. They are fanatic warriors, but tend to be a little flighty in combat – high-strung. Nadraks are not really trustworthy. Marriage is by purchase. Women have no rights.

HOLIDAYS

(*Note*: Erastide is *not* celebrated in the Angarak Kingdoms.)

Festival of Torak – Torak's supposed birthday – a few sacrifices.

Day of the Grief Place – Date of a major battle in Drasnia – an orgy of sacrifice.

Day of the Wounding – The day when Torak was burned by the Orb – several sacrifices.

Day of the Casting Out – The day when Belgarath, Cherek and the boys retrieved the Orb from Cthol Mishrak and Torak destroyed the city – many sacrifices.

POPULATION

Probably 3½–4 million Nadraks.

Mishrak Ac Thull

COINAGE

See Gar og Nadrak. Much barter among the Thulls.

COSTUME

The standard costume of the Thulls is a knee-length belted tunic with elbow-length sleeves (male and female) made of various fabrics. Soft leather shoes. Armor is a chain mail complete with helmet. Weapons are broadswords, maces and axes (weapons of strength) in winter fur cloaks and felt boots.

SOCIAL ORGANIZATION

Thulls tend to be stupid. Village life is about all they are really capable of. Their cities consist of neighborhoods that are little more than villages. Their farms are poor because of the thin topsoil, and the Thulls produce food only through great amounts of back-breaking labor. There is a certain amount of rough, somewhat childish, good humor among them which tends toward the earthy – even obscene.

The major source of income among them is the hiring out as porters to Murgos and Nadraks. This is customary and traditional. Though they *will* fight when banded into military companies under their own leaders, by custom when they are serving as porters they are not required to fight. This is the responsibility of the other Angaraks who have hired them.

Thullish women are sexually voracious, and infidelity is so common that it is not even taken seriously. They are somewhat driven to this by the heavy burden of sacrifice laid upon them by

Torak. The Thulls are sacrificed in numbers sometimes ten times as large as are the Nadraks and Murgos. Since a pregnant woman is exempt, it is prudent for a Thullish woman to keep herself in that condition.

As with the Nadraks, slaves are used as substitutes in the sacrifices. Several Thulls, smarter than the average, have established vast slave-pens to the south of Mishrak Mardu. Worn-out, old or feeble slaves are bought cheap in large numbers from the Murgos and are held in the pens until required. They are sold to Thulls who might need them. It is customary for long caravans of these unfortunates to be driven along behind the Grolims who go about the country selecting sacrificial victims. As soon as he is chosen, a Thull goes to the slave broker and buys a substitute.

Because of the ever-present fear of being chosen, Thulls live in more or less constant fear. Their sometimes homicidal fury is the reaction to this fear. In their dealings, Thulls *have* to make a profit in order to build up a bankroll to buy substitutes. They run away from sacrifice often.

RANK

The King – Hereditary.
Lords of the Marks – Greater or lesser nobles depending on wealth.
Warriors – The standing army of the Thulls. Fairly large. Used to track down runaway sacrificial victims.
Guptors – A Thullish word meaning a wealthy man.
Commons – Farmers, porters, etc.
Slaves – Never used for work. Thulls do all their own. Slaves have only one purpose.

MODE OF ADDRESS

The King – Your Majesty
The Lords – Your lordship
Warriors – Your honor
Guptors – Your honor
Commons – By name
Slaves – Never addressed at all – simply goaded or whipped into motion

MANNERS

Thulls are not bright enough to have very much in the way of elaborate etiquette. They tend to be morose and sour – sullen. The good humor mentioned previously is a kind of release. They fear the Grolims.

Thullish women will quite literally couple at a moment's notice. Always on the look-out for a chance at sex.

The court at Thull Mardu is little more than a large household with the King giving orders like a Sendarian farmer. There is a great lack of formality among them.

HOLIDAYS AND RELIGIOUS OBSERVANCES

See Gar og Nadrak

POPULATION

Probably 5 million Thulls.

Cthol Murgos

COINAGE

See Gar og Nadrak

COSTUME

Murgo men *always* wear armor. Mail-shirts to the knee, breast-plates, pointed helmets, all painted red, covered with black surcoats to mid-calf, substantial boots. Big broadswords and maces in combat, small-sword otherwise, also daggers. Some ornamentation on helmet and surcoat to indicate rank.

Murgo women are *always* kept in harems. Clothing is filmy and diaphanous.

SOCIAL ORGANIZATION

This is a military society and is rigidly organized. Divided into companies, battalions, regiments, etc. All rank is military. The society in the *known* part of Cthol Murgos is in actuality a sham set up to *resemble* a semi-normal society. This is also true of Murgo merchants. They are *all* spies. The seeming society in Rak Goska is a complete stage setting. Murgos are trained there for excursion into the west.

All work in Murgo society is done by slaves.

The *real* cities of the Murgos lie to the south and are unknown to westerners. They are actually base housing type cities – military posts.

Murgo men have more than one wife – up to four. One route to promotion is to produce lots of kids.

There are other peoples (unknown to the west) to the south of Cthol Murgos. These peoples are quite primitive and provide slaves.

There *was* an effort during the Angarak invasion of the 4860s to move a huge column of Murgos through the southern mountains to strike into southern Tolnedra, but the column started out too early and was overwhelmed by a spring blizzard in the mountains. If they had made it, the west would have fallen. There are literally *millions* of Murgos.

Note on Rak Cthol: This ceremonial capital of the Murgos is the ultimate bastion of Angaraks in the west. The Murgos are in charge, and the Kings of Gar og Nadrak and Mishrak ac Thull are subject to the King of Cthol Murgos. *He* gives the orders. These are conveyed to him by Grolims who are not only priests but messengers of Torak as well. Large numbers of Grolims are quartered in Rak Cthol as well as the crack ceremonial divisions of the King of the Murgos. The Ultimate Temple of Torak in the west is in Rak Cthol as well as the court of the King. It is hallowed by the fact that Torak stayed here while planning the invasion of the west. (His normal residence is in Mallorea.)

Here it is that Zedar has his base of operations.* As personal advisor to Kal Torak, Zedar has a great deal of power. He must, however, badger and force the Murgo General-King into doing his bidding.

Also at Rak Cthol selected Grolims study sorcery under Zedar's instruction.

RANKS

The King – Commander in chief.
Generals, Colonels, captains, lieutenants, etc. (Titles of nobility are assigned to various of them for contact with westerners. Those titles have no meaning to the Murgos.)

MODES OF ADDRESS

From the King – My General, My Colonel, etc., 'Sir'
To the King – 'Mighty arm of Torak', 'Your highness'
Ordinary warriors – addressed by rankar
Slaves are merely driven, like cattle

HOLIDAYS AND RELIGIOUS OBSERVANCES

See Gar og Nadrak.
   Murgos are fanatic zealots.

POPULATION

Probably ten million Murgos altogether. Maybe 70,000 in Rak Goska, a half million total in Rak Cthol, the rest to the south.

---

* In the books, there are the additional characters Ctuchik and Urvon.

Mallorea

COINAGE

Varied. Only rarely does a Mallorean coin appear in the west.

COSTUME

Again it varies depending on the latitudes. Mostly Thull-like tunics. Further north, more clothing. Unisex garb.

Malloreans wear plate armor – breastplates. Upper and lower arm guards, upper and lower leg guards. Helmets with visors (buckle on). Large shields, broad-bladed spears, broadsword.

SOCIAL ORGANIZATION

Mallorea is a theocracy totally dominated by the Grolims. Torak's ego is such that he refused to permit the Mallorean Angaraks any nobles or aristocracy. They are all commoners.

There are no cities in Mallorea. They all live on farmsteads or in villages.* The Grolims are administrators of districts and of the large villages. The vast bulk of Malloreans live in semi serfdom.

NOBILITY

See the Grolims. The only rank in Mallorea is in the army. Malloreans *are* permitted to hold military rank.
General – head of a division
Colonel – head of a regiment
Captain – head of a company

MODE OF ADDRESS

To a general – My lord General
To a Colonel – Great Colonel
To a Captain – Master

---

* This changed. Mal Zeth is probably bigger than Tol Honeth.

MANNERS

Malloreans are brusque and even brutal to subordinates and are fawning toward their superiors.

They are a cruel people, a reflection of their religion. When they have a chance to come into contact with strangers they tend to be polite, even friendly, largely because they do not know the precise rank of the stranger.

COMMERCE

The goods from Mallorea are essentially the kinds of goods associated with the orient. Spices, silks, tapestries, carpets, candied fruits, etc. Sugar is a big trade item. There is a great deal of work in fine jewelry.

HOLIDAYS AND RELIGIOUS OBSERVANCES

See Gar og Nadrak.

There are also additional holidays in Mallorea and there is *no* substitution of victims in that land.

POPULATION

Mallorea is about as large as the western sub-continent, and there are approximately 25 million Malloreans.

They could quite easily overwhelm the west by sheer numbers, but the logistics of moving an entire population into position are beyond the capabilities of the Grolims who are not really very good administrators.

The Grolims

WEALTH

The Order (or race, since they are a tribe) is enormously wealthy since taxation – tithing – in Angarak countries is heavy and it all goes to the Grolims.

COSTUME

Monk's robe – black. Hood is always up. Steel mask – polished. The face of Torak. Mask is a complete helmet, hinged and latched – they frequently wear mail under-shirts and carry daggers or swords.

ORGANIZATION

In Mallorea and southern Cthol Murgos there are Grolim communities forbidden to others where the Grolims raise and educate their children and continue their studies. In the western Angarak kingdoms, Grolims have large houses where they can live in some semblance of normalcy.

The *Grolims* have a *Catholic* structure with equivalents to:
Pope – The ultimate high priest.
12 Cardinals – Administrators of large regions.
Archbishop – Administrators of large districts.
Bishop – Administrators of smaller districts.
Monseigneur – Administrators of major towns or cities.
Priest – Priest (or priestess)

These last are the workers – they control villages, also travel as messengers etc., perform the sacrifices, select the victims etc. Keep the Angaraks in line. Some are in the intelligence service, adopt the garb of the people and spy on them or on the west.

RELIGIOUS OBSERVANCES

Angaraks are fearful of their religion – with good reason. The call to the Temple is a call to be sacrificed. A sorrowful horrifying part of their lives. Their relationship to Torak is that of driven slaves. The Grolims, who select those to be sacrificed, are not above using this power for personal revenge. *Some* Grolims can be bribed.

A religion based on fear. Theological offenses are also punishable by death. (Speaking unworshipfully of Torak, striking a Grolim, etc.)

THE SACRIFICE

After suitable invocation to Torak by the priest, the victim is placed naked on the altar, sliced open, and the heart is removed – offered to Torak and then burned in a brazier of hot coals on the altar. Great pits nearby are stoked up with huge fires and the bodies are then burned in the pits. The altars are never washed and the combination of rotten blood and burned flesh makes Angarak temples stink like charnel houses. They are avoided by the people.

They are large buildings of black stone and totally deserted except during the ceremonies.

RANK

The High Priest (Pope) is the Vicar of Torak. He is a dark sorcerer on a par with Belgarath, Zedar and the others, and is also immortal. His name is Ctuchik. He was selected by Torak after the Orb burned him. Taken as his servant and his pupil. Knows the secret of the Will and the Word, but uses more mumbo-jumbo. Calls up demons and monsters to do his bidding. Has found ways to circumvent the restriction on the power of the Word. (He can destroy by creating fire in the body of the victim or creating a spear in his chest, etc.)[*]

The Chosen Ones: The 12 (cardinals) are also sorcerers, though not as powerful. They can alter themselves. A good trick is to expand: move their molecules apart until they're ten times larger. They live for about 1000 years.

The Grolims *all* dabble in some degree of sorcery. Most are limited to simple tricks but some of the higher ranks have fearful powers.

The Grolims have gained control of many of the monsters – though not all. Use monsters as required.

The Grolims are Torak's Gestapo, agents, police, servants, etc. Use as required.

PHYSICAL

The Grolim tribe is tall, lean, swarthy with piercing eyes. Voices behind the masks are hollow, chilling.

Rank is probably indicated by tattoos in some inconspicuous place – no rank on the robes.

POPULATION

All told, there are probably 3–4 million Grolims, widely scattered.

---

[*] This was greatly modified in the writing.

III

THE BATTLE OF VO MIMBRE

Excerpted from the prose epic, *The Latter Days of the House of Mimbre*
By the Arendish bard, Davoul the Lame.*

N O T E   While some aspects of this work are obviously ludicrous, and the
author has taken a great deal of poetic license with facts, the piece has a
certain rude charm. The spells, enchantments, sorcery and other magi-
cal clap-trap, are minimal when compared to other works in which
everyone is a sorcerer, and the Gods themselves strode the battlefield.
All Imperial diplomats, emissaries, ambassadors, trade negotiators and
such functionaries assigned to the court at Vo Mimbre should be thor-
oughly familiar with this work – and most particularly with the portion
excerpted here – before undertaking any official mission to Arendia.
Further, it is considered mannerly and a sign of good breeding to
sprinkle one's speech with quotations from this epic. The Arends are
convinced that this rather pedestrian work is the world's greatest literary masterpiece, and there is even a cult among the nobility which
maintains that Davoul, the author, was divinely inspired at the time of
the writing. The deliberate archaism of Arendish court speech is a
reflection of the 'high style' affected by this author, and officials of the
Tolnedran Empire should strive to match the elevated speech mannerisms of the Arends in all dealings with them. To do otherwise would
be to cast disparagement upon the Empire itself in the eyes of this most
troublesome of people.

* This section is pastiche romance, intended to establish Arendish psychology.

BOOK SEVEN
THE BATTLE BEFORE
VO MIMBRE

Now it came to pass that on the third day of the great battle before the gates of Vo Mimbre, the hosts of the Accursed One had gathered for the final assault upon the city. This, then, was their order of battle. The Murgos, commanded by their fell King, Ad Rak Cthoros, held the left flank beside the River Arend to the east of the city. To the north, the Mallorean Horde under the Accursed Kal-Torak himself held the center before the gates of the city. To the west the Nadraks under Yar Lek Thun and the Thulls under Gethel Mardu held the right flank, encircling the city even again to the river which flowed out west of the city walls. In the center of the Mallorean Horde stood the black iron pavilion of the dread Kal-Torak himself, who had not issued forth during the first two days of the battle.

And on the morning of the third day, a great horn was heard to blow from the forest to the north of the city. And another great horn was heard to answer from the hills to the east. And yet another horn sounded from within the city itself. Only this – nothing more.

Doubts began to assail the Murgos, the Nadraks quailed, and there was fear in the hearts of the Thulls. None knew the portent of the horns, and the dark kings were troubled and sought counsel with Kal-Torak, their over-king and their God, but still he issued not forth from his iron pavilion. The Malloreans clashed their cruel spears against their shields and made fierce outcry to hearten their allies.

Again the horn blew to the north, and again was it answered by a trumpeting from the east and by a brazen reply from the city. And yet was there no movement or sound to reveal the nature of them that sounded those solitary notes.

Nadrak riders went out from the host to the north. Black and grim was their armor, and bright were their swords. They came not back, and the dark forest gave no sound to tell of their fate.

Murgo riders went out from the host to the east. Smokey red were their mail-shirts, and cruel were the maces and the axes of the Murgos. They came not back, and the silent hills gave no token of what had befallen them.

Yet once more the great horn sounded to the north, and yet once more did the eastern hills and even the city reply. And behold, faint and far away from across the plain to the west came an answer of many brazen trumpets, and far out across the plain was there a glinting as of the sun on many waters.

And it came to pass that Zedar, the sorcerer who sat ever at the right hand of the Accursed One, did cast an enchantment and did rise up from the host in the form of a raven that he might espy out the portent of the horns. And he flew unto the east, and behold, a great owl of snowy whiteness did appear in the sky and struck with her cruel talons, and wounded him grievously, and he escaped only with his life.

And Zedar cast another enchantment, and in the form of a great stag went he out from the host again even unto the forest to the north. And behold, a great grey wolf, grizzled and old, appeared at the edge of the forest and harried him back to the host from whence he had come, and the cruel jaws of the wolf did rend his flesh, and he was sore afraid even for his life.

And one last time the great horn blew to the north; and one last time the great horn answered from the east; and one last time the

horn within the city walls replied. And again and nearer now the sound of the many brazen trumpets came from the west, and the glinting of the sun was as upon a great ocean.

And then opened the gates of Vo Mimbre, and there issued forth the mounted Knights of the Mimbrate Arends. Clad in steel were they, and bright were the pennons on their lances, and the iron-shod hooves of their chargers made a great sound, even as the thunder.

And the fell horde of the Mallorean Angaraks, servants of the Accursed One, raised a great cry and clashed their spears on their iron shields, thinking that their enemies were in their grasp and that the city would soon be theirs.

And the Murgos exulted, and the Thulls and the Nadraks also, and all pressed forward that they might quickly overwhelm the Mimbrate Knights and take the city.

With a mighty clash, the Mimbrate Knights struck the forefront of the Host, and the front ranks were overthrown. On they pressed, the cruel, iron-shod hooves of their foaming chargers trampling the living and the dead. And behold, the second rank was overthrown and crushed to earth by the fury of the charge.

Still the Malloreans clashed their spears on their iron shields, and still exulted the Murgos and the Thulls and the Nadraks also, for the numbers of the Mimbrate Knights were diminished, even as the force of a wave is diminished as it rushes upon a strand. And a great joy was in the hearts of the Grolims, the dark priests of Torak, and they urged on the Malloreans and the Murgos, the Nadraks and the Thulls.

And then, even as the watchers from the walls of the city despaired, a great thunder arose from the east, and there burst forth from the low and sullen hills a great charge of many warriors. And in the center the dread long spears of the Drasnians moved like a forest in the wind. And on the flanks the Algar horsemen curved out like two great sickles, and none might withstand them. And upon the Murgos they descended like wolves on the fold, and great was the slaughter and the bloodshed they wrought. And King Ad Rak Cthoros of the Murgos cried out in a great voice to rally his people, and they turned away from the Mimbrate Knights to bear the charge of the Drasnian spears and the long swords of the Algar horsemen. But their axes could not reach past the long spears of the Drasnians, and they fell before them. And their maces were too slow to stem the swift attack of the Algars, and they fell as wheat before the scythe.

Recoiled back then the mail-shirted Murgos and formed they a shield-wall to ward off the Drasnians and the Algars, and behold, there were among them, even in their very midst, Ulgo warriors in curious armor and with strange weapons – long knives with hooks at their points or with edges like saws, and horrid curved things on handles of iron with cruelly pointed spikes that reached into the mail of the Murgos and sought out the life inside – and veiled were the faces of the Ulgo warriors, and the Murgos were sore afraid. And the veiled Ulgos fell upon them, and the shrieks of the maimed and the dying filled the air, and the Murgos were overcome by confusion.

Now it came to pass that Zedar the Sorcerer beheld the faltering of the Murgos and went he even unto the iron pavilion of Kal-Torak and spake unto the Accursed One urging that he come forth and by his very presence overcome his enemies, but Kal-Torak would in no wise do it and remained within the black iron pavilion.

And behold, the earth shook in the west with the heavy feet of the legions of Imperial Tolnedra. And came the legions upon the plain and assumed their battle-order and closed with the Nadraks and the Thulls upon the right flank of the Horde. And Yar Lek Thun, King of the Nadraks, and Gethel Mardu, King of the Thulls, spake with one another and withdrew their forces from that battle which swirled around the Mimbrate Knights that they might better face the Tolnedran Legions.

And there were with the legions Cherek Berserks from the fleet that had borne the might of Tolnedra from Tol Honeth even unto the rapids of the River Arend ten leagues below Vo Mimbre, and the axes and huge broadswords of the Chereks were terrible to behold, and the Nadraks were afraid, and the Thulls quailed.

And the clash of arms resounded to the west also as the legions and the Chereks closed with the Nadraks and the Thulls.

And once again Zedar the Sorcerer went unto the black iron pavilion of the Dread Kal-Torak, and once again besought he the Accursed One to come forth lest the host be overthrown by reason of their enemies upon the left and upon the right and of the Mimbrates who even then made great slaughter in the midst of the Malloreans. And Kal-Torak spake unto him despitefully, saying, 'Art thou so afraid, Zedar, of a handful of Mimbrates? Does thy heart fail thee in the face of the ragged remnants of Drasnia and the tatters of Algaria and the blind creeping things that burrowed forth from the ground in Ulgo? Quailest thou before the fat, over-pampered legions of Tolnedra and a few drunken barbarians from Cherek? My people are Angarak, despoilers of the world. The horde is beyond counting, and I am with them. No might in the world may stand against us – save only Cthrag-Yaska, and he who could raise Cthrag-Yaska against me is no more. Return to the battle, Zedar, or flee and save thy life. I *will* not come forth.'

And behold, it came to pass that from the forest to the north of the city there emerged a silent host that cheered not, nor thundered, nor trumpeted. Grey cloaks wore some or dun or smudged forest-green, and came they from out of the forest in endless waves, grim-faced and silent.

And the heart of Zedar fell as he beheld the coming of the Rivans.

And the rear ranks of the Malloreans turned and ran toward the oncoming foe, but the forest-green warriors were Asturian bowmen, and the Malloreans fell like mown wheat beneath the storm of their arrows. And still the silent Rivans came, and with them the solid men of Sendaria. And they closed with the host and slew the Malloreans with abandon.

And once again Zedar went unto the black iron pavilion of Kal-Torak and spake unto the Accursed One, saying, 'Great Lord, I fear not the remnants of Drasnia nor the tatters of Algaria nor the blind things that creep beneath the earth in Ulgo; nor am I unquiet about the handful of Mimbrate Knights, nor the pampered legions of Tolnedra nor the Berserks of Cherek. Know, however, that thine army is assaulted on the front and on the left and on the right, and lo, now from out the forest behind thee come Asturians and Sendars and them whom most you hate – the keepers of Cthrag-Yaska. Yea, Lord, the Rivans themselves have come to contend with thine host and to cast their defiance in thy teeth.'

Then was the Accursed One wroth, and rose he and called upon his servants to arm him. And he spake unto Zedar the Sorcerer, saying, 'Behold, Zedar, I *will* come forth, that the keepers of Cthrag-Yaska may see me and be afraid. I will raise up mine hand against them and they shall crumble as dry leaves before me. Send unto me the Kings of the Angaraks that I may tell them of my coming.'

And Zedar answered him, saying, 'Behold, Great Lord, the Kings of the Angaraks are no more. King Ad Rak Cthoros of the Murgos lies dead with a hook-pointed Ulgo knife in his bowels. And Yar Lek Thun of the Nadraks perished upon the point of a Tolnedran sword, and Gethel Mardu, King of the Thulls, is cloven – helm to chest – by a Cherek war-axe. And behold, the sons of the Kings also are no more and the generals of the Malloreans also, and there is confusion in the Host by reason of the deaths of the Kings and the sons of the Kings and the generals of the Malloreans, and of the multitudes of the Grolims also.'

And great was the wrath of the Accursed One, and fire was in his right eye and also in the eye that was not, and caused he his servants to bind his shield to his maimed arm, and took he up his dread black sword, Cthrek-Goru, and went forth from his iron pavilion to do war.

And behold, the Host rallied around him who was both King and God, and pushed they back against the Drasnians and Algars and Ulgos upon the left and against the Tolnedrans and Chereks upon the right, and tightened they the ring of swords about the Mimbrate Knights before the gates of the city.

And there came from the north the sound of a great horn, and from the midst of the Rivans a voice called out unto the Accursed One, saying, 'In the name of Belar I defy thee, Torak, maimed and Accursed. In the name of Aldur also, I cast my despite into thy teeth. Let the bloodshed be abated, and I will meet thee – man against God, and I shall prevail against thee. Before thee I cast my gage. Take it up or stand as craven before men and Gods.'

In fury did Kal-Torak smite the rocks about him with his sword, Cthrek-Goru, and fire leapt from the rocks, and the Angaraks and the Malloreans were sore afraid before his wrath.

And Torak spake in a great voice, saying, 'Who among mortal kind is so foolish as to thus defy the King of the World? Who among you would contend with a God?'

And the voice from the midst of the grey-clad Rivans answered, saying, 'I am Brand, Warder of Riva, and I defy thee, foul and misshapen Godling, and all thy stinking Host. Bring forth thy might. Take up my gage or slink away and come no more against the Kingdoms of the West.'

And Zedar the Sorcerer heard this, and he counseled the Accursed One, saying, 'I beseech thee, Oh my Lord, let not thy fury misguide thee. This Rivan is guided by thy kindred. Thy brother Gods do conspire against thee, and this challenge is a trap of their making.'

Again Torak smote the rocks with his great sword, and again the fire leapt from the rocks, and he spake, saying, 'Behold, I am Torak, King of Kings and Lord of Lords. I fear no man of mortal kind nor the dim shades of long-forgotten Gods. I will go forth and destroy this loud-voiced Rivan fool, and mine enemies shall fall away before my wrath, and Cthrag-Yaska shall be mine again and the world also.'

And then strode the Accursed One forth from the Host. Black was his armor, and vast his shield. The dread black sword, Cthrek-Goru, swept like night through the noontide air, and Torak spake, saying, 'Who is *this* who will pit mortal flesh against the will and the invincible sword of the God Torak?'

Then stood forth Brand, Warder of Riva, and his grey cloak shed he away. Mailed he was and helmed in grey steel, and he bare a mighty sword and a shield muffled in rude cloth. And at his side marched a grizzled wolf, and hovered over his head a snowy owl. And Brand spake, saying, 'I am Brand, Warder of Riva. I am he who will contend with thee, Torak. Beware of me, for the spirits of Belar and of Aldur are with me. I alone stand between thee and the Orb for which thou hast brought war into the West.'

And Torak beheld the wolf and spake, saying, 'Begone, Belgarath. Flee if thou wouldst save thy life. It occurs that I may soon have the leisure to give thee the instruction I so long ago promised thee, and I doubt that even thou wouldst survive *my* instruction.'

But the grizzled wolf bared his fangs against him and fled not.

And Torak beheld the owl, and he spake unto her, saying, 'Abjure thy father, Polgara, and come with me. I will wed thee and make thee Queen of all the world, and thy might and thy power shall be second only to mine.'*

But the great white owl shrieked her defiance and her scorn.

'Prepare then to perish all,' quoth Torak, and raisèd up Cthrek-Goru and smote down upon the shield of Brand, Warder of Riva. Many and grievous were the blows they struck, and the Host of the Angaraks and the soldiers of the West stood in amaze as they beheld blows which no mortal might withstand, for the sword of Torak, dread Cthrek-Goru, clave rocks, and the great grey sword of Brand shattered earth. And knew then the multitudes that they beheld not the combat of men but the contention of Gods, and then were they sore afraid.

But the fury of Torak might not be withstood by flesh, and dread Cthrek-Goru did cleave and batter the shield of Brand, and the Warder fell back before the onslaught of the Accursed One. Then howled the grizzled wolf and then shrieked the snowy owl as in one voice that struck the ears of the watchers as it were a *human* voice, and the strength of Brand was renewed.

AND BEHOLD:

The Rivan Warder did unveil his shield, and lo, cast in the center thereof stood a round jewel. Grey it was and like unto the size of the heart of a child. And in the presence of Torak did the stone begin to glow. And brighter and brighter flamed the stone, and the Accursed One fell back before the stone, as one who faces unbearable fire. And shook away Torak his shield, and dropped he away his sword, Cthrek-Goru, and cried out and raised he his hands before his face to

---

* Another aside which proved very important.

ward away the fire of the stone. And his right hand covered his right eye, but lo, the maimed God had no left hand, and the stump thereof was blackened by a fire no mortal had yet endured. And Brand then struck. Two-handed held he his nameless grey sword as a man might hold a dagger, and plunged he the grey sword not at chest armor nor gorget – for knew he that a God may not be smitten save where he hath been injured before. Struck Brand, therefore, at the *Eye* that was *not*. And behold, the point of Brand's sword struck true and did pierce the visor of the Accursed One and passed even into the Eye that was not.

And Torak cried out and grasped the sword and plucked it out and cast it away. Then pulled the God his helm away and cast it aside also, and men saw the seared side of his face which had been marred when he had raised the Orb of Aldur to crack the world. And that face was horrible beyond power to describe it, and the Angaraks recoiled, and the men of the West turned away. And the eye of Torak was seen to weep blood, and raised he up and pushed his arms even into the sky and cried out again. And cried he out one last time as he beheld that jewel which he had named Cthrag-Yaska and which had caused him to be smitten again, and then, as a tree hewn away at the ground, the Dark God fell, and the earth resounded with his fall.

And a great cry went up from the Host by reason of the fall of the Accursed One, and the Angaraks despaired, for their God had fallen. Then fell the armies of the West upon the multitudes of the Host and slew them. And the armies of the Murgos upon the left and of the Thulls and the Nadraks upon the right fled into the river that they might save their lives. But swift is the River Arend at Vo Mimbre, and deep, and the waters swallowed them up. Few only escaped the waters and gained the far shore to flee back through the wilderness to the east. For the hordes of the Malloreans, however, was there no escape, for the armies of the West encircled them, and they were slain – yea, even unto the last man. For Behold, the armies of the West bore torches with them, and when dusky night laid his mantle of darkness upon the plain before the city, set they the torches ablaze that no Mallorean might escape their vengeance. And the watchers within the city wept and came forth to beseech the armies to abate the killings, so great was their pity for the Malloreans. But grim-faced Brand, Warder of Riva and overgeneral of all the armies of the West, hardened his heart against their pleas and abated not the slaughter.

And he spake, saying, 'No more! No more will Angaraks

come into the West. No seed nor root shall escape this cleansing.'

And in the night when the torches had burned low, came forth the scale-armored warriors of Ulgo and sought out the wounded and slew them. And none escaped, for indeed, from the warriors of Ulgo is nothing hidden in the dark.

And when the smoky dawn arose upon the fourth day, the Host was no more, and the multitudes of the slain were lain in heaps upon the plain before the city – yea, as far as the eye could see, the ruin of Angarak did litter the fair plain.

And Brand spake, saying, 'Bring unto me the body of the Accursed One whom I have slain that I might behold Him who would be King and God of all the world.'

But lo! The body of maimed Torak was not to be found among the slain. For it had come to pass that in the night Zedar the Sorcerer who sat ever at the right hand of Kal-Torak had cast an enchantment and had passed unseen through the armies of the West, past Sendar and Tolnedran, past Arend and Drasnian, past Algar and Cherek, past grim-faced Rivan and cat-eyed Ulgo and had borne away the body of the maimed God.

And Brand was troubled and took counsel with his two closest advisers, the grizzled old man whose name none knew and the dark-haired woman with the silver-touched brow who strode through the camp as she were Queen of the World. And between them they cast auguries and were troubled, and the aged man spake, saying, 'Behold, Warder of Riva, thine enemy hath escaped thee. Torak is not dead, but sleeps only and will arise again.'

And Brand spake, saying, 'He is slain. The nameless sword I bear hath bereft him of life. None may withstand such a stroke as the Accursed One was dealt.'

And the aged man spake, saying, 'Be not over-proud, Warder of Riva. Torak, King and God of the Angaraks, is not of mortal kind. He is a God – a dark God and an evil, but a God nonetheless. No stroke by mortal weapon, though it pierce his very heart, may slay him. Even now hath Belzedar, the traitor, borne him away and concealed him lest we find him and chain him against his awakening.'

And Brand was chastened by the words of his counselor, and he spake, saying, 'And when will the Dark God awaken? I must know that I might prepare the kingdoms of the West against his return.'

And the woman spake, saying, 'When once again a King of the Line of Riva sits upon his northern throne; when the fire of Aldur's Orb is rekindled by his touch and the halls of the Rivan King are filled with the light of that Orb, then will the Dark God awaken and come forth from his sleep to do war against the West and against the Rivan King. And then it shall come to pass that they shall meet – even as thou and Torak have met, and one shall slay the other, and the fate of the world shall be decided by that meeting.'

And Brand spake, saying, 'But the line of Riva is no more, and the halls of the Rivan King are dark and unused. How shall the line be renewed when it lies dead? How may a dead tree bear fruit? And if Torak be a God as thou has said, how may even the great sword of the Rivan King overcome him?'

And the woman answered him, saying, 'The dead tree hath borne its fruit, and the seeds thereof have lain concealed many centuries and will for many more. When the time has come, he will arise to claim his own, and the fire of Aldur's Orb will be kindled in rejoicing as a sign unto thy people that their King has returned.'

'And know,' quoth the aged man, 'the Sword of the Rivan King is not a mortal weapon. Aldur's Orb which is its pommel-stone is the creation of the God Aldur, and the two stars which fell and were forged by Riva to make the hilts and the blade were sent by the God Belar, and behold, the Spirits of the two Gods are in the Sword. With that Sword may Torak One-eye be overthrown – and with that Sword only.'

'But the Sword hangs upon the great black rock at the back of the throne in Riva,' quoth Brand. 'The Orb which thou didst command that I put in this shield is no longer attached thereunto. The throne-room of the Rivan King is dank and unused, and the dampness of the sea hath crept in, and the Sword bleeds red rust from its point onto the black face of the rock, weeping away its substance, since the Rivan Kings are no more.'

'Behold, Brand, Warder of Riva,' quoth the woman, ever imperious. 'The Sword of Riva may bleed rust for ten thousand years and lose not one ounce of its substance. It is a holy thing forged by Riva himself, and the Spirits of Belar and of Aldur are in it. It may not pass away, neither may it change nor alter. It abides against the coming of the great battle wherein the fate of the world shall be decided. That is its purpose; for that only was it forged. It is an instrument fated to be raised in the contention of Gods – forged was it to spill out the immortal life of Torak. It hath no other purpose, and it will abide against the time of the accomplishment of that purpose – even if it must be unto the very end of days.'

And Brand was content, and set he his armies to cleansing the battlefield before the city of the wreckage of Angarak, of Murgo and Thull, of Nadrak and Grolim, and of the unnumbered dead of vast Mallorea.

And when it was completed the nobles of Arendia came unto him, saying, 'Behold, the King of the Mimbrates is dead and the war-lord of the Asturians also, for they have slain each other in single combat, so great was their hatred one for the other. Remain with us, Brand, and be thou our King, lest the civil war which hath sundered the Arends for uncounted centuries break forth again and set Arendia aflame.'

And Brand spake, saying, 'Who is the heir to the Mimbrate Throne whom my Kingship would dispossess? And where is the fruit of the Asturian Dukes who would also contend my ascension to the Throne?'

'Korodullin is Crown Prince of the Mimbrates,' quoth the nobles.

'Is there none other?' quoth Brand.

'None, Lord,' quoth the nobles. 'The line ends with him. One sword-thrust and the house of Mimbre is no more.'

Brand looked upon them and spake not.

'And Mayaserana is the last of the Asturian line,' quoth the nobles. 'She is quite young and slender. A sharp knife drawn across her throat will end Astur as easily as Mimbre.'

And Brand spake, saying, 'Bring them to me.' And it was done. And he spake unto them, saying, 'Now ends the bloodshed between Astur and Mimbre. It is my will that thou be wed, one unto the other.'

And Korodullin, Crown Prince of Mimbre, spake hotly, saying, 'Sooner would I die than suffer the dishonor of marriage to some foul whelp of forest brigands.'

And Mayaserana, Duchess of Astur, spake with equal heat, saying, 'Thou mayest command, Great Brand, Warder of Riva, but if rope or knife or spear or high wall or the deep, cold river still have power to take life, thou shalt not bring me breathing unto the marriage bed of some degenerate offspring of thieves and usurpers.'

And Brand was wroth at their pride and their despite unto his will, and he caused them to be imprisoned together in a high tower on the south wall of the city. And the barons of Arendia were gloomy at this and swore that the two would never be reconciled nor would they bend to the will of Brand.

But Brand counseled patience and turned to other matters.

And it came to pass that the Kings of the West gathered in the

great encampment before the City of Vo Mimbre on the plain of Arendia. Splendid was the pavilion in which they met, and mighty were the Kings.

And Ormik, King of the ever-practical Sendars spake, saying, 'Behold, the Kings of the West are assembled. Might we not here resolve those disputes which have divided us and thus wrest from the grim fist of war a felicity for our kingdoms and our people which they have never known? Let us here, my brothers, upon this field of war examine peace.'

And the other Kings marveled at the good sense of the King of the Sendars, for in truth he seemed a foolish man.

But Rhodar, King of Drasnia, spake, saying, 'Not yet is the war against Angarak ended. Still are there Nadrak garrisons in the ruins of Boktor and Kotu, and dark Grolim priests hunt the marshes of Mrin for the sons and daughters of Dras Bull-neck to sacrifice on the altars of Torak One-eye.'

And Cho-Ram, King of Algaria and Chief of the Clan-chiefs spake, saying, 'And still is there war in Algaria. The Stronghold of the Algars is besieged by Murgos.'

But Eldrig, white-bearded King of Cherek spake, saying, 'Dear Brothers, these are but minor internal problems for Aloria. The eviction of a few unwanted guests is not a problem with which we need concern Imperial Tolnedra, Noble Arendia, nor Holy Ulgo. Now that Torak is overthrown, Aloria may dispose of the rags of Angarak at its leisure. The Kings of the West face here a greater destiny. Boundless Mallorea hath sent her unnumbered hordes against us, and Murgo and Nadrak and Thull have tried our strength, and we have overcome them. More than this, we have witnessed here, upon this very field, the overthrow of a God. Surely the hands of the other Gods were in this, and Brand of Riva hath been their instrument. What better omen than this? Know now, dear Brothers, I, Eldrig, King of Cherek, of the blood and bone of Cherek Bear-shoulders, eldest of the Alorn Kings, swear fealty to Brand of Riva as Overlord of the West.' And rose he and saluted Brand, Warder of Riva, with his great war-axe.

And Cho-Ram of Algaria rose also, saying, 'Great indeed is the wisdom of my venerable Brother of Cherek who hath pointed out the will of the Gods. For their guidance was with Brand of Riva as he led us against the hordes of Angarak, and their guidance will surely be with him still in the peace we now face. I, Cho-Ram, Chief of the Clan-chiefs, King of the Algars, descendant of Algar Fleet-foot, also swear fealty to Brand of Riva as Overlord of the West.' And saluted he Brand with his great curved sword.

And then rose Rhodar of Drasnia, saying, 'The children of the Bear-God speak as one. All of Aloria is again one people and one nation. I, Rhodar, King of Northernmost Drasnia, descendant of Dras Bull-neck, pledge fealty to Brand of Riva as Overlord of the West.' And saluted he Brand with his short, broad-bladed sword.

And rose Ormik, King of the Sendars, and troubled was his face, and he spake, saying, 'Dear Brothers, Kings of the West, truly is Brand of Riva a man like unto no other man. Who else among us hath overthrown a God? And I say unto you now, that whatsoever Brand commandeth me to do, that will I do. And wheresoever he leads, there will I follow – yea, be it into fire or into water, and pledge I here fealty unto Brand of Riva – I and all of Sendaria with me. And Sendaria stands with Aloria as one people under the Overlordship of Brand of Riva. *But*, dear Brothers, some there are here who perceive not the glory which we have here beheld. For some it is a simple matter to perceive the touch of the Gods upon a man. For others such perception comes not easy. A miracle can be not seen or can be ignored if the import of the miracle is not to their liking. The force of the West is here upon this field. The war which might here arise could rend us as Boundless Mallorea or the might of Angarak with Fell Torak at their head might never have done. Truly, dear Brothers, might the cities of the West be pulled down and the Kingdoms laid waste and the people harried into the

THE BATTLE OF VO MIMBRE 269

wilderness. Aloria is one and Sendaria with them, but what of Imperial Tolnedra? How speaks Holy Ulgo? What says the Queen of the serpent people in Dark Nyissa? If we war, dear Brothers, what will remain? What spark of humanity will be left to us? If we fall upon each other, may not Mallorean and Murgo, Thull and Nadrak fall upon our remnants and herd our poor survivors into the hands of Dark Grolim priests for their unspeakable rites in celebration of the victory of the Dark God we have here seen overthrown?'

Then rose Podiss, emissary of Nyissa, ambassador of Salmissra, Queen of the Snake People, and spake with great despite unto the Alorn Kings, saying, 'Much have I wondered here at the readiness of Sovereign Kings to submit to the will of one with no name of known heritage. My mistress, Eternal Queen Salmissra of deep-wooded Nyissa, will never submit to the overlordship of a nameless Alorn butcher.'

And wroth was grey-bearded Eldrig, King of Cherek, and Cho-Ram also and equally Rhodar of Drasnia. And Cho-Ram of Algaria spake, saying, 'May it not be that the memory of the emissary of Eternal Salmissra is somewhat short? And that of the snake woman in Sthiss Tor also? Might it not profit her to be reminded of the consequences of offending Aloria? Let us send her the head of this spiteful ambassador that her memory might be refreshed.'

Then rose Mergon, ambassador of Tolnedra to the Court at Vo Mimbre, and spake, saying, 'Highnesses, Great Kings of the North, much wonder have we seen here. Great Brand, Warrior without peer, hath overthrown Dark Torak and well have we avenged the wasting of Drasnia and the invasion of Algaria upon the hordes of Angarak. I greet Brand in the name of his Imperial Majesty, Ran Borune IV, Crown of the third Borune Dynasty, and extend to the Noble Warder of Riva an Imperial invitation to come to the court at Tol Honeth that my Emperor might honor him as befits the foremost warrior of the West. Let us not, however, hasten into unchangeable decisions in the first flush of admiration and gratitude. Noble Brand, I am sure, will be the first to agree that the arts of war and the arts of peace are in no wise similar. Seldom indeed are the two arts linked in the same man. A battle is soon over and a war endures not forever. The burdens of peace, however, grow heavier with the passing of each year. Moreover, I am troubled by this talk of Aloria. Of Cherek I have heard and of Drasnia also and Algaria. And who hath not heard of the Isle of the Winds and the unassailable Riva? But where is this Aloria? What are its boundaries? Where lies this mysterious land of the North? Where is its capital? In truth, Aloria hath not existed since the sundering which took place in the days of Cherek Bear-shoulders and his three mighty sons. I am disquieted by this sudden re-emergence of a kingdom long buried in the mists of antiquity. Imperial Tolnedra must deal with mundane reality. We can send no emissary to the court of the King of the Fairies. We can conclude no treaty with the Emperor of the Moon. With earthly kingdoms only may we have commerce. Myth and legend, however grand, may not enter into the affairs of the Empire lest we become unsettled in our minds, and the solid rock upon which depends the stability of all the West become as insubstantial mist or shifting sand.

'Also, Great Kings and Lords, I am distressed by the evident disregard of long-standing covenants and treaties I have here witnessed. Most solemn agreements have here been breached. Many of you have treaties with the Empire, and those treaties state most clearly that you will have no meetings with other Kings without first informing the Emperor of your intent. Is it wise to tempt thus the might of Imperial Tolnedra?'

And rose grey-bearded Eldrig, King of Cherek, and spake, saying, 'Hearken unto me, Noble Mergon. Upon this field Aloria stands armed. We fear not the might of Imperial Tolnedra. If it please you, you may carry news of our meeting here to Ran Borune. Cherek vessels are swift. It is possible that I myself may be in Tol Honeth to greet you upon your arrival.'

And Cho-Ram of Algaria rose, saying, 'The horses of the Algars are also swift. I too will be in Tol Honeth awaiting you.'

And Rhodar rose, saying, 'I and my pikemen came a thousand leagues to this field. The two hundred to Tol Honeth will not even shake the dust of battle from our feet. I also will await your coming in Tol Honeth.'

Then quoth Eldrig, saying, 'We would instruct your Emperor in geography. The armies of the Alorns assembled are invincible. The boundaries of Aloria are where we say they are, and what we say is to be, will be. And if we must prove this to Ran Borune and to Salmissra, then so be it.'

Then spake the Venerable Gorim of Ulgo, saying, 'Care must we use here, dear Brothers, lest the Spirit of Torak rejoice at our division. Words of spite and of warlike defiance are easy to say in the heat of a moment. They are difficult to unsay even after years of sorrow have proved their folly.

'The Alorn Kings would name Brand of Riva Overlord of the West by reason of his overthrow of the Maimed God Torak – and *also* by reason that he is Alorn. Tolnedra and Nyissa would *honor* Brand for his victory, but would perhaps not wish to submit themselves to his Overlordship – *because* he is Alorn. Might not an accommodation be reached, dear Brothers? Let us give Brand an Imperial Princess of Tolnedra to wed and one third of the treasury of Nyissa as tribute if he will withdraw from the uncomfortable eminence into which he hath been thrust.'

'Never,' hissed Podiss, emissary of Eternal Salmissra.

And troubled was Mergon, ambassador of Tolnedra, and he spake, saying, 'Surely the Gorim of Holy Ulgo speaks in jest. The Imperial Princesses of Tolnedra are the fairest jewels of the Empire. Their bestowing is decided oft-times even before their birth.'

Then Brand, Warder of Riva, who had remained silent, arose and spake, saying, 'Peace, Brothers. No wife do I require, since she who shared my youth and bore my children awaits me in Riva. To me she is a greater jewel than all the princesses of all the empires of the earth. And I require not the treasury of Nyissa – nor of any other kingdom. What should I do with it? The walls of Riva are complete, built by Iron-grip himself, and he it was who clave the rock that the river might come forth to bathe the feet of the city. What need hath a Rivan of treasure? We have one treasure already, and our race hath guarded it with our lives for two thousand years and more. Would you inflict another treasure upon us to guard? How many lives do we have?

'The honor which the Kings of Aloria would do me is beyond my power to bear. I am quite bowed down by the weight of it. But how might I, in far-off Riva, maintain dominion and Empire? How might I know when the people in deepest Nyissa hungered, or the herds in farthest Algaria perished of thirst, or the caverns in Holy Ulgo fell down, trapping the Children of UL beneath the earth? And what of the Gods? Will Nedra permit a son of the Bear-God to hold power in Tol Honeth? Will Chaldan or Issa accept my Overlordship in Arendia or in the land of the Snake-People? And what of mysterious UL? And of Aldur, the God who stands apart? Overlordship may not be bestowed by men, but must come as a duty imposed by the Gods.

'I may not, therefore, accept this honor. And must we all be wary here lest in our seeming power we rise up to such height that the Gods become offended with us; or, if our contentions become too great, might we not see again the disputation of partisan Gods? And if the Gods make war, will they not destroy the world?'

Then rose the Aged Man who had counseled the Warder of Riva

and spake, saying, 'Great is the wisdom of Brand. Hear his words, Oh, Kings and Lords of the West, and offend not the Gods by thine impiety. And yet, might there not be *some* token of gratitude to Brand and to Riva?'

And Gorim of Ulgo looked long at the Aged Man and knew him and spake, saying, 'Thou knowest, Immortal One, that Torak is overthrown, but is not slain.'

'Yes,' quoth the Aged One.

'And thou wouldst fulfill the prophecy?' quoth the Gorim.

'It must be,' quoth the Aged One. 'If we bring not the prophecies into fruition through our own efforts, then will they come to pass in our despite and oftentimes in strange and unseemly ways. The outcome of the great battle is still in doubt, and I would do all that might be done to aid the Champion of the West. If he be not victorious – if he be slain – foul Torak will overcome the world and master it, and all men will be his slaves.'

And the Gorim of Ulgo spake, saying, 'The prophecy is old, and its meaning may have been clouded by the falling of so many dusty years upon it. Art thou certain, Immortal One, that it hath not been twisted by some events of the distant past?'

And the Aged One spake, saying, 'The auguries still hold true. The prophecy is intact. He will rise and will seek out his throne, and a great princess shall be his to wife. And at his coming shall Torak shake off his sleep and come again against the West. And the two shall meet and struggle, and one shall be slain and the other shall be Overlord of all the World.' And he turned unto the Alorn Kings and spake, saying, 'This was not well done, Eldrig of Cherek. He who would twist a prophecy for his own ends casts his impiety into the teeth of the Gods. The final battle is not yet come, and Torak is *not* slain.'

And Eldrig was wroth and rose up as he would smite the Aged One, but the scales fell from his eyes, and he knew the one before him, and he trembled before him, and spake, saying, 'Forgive me, Ancient One, beloved of Aldur and companion of Belar, that I did offend the Gods and thee. I wished only to live in the days of the fulfillment of the prophecy.'

And the Gorim of Ulgo spake, saying, 'Great King of timeless Cherek, the prophecy will be fulfilled. Not in thy time nor in mine, however, shall it come to fruition. But the day will come when the King of the West shall ascend his throne, and the last battle shall be fought, and the fate of the world shall hinge upon that coming and that battle. What we have seen here is prelude. In the fullness of time shall the battle be joined, and we must be content that our part in this is needful and the world is better for our having done what we have done.' And turned he unto the Aged One whose eyes were ever in shadow and spake again, saying, 'And wilt thou abide his coming?'

And the Aged One answered, saying, 'Yea, I will abide – even if it be unto the end of days.'

And the Gorim spake, saying, 'UL is with thee, even as Aldur and Belar. His blessing is upon thee, most Ancient of Men.' And then rose he and spake in a great voice that all assembled might hear, saying, 'Here is promised the Princess of Tolnedra to be wife unto the King of Riva who will be the savior of the world. This is the will of UL and of Aldur and of Belar and of the other Gods also. Let no man gainsay the voices of the Gods, lest the Gods in their wrath rise up and destroy him and all his race.'

And Mergon, ambassador of Imperial Tolnedra, was distressed, and rose he and spake, saying, 'But all the world knows that the Hall of the Rivan King is empty and desolate. No King sits on the Rivan Throne. How may a Princess of Imperial Tolnedra be wed unto a phantom?'

And then spake the woman who was ever at the side of the Ancient One who counseled Brand, saying. 'From this day forward upon her sixteenth birthday shall each Princess of Imperial Tolnedra present herself in the Hall of the Rivan King. In her wedding gown shall she be clad, and three days shall she abide there against the coming of the King. And if he come not to claim her, shall she be free to go wheresoever her father, the Emperor, shall decree, for she shall not be the favored one.'

And Mergon spake, saying, 'All Tolnedra shall rise against such an indignity. It may not be.'

And the woman answered, saying, 'In the day that Tolnedra fails in this shall the West rise up against her, and we will scatter the Sons of Nedra to the winds and pull down thy cities and lay waste thy fields and thy villages. And the people of Nedra shall be as the people of Mara, who are no more. And, like Mara, shall Nedra weep alone in the wilderness that his people are no more.'

And the Kings of Aloria rose, and Eldrig spake, saying, 'To this, pledge I Cherek.' And Cho-Ram said, 'To this, pledge I Algaria.' And Rhodar said, 'To this, pledge I Drasnia.' And Ormik said, 'To this, pledge I Sendaria.' And the Gorim spake, saying, 'I also pledge Holy Ulgo to this. Tell thine Emperor that in the day that he or his line fails in this, in that day shall Tolnedra surely perish.'

And then spake Podiss, emissary of Nyissa, saying. 'And what of my Queen, Eternal Salmissra? What voice hath she in thine ordering of the world?'

Then rose the woman and cast off her cloak. Queenly was her bearing, and her brow was touched as with frost, and she raised up her hands, and behold, the garments of Podiss fell inward as it were the man within had dissolved as snows before the breath of spring. And a serpent emerged therefrom. And the form of the woman became cloudy and indistinct, and there emerged from the mist which surrounded her a great snowy owl, and she did grasp the serpent in her talons and did bear him aloft into the heavens.*

And in the space of a little time did she return, and the woman resumed her proper form and Podiss also. And trembling was he and ashen-faced.

And the woman spake, saying, 'Inform the snake woman in Sthiss Tor what hath befallen thee. Tell her what an easy thing it is for the owl to destroy the serpent. Fail not in this, lest I seek thee out and bear thee again into the sky and dash thee down upon the earth beneath. In the day that Eternal Salmissra raises her hand once more against the Rivan King shall I plunge my talons into her heart and destroy her utterly.'

And the Kings and Emissaries were amazed at the enchantment they had beheld and looked upon the woman in fear and in wonder, knowing that she was a Sorceress.

And spake the Gorim of Ulgo, saying. 'These then are the accords which we have reached here upon the field at Vo Mimbre: The

---

* This was modified.

nations of the West will prepare themselves against the return of the Rivan King, for in the day of his return shall Torak awaken and come again upon us, and none but the Rivan King may overcome him and save us from his foul enslavement. And whatsoever the Rivan King commands, that shall we do. And swear we all fealty here unto the King that shall return. And he shall have an Imperial Princess of Tolnedra to wife and have Empire and Dominion in the West. And whosoever breaketh these accords, will we do war upon him and scatter his people and pull down his cities and lay waste his lands. We pledge it here in honor of Brand, who hath overthrown Torak and bound him in sleep until the One comes who might destroy him. So be it.'

And it was done as the Gorim had said, and all agreed to it and were bound by it.

And in the fullness of time prepared the armies of the West to depart and to return each unto their own kingdom. And before he left called Brand to have the Prince of Mimbre and the Duchess of Asturia brought before him again, and it was done.

And Brand spake, saying, 'I have a mind to see thee wed before I depart. What sayest thou to this?'

And Korodullin of Mimbre spake, saying, 'I am content, for my fair fellow-prisoner hath won my heart, and I will wed none other.'

'And what of thou?' quoth Brand unto Mayaserana, Duchess of Asturia. 'Wilt thou still seek river or rope, knife, or spear to separate thee from thy life that thou mayest avoid thy wedding?'

And she answered, saying, 'Forgive the folly of my childish speech, great Brand. I am a woman now and gladly will I wed noble Korodullin that the wounds of Noble Arendia be healed. And in truth would I wed him even were Arendia not wounded.'

And Brand smiled and caused a great wedding to be prepared, and the people of Arendia rejoiced in the marriage of Korodullin and Mayaserana.

And one last time spake Brand unto the Kings and nobles before he returned to Riva, saying, 'Behold, here has much been wrought that is good. Boundless Mallorea and fell Angarak have been overthrown, and Evil Torak is quelled. His dark presence moves no more in the world. The covenant we have struck between us here prepares the West for the day in which the Rivan King returns and Torak wakes from his long slumber to contest with him for Empire and Dominion. All that may be done in this age to gird the West against that great and final war hath been done. And here have the wounds of Arendia been healed by reason of the wedding of Korodullin and

Mayaserana, and the strife which hath bloodied the fair fields and
forests of Noble Arendia for two thousand years and more is ended.
I am content with it all. Hail then and farewell.'

And he turned from them and rode north with the Aged One and
the Queenly Woman as always by his side. And they did take ship at
Camaar in Sendaria and set sail for Riva, and returned no more to
the kingdoms of the West.

At Tol Honeth

AFTERWORD

To me it has fallen to wrestle the chaos of documents, ancient and modern, herein contained into some kind of order. This has not been a task which I have undertaken willingly. The documents, for the most part, have no verifiable authenticity, and no scholar wishes to have his name appended to such questionable material. Moreover, it is clearly evident that many, perhaps all of the manuscripts in hand were pilfered from one source or another, and I personally find it odious to deal with material so obtained.

Unfortunately, in my capacity as tutor to the Imperial Household, I am subject to Imperial whim. Thus it was that when her Highness, Ce'Nedra, Imperial Princess of Tolnedra, and now (unfortunately) Queen of Riva, charged me with this task, I had no choice but to comply as graciously as possible. This is small reward for the support and protection I gave her on that ghastly journey ten years ago. True to her nature – and, I might add, to the nature of all the Borunes – Princess Ce'Nedra has chosen to ignore one of the most time-honored traditions in the scholarly community. It is customary, if I may be so bold as to point it out to Her Majesty, for an Imperial tutor to be named to a major chair at the Imperial University upon the completion of his service to his pupil. It was for this reason and for this reason only that I accepted my post in the Palace in the first place. I assure her that my fidelity to the near-impossible task of hammering some minimal semblance of education into a willful. arrogant, spoiled and over-pampered pupil had no other motive.

My enemies at this point are undoubtedly gloating over the fate which my frankness here must inevitably bring down upon my head. To immediately rob them of even that minuscule enjoyment, let me state here that it is my intention, when this loathsome chore is completed, to enter the Monastery at

Mar Terin and to pass my final years in peace and quiet with nothing but the shrieks of the spirit of Mara and the wails of the Marag ghosts to disturb my slumbers. From that sanctuary, beyond the reach of Imperial punishment or reward, I shall have that last and best laugh at the discomfort my words here shall cause those who have so cruelly betrayed me.

It is certainly fitting that those remarkable events of ten years ago be recorded by a competent scholar, but this present mass of gibberish is certainly not that record. Once I am safely within the sanctuary at Mar Terin I shall undertake that study. Let the mighty tremble at that prospect. It is my intention to present those events precisely as they occurred. I will not genuflect before some high-sounding but empty concept of Borune dignity, nor will I quiver in awe at the mention of the name of the Rivan King. I know that Ran Borune XXIII is a doddering old fool, a fitting crown to the third (and hopefully last) Borune Dynasty. I know that Ce'Nedra is a spoiled brat. I know that Garion (or Belgarion as he now prefers to be called) is nothing more than a scullery boy who sits by sheerest accident on the throne at Riva. I know that Belgarath is a charlatan or a madman or worse. And I know that Polgara, that impossible woman, is no better than she should be.

But now to the documents in hand. When this mass of disorganized material was delivered to me by the ape-like Barak, I laughed at what was so obviously a fraud. The rambling, self-congratulatory preface by Belgarath provides an immediate clue as to how seriously one should take this entire thing. If we are to believe this absurd testimony, Belgarath is somewhat over seven thousand years old, consorts freely with Gods, converses with beasts and performs miracles with the wave of a hand. I am amazed that even the feeble intelligence of my former pupil accepted so ludicrous a story; for, though she has the typical Borune pig-headedness, she at least had the benefit of my tutelage during her formative years.

The next collection in this welter of documents consists of a series of extracts from the sacred writings of the various peoples of the known world. The manuscripts (all stolen, I'm sure) are hardly subject to verification. The Proverbs of Nedra, for example, are from the list approved by the priests in the Great Temple at Tol Honeth. The Lament of Mara presented here differs only marginally from a copy in my own library. The Book of Alorn is in keeping with the spirit of that barbaric race. The Book of Torak, however, is a translation from old Angarak (a language with which I am unfamiliar) and is subject to all the woeful errors common in translations. And the so-called Book of Ulgo is a patent absurdity. I have always been of the opinion that Ulgos are nothing more than a race of fanatical heretics who should have been forcibly converted to a proper religion centuries ago.

The section dealing with the history of the twelve kingdoms of the West, by contrast, is a solid and respectable piece of work – as well it should be.

The document was stolen from (and still bears the seal of) the Imperial Library at Tol Honeth. My only quarrel with the manuscript is the fact that it is the official version prepared with all that toadying flattery of the House of Borune of which our present Dynasty is so fond.

The final section, the Arendish fairy-tale account of the Battle of Vo Mimbre, is a fitting conclusion to this entire work, since it is filled from beginning to end with utter nonsense.

And now my task is complete. I wish Her Imperial Highness all the joy in it she so richly deserves.

I leave behind me one wish before I depart for Mar Terin. With all my heart I pray to Great Nedra that the Borune Dynasty which has so blighted the Empire be succeeded by the Honethites – a family with a proper respect for tradition, and one which knows how to suitably reward those who have served them.

And now, farewell.

MASTER JEEBERS
Fellow of the Imperial Society
Tutor to the Imperial Household

Done and sealed at Tol Honeth
in the year 5378.

INTERMISSION

Are you still there? What an amazing thing! If you've read the Belgariad, I'm sure you can see now where most of it originated. (If you haven't read the Belgariad, why are you reading this?) The studies you've just so bravely endured gave us the story. Our character-sketches gave us our people. The dialogue grew out of the actual writing. I'm sure you noticed a certain amount of bickering among the troops. Grand and noble companionship *sounds* sort of nice, but both my wife and I have been in the military, so we know how unreal that notion is. Part of our aim was to create an epic fantasy with a heavy overlay of realism. The immediacy – that sense of actually knowing these characters which many readers have noticed – derives from that realism in dialogue and details. We can blame my wife for a lot of that. I'd be trying for 'grand sweep', and she'd jerk me up short with such things as, 'It's all black and white. It needs color.' or 'They haven't eaten for three days.' or 'Don't you think it's about time that they took a bath?' Here I am trying to save the world, and 'Polgara' is nagging me about bathing!

Women! (Does that sound familiar?)

I'd also frequently run into that stone wall named, 'A woman wouldn't talk that way. That's a male expression. Women don't use it.' I'd grumble a bit and then surrender and do it her way. My personal writing strategy is 'Blast on through and get the story in place, and then go back and clean and polish it.' She wants it done right in the first place, and I've learned not to argue with the lady who runs the kitchen – unless I want boiled dog-food for supper.

Now let's answer all the critics who proudly announce that they find our work derivative. What else is new? Chaucer was derivative. So was Shakespeare. The literary value of any story is in its *presentation*. Any plot-line can be reduced to absurdity if one chooses to do so. There's a story, probably apocryphal, which tells us of an early movie producer who simplified all movie plots down to 'Cinderella' and 'Goldilocks'. He'd buy 'Goldilocks', but he wouldn't buy 'Cinderella'.

Back to work. We'd completed the Belgariad, and now we were ready to take on the Malloreon. Most of what we needed was already in place. We had our main characters, our magic thingama-jig, and our cultures of the western kingdoms. Now we needed a new 'Bad-Guy' (or Girl), and a new quest. (I'd also had enough of adolescents by now, and I wanted to see if Garion and Ce'Nedra could function as adults.) Oh, by the way, if anyone out there ever calls those two 'teenagers', I'll turn them into a toad. 'Teenager' is a linguistic abomination devised by the advertising agencies and the social worker industry to obscure an unpleasant reality. The proper term is 'adolescent', and the only good thing about it is that every-body gets over it – eventually. (Or most of them, anyway.)

We extended the geography in our new map, and then it was time to correct the injustice we'd done to the Angaraks. Just because Germany produced Hitler doesn't alter the fact that Germany also produced Kant, Goethe, Beethoven, and Niebuhr. No race or nation-ality has a monopoly on either good or evil. Perfection in either direction simply doesn't exist in the real world, and it doesn't exist in *our* world either. On one occasion Belgarath simplified the whole thing by discarding theology entirely and identifying the contend-ing parties as 'them and us'. You can't get much more to the point than that. We humanized the Angaraks by humanizing Zakath and by stressing the significance of Eriond. The Christ-like quality of Eriond was quite deliberate. Torak was a mistake. Eriond was the original 'Intent of the Universe'. (Deep, huh?)

The tiresome *History of the Angarak Kingdoms* was handed off to the scholars at the University of Melcene, who are just as stuffy and wrong-headed as their counterparts at the University of Tol Honeth. It worked for us in the Belgariad, so it was probably going to work just as well in the Malloreon, (If it ain't busted; don't fix it), and it worked again. Then we substituted *The Mallorean Gospels* for *The Holy Books* in the Belgariad Preliminaries. The intent was the same. Our overall thesis was that there are two worlds running side by side – the ordinary, mundane world, and the theological magic world. When they start to overlap, all hell breaks loose, and you've got story. You're neck-deep in story. Did you want to summarize the twentieth century? Try *that* as a starting point.

To get 'story', we were obliged to become Manichees, maintaining that good and evil are evenly matched. If God is all-powerful, why are we so worried about the Devil? When the medieval Church declared Manicheism to be a heresy, she squirmed a lot, but never did answer that specific question. I won't either.

We also added a note of Existentialism by forcing Cyradis, acting for all of mankind, to make the final choice between good and evil. It makes a good story, but it probably shouldn't be accepted as the basis for a system of personal belief, since it might get *you* into a lot of trouble. If the Pope doesn't get on your case, the Archbishop of Canterbury probably will.

The Malloreon Preliminaries conclude with King Anheg's personal diary, which sort of followed our outline for Book One of the Malloreon. It gives us a condensed chronology, and that's always useful.

As with the Preliminaries to the Belgariad, these Malloreon Prelims had quite a few dead-ends which we discarded during the actual writing. One of the dangers of epic fantasy lies in its proclivity to wander off into the bushes. We have what appears to be the gabbiest of all possible fiction forms, but it requires iron discipline. The writer absolutely *must* stick to the story-line and deviate *only* when an idea or character will improve the overall product. I can't verify this, but I *have* heard that there was a medieval romance that was *twenty-five thousand pages long*!! That's an entire library all by itself. I suspect that if you were to give a contemporary fantasist free rein, he might take a shot at that just to get his name in the *Guinness Book of Records*.

All right, push bravely on. We'll talk again later.

❧IV❧

PRELIMINARY STUDIES FOR THE MALLOREON

A CURSORY HISTORY OF THE
ANGARAK KINGDOMS

*Prepared by the History Department
of the University of Melcene*

Tradition, though not always reliable, places the ancestral home
of the Angaraks in the southern latitudes somewhere off the south
coast of present-day Dalasia. In that prehistoric era, when Angarak
and Alorn lived in peace, the favored races of mankind inhabited
contiguous areas in a pleasant, fertile basin which was forever
submerged by the cataclysmic event known as 'The Cracking of the
World'. It is not the purpose of this work to dwell upon the theological implications of that event, but rather to examine the course of
the history of the Angaraks in the centuries which followed.

The so-called 'Cracking of the World' appears in fact to have been
a splitting of the crust of the primeval proto-continent, and its effects

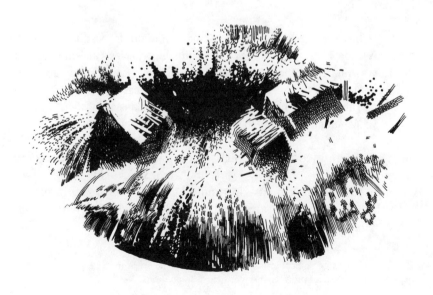

were immediately disastrous. The plasmic magma upon which the great land-mass floated immediately began to extrude itself into that vast split and to force the now-separated continental plates apart. When the waters of the southern ocean rushed into the resulting gap and inundated the rising magma, a continuous violent explosion ripped from one end of the vast fault to the other, forcing the plates even farther apart and setting off a tremendous, rolling earthquake which soon encompassed the entire globe.* Entire mountain ranges quite literally crumbled into rubble, and colossal tidal waves raced across the oceans of the world, forever altering coastlines a half a planet away. The Sea of the East grew daily wider as the elemental violence at its floor rudely shouldered the two continental plates farther and farther apart. The explosive separation of the continents appears to have continued for decades until it gradually subsided and the two great landmasses stabilized in more or less their present location. The world which emerged from this catastrophe was almost totally unlike the world which had previously existed.

During this vast upheaval, the Angaraks retreated northeasterly before the steadily encroaching sea, and they ultimately sought the safety of the higher ground of the Dalasian Mountains in West Central Mallorea. Once the movement of the continental plates had subsided, however, the Angaraks found that the unstable weather generated by the newly-formed Sea of the East made the Dalasian Mountains too inhospitable a place for permanent residence, and they migrated north into the reaches of what is now called Ancient Mallorea.

NOTE When speaking of this era, some confusion is possible. Modern Mallorea encompasses the entire continent, whereas Ancient Mallorea was limited to the northwestern segment of the land mass and was bordered on the south by Dalasia and on the east by Karanda. It is in part the purpose of this study to trace the expansion of the Angaraks which ultimately led to their domination of all of Mallorea.

During the troubled times which accompanied the migration, the presence of Torak, Dragon God of Angarak, was scarcely felt. Although he had previously dominated every facet of Angarak life, the mutilation inflicted upon him by CTHRAG-YASKA (which men in the west call the Orb of Aldur) caused him such unbearable

---

* This is probably a geological impossibility. Volcanoes *do* erupt under the oceans of *this* world, and that does not produce thermonuclear detonations.

suffering that he was no longer able to function in his traditional
capacity as 'Kal', King and God. The Grolim priesthood, demoralized by the sudden incapacity of Torak, was unable to fill the
vacuum, and the leadership of Angarak fell by default into the
hands of the military commanders. Thus it was that the emerging
nation of the Angarak people was administered from the military
headquarters at Mal Zeth. By the time that the Grolims recovered,
they discovered that the military had established de facto rule of all
of Angarak. Shaking off their shock-induced paralysis, the Grolims
set up an opposing center of power at Mal Yaska at the southern tip
of the Karandese Mountains. Had matters remained so, inevitably
there would have been a confrontation between the military and the
priesthood, which in all probability would have destroyed Angarak
in the convulsions of civil war.

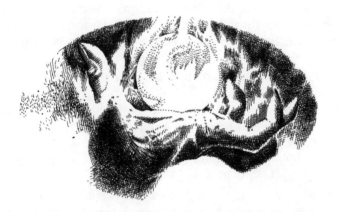

It was at this point, however, that Torak roused himself sufficiently to reassert his authority. During the period of his illness
(perhaps a century or so) the military had become dominant in
Angarak society, and much to the chagrin of the Grolim priesthood,
the awakening God made no effort to re-establish their ascendancy.
Instead of establishing himself at either Mal Zeth or at the ecclesiastical capital at Mal Yaska, however, Torak marched northwest to
establish the holy city at Cthol Mishrak on the northern edge of the
District of Camat. It should be pointed out here that the religious
writings of the period do not reveal the entire story. *The Book of Torak*
states that the Dragon God took his people to Cthol Mishrak and
caused them to build the city following his maiming by Cthrag-
Yaska. The scriptures blur over the hundred year interval during
which the Angaraks spread out over the northwestern quadrant of
Mallorea and implies that those who followed the maimed God

comprised all of Angarak. Civil records of the period, however, reveal that scarcely more than a quarter of the Angarak people followed Torak to Cthol Mishrak. Pleading the necessity of administering and protecting the rest of the nation, the military remained in place at Mal Zeth; and similarly, the Grolim hierarchy, with the equally plausible excuse of the need for overseeing the spiritual requirements of a growing and wide-spread population, continued to occupy Mal Yaska, from which they jealously guarded church interests against military encroachment. Torak, almost totally absorbed in his effort to gain control of the Orb, seemed oblivious to the fact that the majority of the Angarak peoples were becoming secularized. Those who followed him to Cthol Mishrak were, by and large, the often hysterical fringe of religious fanatics which are to be found in any society. Since Torak's attention was almost totally focused upon the Orb, the administration of day to day life in Cthol Mishrak fell to his three Disciples, Ctuchik, Urvon and later, Zedar. This trio, with the zeal which usually marks the Disciple, rigidly maintained the older forms and customs, in effect petrifying the society of Cthol Mishrak in that somewhat pastoral form which had obtained in the Angarak culture prior to the migration to Mallorea. As a result, the rest of Angarak changed in response to external pressures and their new environment, while the society at Cthol Mishrak and environs remained static. It was precisely this divergence which ultimately led to the friction which divides Cthol Murgos and modern Mallorea.

The Grolim hierarchy at Mal Yaska, chafing at what they felt was the usurpation of power by the military, began to take certain steps which once again brought Mallorea to the brink of civil war. While their campaign was scrupulously theological, it was nonetheless quite obviously directed at the military chain of command. The practice of human sacrifice had fallen into a certain disuse during the protracted illness of the Dragon God, but it was now reinstituted with unusual fervor. By carefully manipulating the drawing of lots which selected the sacrificial victims, the Grolims began to systematically exterminate the lower echelons of the officer corps.

The situation soon grew intolerable to the military commanders at Mal Zeth, and they retaliated by leveling fraudulent criminal charges at every Grolim unlucky enough to fall into their hands. Despite the howls of protest from Mal Yaska, where the hierarchy strenuously maintained that the priesthood was exempt from civil prosecution, these 'criminals' were all summarily executed.

Ultimately, word of this surreptitious war reached Torak, and the

God of Angarak took immediate steps to halt the bloodshed. He summoned the Military High Command and the Grolim Hierarchy to Cthol Mishrak and delivered his commands to the warring factions in blistering terms. There were to be no further sacrifices of military officers and no further executions of Grolims. Exempting only the enclaves at Mal Yaska and Mal Zeth, all other towns and districts in ancient Mallorea were to be ruled jointly by the military and the priesthood, the military to be responsible for civil matters, and the priesthood for religious ones. He told them, moreover, that should there be any recurrence of their secret war, he would immediately order the abandonment of all of the rest of Mallorea and command all of Angarak to repair immediately to Cthol Mishrak and to live there under the direct supervision of his disciples.

In retrospect, it is quite obvious that Torak had plans for the future which necessitated both a strong military and a powerful, well-organized Church. At that moment, however, it was only his threat and the cold-eyed stares of the dreaded disciples which whipped the military and the hierarchy into line. Shuddering at the prospect of living in the hideous basin which surrounded the City of Night under the domination of Torak's Disciples, the military and

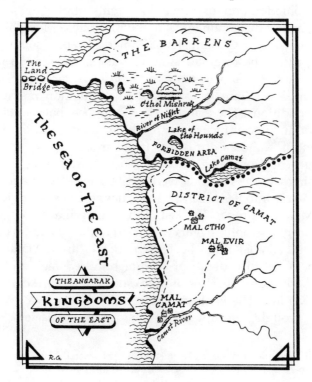

the priesthood made peace with each other, and the matter ended with their return to their separate enclaves where they could exist in at least semi-autonomy beyond the range of Torak's direct scrutiny.

This enforced truce freed the commanders of the army to pursue other matters. It had become evident almost as soon as the Angarak migration had reached the continent that there were other inhabitants of Mallorea. The origins of these people are lost in the mists of pre-history, and scriptural references to them are notoriously inexact. The traditional view that the Gods each selected a people and that the unchosen – or Godless – people were then driven out must, in the light of more modern perceptions, be regarded with some scepticism. Whatever their origins, however, three separate and quite distinct races inhabited the Mallorean continent prior to the coming of the Angaraks; the Dalasians of the southwest, the Karands of the north, and the Melcenes in the east. Once Torak's intervention had established some kind of internal stability in Mallorean society – about nine hundred years after the original Angarak migration – the military at Mal Zeth was forced to focus its attention upon Karanda.

The Karandese were not a wholly unified people, but lived in a loose confederation of seven kingdoms stretching across the northern half of the continent from the Karandese Mountains to the sea lying beyond the mountains of Zamad.* There is some evidence to suggest that the original home of the Karands lay around the shores of Lake Karand in modern Ganesia. Their expansion over the centuries was largely the result of population pressures and climatic conditions. There is abundant evidence that there had long been periodic glacial incursions reaching down onto the plains of north central Mallorea out of the frigid trough lying between the two ranges of mountains in the far north. Retreating before the encroaching ice, the Karands were pushed into Pallia and Delchin and ultimately into Rengel and what is now the District of Rakuth in eastern Mallorea proper. The last of these glacial ages occurred just prior to the catastrophic events which led to the formation of the Sea of the East. At that time the Barrens of Northern Mallorea were sheathed in ice to a depth of several hundred feet, and glaciers extended a hundred leagues or more south of the present shoreline of Lake Karand. The explosive appearance of the Sea of the East, however, brought a abrupt end to the grip of the glaciers. The flow

* This derives from the Anglo-Saxon Heptarchy of pre-Norman England, seven kingdoms that didn't co-exist very well. Their dissension opened the door for the Vikings.

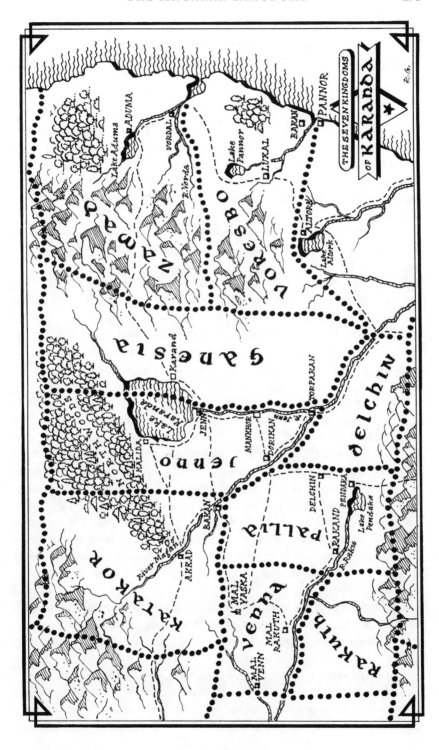

of warm, moist air off the vast steam cloud which accompanied the volcanic formation of the sea poured up through the natural channel lying between the Dalasian and Karandese ranges and initiated a glacial melt of titanic proportions. The suddenly unlocked waters gouged out the huge valley of the Great River Magan, quite the longest and most majestic river in the world.

The Karands themselves, as is so frequently the case with northern peoples, are a warlike race, and their frequent glacier-compelled migrations left them little time for the establishment of the cultural niceties which characterize the nations of more southerly latitudes. Indeed, it has been said with some accuracy that the Karands habitually hover just on the verge of howling barbarism. Karandese cities are crude by any standards, usually protected by rude log palisades, and the sight of hogs roaming at will through the muddy streets is all too common.

By the beginning of the second millennium, incursions by roving bands of Karandese brigands had become a serious problem along Mallorea's eastern frontier, and the Angarak army moved out of Mal Zeth to take up positions along the western fringes of the Karandese Kingdom of Pallia. In a quick punitive expedition, the city of Rakand in southwestern Pallia was sacked and burned and the inhabitants taken captive.

It was at this point that one of the most monumental decisions in Angarak history was made. Even as the Grolims prepared for an orgy of human sacrifice, the military commanders paused to take stock of the situation. The Angarak military had no real desire to occupy Pallia. The difficulties of communication over long distances as well as the wide dispersal of their forces which such an occupation would have involved made the whole notion distinctly unattractive. From the point of view of the military it was far better to keep the Pallian Kingdom intact as a subject nation and to exact tribute than to physically occupy a depopulated territory. No one can be sure to whom the solution first occurred, but the military universally approved.

The Grolims were naturally horrified when the suggestion was first presented to them, but the military was adamant. Ultimately, both sides agreed to place the matter in the hands of Torak himself and to be bound by his decision.

The idea which was presented to the Dragon God was that the Pallian captives should be converted to the worship of Torak rather than being summarily butchered. Though the Grolims were smugly convinced that Torak's devotion was centered upon the Angarak people, certain military commanders had a shrewder conception of the true nature of the Angarak God. Torak, they perceived, was fundamentally a greedy God. He hungered for adoration, and if the case of the Pallian captives – and ultimately of all of Karanda – were presented to him in the light of a manifold increase in the adoration which would be his if he agreed to conversion as opposed to extermination, he could not help but side with the position of the military. Their understanding proved to be correct, and once again the military won out over the shrill protests of the priesthood. It must be conceded, however, that Torak's motives may have been more complex. There can be no doubt that the Dragon God, even at that early date, was fully aware that ultimately there would be a confrontation with the West. The fact that he almost continually sided with the military in their disputes with the Grolims is mute evidence that the God of Angarak placed supreme importance upon the growing army. If the Karandese could be converted to the Worship of Torak, at one stroke he would nearly double the size of his army and his position in the coming conflict would be all the more secure.

Thus it was that the Mallorean Grolims were given a new commandment. They were to strive above all else to convert the Godless Karandese to the worship of the God of Angarak. 'I will have them all,' Torak told his assembled priests. 'Any man who liveth in all of boundless Mallorea shall bow down to me, and if any of ye shirk in this stern responsibility, ye shall feel my displeasure most keenly.' And with that awesome threat still ringing in their ears, the Grolims went forth to convert the heathen.

The conquest of the seven kingdoms of Karanda absorbed the attention of both the military and the priesthood for several centuries. While the Angarak army, better equipped and better trained, could in all probability have accomplished a purely military victory in a few decades, the necessity of conversion slowed their march to the east to a virtual snail's pace. The Grolims, moving always in advance of the army, preached at every cross-road and settlement, offering the Karands the care of a loving God if they would but submit. Karandese society, essentially unreligious, took some time to absorb this notion; but ultimately, swayed by Grolim persuasiveness and by the ever-present threat of the Angarak army poised just to the west, resistance crumbled.

The military victory in Karanda proved to be not only over the Karandese but in some measure over the Grolims as well. The army established puppet-governments in each of the seven kingdoms of Karanda and maintained only a token force in each capital. The Grolims, however, were compelled to be widely dispersed in their ecclesiastical duties in the Karandese kingdoms, and the power of the priesthood was greatly diminished.

In the typical Angarak view, the subject kingdoms of Karanda and their inhabitants were never in a position of equality with Angaraks. Both theologically and politically, the Karandese were always considered second-class citizens, and this general conception of them prevailed until the final ascendancy of the Melcene bureaucracy near the end of the fourth millennium.

The first encounters between the Angaraks and the Melcenes proved to be disastrous. Since the Angarak peoples prior to that time had domesticated only the dog, the sheep, the cow, and the common house-cat, their first encounter with mounted forces sent them fleeing in terror. To make matters even more serious, the sophisticated Melcenes utilized the horse not merely as a mount for cavalry troops but also as a means of drawing their war chariots. A Melcene war-chariot, with sickle-like blades attached to its spinning wheels, could quite literally carve avenues through tightly packed foot troops. Moreover, the Melcenes had also succeeded in domesticating the elephant, and the appearance of these vast beasts on the battlefield added to the Angarak rout. Had the Melcenes chosen to exploit their advantage and to pursue the fleeing Angaraks up the broad valley of the Magan, it is entirely possible that the course of history on the Mallorean continent might have been radically different. Unaccountably, however, the Melcene forces stopped their pursuit at the border between Delchin and Rengel, allowing the Angarak army to escape.

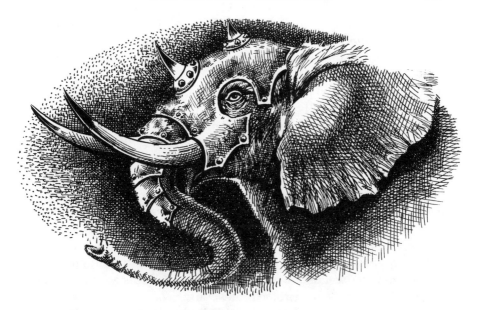

The presence of a superior force to the southeast caused general consternation in Mal Zeth. Baffled by the failure of the Melcene Empire to pursue its advantage and more than a little afraid of their eastern neighbors, the Angarak generals made overtures of peace and were astonished when the Melcenes quickly agreed to normalize relations. Trade agreements were drawn up, and the Angarak traders were urged by the generals to devote all possible effort to the procurement of horses. Once again to the amazement of the generals, the Melcenes were quite willing to trade horses, though the prices were extremely high. The officials of the Empire, however, adamantly refused to even discuss the sale of elephants.

Thwarted in their expansion to the east, the authorities at Mal Zeth turned their attention to the south and to Dalasia. The Dalasians proved to be easy pickings for the more advanced Angaraks. They were simple farmers and herdsmen with little skill for organization and even less for war. The Angaraks simply moved into Dalasia, expanded the somewhat rudimentary cities of the region and established military protectorates. The entire business took less than ten years.

While the military was stunningly successful in the Dalasian protectorates, the Grolim priesthood immediately ran into difficulties. Dalasian society was profoundly mystical, and the most important people in it were the witches (of both genders) and the seers and prophets. Dalasian thought moved in strange, alien directions which the Grolims found difficult to counter. The simple Dalasians rather meekly accepted the forms of Angarak worship – in much the same manner as they scrupulously paid their taxes – but there was, none-theless, a subtle resistance in their conversion. The power of the witches, seers and prophets remained unbroken, and the Grolims worried continually that the sheep-like behavior of the simple Dalasian peasantry masked something subtly more ominous. It seemed almost as if the Dalasians were amused by the increasingly shrill exhortations of the Grolims and that there lurked somewhere beneath the placid exterior an infinitely more profound and sophisticated religion quite beyond the power of the Grolims to comprehend. Moreover, despite rigorous efforts on the part of the Grolims to locate and destroy them, it appeared that copies of the infamous Mallorean Gospels still circulated in secret among the Dalasians.

Had events given them time, perhaps, the Grolims might ultimately have succeeded in stamping out all traces of the secret Dalasian religion in the protectorates, but it was at about this time that a disaster occurred at Cthol Mishrak which was to change forever the complexion of Angarak life.

Despite the most rigorous security measures imaginable, the legendary Belgarath the Sorcerer, in the company of Cherek Bearshoulders, King of Aloria, and of Cherek's three sons, came unobserved to the Holy City of Angarak and stole the Orb of Aldur from the iron tower of Torak in the very center of the City of Night. Although a pursuit was immediately mounted to apprehend the thieves, they were able, through some as yet undiscovered sorcery to utilize the Orb itself to make good their escape.

The anger of the Dragon God of Angarak knew no bounds when it became evident that Belgarath and his accomplices had escaped with the Orb. In an outburst of rage, Torak destroyed Cthol Mishrak and immediately began a series of fundamental changes in the basic structure of the Angarak society which had dwelt in the city and the surrounding countryside. It appears that Torak suffered a peculiar blindness about the nature of human culture. To him people were only people, and he gave no consideration to distinctions of rank. Thus it was that as he ruthlessly divided the citizens of Cthol Mishrak into the three tribes which were to be forcibly migrated to the western continent to establish an Angarak foothold there, he utilized the most obvious distinctions between them as a means of effecting that division.

Unfortunately, the most immediately discernible difference between men is one of class. The cultures which were exported to the west, therefore, were profoundly unnatural cultures, since the division along class lines absolutely disrupted anything resembling normal human society. Even the most cursory familiarity with the dialect which had evolved in Cthol Mishrak reveals the fundamental differences between the three western tribes. In that dialect the word 'Murgo' meant nobleman; the word 'Thull' meant serf or peasant; and the word 'Nadrak' meant tradesman. These, of course, were the names Torak assigned the three tribes before he sent them into the west. To insure their continuing enthusiasm for the tasks he had set them, moreover, he dispatched the Disciple Ctuchik, along with every third Grolim in all of Mallorea to accompany them on their migration. The abrupt decimation of Grolim ranks profoundly disrupted the power of the Church in ancient Mallorea and in the subject kingdoms to the east and marked yet another step toward the secularization of Mallorean society.

The great trek across the land bridge to the western continent cost the western tribes of Angarak nearly a million lives, and the lands which awaited them were profoundly inhospitable. The Murgos (in keeping with their position as the aristocracy) took the lead in the march, and thus it is that their lands are most far removed from the natural causeway formed by the land bridge. The Thulls, still subservient to their former masters, followed closely behind. The Nadraks, on the other hand, seemed quite content to remain as far from Murgo domination as possible. It was, quite naturally, the Nadraks who most quickly adjusted to the new conditions in which they found themselves. A fundamentally middle-class society has little need for serfs and even less for overlords. Thullish society could function, albeit marginally. For the Murgos, however, the new situation was very nearly a disaster. Since they were aristocrats (i.e. the warrior class), their society was organized along military lines with position stemming in large measure from military rank. Moreover, their decisions were frequently based upon military considerations. Thus, their first major stopping point in their migration to the south was at Rak Goska. Rak Goska is admirably situated from a military standpoint. As a location for a functioning city, however, it is a catastrophe. The surrounding territory consists of the bleak, unfarmable wastes of Murgos, and all food, therefore, must be imported. To make matters even worse, Murgos make very poor farmers. At first, the Thulls were more than willing to supply the needs of their former masters, but as time and distance blurred the former ties between the two nations, the Thullish contributions to Murgo well-being diminished to a trickle. The starving Murgos

responded with a series of punitive expeditions into Mishrak ac
Thull until a stern command from Torak (issued by Ctuchik) halted
that practice. The situation of the Murgos was rapidly growing
desperate. It was at this point that they first encountered the oily
Nyissan slave-traders. Nyissans had long conducted slave-raids into
the southern reaches of the continent, which was inhabited by a
simple, quite docile race of people apparently somewhat distantly
related to the Dalasians of southwest Mallorea. The first purchase of
a slave by a Murgo aristocrat forever established the pattern of
Murgo society. The information gleaned from the Nyissans made
them aware of the lands and peoples lying to the south and they
immediately began their conquest of that region as part of their
search for an uninterrupted food supply.

Once the Murgos passed the desolate wastes of Goska, they found
themselves in a fertile land of lakes, rivers and forests. They also
found a ready supply of slaves. The native populations, viewed by
the Murgos as little more than animals, were brutally rounded up
and herded into huge encampments from which they were parceled
out to work the farmlands in the emerging Murgo military districts.
In typical Murgo fashion, the regions in the south were organized
along military lines, and each district was administered by a general.

A peculiarity of the Murgos has long been a singular lack of any
sense of personal possession – particularly when dealing with land.
A Murgo simply cannot conceive of the notion of personally owning
land. The conquered territories of the south belonged, therefore, to
Murgodom in general. A Murgo's primary loyalty is to his immediate superior, and he does not want to own land, since the responsibility of ownership might divide that loyalty. Thus, Cthol Murgos
is divided into military districts administered by army corps.
Each corps (and ultimately the corps commander) has a specific
geographic region of responsibility. The land is further subdivided
into division areas, regimental areas, battalion areas and so on.
Individual Murgo soldiers act primarily as overseers and slave-
drivers. Murgo population centers thus more closely resemble military encampments than they do cities. Housing is assigned to
individual soldiers on the basis of rank. While such a society seems
bleak and repugnant to Westerners and Malloreans alike, one must
nonetheless admire the Murgo tenacity and sense of self-sacrifice
which makes it function.

Since one of the primary concerns of an aristocratic class is the
protection of bloodlines, and since Murgos live in what is quite literally a sea of slaves, Murgo society rigidly enforces separation

between slave and master. Murgo women in particular are totally isolated from any possible contact with non-Angaraks, and this obsession with racial purity has quite literally imprisoned them within the confines of special 'women's quarters' which lie at the center of every Murgo house. Any Murgo woman even suspected of 'consorting' with a non-Murgo is immediately put to death. Moreover, any Murgo male, regardless of rank, who is caught in delicate circumstances with a foreign woman suffers the same fate. These laws, since they have existed since the end of the second millennium, have guaranteed a remarkably pure strain. The Murgo of today is probably the only uncontaminated Angarak on the face of the globe. In time this obsessive concern with racial purity became viewed by Murgos as a quasi-religious obligation, and no attempt was ever made in the western hemisphere to convert non-Angaraks as became the practice in Mallorea.

It was perhaps the Disciple Ctuchik who was ultimately responsible for giving an elemental class prejudice the force of religious sanction. Ctuchik, mindful of the deterioration of Church authority in Mallorea as a result of the growing secularization and cosmopolitanism of Mallorean society, issued his pronouncements on the subject from his theological capital at Rak Cthol in the wasteland of Murgos. He reasoned (probably correctly) that a society faced with both a legal and religious obligation to avoid contact with foreigners would not encounter those new ideas which so seriously undermine the power of the Church. There is, moreover, some evidence which suggests that Ctuchik's decrees were in some measure dictated by the increasing friction between him and his two fellow Disciples, the newly converted Zedar, and Urvon. Urvon in particular had embraced the idea of converting non-Angaraks with great enthusiasm, reasoning that this could only increase the authority of the Church. Zedar, of course, was an enigma, and was soundly detested by Ctuchik and Urvon both. It was to counter Urvon, however, that Ctuchik strove to maintain Murgo purity. It is entirely possible that Ctuchik reasoned that following Torak's ultimate victory, the maimed God would welcome the delivery of an absolutely pure Angarak strain to function as the ultimate overlords of a captive world.

Whatever may have been Ctuchik's ultimate motivation, Murgos and western Grolims vigorously contend that Mallorean cosmopolitanism is a form of heresy, and they customarily refer to Malloreans as 'mongrels'. It is this attitude, more than anything else, which has led to the ages-old hatred existing between Murgo and Mallorean.

Following the upheaval which accompanied the destruction of Cthol Mishrak, Torak himself became almost totally inaccessible to his people, concentrating instead upon various schemes to disrupt the growing power of the kingdoms of the West. The God's absence gave the military time to fully exploit its now virtual total control of Mallorea and the subject kingdoms. One of the oddities of this period was the lack of a supreme commander at Mal Zeth. Although powerful men had dominated the high command from time to time, the authority of the military was normally dispersed among the senior generals, and this condition prevailed until very nearly the end of the fourth millennium. Now that their authority in ancient Mallorea, Karanda and Dalasia was firmly established, the High Command once again turned its attention to the problem of the Melcene Empire.

As trade between the Melcenes and the Angaraks increased, so did Angarak knowledge about their eastern neighbors. The Melcenes had originally inhabited the islands off the east coast of the Mallorean Continent, and had, until the catastrophe caused by the separation of the two continents, been quite content to ignore their mainland cousins. The vast tidal waves (estimated to have been a hundred feet high) which swept across the oceans of the world during the readjustment of the two great land-masses, however, swallowed up more than half of their islands, leaving the survivors huddled fearfully together in the uplands. Their capital at Melcene itself had been a city in the mountains where affairs of state could be managed without the debilitating effects of the climate in the tropical lowlands. Following the catastrophe itself, however, Melcene was a shattered city, destroyed by earthquake and lying no more than a league from the new coast. After an intense period of rebuilding, it became abundantly clear that their tremendously shrunken homeland would no longer support a burgeoning population. With typical Melcene thoroughness, they attacked the problem from every possible angle. One thing was absolutely certain; they had to have more land. The Melcene mind is a peculiarly compartmentalized one, their answer to any problem is to immediately form a committee. The 'newlands' committee which was drawn up to present possible solutions to the Emperor arrived at its final proposal only after considering every possible alternative. They concluded that, since they could not make new land, they would be forced to either buy or take lands from someone else. Since southeastern Mallorea lay closest at hand and was populated by people of their own race, it was to that region that the Melcenes turned their

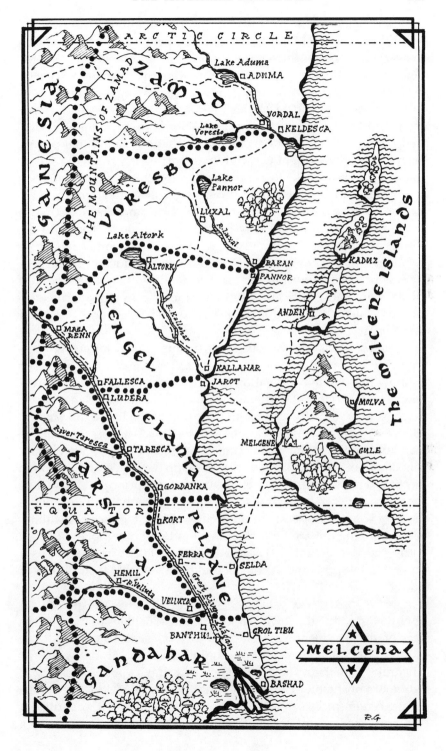

attention. There were five rather primitive kingdoms in southeastern and east central Mallorea occupied by peoples of the same racial
stock as the Melcenes themselves; Gandahar, Darshiva, Peldane,
Cellanta, and Rengel. These kingdoms were overrun one by one by
the Melcenes and were absorbed into their growing empire.

The dominating force in the Melcene Empire was the bureaucracy. Unlike other governments of the time, which frequently oper-
ated on royal whim or upon the accumulation of personal power,
the Melcene government was rigidly departmentalized. While there
are obvious drawbacks to a bureaucratic form of government, such
an approach to administration provides the advantages of continu-
ity and of a clear-eyed pragmatism which is more concerned with
finding the most practical way to getting a job done than with the
whim, prejudice and egocentricity which so frequently mars more
personal forms of government. The Melcene Bureaucracy in particular was practical almost to a fault. The concept of an 'aristocracy of
talent' dominated Melcene thinking, and if one bureau chose to
ignore a talented individual – of whatever background – another
was almost certain to snap him up.

Thus it was that the various departments of the Melcene government rushed into the newly-conquered mainland provinces to
winnow through the population in search of genius. The 'conquered'
people of Gandahar, Darshiva, Peldane, Cellanta and Rengel were
thus absorbed directly into the mainstream of the life of the Empire.
Always pragmatic, the Melcenes left the royal houses of the five
mainland provinces in place, preferring to operate through established lines of authority rather than to set up new ones, and, although
the title 'king' suffered reduction to the title 'prince', it as widely
considered more prestigious to be a 'prince of the Empire' than a
'king' of some minor east-coast kingdom. Thus, the six principalities
of the Melcene Empire flourished in a kind of brotherhood based on
hard-headed practicality. The possession of talent in Melcena is a
universal passport, and is considered more valuable than wealth or
power.

For the next 1800 years the Melcene Empire prospered, far
removed from the theological and political squabbles of the western
part of the continent. Melcene culture was secular, civilized and
highly educated. Slavery was unknown, and trade with the
Angaraks and their subject peoples in Karanda and Dalasia was
extremely profitable. The old Imperial capital at Melcene became a
major center of learning. Unfortunately, some of the thrust of
Melcene scholarship turned toward the arcane. Their practice of

Magic (the summoning of evil spirits) went far beyond the primitive mumbo-jumbo of the Morindim or the Karandese and began to delve into darker and more serious areas. They made considerable progress in witchcraft and necromancy. Their major area of concentration, however, lay in the field of alchemy. It is surprising to note that some Melcene alchemists were actually successful in converting base metals into gold – although the effort and expenditure involved made the process monumentally unprofitable. It was, however, a Melcene alchemist, Senji the Clubfooted, who inadvertently stumbled over the secret of the Will and the Word during one of his experiments. Senji, a 15th century practitioner at the University in the Imperial city was notorious for his ineptitude. To be quite frank about it, Senji's experiments more often turned gold into lead than the reverse. In a fit of colossal frustration at the failure of his most recent experiment, Senji inadvertently converted a half-ton of brass plumbing into solid gold. An immediate debate arose among the Bureau of Currency, the Bureau of Mines, the Department of Sanitation, the faculty of the College of Alchemy and the faculty of the College of Comparative Theology about which organization should have control of Senji's discovery. After about three hundred years of argumentation, it suddenly occurred to the disputants that Senji was not merely talented, but also appeared to be immortal. In the name of scientific experimentation, the varying Bureaus, Departments and faculties agreed that an effort should be made to have him assassinated.

A well-known defenestrator was retained to throw the irascible old alchemist from a high window in one of the towers of the University. The experiment had a three-fold purpose. What the various Departments wished to find out was: (a) If Senji was in fact unkillable, (b) what means he would take to save his life while plummeting toward the pavement, and (c) if it might be possible to discover the secret of flight by giving him no other alternative. What they actually found out was that it is extremely dangerous to threaten the life of a sorcerer – even one as inept as Senji. The defenestrator found himself translocated to a position some fifteen hundred meters above the harbor, five miles distant. At one instant he had been wrestling Senji toward the window; at the next, he found himself standing on insubstantial air high above a fishing fleet. His demise occasioned no particular sorrow – except among the fishermen, whose nets were badly damaged by his rapid descent. In an outburst of righteous indignation, Senji then proceeded to chastise the Department heads who had consorted to do violence to his person. It was finally only a personal appeal from the Emperor himself that persuaded the old man to desist from some fairly exotic punishments. (Senji's penchant for the scatological had led him rather naturally into interfering with normal excretory functions as a means of chastisement.) Following the epidemic of mass constipation, the Departments were more than happy to allow Senji to go his own way unmolested.

On his own, Senji established a private academy and advertised for students. While his pupils never became sorcerers of the magnitude of Belgarath, Polgara, Ctuchik or Zedar, they were able to perform some rudimentary applications of the Will and the Word which immediately elevated them far above the magicians and witches practicing their art forms within the confines of the University.

It was during this period of peace and tranquillity that the first encounter with the Angaraks took place. Although they were victorious in that first meeting, the pragmatic Melcenes realized that eventually the Angaraks could overwhelm them by sheer weight of numbers.

During the period when the Angaraks turned their attention to the establishment of the Dalasian protectorates and Torak's full concentration was upon the emerging Angarak kingdoms on the western continent, there was peace between the Angaraks and the Melcenes. It was a tentative peace – a very wary one – but it was peace nonetheless. The trade contacts between the two nations gave them a somewhat better understanding of each other, though the sophisticated Melcenes were amused by the preoccupation with religion which marked even the most worldly Angarak. Periodically over the next eighteen hundred years, relations between the two countries deteriorated into nasty little wars, seldom longer than a year or two in duration and from which both sides scrupulously avoided committing their full forces. Obviously neither side wished to risk an all-out confrontation.

In the hope of gaining more information about each other, the two nations ultimately established a time-honored practice. Children of various leaders were exchanged for certain periods of time. The sons of high-ranking bureaucrats in the city of Melcene were sent to Mal Zeth to live with the families of Angarak generals, and the sons of the generals were sent in turn to the Imperial capital to be raised there. The result of these exchanges was to produce a group of young men with a cosmopolitanism which in many was later to become the norm for the ruling class of the Mallorean

Empire.* It was one such exchange toward the end of the fourth millennium which ultimately resulted in the unification of the two peoples. At about the age of twelve, a youth named Kallath, the son of a high-ranking Angarak general, was sent to the city of Melcene to spend his formative years in the household of the Imperial Minister of Foreign Affairs. The Minister, because of his position, had frequent official and social contacts with the Imperial Family, and Kallath soon became a welcome guest at the Imperial palace. The Emperor Molvan was an elderly man with but one surviving child, a daughter named Danera, who, as luck would have it, was perhaps a year younger than Kallath. Matters between the two young people progressed in a not uncommon fashion until Kallath, at the age of eighteen, was recalled to Mal Zeth to begin his military career. Kallath, obviously a young man of genius, rose meteorically through the ranks, reaching the position of Governor General of the District of Rakuth. He was by then twenty-eight, becoming thereby the youngest man ever to be elevated to the General Staff. A year later Kallath journeyed to Melcene, where he and Danera were married.

Kallath, in the years that followed, divided his time between Melcene and Mal Zeth, carefully building a power-base in each capital, and when Emperor Molvan died in 3829, Kallath was ready. There had been, of course, others in line for the Imperial throne, but during the years immediately preceding the old Emperor's death, most of these potential heirs had died – frequently under mysterious circumstances. It was, nonetheless, over the violent objections of many of the noble families of Melcena that Kallath was declared Emperor of Melcena in 3830. These objections however, were quieted with a certain brutal efficiency by Kallath's cohorts.

Journeying the following year to Mal Zeth, Kallath brought the Imperial Melcene army with him as far as the border of Delchin, where they stood poised. At Mal Zeth, Kallath delivered his ultimatum to the General Staff. His forces at that time were comprised of the army of his own district, Rakuth, as well as those of the eastern principalities in Karanda, where the Angarak military governors had already sworn allegiances to him. These forces, coupled with the Melcene Army on the Delchin border, gave Kallath absolute military supremacy on the continent. His demand to the General Staff

---

* This was a common practice in antiquity. Attila the Hun, for example, spent several years of his childhood in the City of Rome. The idea was to civilize and Christianize him. It didn't work out that way, however.

was simple: he was to be appointed Overgeneral-Commander-in-Chief of the Armies of Angarak. There were precedents, certainly. In the past, an occasional brilliant general had been appointed to that office, though it was far more common for the General Staff to rule jointly. Kallath's demand, however, brought something new into the picture. His position as Emperor of Melcena was hereditary, and he insisted that the office of Commander-in-Chief of Angarak also be inheritable. Helplessly, faced with Kallath's overpowering military forces, the Angarak generals acceded to his demands. Kallath stood supreme on the continent. He was Emperor of Melcena and Commander-in-Chief of Angarak.

The integration of Melcena and Angarak which was to form modern Mallorea was turbulent, but in the end it can be said that Melcene patience won out over Angarak brutality. Over the years it became increasingly evident that the Melcene bureaucracy was infinitely more efficient than Angarak military administration. The first moves by the bureaucracy had to do with such mundane matters as standards and currency. From there it was but a short step to establishment of a continental Bureau of Roads. Within a few hundred years, the bureaucracy had expanded until it ran virtually every aspect of the life of the continent. As always, the bureaucracy gathered up every talented man in every corner of Mallorea, regardless of his race, and it soon became not at all uncommon for administrative units to be comprised of Melcenes, Karands, Dalasians and Angaraks. By 4400 the ascendancy of the bureaucrats was complete. In the interim, the title 'Commander-in-Chief-of-Angarak' had begun to gradually fall into disuse, in some measure perhaps because the bureaucracy customarily addressed all communications to 'The Emperor'. Peculiarly, there appears not to have been a specific point at which 'The Emperor of Melcene' became the 'Emperor of Mallorea', and such usage was never formally approved until after the disastrous adventure in the west which culminated in the Battle of Vo Mimbre.

The conversion of the Melcenes to the worship of Torak was at best superficial. The sophisticated Melcenes pragmatically accepted the forms of Angarak worship out of a sense of political expediency, but the Grolims were unable to command the kind of abject submission to the Dragon God which had always characterized the Angarak.

In 4850, however, Torak himself suddenly emerged from his eons of seclusion. A vast shock ran through all of Mallorea as the living God of Angarak, his maimed face concealed behind the polished

steel mask, appeared at the gates of Mal Zeth. The Emperor was disdainfully set aside and Torak once again assumed his full authority as 'Kal' – King and God. Messengers were immediately sent to Cthol Murgos, Mishrak ac Thull and Gar og Nadrak, and a council of war was held at Mal Zeth in 4852. The Dalasians, the Karands and the Melcenes were stunned by the sudden appearance of a figure they had always thought was purely mythical, and their shock was compounded by the presence of Torak's Disciples, Zedar, Ctuchik and Urvon. Torak was a God, and did not speak except to issue commands. Ctuchik, Zedar and Urvon, however, were men, and they questioned and probed and saw everything with a kind of cold disdain. They saw immediately what Torak himself was strangely incapable of seeing – that Mallorean society had become almost totally secular – and they took steps to rectify that situation. A sudden reign of terror descended upon Mallorea. The Grolims were quite suddenly everywhere, and secularism was, in their eyes, a form of heresy. The sacrifices, which had become virtually unknown, were renewed with fanatic enthusiasm, and soon not a village in all of Mallorea did not have its altar and its reeking bonfire. In one stroke the Disciples of Torak overturned eons of rule by the military and the bureaucracy and returned the absolute domination of the Grolims. When they had finished, there was not one facet of Mallorean life that did not bow abjectly to the will of Torak.

The mobilization of Mallorea in preparation for the war with the west virtually depopulated the continent. The Angaraks and the Karands were eventually marched north to the land bridge crossing to northern most Gar og Nadrak, and the Dalasians and Melcenes moved to Dal Zerba, where fleets were constructed to ferry them across the Sea of the East to southern Cthol Murgos. Torak's overall strategy was profoundly simple. The northern Malloreans were to join with the Nadraks, the Thulls and the northern Murgos for the strike into Drasnia and Algaria; the southern Malloreans to join forces with the southern Murgos, await Torak's command, and then march northwesterly. The goal was to crush the west between these two huge armies. The disaster which overtook the northern column at Vo Mimbre was in large measure set off by the lesser-known disaster which befell the southern forces in the Great Desert of Araga in central Cthol Murgos. The freak storm which swept in off the Great Western Sea in the early spring of 4875 caught the southern Murgos, the Melcenes and the Dalasians in that vast wasteland and literally buried them alive in the worst blizzard in recorded history. When the storm finally abated after about a week, the southern column was mired down in fourteen-foot snowdrifts which persisted until early summer. And then, with a sudden rise in temperature, the snow-melt turned the desert into a huge quagmire. It is now quite evident that the storm and the conditions which followed were not of natural origin. None of the various theories put forth to explain it, however, is quite satisfactory. Whatever the cause, the results were one of the great tragedies in human history. The southern army, trapped in that wasteland first by snow and cold and then by an ocean of mud, perished. The few survivors who came straggling back at the end of the summer told tales of horror so ghastly that they do not bear repeating.

The two-fold catastrophe which had occurred in the west, coupled with the apparent death of Torak at the hands of the Rivan Warder, utterly demoralized the societies of Mallorea and of the western Angarak Kingdoms. Expecting a counter-invasion, the Murgos retreated into fortified positions in the mountains. Thullish society disintegrated entirely, reverting to crude village life. The somewhat more resilient Nadraks took to the woods, and much of the independence of the modern-day Nadrak derives from that period of enforced self-reliance. In Mallorea, however, events took a different course. The doddering old Emperor emerged from retirement to reassume authority and to try to rebuild the shattered bureaucracy. Grolim efforts to maintain their control were met with universal hatred. Without Torak, the Grolims had no real power. Though most of his sons had perished at Vo Mimbre, one gifted child remained to the old Emperor, the son of his old age, a boy of about seven. The Emperor spent the few years remaining to him instructing, schooling and preparing his son, Korzeth, for the task of ruling his far-flung Empire. When advanced years finally rendered the old Emperor incompetent, Korzeth, then aged about fourteen, callously deposed his father and ascended the Imperial throne.

In the years following Vo Mimbre, Mallorean society had fractured back into its original components of Melcena, Karanda, Dalasia and ancient Mallorea. Indeed, there was even a movement in some quarters to further disintegrate the nation into those prehistoric kingdoms which had existed on the continent prior to the coming of the Angaraks. This movement toward separatism was particularly strong in the principality of Gandahar in southern Melcena, in Zamad and Voresebo in Karanda and in Perivor in the Dalasian protectorates. Deceived by Korzeth's youth, these separatist regions rashly declared independence from the Imperial throne at Mal Zeth, and other districts and principalities, notably Ganesia, Darshiva and Likandia gave strong indications that they would soon follow suit. Korzeth moved immediately to stem the tide of revolution. The boy-emperor spent the rest of his life on horseback in perhaps the greatest internecine blood bath in history; but when he was done, he delivered a reunified Mallorea to his successor on the throne.

The new Emperors of Mallorea, the descendants of Korzeth, brought a different kind of rule to the continent. Prior to the calamity in the west, the Emperor of Mallorea had quite often been little more than a figurehead, and power had largely rested in the hands of the bureaucracy. Now, however, the Imperial throne was absolute. The center of power shifted from Melcene to Mal Zeth in keeping with the largely military orientation of Korzeth and his descendants. As is almost always the case when power is consolidated in the hands of one supreme ruler, intrigue became commonplace. Plots, ploys, conspiracies and the like abounded as various functionaries schemed to discredit opponents and to gain Imperial favor. Rather than move to stop these palace intrigues, the descendants of Korzeth encouraged them, shrewdly perceiving that men divided by mutual distrust and enmity would never unite to challenge the power of the throne.

'Zakath, the present Emperor, assumed the throne during his eighteenth year and gave early promise of enlightened rule. He appeared to be intelligent, sensitive and capable. It was a profound personal tragedy, however, which turned him from that course and helped to make him a man feared by half the world. In order for us to understand what happened to 'Zakath, we must first examine what was taking place in Cthol Murgos. As is generally the case when a nation survives for more than a few centuries, the Kings of

Cthol Murgos may most conveniently be considered in dynasties.

Upon their first arrival in the west, the Murgos had debated the actual necessity for a king. Their aristocratic background, however, coupled with the fact that the nations around them all had kings, made the establishment of a Murgo throne inevitable. At first the Kings of Cthol Murgos were for the most part ceremonial, with the real power residing in the hands of the commanding generals of the nine military districts. The military commander of the District of Goska was elevated to the throne largely because he commanded the oldest military district in the kingdom and because it was decided early on that Rak Goska would be the capital the nation would present to the world.

In time, however, the Goska Dynasty became corrupt. The trappings of power with no real power behind them all too frequently leads to self-indulgence. While other kingdoms endure periodical bad kings in the hope of better successors, Murgos tend to be more abrupt. Thus, after several centuries of misrule by the admittedly limited kings of the Goska Dynasty, the military commanders of the other eight districts ruthlessly moved against the King and exterminated him, together with all his heirs, ministers and functionaries. The palace coup was followed by several decades of rule by a military Junta until, once again in need of a figurehead to present to the outside world, the generals offered the crown to the most capable of their number, the commander of the District of Gorut. The General of Gorut, however, declined to accept the crown unless the position of king was given a bit more meaning. This procedure has been repeated with every dynastic change-over until presently the King of Cthol Murgos is the most nearly absolute monarch in the world.

The near-disaster which has enveloped Cthol Murgos for the past several centuries has been the result of an hereditary affliction strongly prevalent in the Urga Dynasty. The Urgas came to the throne with much promise, but the inherited affliction appeared in the second King, and has been almost inevitable in every Urga King since. The insanity in the house of Urga is difficult to diagnose, but it is characterized by extreme hysteria, suspicion, rapid fluctuation of mood, and ritualized behavior. In no Urga King have these symptoms been more pronounced than in the present occupant of the throne, Taur Urgas, the tenth Urga King.

The reign of Taur Urgas of Cthol Murgos has been marked by the fear and suspicion which are so characteristic of his disease. Though the mad King fears and hates all Alorns (the Algars in particular), as have all members of his family, Taur Urgas carries his suspicions even further. He is fearful of a possible alliance between Tolnedra, Arendia and the Alorn Kingdoms, and he has saturated the west with his agents with instructions to stir up as much discord as possible. The secret fear which haunts the sleep of Taur Urgas, however, is the dread that Mallorea might move to play a greater role in the destiny of the kingdoms of the western continent. It is evident that the discovery in his youth that Mallorea was at least twice the size of Cthol Murgos filled Taur Urgas with an unreasoning fear and hatred. The contempt with which the average Murgo views the Malloreans has in the case of their King crossed the line into open hostility.

Thus, when the young Emperor 'Zakath ascended the throne at Mal Zeth, Taur Urgas immediately instructed his agents to provide him with the details of the new Emperor's background, education and temperament. Their reply filled the King of the Murgos with alarm. It appeared that 'Zakath was precisely the kind of man Taur Urgas had feared would be the new ruler of the world's most populous nation. Desperately, the King of the Murgos cast about in search of a way to neutralize the Mallorean's obvious talents.

The opportunity Taur Urgas had been awaiting came when reports filtered back to Rak Goska that 'Zakath was in love – or at least strongly attracted. The lady in question was a Melcene girl of high degree with a powerful family which had nonetheless fallen upon difficult times. The conditions were perfect for the Murgo King. Calling upon the almost unlimited wealth of blood-red gold which yearly poured from the mines of Cthol Murgos, Taur Urgas bought up all of the outstanding debts of the Melcene girl's family and began applying pressure upon them for repayment. When the family was sufficiently desperate, Taur Urgas, acting through his agents, presented his proposal. The girl was to encourage 'Zakath's attentions and to lure him into marriage by whatever means necessary. She was then to exert all her influence upon the young man to prevent his ever considering adventures in the west, and failing that, a Nyissan poison was provided and the girl was to be instructed to kill her husband.

The failure of the plan was largely the result of a basic Murgo inability to understand the complexities of Mallorean intrigue. Murgos appear to automatically assume that everyone they bribe will remain bribed. In Mallorea, however, such integrity is the exception rather than the rule. Thus, a relatively minor participant in Taur Urgas's scheme soon found an opportunity to sell the information to certain officials in the government of Emperor 'Zakath. When the entire matter was placed before the Emperor, the young man, in a sudden fit of outrage, ordered that all participants in the intrigue be rounded up and immediately be put to death. Certain evidence emerged after the order was carried out which suggested strongly that the Melcene girl (for whom 'Zakath appeared to have a genuine affection) was not only innocent of any participation in the Murgo scheme, but may even have been totally unaware of it. When this tragic information was conveyed to the young Emperor, he very nearly went mad with grief, and when he finally recovered, his personality was so altered that even his own family could not recognize him as the same man. The previously open and gregarious young man is now quite often surreptitiously referred to as 'the man of ice'.

'Zakath's first act upon his recovery was to direct the now-famous letter of remonstrance to Taur Urgas. The letter read as follows:

To His Majesty, Taur Urgas of Murgodom,

I was unamused by your recent attempt to influence Mallorean internal affairs, your Majesty. Were it not for current world conditions which require that there be no apparent rupture between the two major Angarak powers, I would bring the entire weight of the Mallorean Empire down upon you and chastise you beyond your imagining for your offense.

To insure that there will be no recurrence of this affair, I have taken all Murgos within my boundaries into custody to serve as hostage to your continued good behavior. I am advised that several of these internees are closely related to you. Should you instigate further adventures in my realm, I shall return your kinsmen to you – piece by piece.

In the past, your madness has filled your world with imagined enemies. Rejoice, Taur Urgas, and put aside your insanity, for you now have a real foe, far more deadly than any of the phantoms of your lunacy. You may be assured that as soon as world conditions permit, I will descend upon you and the stinking wasteland you call your Kingdom. It is my firm intention to destroy you and the vile race you rule. When I am done, the name 'Murgo' will be forgotten.

Keep a watchful eye over your shoulder, Taur Urgas, for as surely as the sun rises tomorrow, one day I will be there.

With My most heartfelt contempt,
'Zakath,
Emperor of Mallorea

When Taur Urgas read this letter, his advisors found it necessary to physically restrain him to prevent his doing himself injury. Though it is possibly an exaggeration, some witnesses maintain that the Murgo King actually began to froth at the mouth, so great was his rage. It must be admitted that the letter of 'Zakath was probably the most strongly-worded which any sovereign has ever directed at another, however, and it signaled the beginning of preparations in the two nations for that war which was now absolutely inevitable.

Occasionally the Murgo King was impelled by his growing insanity to take some kind of action against his implacable enemy. While these actions were usually rather petty, 'Zakath's response was always the same. Not long after such incidents, Taur Urgas would receive the dismembered body of some cousin or nephew. Since the Murgo obsession with race is exceeded only by their attachment to family, nothing 'Zakath could have done could have injured Taur Urgas more, and as the years passed, the hatred of the two grew stronger until it became in the mind of each man virtually an article of religion.

The tragically altered Emperor of Mallorea has become obsessed with the concept of power, and the idea of becoming Over-King of all of Angarak has dominated his thinking for the past two decades. Only time will determine if 'Zakath of Mallorea will be successful in his bid to assert his dominance over the western Angarak kingdoms, but if he succeeds, the history of the entire world may well be profoundly altered.

V

THE MALLOREAN GOSPELS

BOOK 1

THE BOOK OF AGES

Now These are the Ages of Man:

I N THE FIRST AGE was man created, and he awoke in puzzlement and wonder as he beheld the world about him. And those that had made him considered him and selected from his number those that pleased them, and the rest were cast out and driven away. And some went in search of the spirit known as UL, and they left us and passed into the west, and we saw them no more. And some denied the Gods, and they went into the far north to wrestle with demons. And some turned to worldly matters, and they went away into the east and built mighty cities there.

But we despaired, and we sat us down upon the earth in the shadow of the mountains of Korim, which are no more, and in bitterness we bewailed our fate that we had been made and then cast out.

And it came to pass that in the midst of our grief a woman of our people was seized by a rapture, and it was as if she were shaken by a mighty hand. And she arose from the earth upon which she had sat and she bound her eyes with cloth, signifying that she had seen that which no mortal being had seen before, for lo! She was the first Seeress in all the world. And with the touch of vision

still upon her she spake unto us in a great voice, saying:

'Behold! A feast hath been set before those who made us, and this feast shall ye call the Feast of Life. And those who made us have chosen that which pleased them, and that which pleased them not was not chosen.

'Now we are the Feast of Life, and ye sorrow that no guest at the feast hath chosen ye. Despair not, however, for one guest hath not yet arrived at the feast. The other guests have taken their fill, but this great Feast of Life awaiteth still the beloved guest who cometh late, and I say unto all the people that it is he who will choose us.

'Abide therefore against his coming, for it is certain. The signs of it are in the heavens, and there are whispers which speak of it within the rocks. If earth and sky alike confirm it, how can it not come to pass? Prepare then for his coming. Put aside thy grief and turn thy face to the sky and to the earth that thou mayest read the signs written there, for this I say unto all the people, it is upon ye that his coming rests. For Behold, he may not choose ye unless ye choose him. And this is the fate for which we were made.

'Rise up, oh my people. Sit no more upon the earth in vain and foolish lamentation. Take up the task which lies before ye and prepare the way for him who will surely come.'

Much we marveled at the words which had been spoken to us, and we considered them most carefully. And we questioned the Seeress, but her answers were dark and obscure. And we perceived that a danger lurked within the promise. And we turned our faces to the sky and bent our ears to the whispers which came from the earth that we might see and hear and learn. And as we learned to read the book of the skies and to hear the whispers within the rocks, we found the myriad warnings that two spirits would come to us, and that the one was good and the other evil. And we redoubled our efforts so that we might recognize the true spirit and the false in order to choose between them. And as we read the Book of the Heavens we found two signs; and as we listened to the earth we heard two voices; and we were sorely troubled, for we could not determine which sign was the true sign nor which voice the true voice. Truly, evil is disguised as good in the Book of the Heavens and in the speech of the earth, and no man is wise enough to choose between them unaided.

Pondering this, we went out from beneath the shadow of the mountains of Korim and into the lands beyond, where we abode. And we put aside the concerns of man and bent all our efforts to the task which lay before us. And we sought out all manner of wisdom to aid us in distinguishing the true God from the false when the two should come to us, each saying, 'I am the way.' Our witches and our seers sought the aid of the spirit world, and our necromancers took counsel with the dead, and our diviners sought advice from the earth. But lo, the spirits knew no more than we, and we found that they were as confused and troubled as we.

evil is disguised as good in the Book of the Heavens

Then gathered we at last upon a fertile plain to bring together all that we had learned from the world of men, the world of the spirits, the Book of the Heavens and the voices of the earth. And Behold, these are the truths that we have learned from the stars, from the rocks, from the hearts of men and from the minds of the spirits:

Know ye, oh my people, that all a'down the endless avenues of time hath division marred all that is – for there is division at the very heart of creation. And some have said that this is natural and will persist until the end of days, but it is not so. Were the division destined to be eternal, then the purpose of creation would be to contain it. But the stars and the spirits and the voices within the rocks speak of the day when the division will end and all will be made one again, for creation itself knows that the day will come.

Know ye further, oh my people, that two spirits contend with each other at the very center of time, and these spirits are the two sides of that which hath divided creation. And in a certain time shall those spirits meet upon this world, and then will come the time of the choice.

And if THE CHOICE be not made, the spirits will pass on to another world and confront each other there, and this world will be abandoned, and the beloved guest of whom the Seeress spoke will never come. For it is this which was meant when she said unto us: 'Behold, he may not choose ye unless ye choose him.' And the choice which we must make is between good and evil – for there is an absolute good and an absolute evil, and the division at the heart of creation is the division between good and evil, and the reality which will exist after we have made THE CHOICE will be a reality of good or a reality of evil, and it will prevail so until the end of days.

Behold also this truth; the rocks of the world and of all other worlds murmur continually of the two stones which lie at the center of the division.* Once these stones were one, and they stood at the very center of all of creation, but, like all else, they were divided, and in the instant of division were they rent apart with a force that destroyed whole suns. And where these stones are found, there surely will be the next confrontation between the two spirits. Now the day will come when all division will end and all will be made one again – except that the division between the two stones is so great that they can never be rejoined. And in the day when the division ends shall one of the stones cease forever to exist, and in that day also shall one of the spirits forever vanish.

now the Second Age of man began in thunder and earthquake

These then were the truths which we gathered from the stars and from the rocks and from the hearts of men and from the minds of the spirits. And it was our discovery of these truths which marked the end of the First Age.

Now the Second Age of man began in thunder and earthquake, for lo, the earth herself split apart, and the sea rushed in to divide up the lands of men even as creation itself is divided. And the mountains of Korim shuddered and groaned and heaved as the sea swallowed them. And we knew that this would come to pass, for our seers had warned us that it would be so. We went our way, there-

---

* The Orb and the Sardion.

fore, and found safety before the world was cracked and the sea first rushed away and then rushed back and never departed more.

And it was in the Second Age that we saw the coming of the chosen ones who had been selected by the Seven Gods. And we studied them to determine if there were yet some mark upon them to distinguish them from the rest of mankind, but we found no such mark or sign. And our seers communed with the minds of the seers of our brothers who had gone into the west before the seas came in to divide the lands of men. And our brothers in the west also studied the chosen ones of other Gods, and their seers spake unto the minds of our seers, and they said that they – even as we – could find no mark or sign. And our brothers in the west looked at the chosen of the Bear God and the Lion God and the Bull God and the Bat God and the Serpent God and found no mark or sign, and we looked at the children of the Dragon God, and it was the same, even though the Dragon God's people warred with the people of the other Gods.

Yet was there another God, and some men thought that this God dwelling in solitude might indeed be the God who would in time take up all of the unchosen people. And our brethren in the west went up to the Vale in which he dwelt with his disciples and prostrated themselves before him and besought him that he disclose to them the secrets locked in the future. And the God Aldur spake kindly unto them and counseled them, saying: 'Abide against the coming of the Beloved One, and know that my brothers and I, and our people as well, strive to insure his coming – and our striving and our sacrifice is for ye, who are destined to become the Chosen of Him who is yet to come.'

And one of our brethren spake, asking the God thus: 'And what of the Dragon God, Lord, that is Thine enemy? Doth he also strive for the coming of the Beloved One?' And the face of Aldur grew troubled, and he spake, saying: 'My brother Torak doth indeed strive, though he knoweth not the end toward which he moves. I counsel ye to dwell in peace with the children of the Dragon God, for ye dwell in lands which shall be theirs, and they will be Lords over ye. Should ye resist them, they will cause ye great suffering. Endure that which they lay upon ye and abide in patience as ye continue the tasks which have been given ye.'

And the Seers of the West disclosed what Aldur had told them unto the minds of the seers who dwelt among us, and we took counsel with the seers and considered how we might least offend the children of the Dragon God so that they would not interrupt our studies. In the end we concluded that the warlike children of Angarak would be least apprehensive about simple tillers of the soil living in rude communities on the land, and we so ordered our lives. We pulled down our cities and carried away the stones, and we betook ourselves back to the land so that we might not alarm our neighbors nor arouse their envy.

And the years passed and became centuries, and the centuries passed and became eons. And as we had known they would, the children of Angarak came down amongst us and established their overlordship. And they called the lands in which we dwelt 'Dalasia', and we did what they wished us to do and continued in our studies.

Now at about this time it came to pass in the far north that a Disciple of the God Aldur came with others to reclaim a certain thing which the Dragon God had stolen from Aldur. And that act was so important that when it was done the Second Age had ended and the Third Age had begun.

Now it was in the Third Age that the priests of Angarak, which men call Grolims, came to speak to us of the Dragon God and of his hunger for our love, and we considered what they said even as we considered all things men told us. And we consulted the Book of the Heavens and confirmed that Torak was the incarnate God-Aspect of one of the spirits which contended at the center of time. But where was the other? How might men choose when but one of the spirits came to them? How might man select the Good and abjure the Evil when he could in no wise compare them? The spirit infusing the Dragon God could not help us in our choice, for that spirit perceived its goal as good and could not comprehend the possibility that it might be evil. Then it was that we understood our dreadful responsibility. The spirits would come to us, each in its own time, and each would proclaim that it was good and the other was evil. It was man, however, who would choose. And some there are who believe that it is man's choice which will determine the outcome. And we took counsel among ourselves and we concluded that we might accept the forms of the worship which the Grolims so urgently pressed upon us. This would give us the opportunity to examine the nature of the Dragon God and make us better prepared to choose when the other God appeared.

for the pupil may corrupt the intent of the master

Now the forms of worship which the Grolims practiced were repugnant to us, but we placed no blame for those forms at the feet of Torak, for the pupil may corrupt the intent of the master and do in his name that which the master had not intended. And so we observed, and we waited, and we remained silent.

In time the events of the world intruded upon us. The children of the Dragon God, whom men called Angarak, allied themselves by marriage with the great city-builders of the east, who called themselves Melcene, and between them they built an empire which bestrode the continent. Now the Angaraks were doers of deeds, but the Melcenes were performers of tasks. A deed once done is done forever, but a task returns every day. And the Melcenes came among us to seek out those who might aid them in their endless tasks. And we aided them in some measure, but concealed our true nature from them. Now as it chanced to happen, one of our kinsmen who had been selected by the Melcenes to aid them had occasion to journey to the north in performance of a duty which had been laid upon him. And he came to a certain place and sought shelter there from a storm which had overtaken him. Now this certain place was in the care of the Grolims, but the master of the house was not Grolim nor Angarak nor any other man. Our kinsman had come unaware upon the house of Torak; and as it happened Torak was curious concerning our people, and he sent for the traveler, and our kinsman went in to behold the Dragon God. And in the instant that he looked first upon Torak, the Third Age ended and the Fourth Age began. For lo, the Dragon God of Angarak was not one of the Gods for whom we waited. The signs which were upon him did not lead beyond him, and our kinsman saw in an instant that Torak was doomed and that which he was would die with him.

And then we perceived our error, and we marveled at what we had not seen – that even a God might be but the tool of Destiny. For Behold, Torak was of one of the two Fates, but he was not the entire Fate. And as we grew to understand this difficult truth, we realized that the two contending Necessities contained the ultimate power in the Universe and that even the Gods must bow before them. Now the world moved on as we pondered this, and we observed the touch of the two Fates as they guided and turned events into the unalterable courses which must in the fullness of time collide.

Now it happened that on the far side of the world a king was slain, and all his family with him – save one. And this king had been the keeper of one of the two stones which lie at the center of the division which mars creation. And when word of this was brought to Torak, he exulted, for he believed that an ancient foe was no more. Then it was that he began his preparations to move against the kingdoms of the west. But the signs in the heavens and the whispers in the rocks and the voices of the spirits told us that it was not as Torak believed. The stone was still guarded and the line of the guardian remained unbroken, and Torak's war would bring him to grief.

And now for the first time we began to feel the echoes of another presence, far away. Faintly down through the years we had felt the movements of the First Disciple of the God Aldur – whom men and Gods call Belgarath. Now we perceived that he had been joined by another – a

woman – and between them they moved to counter the moves of Torak and of his minions. And we knew this to be of the greatest significance, for now events which had previously taken place among the stars had moved to this world, and it was here that the final meeting would take place.

The preparations of the Dragon God were long, and the tasks he laid upon his people were the tasks of generations. And even as we, Torak watched the heavens to read there the signs which would tell him when to move against the west. But Torak watched only for the signs he wished to see, and he did not read the entire message written in the sky. Reading thus but a small part of the signs, he set his forces in motion upon the worst possible day. Perceiving this, we took counsel with each other. Though our people were perforce gathered up in the great army which was to attack the west, we felt that we should not interfere with the course of either Fate. A different task had been selected for us, and if we were to perform it, we must needs allow the courses of the Fates to continue unhampered. We were troubled, however, that other men and even Gods could not read those messages in the skies which were to us as clear as if they had been engraved upon stone.

And, as we had known it must, disaster befell the armies of Torak there on the broad plain lying before the city of Vo Mimbre. And we mourned with all of Mallorea, for hosts of our kinsmen perished there. There it was also that the Dragon God of Angarak was overthrown by the power of the stone, and he was bound in sleep to await the coming of his enemy.

And now was the course of events in the hands of the Disciples of Gods rather than of the Gods themselves. And the names of the Disciples rang from the stars, and we read the accounts of their exploits and of their ordering of events in the Book of the Heavens. Now the Disciples of Torak were Ctuchik and Zedar and Urvon, and their enchantments and sorceries were mighty; but the Disciples of Aldur, who countered those acts with sorceries of their own, were Beltira and Belkira and Beldin. And the most powerful of all the sorcerers was Belgarath, whom men called eternal, and close to him in power stood his daughter, Polgara the Sorceress. Then it was that a whisper began to reach us with yet another name. As all the twisted skeins of events moved into those final channels from which there can be no turning the whisper of that name became clearer to us. And upon the day of his birth, the whisper of his name became a great shout, and we knew him. Belgarion the Godslayer had come at last.

and all the light in all of creation went out

And now the pace of events, which had moved at times with ponderous tread, quickened, and the rush toward the awful meeting became so swift that the account of it could not be read in the stars, for the Book of the Heavens is so vast that it takes lifetimes to read a single page. But we could hear Belgarion's power stirring, and the thundershocks of his first efforts were terrible. And then upon the day which men celebrate as the day when the world was made, the Orb of Aldur, which the men of Angarak call Cthrag-Yaska, was delivered up to Belgarion; and in the instant that his hand closed upon it, the Book of the Heavens filled with a great light, and the sound of Belgarion's name rang from the farthest star.

Events now moved so swiftly that we could only guess at their course. We could feel Belgarion moving toward Mallorea, bearing the stone with him, and we could feel Torak stirring as his sleep grew fitful. We could also feel the movements of armies, but Belgarion led no army. A great battle was joined in the West, but the outcome of that battle had no bearing upon that which was about to happen.

Finally there came that dreadful night. As we watched helplessly, the vast pages of the Book of the Heavens moved so rapidly that we could not read them. And then the Book stopped, and we read the one terrible line, 'Torak is slain,' and the Book shuddered, and all the light in all of creation went out. And in that dreadful instant of darkness and silence, the Fourth Age ended and the Fifth Age began.

And Behold, when the light returned, we could no longer read the Book of the Heavens! Its language, which had been clear to us, was now foreign and obscure, and we were compelled to begin once again to piece together its meaning even as we had during the First Age. And when we could once again read the pages written in the stars, we found therein a mystery. Before, all had moved toward the meeting between Belgarion and Torak, but now events moved toward a different meeting. There were signs among the stars which told us that the Fates had selected yet other aspects for their next meeting, and we could feel the movements of those presences, but we knew not who or what they might be, for the pages which told of their births or origins had been forever lost to us during those years when the Book spake in an alien tongue. There was, moreover, a great confusion in the signs which we read, for the Book seemed to say that the Keeper of the Orb was destined to succeed Torak as the Aspect of the Second Fate which was called the Child of Dark. But this we knew to be impossible, for Belgarion was the Keeper of the Orb, and Belgarion was the Child of Light. Further, we read that the mothers of the Child of

yet we felt a presence, shrouded and veiled in darkness

Light and the Child of Dark would guide them to the meeting, and the signs said most clearly that Polgara was the mother of the Child of Light. But Polgara's Destiny was to be forever childless, and this had been in her stars since before her birth.* Moreover, even should the impossible occur and Belgarion be won over to the other Fate and, like Zedar, become Apostate, Belgarion's mother, Ildera, had died when he was but an infant. Yet we felt a presence, shrouded and veiled in darkness, moving through the affairs of men, and the moon spake most clearly, advising us that this dark presence was a woman, and that her power was even as great as Polgara's. But this Mother of Dark was also childless.

And the riddles of the stars baffled us and left us as helpless as the unlettered serf for whom the lights in the

---

* Eriond changed this.

night sky were only stars and for whom the voices in the earth were only the sighing of wind or the beat of rain-drops. One thing we saw most clearly, however. The Ages of Man grew shorter as each one passed, and the EVENTS which were the meetings between the two Fates were growing closer and closer together. Once there had been time for leisurely consideration of all that we had learned, but now we knew that we must hasten, lest the EVENT come upon us all unaware.

And so it was in the tenth year following the death of Torak that we met at Kell, and there we determined that we could no longer stand idly aside, observing the course of EVENTS. The time for study had passed; now the time had come to act. It was decided that, since the signs in the Book of the Heavens had become an enigma, we must in some way control or goad or deceive the participants in the next EVENT to go to a place which we knew. Thus, though we could not know what the EVENT was to be, we could know when and where it was to take place.

And we communicated this decision to the mind of a Seeress who dwelt in the lands to the west of the great sea which had divided the lands of this world, and we besought her that she go up unto the Vale of Aldur, where dwelt the Sorceress Polgara with her husband and a foundling Belgarion had rescued from the Disciple Ctuchik, and to speak to Polgara in such wise that she must perforce set out upon the journey which must inevitably bring her to a place of our choosing. And the Seeress in the lands of the west agreed to our request, and she set forth upon the journey with only her silent guide for company.

And we all then turned to our preparations, for much remained to be done, and we were all resolved that this EVENT should be the last. Whatever the outcome should mean for this world, the division of creation had endured for too long, and we were determined that with this meet-ing between the two Fates, the division would end and all would be made one again.

BOOK 2

THE BOOK OF FATES

Now These are the Fates we have known:

I N THE DAYS before the world was divided, a spirit came unto us and told us of the Feast of Life and of the Beloved Guest who would one day come to partake of that feast. And the spirit spake also to us of signs in the heavens and whispers within the rocks which foretold the coming. And we lifted our eyes to the sky to read, and we bent our ears to the earth to hear, and we learned that a false voice would speak to us and try to lead us away from the truth. For behold, the fate of man is not a clear and straightforward path. Two fates await us, and the one is true and the other false. And we turned all our effort and all our care to the task of determining which fate was true and which fate false. But the Book of the Heavens, which told us so much, spoke not to that. Clearly we could read there that which would happen should we follow truth and that which would happen should we follow falsity, but the great book written in the stars spoke no word concerning which fate was which. And we were puzzled and fearful lest we choose awry.

And we went away from the place where this had been revealed to us and took up the great task which had been

placed upon us. Clearly, it is the task of our people to learn all that may be learned of the two Destinies which divide creation and to judge between them and determine which is the path of truth. And we sought out the wisdom of spirits and the wisdom of other men and even the wisdom of Gods and Prophets. And men and spirits and Gods and Prophets gave us their wisdom, and behold, they knew no more than we. All believed that the fate they followed was the true Fate, but none could offer certainty or proof. Thus it was that the task remained before us. And we took counsel with each other, for we saw that others, by reason of their adherence to one fate or the other could read the Book of the Heavens only indistinctly, but that we, who still sought truth, could read it clearly. And the burden of our task grew heavy, for truly, in our choosing we choose for all of man.

To aid us to choose aright we turned to the pages of the book of the stars that speak of beginnings. And on the first page of the Great Book it is written that at the beginning there was but one Destiny and one Fate for all that had ever been made, and the fate was a purpose and a necessity. But it came to pass in the timelessness which existed before there was any man to consider the meaning of time, that a Second Destiny came into being, and it was also a necessity and a purpose. And the second purpose was at odds with the first, and the pull of the one against the other strained the very fabric of creation. And out of that stirring there came to be awareness, for each Destiny became aware of the other. And they became mortal foes, for each stood athwart the path of the other, and so long as both existed, neither could be fulfilled. And each Fate put its hands upon events to twist them and turn them so that the other fate might be defeated. Great forces were set in motion which must inevitably collide; and the two Fates spake unto those who would be their instruments.

all believed that the fate they followed was the true Fate, but none could offer certainty or proof

The voices of these two Great Destinies and the words they speak are called Prophecy, and a Prophecy must be fulfilled. Were there but one voice and one Destiny, our task would have ended with the discovery of that

voice. But there are two voices and two Prophecies, and all of creation is a battleground between them. And the Prophets of the First Destiny proclaimed that the other Fate was an error and an abomination; while the Prophets of the Second declared that the First Fate had been the embodiment of evil which had now been supplanted by truth.

And we considered these Prophecies and teachings, and it was possible that an error could lead inevitably to evil, but it was also possible that evil might have existed from the beginning of time in order to be corrected.

and the
lands
parted like
cloud
before
Torak and
the stone
he raised

Now at about the same time that we learned of the two great voices and the two Destinies, it came to pass that the world was also divided, even as the rest of creation, and behold! The dividing of our world came about as the result of the touch of one Destiny upon the other, for the God of the people called Angarak was the fruit of the Second Fate, and the stone which he raised was the instrument of the First Fate. So vast was the force of their coming together that earth herself could not bear the weight, and the lands parted like cloud before Torak and the stone he raised, and the seas came in, and that which had been one became two.

And when the movement of the seas and the dry lands had subsided, there were two places where men dwelt, and the men in one of those places followed the First Destiny, and the men in the other place followed the Second. And we marveled at the perfection of this. Yet as we considered what had taken place, we found a flaw in it, for there was not symmetry within it. The God of Angarak and the stone which men call the Orb are not equal. For Torak is one aspect of the Second Destiny, and the Orb is a different aspect of the First. And we concluded that there must be a symmetry between the two – that there must somewhere be a God to match Torak and that somewhere there must be a stone which will represent the aspect of the Second Destiny which the Orb represents for the First. And as we turned this over in our minds, it became clear to us that when any aspect of the

one Fate meets the same aspect of the other, that meeting will be the final meeting between the two, and one will triumph and one perish – but should we be unable to perform our part in this meeting, all that is will perish. Thus it was that we became aware that it would be upon this world that the ultimate contest between Good and Evil was destined to take place, and that we must prepare ourselves to do that which must be done.

And we bent our efforts to find the stone which had been revealed by the flaw in the event which men call the Cracking of the World, for we reasoned that the coming together of the two stones was the most likely form of the final conflict, and could we find the other stone, we might be able to keep the two separate until we were ready for their meeting. But the Book of the Heavens spoke obscurely and the voices of the rocks muttered indistinctly, and our search proved in vain. Finally we realized that the two contending Destinies were concealing certain aspects of themselves from each other and from the eyes of men.

With the beginning of the Third Age, which came into being when Belgarath and certain Alorns recovered the Orb of Aldur from the City of Endless Night, there dawned the great Age of Prophecy. And the fervor of Prophecy descended upon the maimed God of Angarak, and he spake in an ecstasy, and his words were the words of the Second Destiny. And we waited, for we knew that the First Destiny must also speak – for the word sets forth the meaning of the Event, and each Destiny must put its own meaning to the Events which inevitably must come to pass. Then from far to the north in the lands called the Kingdoms of the West came the voice of the First Destiny. And all in amaze we heard that voice – for Behold, the First Fate spake not in the voice of a God, but in the voice of an idiot.

In a rude village on the banks of the River Mrin there dwelt a man so like a beast that his family kenneled him. He spoke no human speech, but rather howled and whined like a very dog. And yet in his thirtieth year the power of Prophecy came to him, and the rapture

descended upon him, and he began to speak. And as chance had it, the King of that land was one of the sons of Bear-shoulders, and he had gone with his father and ancient Belgarath to the City of Endless Night to reclaim the Orb. Now this King – whom men called Bull-neck – had been warned by Belgarath to listen for the Voice of Prophecy and to record it when it came. And so it was that King Bull-neck sent scribes to the village of the Prophet to record his words.

And we marveled at this, for the God of Angarak dwelt in a great palace high in the mountains of Karanda, and the Prophet of the River Mrin dwelt in a mud and wattle kennel by the riverbank, and yet the rapture of Prophecy was equally upon them – and it seemed in some wise that the higher and more exalted Torak became, the lower and more degraded became the one who spoke the Prophecies of the Destiny which opposed him. And behold, in his final days, after he had Prophesied for twenty years, the mind of the Prophet of Mrin broke entirely, and his idiocy became tainted with madness, and King Bull-neck perforce was obliged to have him chained to a post before his kennel lest he do himself injury or run into the fens to live with the beasts.

And from afar we watched and we waited, and when the rapture of Prophecy had passed we sent certain of our number to copy down the Prophecies of the idiot of Mrin and the God of Angarak that we might compare them and learn from them.

And there were lesser Prophecies as well during this time. The First Destiny spake through the mouth of a merchant of Darine in far-off Sendaria, and the Second Destiny spake from the mouth of a slave at Rak Cthol in the wasteland of Murgos. And a scholar in Melcena was seized by an ecstasy and spake in the voice of the First Destiny for three hundred and nine hours – and then he died. And a seaman and warrior of the far northern kingdom of Cherek leapt from his sleep aboard a Cherek warboat to speak Prophecies of the coming of Torak, and his shipmates bound him in chains and cast him into the sea.

And there was in all of this a design which we could not perceive. The Destinies which contended with each other at the center of creation moved mysteriously to counter each other, and whom they chose to speak and where the Prophecies were spoken were as vital as what was said – and it was beyond our understanding.

But with the beginning of the Fourth Age, the time of Prophecy ended and the time of EVENT began. And the first EVENT was the slaying of the King of Riva, who was the keeper of the Orb. And Torak exulted in the death of the King of Riva, which Zedar the Apostate had caused to come to pass. But the Dragon God knew not that by that act had his own fate been sealed. For behold, the death of the Rivan King consumed the heart of Polgara the Sorceress with eternal hatred for the maimed God, and if he could not win Polgara's love, he was doomed.

with the beginning of the Fourth Age, the time of Prophecy ended

And the next EVENT was the coming of Angarak against the Kingdoms of the West. And upon the field at Vo Mimbre was Torak overcome by the power of the Orb and bound by it to await the coming of his enemy.

And EVENTS, both large and small, followed the overthrow of Torak, and we saw in the course of those EVENTS the hands of the two Fates, and we saw also the intricate moves of their eternal game. But no EVENT resounded more in the stars than the birth of Belgarion. And in his sixteenth year he put forth his hand to claim the Orb, and when his hand touched it, all of creation rang like some vast bell.

And now the EVENT for which the universe and Time itself had waited drew near, and the two Destinies confronted each other in the ruins of the City of Night. And it came to pass that Torak, Dragon God of Angarak, was slain by the hand of Belgarion, the Keeper of the Orb. And that EVENT signaled the beginning of the Fifth Age.

And the Fifth Age began in darkness and confusion, for the Book of the Heavens had changed in the instant of Torak's death, and we could no longer read it. Moreover, with the death of Torak we felt a shudder pass through all of creation, and we were chagrined, for one of the

Destinies appeared to have been vanquished – and we had not yet chosen between them. The First Destiny had been fulfilled and the Second had failed, but we still did not know which was Good and which was Evil. And if the Prophecies of Torak had been the voice of truth, then Good had passed forever from creation, and we were doomed to eternal Evil.

Desperately we sought to learn anew the language of the Great Book of the Heavens, but one of our number, who had ever bent his attention to the voices within the rocks, came to us and spake, saying: 'Behold, the rocks still speak with two voices.' And the spirits also spake unto us, saying: 'Behold, the Child of Light and the Child of Dark still contend with each other in the spirit world.' And as the Book of the Heavens became clear once more, we read with astonishment that the two Destinies continued their endless game. In the meeting between Belgarion and Torak one aspect of the one Destiny perished. And we perceived that other such meetings had taken place – and that still more would. Even now, a new aspect of the Destiny which had failed with the death of Torak had begun to move about the world – and in some regard this aspect seemed a dark reflection of Polgara the Sorceress. And we shuddered at the prospect of the meeting between this dark shape and terrible Polgara.

And as the Book of the Heavens became clearer, we read there that the struggle between the two Destinies will continue for so long as the two stones which once were one still exist. For even as the stones were once the center of all creation, each is now at the core of a different Destiny, and so long as both exist, the endless struggle will go on.

And we searched even more urgently for that stone which is the counter to the Orb, for Behold, the Orb is in the hand of Belgarion, and he is a mighty sorcerer. Should the two stones be drawn together for their final confrontation, the hand of Belgarion will surely enter into the struggle, and we do not know if this is as it should be – but how might we deny to mighty Belgarion anything he chooses to do?

The second stone is here. The rocks of this world reverberate with the sound of its presence. The two stones move toward each other as inexorably as the Fates they represent. We must find the second stone, and we must delay Belgarion lest he bring the Orb into the presence of the other stone before we have made our choice. For should the meeting take place before we have chosen, all of creation will perish.

BOOK 3

THE BOOK OF TASKS

Now These are the Tasks which have been set us:

ONCE WE SAT UPON THE EARTH in the shadow of the mountains of Korim, which are no more, and we made great moan that we had been made and cast out. And even as we grieved, the gift of sight came to one of our people, and she became a Seeress, and she spake unto us of the Feast of Life and of the Beloved Guest who would one day arrive to partake of that feast. And she exhorted us to prepare for his coming. She told us of the signs in the sky and in the earth and commanded that we learn to read those signs in order that we might choose between the two who would one day come to us.

So it was that we turned our faces first to the heavens, and we despaired for there seemed no sign there. But lo! a great light streamed across the night sky, trailing clouds of fire behind it like a veil. And in those clouds of fire read we the first word in the Book of the Heavens, and the word we read was 'Peril'. Painfully we began to piece together the message written in the stars. And as we labored at this, others of our number strove to hear the voices which whispered within the rocks. Now there were whispers which all men might hear, but they spoke in a

language which no man could translate. But lo! in a
certain time the earth was seized by the throes of earthquake, and the whisper of the rocks became a shriek, and
in that shriek we found the first word of the language of
the rocks, and the word we heard was 'peril'.

For centuries we struggled with the signs among the
stars that we might read them, and for centuries we wres-
tled with the whispers in the rocks that we might hear
them more clearly and translate them. And in time it
came to pass that one amongst us lifted his face to the sky
and read clearly there the message of the stars. And the
message read: 'Peril lies at the heart of the choice, for
should ye choose awry, all of creation will be bent to the
design of EVIL, and GOOD shall perish and be no more.'
And at the same time, another of our scholars arose and
went to a certain rock and laid his ear against it, and he
heard therein the voice of the rock speaking clearly unto
him. And the rock said: 'Peril lies at the heart of the choice,
for should ye choose awry, all of creation will be bent to
the design of EVIL, and GOOD shall perish and be no
more.'

And as we studied further, the Book of the Heavens
became more clear, and the Voice of the Earth more audi-
ble. But the pages written in the stars and the volumes
spoken from the earth provided no aid to us in the choice
which we must make. Both earth and sky warned repeat-
edly that two would come to us, and that one was good
and one was evil and that we must choose between them,
but neither earth nor sky would advise us which was
which. And we sent scholars into other realms of knowledge to seek the answer we must have. And some of them
communed with the dead and others spoke with spirits
and with beasts and with trees. And our seers cast their
sight into the far future and the distant past, but nowhere
could we find the answer.

And upon a certain day we gathered together upon the
plains of Temba to consider our task and what we might
do to complete it. And we brought together all that we
had learned from earth and sky, from the living and the

dead, from the spirits and the beasts and the trees. And when it was all before us, we were amazed that we had discovered so much, for often what the sky did not say, the earth did, and if neither earth nor sky spoke to a matter, the spirits did. And when it was all joined together we discovered that our first task was complete. We had learned of the division which marred creation; we have learned of the two spirits at the core of the division; and we have learned of the two stones which once were one but will never be rejoined.

And as we contemplated this, an aged man arose from our midst and did bind his eyes with a cloth and spake unto us in the voice of vision, saying:

'BEHOLD! Thy first task is complete, and now thou wilt turn unto the second. The two spirits which mar creation with Division contend with one another upon this earth even now. One of the two stones is here and the God-form of the other Destiny also. Even now the God raises the stone against the earth. Seize upon this opportunity to study the two Fates. Learn all that may be learned of them that thou might make the choice between them.'

And even as the seer set this task upon us, the earth heaved and split asunder as the God and the stone joined to crack the world. And we turned all of our effort to the study of the two Destinies which were revealing themselves by their acts. The First Destiny we found to be obdurate and unforgiving, and some among us seized upon this, saying: 'Surely this Destiny must be the Evil one, since Good cannot be so.' But we pointed out to them that we had considered only the aspect of the Fate which was represented by the stone, and it is most natural for a stone to be obdurate and unforgiving. And in like manner we found the Second Destiny filled with pride of Self and with a great longing for praise and adulation; but these were the natural attributes of a certain kind of God, and it was such a God which represented the God-aspect of the Second Fate.

And so we bent our minds to the task of seeing beyond the aspects to the true nature of the two Fates. And in the

often what the sky did not say, the earth did

Book of the Heavens we found the pages which spoke of the First Destiny before the arrival of the Second. The fate then of all that was all that is and all that is yet to be bent toward one EVENT, which was to come at a certain time and was to be the fulfillment of creation. And then we turned to the pages which spoke of the Second Destiny before it became aware of the existence of the First; and Behold! the Second Destiny also moved inexorably toward one EVENT. At a certain time the two Fates will confront each other in all their aspects and the fate of creation will be chosen.

And as we learned more, we discovered more and more of the aspects of the two Destinies; and we found them always to be in balance. For the one stone there was another; for the God, there was another God; for the hero, a hero; for the woman, a woman; for the sword, a sword. In all things were the two Fates so balanced that the weight of a single feather might tip the course of the ultimate EVENT.

for the one stone there was another; for the God, there was another God

And behind it all we found that the First Destiny of creation was unchanging and immutable, permanent and unmoving. The Second Destiny we found to be bent on change and alteration, transmutation and progression. And we saw evidence of these differences in all of the acts of the two Destinies, and we argued among ourselves concerning the nature of GOOD and the nature of EVIL, and at last we were still unsure and unable to state with certainty that change was good or evil or that absolute immutability was the Fate we should choose.

And even as we considered all that we had learned, ancient Belgarath, himself one aspect of the First Destiny, moved to retrieve his master's Orb from the City of Endless Night. And as the morning of that day dawned, a Seeress we had not known before came down from out the mountains bordering upon Darshiva, and the voiceless man who guided her was of a strange race. And the Seeress raised her voice and laid our third task upon us.

'Behold,' she said, 'the Third Age of man has begun, and this is the Age of Prophecy. And it shall be thy task to

gather up all the Prophecies which are spoken by the one
Destiny or by the other. Seek ye, therefore, among the
lands of all men for the Prophets who will speak the
words of the Fates, and gather up all that is said and carry
the words of Prophecy to the speakers, who will wrest the
meaning from them.' And so saying the nameless Seeress
turned and went her way, and we saw her no more.

And the task the Seeress had lain upon us was long and
hard, for Prophecy hovers ever on the verge of madness,
and we were perforce obliged to seek out every madman
in all the kingdoms of the world and to take down all the
ravings of gibbering insanity. And some of the words of
the madmen of this world seemed to be the words of Fate,
and some of the words of true Prophets seemed to be the
ravings of the deranged, and we knew not which was the
Voice of Prophecy and which the Voice of Madness. And
so, that we leave no true Prophecy ungathered, we carried
all such mouthings back to the Seers at Kell, where they
winnowed Prophecy from madness.

And sometimes we despaired, for the times themselves
seemed mad. And we found, moreover, that sprites and
Devils oft-times in mockery would speak through innocent mouths in the tones of Prophecy to lead us astray. But
we persevered, and when the Age of Prophecy ended, we
for the found that of all that we had gathered, scant few grains
times were the true voices of the Fates, and all that remained
themselves was dross, and the knowledge was bitter to us.
seemed And in the midst of our sorrow the Seeress Onatel came
mad to us with words of comfort, saying:

'Grieve not, nor let your shoulders be bowed down in
despair, for the greatest task lies yet before ye, and all that
has gone before is a preparation and a testing. And this is
the task which ye must perform. All that is needful has
been given. In this Age must ye make the Choice.'

And we heard her words in astonishment, for we knew
not that the Third Age had ended and the Fourth Age had
begun. But in time our kinsman returned from the north
and told us what he had seen in the house of Torak, and
we began to understand. Torak was not the culmination of

the Fate which ruled him, and we must look further to find the God who would one day come to us. Yet the Seeress Onatel had told us that we had all that was needful to make the choice. How could we choose between two Gods who had not yet come to us? Clearly we had received some knowledge which we had overlooked – some sign which had escaped us. And so we gathered on the plains of Kell to consider all that we had learned.

And in time we despaired, for we found no certainty in all that we had gathered – no truth which emerged which could guide us without the possibility of error. And again the Seeress Onatel came to us, saying:

'Behold! I will tell you a mystery. The choice will be made by one of ye – not by all. And the choice between the two Fates will not be made in wisdom, but in desperation. At a certain time, the Fates will confront each other, and one of ye will see at last what none have seen as yet, and that one will choose.' And with that Onatel left us.

And we reasoned that the Fates must meet in one of the great EVENTS which were written large in the Book of the Heavens, and we journeyed about the world to be present at those EVENTS. One of our number was present when the Rivan King was slain, but there was no choice to be made at that EVENT. And one of us was present when Torak set his forces in motion against the West. And one stood nearby at Vo Mimbre when maimed Torak met in single combat with the Warder of Riva and was struck down by the power of the Orb. And one of us was in the rude village where Belgarion was born and not far from the burning house in which the Godslayer's parents perished. We were at Riva when the Orb was delivered into Belgarion's hand and hovered for an instant on the verge of choice, but forbore a moment and the EVENT slipped past us.

Then came we at last to accursed Cthol Mishrak in the diseased basin where it lies, and once again the moment escaped us. For behold, the EVENT in that place was not the death of Torak at the hands of Belgarion, but rather it came and passed in the moment that Polgara spurned the

God of Angarak. And as Torak fell and all of creation shuddered to a stop, we feared that it might never again grow light. The EVENT had passed and we had not chosen, and we had always believed that in that instant all must be destroyed.

And we came away from Cthol Mishrak shaken and afraid. Had our failure to choose been in fact the choice of EVIL over GOOD? We knew not, and fearfully we watched the Book of the Heavens for some new and dreadful sign.

And at last there came to us the seer Gazad, and his face was stern and angry, and he spake rebukingly to us, saying:

'Behold! Ye have failed in the task which was lain upon ye by Onatel. All of creation has been marred by your failure. Your task remains the same. Choose! Fail not again, for in your next failure, all that is or was or is yet to be shall perish, and creation shall be no more.'

And the words of Gazad scourged us, and he drove us ever into new efforts to complete the task which we had failed to complete in the previous Age. And as a part of this task we strove more urgently to find that other stone which counters the Orb of Aldur, but the Destiny of which **they must be** the stone is the center moved ever to conceal the stone **enlisted by** from us and from all men and Gods. None among us was **subterfuge,** powerful enough to break through the barriers of mind **and this is** and spirit with which the Destiny protected its secret, and **perilous** we determined at last to follow a dangerous course. Of all **indeed** the power in this world, that which lay in the hands of Belgarath, Polgara and Belgarion was the greatest. Could

we in some way enlist their aid in our search for the other stone, we might succeed; but in so doing we must conceal our intent from them, for they were the servants of the First Destiny. Should they find the other stone before we, they will surely attempt to destroy it, and this cannot be permitted. Thus they must be enlisted by subterfuge, and this is perilous indeed. Moreover, we must seek out and identify the shadowy, veiled woman who is even now moving and shaping EVENTS to her own purposes.

These, then are portions of our great task. Let each strive

with all his might to accomplish that which is assigned to him, but keep ever in mind that the paramount task is to choose, and should circumstances compel it, any one of us might be forced to make the choice unaided and alone. Share all of thy knowledge with thy brothers and sisters therefore, for should one of them be compelled to make the choice, it may be that some fragment of knowledge withheld could cause them to choose awry. For Behold, the choice, once made, can never be unmade, and what ye choose shall endure until the end of days.

BOOK 4

THE BOOK OF GENERATIONS

Now These are the Generations of the Seers:

KNOW BEFORE ALL ELSE that thou art not exalted above others by the sight. We know not from whence it comes; we know not why some are chosen to receive it and others are not. Know also that the sight is not thine instrument. Thou art but the tool of the sight, and it will use thee for its own purpose, and thou wilt never know what that purpose may be. Submit, therefore, in humility and in patience.

The sight first came to the woman called Ninal. Now Ninal had been a wife and a mother, but when the sight came to her, she turned forever from her husband and children. And the rapture of seeing brought her to her feet, and to darken her eyes against the common light of day that she might more clearly see what the sight revealed to her, she bound a cloth about her eyes. And from that day until her last, Ninal never again unbound her eyes. And she spake unto the people of what had been revealed to her. And the people listened in wonder as she told them of the Feast of Life and of the Beloved Guest who would one day come. And all knew that her words were truth

because of the way her voice reached into their hearts. And when Ninal had finished speaking, the people stood in awe of her – all save one.

Among the people at that time there was an unfortunate man called Jord. And he was taller than any other man and his thews were mighty. But Jord had never spoken or uttered a single sound since the day of his birth. And Jord took up a staff from the earth and went with it to Ninal and put her hand upon the staff and led her out from the midst of the people. And ever after, Ninal and Jord dwelt apart from the people, and he cared for her and protected her from all harm, and though she may have revealed many secrets to him, those secrets were forever locked behind his silent lips. And it hath ever been thus: for every Seer upon whom the sight descends there is a mute to be the guide and protector.

In the years that followed the great revelation, the Seeress Ninal spoke unto the people many times, and the words she spoke were sometimes clear and sometimes dark and obscure. And in time the Sight descended upon others, and they too bound their eyes against the common light that they might better see; and for each of them as well a mute came forth to guide and protect. Now some of the Seers spoke of the revelation which had come to Ninal, and others spoke to other matters. Some spoke clearly while the words of others were a mystery.

But because she was the first and because the great revelation came first to her, the Seers of the First Age of man are called the Generations of Ninal in her honor. And when she was old and filled with years, the Seeress Ninal died, and within the same hour mute Jord also passed from this earth, and they were buried side by side in great honor.

And the Seers aided the scholars who sought to read the Book of the Heavens and those who sought to translate the words spoken in the voices of the rocks. And we discovered that the Seers could speak to each other over great distances and that they seemed all to share in one univer-

sal soul which was the source of the Sight; but they spoke not of this, and our questions remained unanswered.

Now it came to pass that the Generations of Ninal ended with the end of the First Age, and the Generations of Vigun began. The Seer Vigun arose and spoke to us upon the day when the Dragon God of Angarak raised the stone which he called Cthrag-Yaska and by its power cracked the earth asunder. And with the cracking of the earth the First Age ended and the First Fate and the First Task, and it became the concern of the Second Generation to seek out the children of the Gods to learn from them the things which they knew of the Gods and of the two Fates which contended for the mastery of creation.

And the Seers of the Generations of Vigun were called the searchers, for they wandered up and down the world, touching the minds of the children of the Gods to learn from them. And the searchers found many strange things concerning the Gods, for Behold! Each God was so caught up in a single idea that he was in all other ways incomplete. But when at last the searchers went up unto the Vale where the God Aldur dwelt with his Disciples, they found a God caught up with the idea of knowing, and the despair which had descended upon them was banished as they came into contact with the mind of Aldur. And Aldur comforted them with his wisdom and counseled them to endure the coming of the Angaraks, who would soon invade their lands. And when they went away, one of their number remained behind for a time. And this was the Seeress Kammah, who awaited the return of the first Disciple of Aldur and she who was to be his wife. And when Belgarath, his task completed, returned to the Vale, his only companion was a snowy owl. And Kammah perceived this in wonder and even unbound her eyes so that they might confirm by common sight what that other Sight had revealed. And Behold! Poledra was an owl, and the Sight revealed to Kammah that she was also a wolf, but that one day she would become a woman and wife to Belgarath. And Kammah began to tremble and she fell

it became the concern of the Second Generation to seek out the children of the Gods

down upon the earth in the presence of Poledra, for the vision which came to her shook her very soul. Kammah knew in that instant that Poledra would bear two daughters, and that the one would wed the King who would be the Guardian of the stone called the Orb, and that from their line would spring the Godslayer whom men would call 'Belgarion'. The other daughter of Poledra, Kammah perceived, would be the mightiest Sorceress the world would ever know, and the name 'Polgara' would be inscribed beside that of 'Belgarath' in the Book of the Heavens. But it was not Polgara's power which so awed Kammah. Rather it was the knowledge that the childless Sorceress would be mother to Belgarion, and even more so to the Beloved Guest who would one day come to the Feast of Life.

And of all the things which were learned by the Seers of the Generations of Vigun, this was the most important. And the Seers of the lands of the east and of the lands of the west contemplated it in wonder until the end of the Second Age.

Now, as all men know, the Third Age began when ancient Belgarath, in the company of the King of the Alorns and the King's three sons, went up unto Cthol Mishrak, the City of Endless Night, to reclaim the Orb of Aldur from the iron tower of the maimed God of Angarak. But what some men do not know is that at the same time – indeed within the same moment – another EVENT of equal importance took place half around the world in the Vale of Aldur. There it was at that particular time that Poledra, Wolf-wife to Belgarath, labored and brought forth twin daughters and died in bearing them. And the birth of Polgara and Beldaran and the death of Poledra shaped the future as much as did the recapture of the Orb. And as we read in wonder of these EVENTS in the Book of the Heavens, a strange Seeress came down to us from the mountains above Darshiva, and she spake unto us, laying upon us the task of gathering. And we went up and down in the world, gathering the Prophecies whispered into the

hearts of diverse men by the two Fates which rule creation.

And Behold, there arose yet another generation of Seers to consider the Prophecies and to speak of their meaning. And these were the Generations of the unknown Seeress, whom men called the Speakers. And we carried to the Speakers both Prophecy and the ravings of the demented, for we determined that no possible word of either Fate should escape us. And the Speakers who were of the Generations of the unknown Seeress went down to the city of Kell, where the priests of the God of Angarak feared to come, and there they received what we had gathered. And we beheld there a wonder, for the documents which reported our gatherings were delivered into the hands of the mutes who guarded the Seers, and the mutes read the documents. And if the Seer spake not, the document was known to be false, and the mute who had read it committed it immediately to the fire. But if the document was truly Prophecy – of either of the two Fates – the Seer would begin to speak almost as soon as the mute began to read. And we perceived from this that the Seers communed with the minds of their silent guides, and despite the binding of their eyes, they were not blind, but saw rather through the eyes of their mute protectors.

Now from all that we gathered, but little was truly Prophecy, and the Prophecies all spake the same story – that one day the Child of Light and the Child of Dark would meet and that in their meeting would be decided the Fate of all creation. And this was bitter to us, for we had known of it before, having read the self-same words in the Book of the Heavens. But the aged Seer Encoron of the Generations of the unknown Seeress spake in his last days, and at last we understood the meaning of what was taking place and had been since the beginning of time.

'Variations,' quoth Encoron. 'Each EVENT is but a variation of the same EVENT which hath repeated itself innumerable times down through all the ages. The Child of Light and the Child of Dark will meet – as they have met times beyond counting before. And they will continue to

meet in these endless variations of this same EVENT until at one meeting a choice is made between them.'

'What is the choice, Master?' we urged him, 'and who must make it?'

But he spake not, and his mute guardian sighed and gently laid his master in a posture of repose. Then he also laid himself upon the earth beside his master and he also died.

And at the beginning of the Fourth Age the Seeress Onatel came, and she also spake of the choice. And the Seers of the Generations of Onatel probed with their minds toward the very center of Prophecy and of the Destiny which was at the core of Prophecy. But the visions came darkly and seemed without meaning. We saw the whirling of stars and entire worlds suddenly touched into fire, but none knew what such visions meant. And at last came Dallan, a Seer of the Generations of Onatel, and he spake the great truth unto us, saying:

'Behold what I have seen. The life of man is but the winking of an eye, and the life of a star is but a breath in length. The contention between the two Fates hath endured throughout eternity, and the outcome will encompass EVENTS so vast that thine imagining cannot grasp them. Should the Fate which is EVIL triumph over the other Fate, the result will not so much rebound upon the lives of men, but rather shall be seen among the stars. And if the stars perish, all will perish.'

And then at last we understood. The choice between GOOD and EVIL was a choice between existence and destruction for all of creation, and GOOD and EVIL were but human terms, and had no meaning among the stars. That which might be foulest evil in the eyes of men might well be that which would save creation from destruction. And as we considered this, we grew afraid, for Behold, it was our stern duty to protect creation – even should our choice enslave or even destroy mankind.

And thus it was when we saw in the Book of the Heavens that the time was drawing nigh for the meeting

between the Child of Light and the Child of Dark, sent we five Seers of the Generations of Onatel to Cthol Mishrak, the City of Night, to make the choice.

But the moment for the choice came and passed – for lo, we had believed that the EVENT was to be the meeting between Belgarion and Torak, but it was not. The EVENT which slipped so swiftly past us was the spurning of Torak by Belgarath's daughter, Polgara.

And, sorrowing that they had failed in their task, the five Seers of the Generations of Onatel returned to Kell, and the Fifth Age had already begun.

And the Fifth Age was the Age of the Generations of Gazad, the stern Seer who berated us that we had failed in our task. And the Generations of Gazad were to be known as the Choosers, and they moved into the affairs of this world as none of us had done before. The necessity for choice now lay heavily upon us, and the time of indifferent contemplation of EVENTS had passed. Now is the time to act, to shape EVENTS rather than to be shaped by them. We must move the figures on the board of time ourselves and place them in such fashion that the final meeting will take place at a time and place of our choosing. For Behold, should this meeting pass without our choosing, all that was, is and shall be must surely perish.

we must move the figures on the board of time ourselves

BOOK 5

THE BOOK OF VISIONS

Now These are the Five Visions:

*B EHOLD! A GREAT LIGHT came into mine eyes, and I was dazzled by it and could not see; but in time, as mine eyes grew accustomed to the brilliance, I saw a great table lain with fine cloth and dishes of gold. And I saw the seven guests at the feast and the empty seat for the beloved one who had not yet come. And the seven guests ate that which pleased them and looked about often for the one who had not yet arrived. And I looked upon this in puzzlement, for I knew not why it should be shown to me.

And I became aware of a robed and hooded figure stand-ing by my left hand and another upon my right, and both figures insisted with imperious gesture that I continue to watch the feast. And in time, the seven guests

* This is the vision of Cyradis.

rose from the table, having eaten their fill, and lo, much of the feast remained, and still was I filled with wonder and puzzlement.

And then the figure upon my right spake unto me, saying: 'This is the Feast of Life, and the seven guests are the seven Gods, who have chosen that which pleased them.'

And the figure upon my left spake also unto me, saying: 'One guest hath not yet arrived at the feast, and that guest is also a God. And when he cometh, he will choose all that the other guests have not taken.'

And still I perceived not the meaning of their words, yet felt I the enmity which stood between them. And each strove to some great end but failed in its accomplishment because of the other. And then they turned their shadowed faces to me and spake unto me in one voice, saying: 'The choice is upon thee, for two guests shall come to the Feast of Life, and thou shalt bid one stay and the other go, and it shall be as thou shalt decide. And thy choice shall be for all that was, all that is and all that is yet to be.'

and I will make this choice for all of creation

And I was bowed down by the weight of the burden they had placed upon me, for now at last I understood the vision and why it had been sent. The figure upon my right and the figure upon my left were the Destinies which had striven the one against the other adown all the endless corridors of time, and each was as strong as the other, and they remained locked, each in the grip of the other. And all that was, all that is, and all that is yet to be is divided equally between them. So equal is this division that the weight of my choice between them will tip the balance, and I will make this choice for all of creation. And I turned to the figures in anguish to protest the burden, that I was not

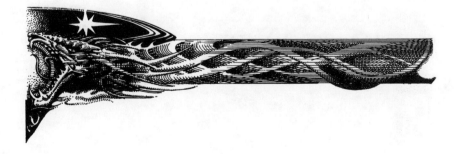

wise enough to decide, and they replied, saying: 'No man nor God nor spirit is wise enough for this choice. Thy selection for this task was at the whim of random chance. We care not how the choice is made, only that it be made. The division strains the very fabric of creation, and if the division doth not soon end, all of creation will perish. Choose wisely; choose ill; choose by whim alone – but choose!'

And at these words I fell into a swoon and saw no more.

All as in a dream I wandered across a barren heath under a lowering sky. And by the tokens which tell of such things I knew that a great storm was approaching and that I must seek shelter. And behold, the thought had scarcely entered my mind when I saw at the farthest edge of that heath a great house, and I hastened toward it to take shelter therein from the gathering storm. But as I approached the house I found that less and less I liked its aspect. Grim and bleak it crouched at the very edge of the precipice which marked the end of the heath. The storm which pursued me, however, gave me no choice, and I reached the door of the house but scant seconds before the deluge.

The servant who admitted me was civil enough, though impatient. He led me through the gloomy corridors of the grim house to a great dining hall with a huge table upon which sat a single plate, and he bade me sit at the table and brought me meat and drink. And as I ate, I questioned him closely concerning the house and its owner, and he replied most strangely, saying:

'The house hath been here since before the beginning of

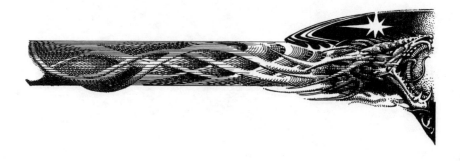

time, and it hath two owners – the same two who caused it to be built.'

His words amazed me, and I protested that no house can endure so long and that certainly no mortal hath lived since before the beginning of time. But he received my protests in silence as if they were unworthy of reply, and he bade me make haste at my meal since I was to be taken immediately to the owners of the house.

venture not near the window lest the void beyond it destroy thy mind

When I had finished, he led me once again through the dim corridors and brought me at last to a strange room. Behold, a great window formed one wall of the room and overlooked the void upon which the house sat, and by that window stood a table, and at the table sat two robed and hooded figures. And on the table was laid a game of enormous complexity.

Now the servant cautioned me in whispered tones, saying: 'Speak not, lest ye disturb the game which these two have played for all eternity, and venture not near the window lest the void beyond it destroy thy mind.'

I replied with some asperity, stating that I had viewed chasms before and that my mind was therefore in little danger. And the servant looked at me in amazement and said, 'Knowest thou not to what house thou hast come? This is the house which stands at the very edge of creation. Beyond that window lies no mere chasm, but absolute nothingness. I know not why thou hast been brought unto this lonely house. I know only that thou art to observe the game until the storm which brought thee here abates, and then thou art to go thy way.'

And so it was that throughout the long night I watched the two faceless players at the game which I could not begin to comprehend. And the moves which they made had no meaning to me. If the one moved a king, the other

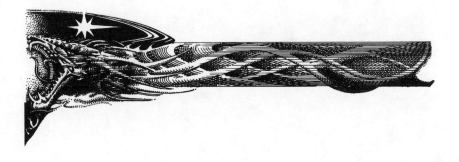

countered by moving a comet or a sun or a grain of sand. And there were beggars and thieves and harlots on the board as well as kings and knights and queens. And sometimes the players moved rapidly and sometimes they pondered long between moves. And I watched their play and spake not throughout the long night.

And when morning came, the servant returned and led me down the gloomy halls of the house which stands at the edge of creation. And when he opened the door I saw that the storm had passed. And I turned to the servant and I said, 'What is the game they play?'

And he answered, saying, 'It is the game of the two Fates. All the pieces contain two possibilities and all are interconnected. When one piece is moved, all other pieces also move. The two players no longer even strive to win the game, but merely attempt to maintain the balance between them.'

'Why do they continue to play then?'

'Because they must. The game must be played to its conclusion, though it last until the end of days. Thou wert brought to this place because it may be that thou or one who might come after thee will one day make some move in this eternal game. I know not, and I care not. My care is to tend the house, and I have done so since it was built. Now go thy way.' And so saying, he closed the door, leaving me standing alone upon the doorstep.

Now the morning was bright, and the birds sang sweetly, and I strode across the heath at a goodly pace, and by midafternoon I found the path which led me back to my own country.

when one piece is moved, all other pieces also move

*

*At a certain time I found myself weary and alone in a dusky wood, having strayed, it seems, from the true path. Yet I knew not why I was there nor whither I had been bound when I lost my way. As night descended upon that gloomy wood, I despaired of finding the path again ere it grew dark, and as best I could I composed myself for sleep, wrapped in my cloak and with my back resting against the bole of a great tree.

If I slept or no, I shall never know, for it seemed that I came awake of a sudden in the broad street of a populous city, and excited crowds were all hurrying toward the central square, and I, perforce, was borne along with them, so great was the press. Turning to the man pushing along beside me, I asked as politely as possible what event had so moved this multitude of people that they should strive all at once to gather in the square.

'She comes,' he replied in ardent tones.

I confessed to him that I was a stranger in his city and that I knew not to whom he referred.

'Why, she, of course,' quoth he, '– the paramount Lady of all the world. Men say she is a thousand years old, and wise beyond belief.'

'Is it wise of us, then,' I said to him, 'to intrude ourselves upon her in such numbers? For if it be true that she is so deeply sunk in eld, she will surely be frail and infirm, and will not welcome the noise and confusion of so great a multitude.'

My companion, however, was swept from my side by the press of the crowd, and I heard not his reply.

* Read the opening canto of *The Divine Comedy* for a comparison.

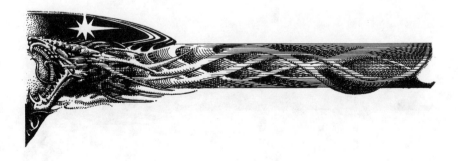

At length I reached the great square, whither all in that
city had been hastening, and to my disappointment, I
found that the venerated lady had not yet arrived. And I
concluded that my informant may have spoken in jest, for
as I had leisure to consider his words, I realized that what
he had told me was an absurdity, for no man or woman,
however noble or powerful, could endure the weight of a
thousand years. And almost I laughed that I had for a
single instant considered it possible.

And then from out an azure sky there came on silent
wings the form of a great snowy owl, and to my surprise
she descended from aloft into the very center of the populous square. And at the last moment she flared her great
pinions, and at the same time a strange shimmering
seemed to engulf her – not unlike the disturbance of air
above heated rock. Now when that peculiar shimmering
had passed, I beheld with astonishment that the owl had
vanished and that in its place stood the most beautiful
woman I have ever seen. Gowned all in blue, she swept
the square with imperious gaze, and all present bowed
and abased themselves before her. I alone, struck dumb
and motionless by her beauty, bowed not nor acknowledged her with any display of respect. Seeing this, she
approached me, her expression quizzical and the faintest
trace of a smile hovering about her lips. And as she came
nearer, I saw that her raven hair was touched at the brow by
a single lock of snowiest white. Her glorious eyes fell full
upon me, and I confess that my heart stopped within me.

And then she spake unto me, saying, 'Why art thou
pale, youth? Hast thou never before seen such simple
sorcery?'

'My lady,' I stammered, 'forgive me. It is not thy
sorcery which hath robbed my limbs of their ability to
move, it is thy beauty.'

And she smiled at me and said, 'Thou art a well-spoken youth.'

Emboldened by her encouragement, I blurted, 'Truly, my Lady, thou art the most beautiful of all women.'

And a secret little glow of pleasure touched her eyes at my words, and she reached forth and gently touched my cheek, and she replied, saying, 'Yes, fond youth, I know.'

And then she looked at me gravely, and she spake further, saying, 'Thou art a stranger here, and thou know-est not how or why thou camest to this place. It will not be long ere thou awaken.'

'Ah,' I said, my heart wrenching within me. 'Is this then but a dream?'

I beheld upon the coverlet of my bed a single soft white feather

'Nay, dear youth,' she replied, 'this is more real than the world from which thou hast come. Return to thy people and tell them what thou hast seen, and tell them that they may know that the time for the Choice hath arrived when they see me abroad in their lands. For I shall not come into the lands of thy people until it is time for them to choose, and they may take my coming as a sign.' And so saying, she touched my cheek again, turned and vanished. And so great was my emotion that I fell down in a swoon.

And Behold, when I awoke, I was not in the populous city nor in the dismal wood where I had lost my way, but was once again in mine own house and mine own bed. And I concluded that what I had seen had been but a dream – but then I beheld upon the coverlet of my bed a single soft white feather, and I knew that the Lady of my vision had spoken the truth and that I had truly seen her and that one day she would come down into the country of my birth to demand a choice of my people.

Once, when I had gone into the West upon certain duties, it came to me that I must journey up unto the Isle of the

Winds to behold a wonder that I might tell my brothers and sisters of it when I returned at long last to Kell.

It was the worst time of the year for a journey, for the sea raged and the wind oft-times threatened to drive the boat which bore me to the distant isle beneath the hungry waves. At length, however, I landed upon the strand at the city of Riva upon the very eve of that holiday which all men in the west observe. And the city was alive with the news that the Orb of Aldur, which had been stolen away, was to be restored on the morrow, and I contrived to be present in the Hall of the Rivan King to witness the restoration, for I believed that this was the wonder I had been sent to witness.

But lo, as the child who bore the Orb and the young Sendar who guided the child's steps entered the Hall, a rapture seized me and all unbidden, the Vision descended upon me, and I saw that the young Sendar was clothed all in light, and when the child presented the Orb to him, I heard a chorus of a million voices resounding from the farthest star, and I knew that Belgarion had come at last. And as the young man affixed the Orb to the pommel of the great sword, and the blade leaped into flame to declare his identity to those in the Hall and to all of mankind as well, my vision continued, for lo, all unnoticed, the child who had carried the Orb turned, and I saw his face bathed in ineffable glory, and I knew that I beheld the face of one of the two Gods between whom we must one day choose. And because of what I had just seen, my eyes grew dark and I fell down in a swoon.

*

I wandered as in a dream through the marshes of Temba and came at last to the shore where a small boat awaited me. And all unbidden I stepped aboard the boat which then without oars or sails bore me out to sea. At length the boat brought me to a shoal, and I saw ahead of me a grim reef of ancient rock where the sullen sea beat itself to frothy tatters. And, as one compelled, I debarked upon that reef to wander through a wilderness of brine-crusted rock until I came at last to a fissure which tended downward into the darkness beneath.

there in the dimness I beheld the ruins of an ancient temple

Fearfully I descended into that grim cavern, and there in the dimness I beheld the ruins of an ancient temple, and on the steps thereof I beheld the hooded and veiled form of a woman. And her aspect chilled my blood within me. Wordlessly she pointed to the door of the temple, commanding me to enter, and, unable to resist, I did as she ordered.

Within the temple I beheld an altar and resting thereupon I beheld a dark stone of some size. And I wondered why I had been brought to this place. But as I stood, the woman came forward, and in her arms she bore a newborn infant. And as she approached the altar, the stone thereon began to glow with a dim fire, and it seemed that of a sudden I could see within the stone and what I saw there terrified me. And the woman reached forth the newborn child as if she intended to press it into the stone itself, and Behold, the stone opened to accept the child. But of a sudden I beheld the grim form of Belgarion the Godslayer standing before the woman. With his face contorted in anguish and with tears streaming from his eyes, he raised his flaming sword to smite down the woman and the child in one dreadful blow. And as I cried

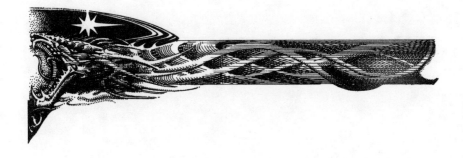

out to stop him, the sound of my voice shattered the vision which had come unbidden to me and I awoke shrieking in terror.

But truly I tell thee, my brother, my vision was not a misty imagining but a truth as solid as the earth upon which thou standest. Hear my words, for they are truth. The shoal and the reef are there, and the temple within the cavern doth truly exist. And within the temple lies the stone. One day will the woman and the child and the Godslayer himself come to that dim place, and at that moment must the choice be made, for that is the EVENT toward which all hath been moving since before the beginning of time.[*]

---

[*] The Mallorean Gospels took three months to write. It was worth the time and effort, since in a rather obscure way these Gospels provided a philosophical basis for The Malloreon. This is what Cyradis believed, and Cyradis was ultimately the core of Malloreon.

❧VI❧

A SUMMARY OF CURRENT EVENTS

5376-5387

From the Personal Journal of King Anheg of Cherek[*]

~~~

5376

I N THE SPRING of the year following the Battle of Thull Mardu and the enormous events which took place at Cthol Mishrak, we gathered – all of us – at Riva for the wedding of young King Belgarion and the Imperial Princess Ce'Nedra. I have some personal reservations about the wisdom of so closely allying the house of the Keeper of the Orb with the Imperial House of the Tolnedran Empire; but, since Ran Borune is elderly and the last of his line, I suppose no great harm can come of it. Moreover, despite her occasional flightiness, I found Ce'Nedra to be a remarkable young woman. It may well prove that the strong-willed girl will complement Belgarion's somewhat diffident nature, which has given us all some concern. Their marriage promises to be stormy, but I expect that my young friend will seldom be troubled with boredom. As for me, I'd sooner shave off my beard than have such a wife.

* I always liked Anheg. He has his faults, but he's a lot of fun.

In the summer of this year word reached us that 'Zakath had brought his siege of Rak Goska to a successful conclusion. His capture of the city, by all reports, was particularly savage, even for an Angarak. I have no great sympathy for Murgos, but I suspect that 'Zakath may live to regret his butchery of the inhabitants of Rak Goska. King Urgit, the son of Taur Urgas, unfortunately escaped, and he is certain to use the atrocity to fan Murgo sentiments to a white heat. I plan to sit quietly on the sidelines, cheering both sides on in their war of mutual extinction and permitting myself the private luxury of gloating. I know that gloating is an unattractive thing for a king to do, but a man needs some vices, after all.

Late in the fall, I received a letter from my good friend, General Varana, which gave me almost as much pleasure. The insufferable ass whom the Honeths were touting as Ran Borune's successor was neatly poisoned by a Horbite assassin, may Belar bless him! The Honeths are confounded, and Ran Borune is almost beside himself with glee. For once, I wholeheartedly share in the Emperor's delight. I think I could almost grow to like that sly little old fox.

Word has reached us that the strange fellow, Relg, and the Marag woman Belgarath found in the caves beneath Rak Cthol have produced their first child, a son. The boy, we are told, has blue eyes – a fact which for some reason has sent the Ulgos into a frenzy of celebration. My cousin Barak tells me that this has something to do with their religion. I didn't pursue the matter further, since questions of religion have always made my head ache. Barak, incidentally, has shown no further indications that he plans to turn into a bear on a regular basis. I'm profoundly grateful for his restraint in this regard. The difference between Barak and a bear is not really that extensive, but it's a bit embarrassing to admit close kinship to something that really belongs out in the forest.

5377

*I*SLENA and I spent Erastide with Rhodar and Porenn at Boktor and have only just returned to Val Alorn. Rhodar seems even more mellowed, and he dotes on his new son, of course. He tells me that his vagrant nephew, Kheldar, has joined forces with one Yarblek, a Nadrak who appears to be almost as big a thief as himself. In a brilliant stroke the pair of them have managed to capture the Nadrak fur market.

Also while we were at Boktor, Cho-Hag sent us the news that Hettar and Belgarion's cousin, Adara, had produced him a grandson. Everyone seems to be having children lately. One hopes that Belgarion and his little queen will get into the spirit of things. I know that we'll all rest more securely once the line of Riva is perpetuated.

In the kingdoms of the south events, as always, turn on politics. My cousin Grinneg, our ambassador at Tol Honeth, advises me that General Varana, acting as Ran Borune's special envoy, has concluded a very advantageous trade agreement with Sadi, Chief Eunuch at Queen Salmissra's court in Sthiss Tor. I'm sure the Empire will grow richer, but I don't envy them the pleasure of dealing with the snake people.

Young King Korodullin, with surprising astuteness, has appointed Count Reldegen Governor General of Asturia. I've met Reldegen, and he seems to have normal good sense – which in Arendia makes him an absolute genius. One can hope that the appointment will ease the tensions between Mimbre and Asturia – at least to the point where there is no longer open war on the Arendish plain.

This summer, our young Belgarion and his queen are making the grand tour, visiting all the capitals of the west. The move is politically sound, I think. Belgarion has made no effort to emphasize his title, Overlord of the West, and it's probably time to remind a few people that he's still there. The advantage of having done nothing, however,

is that he's made no mistakes and hence no enemies. Moreover, a great deal of good will for him still exists. Personal visits will enhance that good will. I look forward to seeing them. I am particularly interested in Ce'Nedra's waist-line. One hopes that she has begun to pick up a bit of weight. Ten or fifteen pounds on that girl would set my mind at ease considerably.

The visit of the royal pair was pleasant. Garion (Belgarion actually – it's hard to remember the formal name when you've just talked with him) seems to have matured a bit and to have become more decisive. I suspect that a part of his retiring nature may have been the result of Polgara's presence. That lady can be rather overpowering at times. I'm sure that the necessity of asserting his authority over his wife has given his backbone a bit of steel. Ce'Nedra, alas, remains as slender as a willow.

Just before the winter storms set in, word reached us from the south that 'Zakath* has captured the Murgo city of Rak Hagga, a major population center lying perhaps a thousand leagues to the south of Rak Goska. Unless something happens to halt his conquest down there, we may be obliged to take steps against him. His motives are obscure, and his army a bit too large for my comfort.

5378

MY apprehensions about 'Zakath appear to have been unfounded. King Urgit of Murgodom, who appears not to share his late father's headlong insanity, cleverly retreated before the advancing Malloreans, drawing them into the vastness of the great southern forest lying mainly in the Military District of Gorut. There, using the trees for concealment, Urgit had placed the bulk of the

---

* We dropped the apostrophe at the beginning of Zakath's name, although it was an indication that 'Kal' had been omitted ('Kal Zakath' hints around the edges of Zakath's insanity. Right at first he was at least as mad as Taur Urgas).

Murgo army. As 'Zakath approached Rak Gorut, Urgit fell upon him and massacred half his army. It is difficult for me, as I look out at the snow which chokes the streets of Val Alorn, to adjust myself to the fact that it is summer in those southern latitudes where Urgit and 'Zakath contend with each other across alien landscapes whose harsh names in the Angarak tongue seem made up of the echoes of nightmare. I suspect that this is because at heart I am a simple man and that there lurks within me the unyielding belief that the world is flat and the seasons everywhere the same and that the sun rises upon every inch of the world at the same time. Ah well.

This spring, Ran Borune became gravely ill, though not even Rhodar's most clever agents in the palace at Tol Honeth have been able to determine the precise nature of his malady. Surprisingly, the old fox retains enough of his mental faculties to realize that he is no longer able to conduct the day-to-day business of the Empire. He has appointed General Varana Imperial Regent, and he concerns himself only with the most pressing of affairs. Varana's participation in the Battle of Thull Mardu has made him something of a national hero in Tolnedra, so the Emperor could not have chosen more wisely.

I traveled this summer to Riva for the meeting of the Alorn Council. Since Torak is dead, our meeting had none of the urgency which had marked those previous, and the entire affair was something more in the nature of a social get-together rather than a council of war. How strange it is to return to Riva now that peace is finally here. Belgarion appears to be maturing, growing as it were, into his crown. I like that young man. If I had a son, I would wish him to be no different. Perhaps if Islena had not that morbid fear of childbirth, I might have had such a son. We all gently jibed at the young King for his failure to produce an heir to his throne, and our jesting put him, I think, a bit out of sorts. He is, perhaps, a bit too sensitive about jokes at his expense, but time will toughen his soul. Belgarath, who came late, was the same as always, as unchanging as the very rocks, but Rhodar appears to be declining. He suffers

from shortness of breath and has become dropsical. He can no longer negotiate stairs, though his mind remains alert.

While we were at Riva, a messenger arrived from Arendia to inform Belgarion that his close friend Lelldorin and his Mimbrate bride had just had their first child, a girl. In the celebration which followed, I managed to get the somewhat overly sober young monarch roaring drunk. It's important to see how a man behaves when he's drunk, if you really want to get to know him. Once you get a gallon or so of good ale into Belgarion, he's quite a different young fellow. He sings abominably, however. The following morning, his suffering was truly pitiable. The boy obviously needs practice. Social drinking is an important part of a monarch's repertory.

5379

I WAS greatly saddened early this year to learn of the sudden death of my friend, Rhodar of Drasnia. We were brother Alorn monarchs, comrades in arms and dear personal friends. His sly wisdom, his unfailing good humor and his true courage made him a rock upon which we all leaned in troubled times. There is of a sudden a huge vacancy in the world, and I feel it profoundly. Porenn has undertaken the regency in behalf of her young son. This causes me some concern, since Porenn is a trifle too much a creature of the Drasnian Intelligence service to make me altogether comfortable.

Meanwhile, we have learned that 'Zakath is retreating northward, having abandoned the city of Rak Hagga and apparently intending to winter in Rak Cthan near the equator. To compound his difficulties, there are rumors that civil war has broken out in Mallorea. There appear to be strong separatist sentiments in the Seven Kingdoms of Karanda in north central and east-central Mallorea. Should this oblige him to return home to mend his fences, I believe it will mark the end of his adventures on this continent.

I visited Fulrach early this summer to consult with him concerning events in Drasnia and southern Cthol Murgos. Sendaria is of enormous strategic and logistic importance in the overall posture of the Alorn Kingdoms, so cordial relations between Fulrach and me are essential. An epidemic of hog-cholera has broken out in Sendaria, however, and I found Fulrach totally preoccupied with the problem. I expect that the price of bacon and ham will soar before winter.

Astounding news from Tol Honeth! General Varana, in an effort at conciliation, called a meeting at the palace to propose a series of steps which would lessen the tensions surrounding the succession to the Imperial throne. The Grand Dukes of all the major houses of Tolnedra were present, as well as the Council of Advisors. The Council, obviously aware that Varana's proposals would seriously cut into the bribes they were receiving from the great houses, shrilly attempted to shout him down. Varana, normally as patient as a stone, eventually grew irritated; and, acting in his official capacity as regent, he dissolved that body! The Council rashly declared that they would refuse to accept his decree, and he immediately threw the entire lot of them into the Imperial dungeons. Since the die had been cast at that point, Varana, with a certain pragmatism typical of the military mind, took all the Grand Dukes of Tolnedra into protective custody, holding them in comfortable, though well-guarded, apartments in the palace. Then, following the inescapable logic of the situation, he somewhat reluctantly assumed full command of the Tolnedran Empire as military dictator. The entire world trembles under the impact of these events. Much as I dislike the Empire, I must admit that Tolnedra is a tremendously stabilizing factor in world affairs. If she crumbles, the Gods alone know what will happen.

I am advised that the woman, Taiba, who appears to be as fertile as a rabbit, bore Relg, the Zealot, a second child (a girl) in late 5377 and that now she has just delivered another girl. Given Relg's tendencies toward extreme

asceticism, I'd be curious to know exactly what blandishments she used to lure him to her bed. I mentioned this jocularly to Islena, and she replied with uncharacteristic heat, calling me (among other things) a lewd and disgusting degenerate. Oddly enough, I found the conversation more exhilarating than any I've had with her in years.

5380

*I*SLENA continues to behave peculiarly. If I had the time, I'd investigate to find out what's at the bottom of her problem.

Trouble in Cthol Murgos! 'Zakath has landed a huge armada on the south coast of the Military District of Hagga and has caught Urgit squarely between two huge Mallorean armies. The battle took place on the border between Hagga and Cthan, and our informants advise us that Urgit was disastrously defeated, barely escaping with his life. 'Zakath has retaken Rak Hagga, and my belief that he was done in this part of the world seems to have been grossly premature. I think that I'd better have a long talk with Belgarion. Things in the south are reaching the point that we're going to have to take steps.

Matters in Tolnedra have deteriorated even further, I'm afraid. Ran Borune has 'adopted' Varana and has declared the general to be his official and legal heir. The other great houses are shrieking in protest, but the Emperor holds firm. I personally feel that Varana would be an excellent choice for the throne, but I fear that his elevation will cause such tremendous turmoil in Tolnedra that the advantages of having so able an Emperor will be offset by the strife which now seems inevitable. Were times less troubled, I might take pleasure in watching the Tolnedrans go up in flames. The Empire has had too much sway in the affairs of other nations to suit me. But with 'Zakath loose in southern Cthol Murgos, this is not the time for any of us in the west to be distracted by internecine bickering.

MY ISLENA IS PREGNANT! What an amazing thing! Either she has overcome her fear of childbirth or one of the nostrums she routinely takes to prevent pregnancy failed her. She refuses to discuss the matter. Merel, Barak's wife, is constantly at her side to shore her up in moments of weakness. There is a woman that is made of steel. Sometimes she even intimidates me. She purrs like a kitten when Barak is around, however. I will never understand women. After all these years, I'm going to be a father. Barak and I are now going to go out and get disgustingly drunk.

The commercial empire of Prince Kheldar and his Nadrak accomplice has swelled beyond the bounds of good taste. They totally dominate trade along the North Caravan Route, and they have hired the shipyards at Yar Marak to build them a fleet of merchant vessels so that they might plunder Mallorea. The rascally Kheldar came to Cherek like a thief in the night and hired away every ship-builder he could find. So total was their defection that I couldn't even get a row-boat built in the yards at Val Alorn if I needed one. It's a sad reflection on the times when money commands more respect than patriotism or loyalty to one's nation and one's King. Islena swells like a big-bellied sail, and she has developed an insatiable craving for strawberries. Where am I going to find strawberries at this time of year?

I have sent this day a remonstrance to Prince Kheldar. I should have realized that the boats he was building were only a prelude. He has now begun recruiting sailors. I don't have enough good men left in Cherek to man the fleet. The wages he offers are absolutely outrageous. I'd have to strip my treasury to match them. He goes too far. He goes too far. I never really liked him anyway.

Polgara has graciously sent Islena whole baskets of strawberries from her own garden. How she made the bushes bear in the fall is quite beyond me. After eating only two, however, Islena lost interest in them. What am I going to do with all those strawberries?

Ariana, wife of Lelldorin of Wildantor, has given birth to their first son. I hope that's a good sign.

I HAVE A SON! – a great squalling boy with black hair and lungs like a set of bellows! May Belar be blessed! As is our custom, Barak and I took him immediately to the harbor and dipped his feet into the salt water of the sea so that he will ever be a sailor. Upon our return, my cousin and I broached a hogs-head of fine old ale to aid us in our consideration of a suitable name for him. The ale, unfortunately, hampered my creativity, and my Earls advise me that sometime after midnight I poured beer on my son and named him Anheg, after myself. Oh well, Anheg II isn't such a bad name, I suppose. Islena's labor lasted only a day and a half, scarcely worth mentioning. She is dramatizing it all out of proportion, however, and I try to humor her. She did, after all, do a fairly good job of carrying my child, and I suppose I owe her something for that.

5381

'ZAKATH has returned to Mallorea and has crushed the rebellion in Karanda. I'm told that his suppression of dissident factions in Zamad, Ganesia and Voresebo was particularly savage. Will nothing halt the man's run of good luck? I suppose we can expect him back on this continent again before long. My son has his first tooth! He bit me with it this morning – not hard enough to draw blood, but he was trying.

Ran Borune died this spring. The state funeral was huge. I rather liked him, all things considered, but events in Tolnedra have soured noticeably in the years of his decline. Varana, never one to miss a strategic opportunity, had himself immediately crowned Emperor of Tolnedra. Technically his name is Ran Borune XXIV, but we all still call him Varana. The great houses, of course, are all outraged, but Varana controls the legions, and that is where the real power in Tolnedra lies. The Honeths, the

Horbites and the Borunes have all (grudgingly) taken the customary oath of allegiance. The Vordues, however, steadfastly refuse to swear fealty. I suspect that my friend will be obliged to clear that up before his claim to the throne is finally secure.

A returning sailor has informed me that Prince Kheldar, acting for all the world like a head of state, has paid an official visit to 'Zakath at the Mallorean Imperial capital at Mal Zeth. The sailor was not privy to the details of their conversations, but his descriptions of Kheldar's glee following the meetings can only lead me to believe that the wily little thief has concluded some very advantageous trade agreements with the Mallorean throne. I can only hope that Kheldar won't forget that he's an Alorn.

Trouble in Arendia again. The Baron of Vo Ebor, seriously wounded at the Battle of Thull Mardu, passed away this preceding winter. His heir, a nephew, asserted his authority as the new baron and promised the hand of the widow Nerina to one of his cronies. Mandorallen, the Baron of Vo Mandor, chose at that point to intervene. He marched into the barony of Vo Ebor and took the sorrowing baroness into 'protective custody'. Several knights rashly attempted to impede the great man's progress. The casualties, I understand, were extensive. Once again the Arendish potential for disaster has asserted itself. A state of war now exists between the two baronies, and the rest of the Mimbrate nobility is choosing up sides. Mandorallen is forted up at Vo Mador, paying court to his captive lady, and the new Baron of Vo Ebor, who, it appears, will recover from his wounds, is howling for his head. Korodullin is beside himself, and Lelldorin of Wildantor, ever an enthusiast, is recruiting an army in Asturia to march to the aid of his old comrade in arms. Arends can get into more trouble by accident than most of us can on purpose.

Taiba, wife of Relg the Zealot, gave birth to twin daughters this fall. She appears to have every intention of repopulating Maragor singlehandedly. The customary

presents on each such occasion are beginning to cut into my pocket rather deeply.

My son is walking now. In celebration, I gave him one small cup of mild beer. Now Islena isn't talking to me.

5382

*V*ARANA'S difficulties in Tolnedra are multiplying. The Vordues steadfastly refuse to admit his legitimacy, and refuse to allow Imperial Tax Collectors into northern Tolnedra. They have instead usurped tax-gathering, and these technically Imperial funds are pouring into the treasure-vaults in the cellars of the Vordue family palaces. The power to tax is the ultimate power of any government, and any interference with tax-gathering is tantamount to an open declaration of war upon the central government. All of Tolnedra holds its breath to see how Varana will respond to the challenge of the Vordues. His situation is difficult. He is reluctant, obviously, to command the legions into the northern provinces to enforce his authority by the sword. His claim to the throne is tenuous at best, and harsh measures against the Vorduvian insurgents would quickly give him a reputation as a tyrant. He cannot, however, allow this challenge to pass unanswered. I sympathize with him in this difficult time.

At the request of King Korodullin of Arendia, Belgarion of Riva sailed to that kingdom to mediate the dispute between the Baronies of Mandor and Ebor. He came upon them as they were engaging upon the plains of southern Arendia. At first, the din of battle drowned out our young friend's voice as he attempted to call a halt to the hostilities. Presently, he grew irritated. I suspect this to be a trait of his family. I have noted that same irritability in Belgarath on numerous occasions. At any rate, Belgarion drew his sword. Now this is a spectacle which will stop any man from doing anything in which he is currently engaged. The sword, of course, immediately leapt joyously into flame. The sight of Belgarion, his burning sword held aloft, his face angry and his eyes ablaze, caused a great consternation among the two armies. To emphasize his dissatisfaction with their behavior, the young King of Riva called upon his power of sorcery. The first thunder-clap he called down shook the earth as far as Vo Mimbre and tumbled fully armed knights from their saddles. The second ripped open the sky and engulfed the entire battlefield in an unbelievable down-pour of rain and hail. With a single word he stopped the torrential rain and then spoke to the two armies in a voice which could be heard clearly three leagues away. His words are clearly engraved upon the memories of all who were present.

'Stop this foolishness at once!' he commanded them. He then pointed his sword at the Baron of Vo Ebor. 'You,' he said, 'come here.' The Baron tremblingly approached him. 'You,' he said then to Sir Mandorallen, 'I want you over here, too.' Palefaced, the great knight obeyed. Belgarion then proceeded to give the two a blistering dressing-down. Finally, after he had reduced the pair of them nearly to tears, he ended their war with a series of blunt commands. To the Baron of Vo Ebor he said, 'You will immediately surrender any and all claims of author-ity over the person and future of the Baroness Nerina.' To Sir Mandorallen he said, 'You will return immediately to Vo Mandor, where you will marry the lady in question. You will – here and now – relinquish any and all territorial claims on behalf of the Baroness. In short, gentlemen, the Baron gets the land, and Mandorallen gets the lady – and that is that!' He then glared at them. 'Now go home,' he said. 'I'm sick of looking at both of you.' And that ended the civil war.

The Baroness Nerina, an Arend to the bone, protested vigorously when Belgarion and Mandorallen advised her that she was that day to be married to the man she had loved for all those years. Quite clearly she saw all those

splendid opportunities for tragic suffering flying out the window. Belgarion, however, would have none of that. Bluntly he silenced her and then quite literally drove the pair of them before him to the chapel and stood threateningly over them while the priest of Chaldan performed the ceremony. Thus ended one of the great tragic love-stories of contemporary history. The melancholy Baroness is now radiant; gloomy Mandorallen now smiles foolishly all the time; and Belgarion returned to Riva with a self-congratulatory smirk on his lips.

The incident provides a certain insight into our Belgarion's character which is quite instructive. He is an extraordinarily long-suffering fellow, but he will only allow things to go so far before he takes steps. Once he decides that the time has come to act, nothing in the world can stand in his path. I must remember never to cross him.

In Algaria, Hettar and Adara have had their second child, a girl. Everyone in the whole world seems to be having children – except for Belgarion and Ce'Nedra. I wonder if they're doing something wrong.

5383

'ZAKATH has returned to his campaign in southern Cthol Murgos. His absence gave King Urgit time to gather up the shattered remnants of his army and to reorganize them. He has no hope, of course, of meeting 'Zakath on the open plains of southeastern Cthol Murgos. Such an encounter would be disastrous for him and would mark the end of the Murgo nation. He has instead, wisely I think, retreated into the mountains of Araga and of Urga on the west coast. Murgos are splendid mountain fighters, but, as Cho-Hag found on the plains of Algaria and as we all discovered at Thull

Mardu, they do not do so well in open country. 'Zakath will be forced to chase the Murgos in terrain of their choosing. Such campaigning is likely to take generations. I'm rather pleased about that idea, and I wish both sides enormous success in their efforts to exterminate each other.

Varana has approached the Vordues in a conciliatory fashion, obviously hoping to head off civil war in Tolnedra. They have coldly rejected his offer. It is quite rapidly reaching the point where he will have to move decisively or his entire nation will disintegrate before his eyes.

Belgarath passed through on his way to Riva. I have seldom seen him so angry. Belgarion's impromptu thunderstorm last year appears to have had some far-reaching and near-disastrous effects on the continental weather-patterns, and Belgarath is furious. I do not envy my young friend the upcoming meeting with his grandfather. When provoked, the old man can peel off whole yards of skin, and he is at present mightily provoked.

Prince Kheldar, still behaving for all the world like a visiting monarch, has visited Melcene, the home of the Mallorean Bureaucracy. He has established relations with the Bureau of Commerce there. If he is not so already, I suspect that it will not be long before the little bandit is the wealthiest man in the world. It makes me positively sick to think about it.

Taiba and Relg have moved with their growing family to Maragor for reasons far too obscure for me to comprehend. The Tolnedrans, who have lurked hungrily on the borders of that haunted region, took this as a sign that the ghosts had departed. When they dashed in to gather up the gold lying all over the ground, however, they discovered that they had been grossly in error. The few who returned were all hopelessly insane. It appears that Mara still stands watch over Maragor.

5384

*I*T IS NOW eight years since the marriage of Belgarion and Ce'Nedra, and they remain childless. The business is rapidly becoming a matter of urgency. The Rivan King is the Keeper of the Orb, and he must have an heir. Even though Torak is gone, the forces ranged against us are too powerful for us to even consider facing them without the aid of the Orb, and only the King of Riva can wield it. I therefore summoned Brand and Cho-Hag and Porenn to Val Alorn this spring so that we might discuss the matter and decide what must be done. The immediate solution, of course, is for Belgarion to take another wife. Ce'Nedra's barrenness is certainly reason enough for him to set her aside. He is extremely fond of her, however, and the proposal would have to be broached with some delicacy. Porenn raised all manner of objections. Although she is extraordinarily able as a ruler, she is nonetheless still a woman, and is therefore unable to see such matters without emotionality creeping in. She pointed out most eloquently that she herself had been childless for several years following her marriage to Rhodar and that it had been only with the guidance of Queen Layla that she had been able to become pregnant. She urged that before we suggest divorcement to Belgarion, we should consult with Layla and enlist her aid. She went on to suggest that should Layla fail, we should then appeal directly to Polgara, who now lives in the Vale with her husband, Durnik, and the strange, beautiful foundling they call Errand. Rhodar's tiny little widow can be extremely forceful when she takes it into her head to be so. She stubbornly insisted that we take no steps with Belgarion until both Layla and Polgara have been unable to remedy Ce'Nedra's childlessness. By custom, no action may be taken in concert by the Alorn rulers unless all of us agree, so Porenn had us over a barrel. She declared that she would refuse to agree until we met her conditions, and she even offered to go to

Layla herself to present our request to the Sendarian Queen. Brand, of course, had no official standing at our meetings, but was present to protect Rivan interests in discussions to which Belgarion should probably not be privy. Brand has aged noticeably since the Battle of Thull Mardu. The death of his youngest son appears to have struck him to the heart. Cho-Hag, however, remains much the same – although his face is so weather-beaten that it would be well-nigh impossible to detect signs of aging upon it.

Following our meetings, Porenn traveled to Sendar, and there she placed the entire business so forcefully to Layla that Fulrach's plump little queen put aside her morbid fear of sea travel and left immediately for Riva to consult with Queen Ce'Nedra. I hope her efforts will be successful. Peculiarly, I find that I love the little Rivan Queen. She can be absolutely impossible, but at the same time completely adorable. Belgarion would be much poorer without her.

The Vordues have set up what they call 'the Kingdom of Vordue' in northern Tolnedra. Varana is going to have to do something about that.

This fall Prince Kheldar returned from Mallorea and, somewhat surprisingly, traveled directly to Boktor for discussions with Porenn rather than return to his base of operations in Gar og Nadrak. She advises me that our wily little friend traveled through the Dalasian protectorates in southwest Mallorea after his departure from Melcene and that what he saw there frightened him. I can't for the life of me imagine anything sufficiently awful to frighten Kheldar. I think I'd better investigate.

I've underestimated Varana. He's almost as foxy as Ran Borune was. He has concluded a secret agreement with King Korodullin, and the Mimbrate Knights have been unleashed upon the 'Kingdom of Vordue'. Varana steadfastly withholds the legions, piously proclaiming that he will not commit them against their own countrymen. The Mimbrates are tearing up Vordue, and it will only be a matter of time before the Vorduvians will be forced to

appeal to the Imperial Throne for protection. Varana will thus crush their rebellion without so much as dirtying his hands. Absolutely brilliant!

5385

KING DROSTA LEK THUN, the scabby monarch of Gar og Nadrak, has expropriated the holdings of Prince Kheldar and Yarblek. Kheldar, who was in the Vale of Aldur consulting with Belgarath and Polgara about what he saw in Dalasia, is positively livid with rage. I hold no particular brief for Drosta's high-handed banditry, but I do take a certain amount of pleasure at Kheldar's discomfort. The little thief was growing a bit too high and mighty for my taste. Driven a bit wild by Drosta's open theft, Kheldar has forwarded a formal declaration of war to the palace at Yar Nadrak. How can a private citizen declare war on an entire kingdom? It's an absurdity. Kheldar, however, appears to be dead serious about it, and he's moving about in the west, recruiting an army in preparation for mounting an invasion. Drosta laughs uproariously, but if I were in his shoes, I'd be a little nervous. Even with his Nadrak holdings out of reach, Kheldar has vast sums at his disposal, and mercenaries are flocking to his banner.

The Mimbrate Knights are savaging Vordue. They try, insofar as possible, to avoid bloodshed in their encounters. Property damage, however, mounts into the millions. The Mimbrates move in, evacuate the towns and villages, and then burn them. Stone buildings are pulled down and the furnishings and other contents thrown onto huge bonfires. Homeless refugees wander about in northern Tolnedra, cursing the Vordues and sending appeals for aid to Emperor Varana. Varana, however, is sitting tight in Tol Honeth, waiting for the Vordues to capitulate.

It appears that Layla has failed. Ce'Nedra remains

childless. We must now convince Belgarion to take his Queen to the Vale. Polgara is our last hope.

'Zakath has completed his conquest of the plains regions of southern Cthol Murgos. Urgit's army, however, has taken up strong positions in the mountains. 'Zakath is preparing for a long, difficult campaign. We can hope that it will take him the rest of his life.

5386

COUNT Reldegen, the able Governor-General of Asturia, has journeyed southward at the request of both parties to mediate the dispute between Emperor Varana and the Vordues. I'm not certain who first suggested him, but the suggestion was a stroke of genius. I've met Reldegen on a couple of occasions, and I've never met a more fair-minded and impartial man. The fact that Varana and the Vordues are seeking a mediator is ample evidence that their 'war' is winding down. Quite obviously, Varana has won, and Reldegen's good offices will be somewhat in the nature of a formality – a face-saving gesture to make total surrender more palatable to the Vorduvians. Varana got what he wanted, and he sees no necessity for rubbing the Vordues' noses in his victory.

Once again we have disturbing news out of southern Cthol Murgos. The region was apparently inhabited before the Murgos came, and the indigenous population was enslaved. Despite the eons of slavery, however, it appears that those people have managed to keep their racial identity intact. Because of their peculiar racial notions, Murgos scrupulously avoid contact with their slaves, hence they are almost totally unaware of what is really going on in their slave-pens. The Malloreans, however, are more curious. The Melcenes in particular seem to automatically begin to search through any new population they encounter in the search for what they call 'talent'. Drasnian

intelligence agents, operating at great risk in 'Zakath's army, have begun to send back reports of a highly disturbing nature. The Malloreans are aghast at what they have discovered. They have found a sort of religion among the slaves in southern Cthol Murgos. In itself this would not be particularly significant, but what has so alarmed the Malloreans is that this subterranean religion is absolutely identical to the one which exists in the Dalasian protectorates of southwestern Mallorea. This despite the fact that the two regions have been totally separated from each other since the cracking of the world almost 5400 years ago. What seems to upset the Malloreans the most is the fact that a document referred to as 'The Mallorean Gospels' is circulated among the slaves. Mallorean Grolims have been attempting for centuries to destroy all existing copies in Dalasia, and now the self-same work appears in southern Cthol Murgos – with no possible explanation for its presence. I am afire with curiosity. I must have a copy of these 'Mallorean Gospels'. I will not rest easy until I have read them.

This spring Belgarion issued a general invitation to the monarchs of the entire world to attend a conference in the city of Sendar. To take the note of peremptoriness from the invitation, he urged those monarchs unable to attend to send envoys. The avowed purpose of this conference is 'to examine world tensions and to seek peaceful solutions to frictions between nations.' This is an ambitious proposal, but one which derives more from idealism than from any sense of how the world really operates. Our Belgarion still has a great deal of growing to do, I fear. I will attend his conference, however, (scheduled for mid-autumn). I look forward to meeting rulers of nations and principalities lying on the far side of the world.

The conference,* rather naturally, produced almost no

---

* This was heavily revised, eliminating the meeting between Belgarath and Urvon and the confrontation between Polgara and Zandramas. The conference did not happen, and Cyradis visited the town of Rheon after Garion had put down the Bear-cult uprising at the end of *Guardians of the West*.

concrete results. Belgarion, however, seems not particularly disappointed. The fact that we did talk to each other seems to be enough to satisfy him. Many of the world's rulers were, of course, unable to attend. Urgit was not present, nor was 'Zakath. Surprisingly, however, both sent envoys. The King of Darshiva is in his eighties, and his envoy expressed the old man's regret at being unable to attend. The King of Jenno, one of the seven kingdoms of Karanda, is under house arrest for some misfeasance of office. (How can you arrest a king?!!) A number of the visitors at the court of Fulrach, who acted as official host, had no royal title but were of sufficient stature that no one questioned their right to be present. Belgarath attended, as did Polgara, Durnik and the foundling, Errand. From Mal Yaska, the holy city of the Mallorean Grolims, came Urvon, the third disciple of Torak. The meeting between Urvon and Belgarath was chilling. I don't believe they've ever met, but they have known of each other for eons. I'm certain that Urvon had no love for Ctuchik and Zedar, his fellow disciples, but the fact that Belgarath destroyed them both in little more than a single year must give Torak's sole remaining disciple certain qualms. Moreover, I'm certain that Urvon came into the presence of Belgarion with some highly charged emotions. Belgarion did, after all, kill Urvon's God. Accompanying Urvon was a strange veiled and hooded woman. I do not know in what capacity she was present. I rather strongly doubt that she was Urvon's mistress. She seems to have been along as an advisor of some sort. None of us ever spoke to her or saw her face. The single look which passed between her and Polgara, however, froze my blood.

Another peculiar visitor – also a woman – came with her eyes bound and escorted and guided by a towering and awesomely muscled mute. When we politely questioned her presence, she declared in a firm, clear voice, 'I am here as a representative of my people, and I am here to observe.' When we pressed her concerning exactly who her people were, she replied in that infuriating way some women have,

'I'm sorry, but I'm afraid you wouldn't understand.' I witnessed also a peculiar little ceremony involving the three women. Urvon's companion, her face still heavily veiled, approached the blind-folded woman and acknowledged her with the briefest of nods. Then Polgara also approached, and she too nodded. Astonishingly, the totally blind-folded woman – I know she could not see – responded to each nod. There was no trace of cordiality in those greetings, however. They were not unlike the curt nods exchanged by men about to engage in a duel. I'm not certain what's going on, but I'm most definitely certain that I don't want to be in the way when whatever it is happens.

One good thing that did come of the conference is that Belgarion managed to make peace between Drosta and Kheldar. The peace was not to the liking of either party, but in the end, both of them bowed to the Rivan King's will. Drosta will be allowed to keep the expropriated holdings, but he will be obliged to pay Kheldar and Yarblek a certain royalty percentage, such amounts to be determined by a Rivan accountant. Thus, Drosta has to operate his stolen holdings at his own expense and pay a royalty; Kheldar and Yarblek have no operational expenses, but their profits are substantially reduced. It's an interesting arrangement, but it will only succeed for as long as Belgarion stands over all parties with a club.

5387

*T*HE die is finally cast. Brand approached Belgarion with a near-ultimatum, pointing out that producing an heir is the King's foremost responsibility. Belgarion agreed to consult with Polgara about the problem of Ce'Nedra's childlessness. Brand then regretfully stated, 'Should Polgara's aid fail, it will be necessary for you to put aside your barren Tolnedran queen. We will then conduct a search to find a fertile Alorn girl for you to marry.' In some unknown way, Ce'Nedra overheard this statement. The scene which followed, I'm told, was absolutely dreadful.

It is difficult to foretell what the future will bring. I had thought that with the death of Torak, the world might return to that golden age which had existed before the God of Angarak took the Orb and used it to crack the world. The peace of that simple former age will never return, I'm afraid. The cracking of the world seems to have been more than just a physical event. The hearts of men were also divided, and we will never again return to our previous innocence. In some ways that's a shame, but I'm not entirely sure I'd care for a bovinely placid world. The world we have now is full of dangers, but at least it is not dull.

ANHEG I,
KING OF CHEREK*

* The amount of labor involved in creating a world tends to make most fantasists a little reluctant about manufacturing another one. An accidental conversation between my agent and another publisher, however, resulted in Elenium/Tamuli, and I discovered that building the second world isn't nearly as difficult as that first one was. I built the world of Elenium in six weeks. Experience *does* pay off, I guess. Alternating between two entirely different worlds as we did when Malloreon and Elenium were coming in tandem, however, is an open invitation to schizophrenia. It splits your head right down the middle. I found myself unconsciously reaching for Sparhawk when I was in the middle of a Garion book. Maybe someday we'll manufacture a third world just to find out if we still know how to do it. We'll see.

AFTERWARD

Wasn't that educational? My training (regardless of what it might say on my academic degrees) was in the field of literary criticism, a field which has strayed from its original purpose, I think. The great critics of the eighteenth century believed that a close examination of the classics would improve current writing, and that the purpose of criticism was to produce 'how to write good stuff' essays. Criticism should be distinguished from book reviews. 'My favorite writer is better than your favorite writer' is just a trifle juvenile, and 'I could write a better book than this if I really wanted to' is even worse.

As I said earlier, this collection provides a kind of running description of a process. It included a lot of groping. Some things that *looked* very interesting just didn't work. Other things jumped off the page right in the middle of the actual writing. Not infrequently, the story would take the bit in its teeth and run away, dragging us along behind it.

As I've mentioned before, when the urge to write an epic fantasy seizes the unwary reader, he will usually rush to his typewriter, and that's his first mistake. If he leaps into the swamp right away, he'll probably produce a chapter or two and then find that he's run out of story, largely because he doesn't know where he's going.

Papa Tolkien once wrote, 'I wisely started with a map.' I'm not sure how wise *my* doodle was, but my inadvertent following of the same path *also* dictated much of our story. People who live on a rocky seacoast usually become sailors (translation: pirates). People who live on large open grasslands usually need horses, and usually get involved with cattle. People who live in natural converging points – river fords, mountain passes, and the like – usually become traders or merchants. Geography is very important in a story.

One of the items ticked off by Horace in his *Ars Poetica* was that an epic (or a drama) should begin *in medias res*, (in the middle of the story). Translation: 'Start with a big bang to grab attention.' Fantasists tend to ignore grandfather Horace's advice and take the *Bildungsroman* approach instead. This German term can be translated as 'Building (or growing up) romance'. (Note that most European languages don't use the word 'Novel'; they still call these things 'romances'.) The 'growing up' approach is extremely practical for a fantasist, since all of our inventions have to be explained to our 'dumb kid' hero, and this is the easiest approach to exposition.

Some of you may have noticed that we *did* follow Aristotle's advice in the Elenium/Tamuli. That one *did* start *in medias res*, and it seemed to work just as well. Would you like another test? How about, 'Explain the theological differences between Eriond and Aphrael'?

To counter the 'Gee Whiz! Look at that!' sort of thing that contaminates fantasy, the fantasist should probably grind his reader's face in grubby realism. Go ride a horse for a day or two so you know what it feels like. Saddle sores show up on *both* sides of the saddle. Go to an archery range and shoot off a couple hundred arrows. Try it without the arm-guard a few times. The bow-string will act much like a salami-slicer on the inside of your left forearm, and it'll raise blisters on the fingertips of your right hand. Pick up a broadsword, swing it for ten minutes, and your arms will feel as if they're falling off. Those things were built to chop through steel. They're very heavy. Go out and take a walk. Start at daybreak and step right along. Mark the spot where you are at sunset. Then measure the distance. That's as far as your characters will be able to walk in one day. I used twenty miles, but I've got long legs. Ask a friend not to bathe for a month. Then go sniff him. (Yuk!) When you write dialogue, read it aloud – preferably to someone else. Ask if it *sounds* like the speech of a real live human being. The spoken word is different from the written word. Try to narrow that difference.

Next, learn how to compress time gracefully. You can't record your hero's every breath. 'Several days later it started to snow' is good. It skips time and gives a weather report simultaneously. 'The following spring' isn't bad. 'Ten years later' is OK *if* you're not right in the middle of something important. 'After several generations' or 'About the middle of the next century' skip over big chunks of time.

I've devised a personal approach which I call 'authorial distance'. I use it to describe just how close I am to what's happening. 'Long distance' is when I'm standing back quite a ways. 'After Charlie got out of prison, he moved to Chicago and joined the Mafia', suggests that I'm not standing in Charlie's hip pocket. 'Middle distance', obviously, is closer. 'The doors of Sing-Sing prison clanged shut behind Charlie, and a great wave of exultation ran through him. He was free!' That's sort of 'middle', wouldn't you say? I refer to the last distance as 'in your face'. 'Charlie spit on the closing gate. "All right, you dirty rats, you'd better watch out now," he muttered under his breath. "Someday I'm gonna come back here with a tommy-gun an' riddle the whole bunch of youse guys." Then he swaggered off toward the long, black limo where Don Pastrami was waiting for him.' 'In your face' means that you're inside the character's head. Be advised, though, that it uses up a lot of paper. (See *Belgarath the Sorcerer* and *Polgara the Sorceress*. First person is *always* in your face.)

I try, not always successfully, to keep chapters within certain parameters as to length – no less than fourteen pages, or more than twenty-two – in typescript. I try to maintain this particular length largely because I think that's about the right length for a chapter. It *feels* right. Trust your gut-feel. Your guts know what they're doing even if you don't.

Don't write down to your readers. Don't do a re-write of *Run, Spot, Run!* Belittle your readers and you belittle your work and yourself. Epic fantasy is genre fiction; so are mysteries, westerns, spy books, adventure novels and bodice-rippers. This does *not* mean that we can ever afford to say 'Aw, hell, that's good enough,' because it won't be. Write anything you put on paper as good as you can possibly make it. 'Good enough' stinks to high heaven, and 'It's only a fantasy, after all,' will immediately enroll you in that very large group known as 'unpublished writers'.

Everybody in the world probably believes that his own language is the native tongue of God and the angels, so I'll offend people all over the globe when I assert that English is the richest language in human history. Its richness doesn't derive from its innate beauty or elegance of expression. Its structure is Germanic (Frisian, basically, with strong overlays of other Scandinavian tongues). West Saxon, the language of King Alfred, wasn't really all that pretty to listen to, and it'll sprain your tongue while you're learning to speak it. English is a rich language because the English were the greatest pirates in history. They stole about one fifth of the world, *and* they stole words and phrases from *most* of the languages of the world as they went along – French, Latin, Greek, Hindi, Zulu, Spanish, Apache – you name it; the English stole from it. My eight years of exposure to college English gave me an extended vocabulary (my cut of the loot, you might say), and when it's appropriate, I'll use it. The youthful, marginally educated reader is going to have trouble with such sentences as 'Silk's depredations were broadly ecumenical.' That might seem a little heavy, but it said exactly what I wanted it to say, and I chose not to rephrase it to make it more accessible to the linguistically challenged. If you want simple, easy books, go read 'The Bobbsey Twins at the Seashore'. How's that for towering arrogance?

In line with that thought, I'll take one last pass at that 'I get letters' business. Some I've received have candidly admitted, 'I didn't really like to read before I got into your stories, but now I read all the time.' Let television tremble. Big Dave and Little Leigh are coming to black out those screens. Maybe that's our purpose in life. We're here to teach whole generations how to read – not everybody, perhaps, but enough to possibly make a difference. 'They left the world better than they found it,' sounds like a tombstone, but there are worse things you can say about people, wouldn't you say? Egomaniacal, huh? But egomania is a requirement for any writer. You *have* to believe that you're good and that people will want to read your stuff. Otherwise, you'll give it up after your first rejection slip. Always remember that *Gone with the Wind* was rejected by thirty-seven publishers before it was finally accepted, and short of the Bible, there are probably more copies of that book in print than any other in publishing history – or so I've been told.

I'll close with a recommendation. My personal favorite fantasy author is Lord Dunsany. He teaches me humility, since he does more in four pages than I can do in four hundred. Read *The Book of Wonder*. Get to know Slith, Thangobrind the jeweler, Pombo the Idolater, and Nuth. Ponder the fate of people who jump off the edge of the world. Consider the folly of messing around with Hlo-Hlo, the Spider idol. Journey across the Plains of Zid, through the cities of Mursk and Tlun, around the shoulder of the Peak of Mluna that overlooks the Dubious Land, and cross the bridge from Bad to Worse.

Go ahead. I dare you.

THE END